Destiny
BRIDES

A BRIDE'S DILEMMA IN FRIENDSHIP, TENNESSEE

by Diana Lesire Brandmeyer

Dedication

God has placed amazing women in my life
to help me on my journey.

Barbara Schlapkohl, Barb Friederich, Luanne Burkholder, Brenda Singleton, Terry Stretch, Debbie Wright, Patty Wiesner, and Marty Lintvedt—thank you for carrying me in prayer. Jennifer Tiszai, without you this book wouldn't be.

Destiny
BRIDES

DIANA LESIRE BRANDMEYER
& MURRAY PURA

BARBOUR
PUBLISHING

A Bride's Dilemma in Friendship, Tennessee © 2012 by Diana Lesire Brandmeyer
A Bride's Flight from Virginia City, Montana © 2012 by Murray Pura

Print ISBN 978-1-62416-736-2

eBook Editions:
Adobe Digital Edition (.epub) 978-1-62836-261-9
Kindle and MobiPocket Edition (.prc) 978-1-62836-262-6

All scripture quotations are taken from the King James Version of the Bible.

This book is a work of fiction. Names, characters, places, and incidents are either products of the author's imagination or used fictitiously. Any similarity to actual people, organizations, and/or events is purely coincidental.

Published by Barbour Publishing, Inc., P.O. Box 719, Uhrichsville, Ohio 44683, www.barbourbooks.com

Our mission is to publish and distribute inspirational products offering exceptional value and biblical encouragement to the masses.

 Member of the
Evangelical Christian
Publishers Association

Printed in the United States of America.

Prologue

Travis Logan leaned over the deck railing and watched the river swirl and froth as the steamboat shoved its way through the muddy Mississippi. An older gentleman stood next to him. Travis hadn't seen him on board before. "Nice out here on the water."

"Better than down below." The man swayed.

"Are you feeling okay, sir?" Travis reached over and steadied him while he grasped the railing.

"Must be the motion. It's the first trip I've taken on a big ship." The man's knuckles were white.

The man did look a bit green. Some people couldn't handle the rhythm of the ship. "The fresh air should help." Travis relaxed. Other than suggesting a piece of ginger to settle the man's stomach, there was little he could do for seasickness as a doctor. And he'd left that life behind. Now a horse claimed his thoughts and his future. He walked a few paces away and then stopped. He should offer the man some assistance, maybe collect a family member? He turned back to ask, "Can I get someone for you?"

The man released the rail and dropped to the steamboat deck with a thud.

Travis's physician training kicked his future out of the way.

He automatically knelt and felt for a pulse. It was there. Weak, but there.

"Sir, can you hear me?"

No response came from the man. Sweat beads swelled on his forehead and dripped down his neck. Either the man had succumbed to heatstroke, or worse, had some kind of fever. Pricks of fear stabbed Travis's neck. He'd been at the bedside of too many men who succumbed to a fever during the War Between the States. And he couldn't prevent their deaths.

Feet shuffled around him as a small crowd of passengers gathered in a half circle to gawk and whisper.

"Someone go after the ship's doctor." He didn't mind giving that order. It would be best for the man and Travis.

"Doctor got off at the last stop in Cairo, Illinois. We're picking up the new one in St. Louis," a deckhand propping himself up with a mop called from behind the crowd.

Travis's jaw tightened. "Anyone know this man's name? Where his cabin is?" He searched faces for some indication of recognition and saw none.

There were mumbles as the man's identity was discussed, but no clear response came other than he'd been seen boarding the ship in Memphis alone.

A flock of seagulls squawked as they flew overhead, casting shadows that flittered across the unconscious man's face.

"Is there an infirmary at least? Perhaps the captain can look in on him." Travis didn't want to announce he was a doctor. If he did, he'd likely be pressed into service until St. Louis.

"There's a room he used a few floors below deck."

"Let's take him there then. I'll help you get him there."

He hoped the captain would take charge of the patient, leaving Travis to go back to planning his life as a horse breeder.

The deckhand propped his mop between a brass spittoon and the rail. The wooden handle clunked against the brass.

Travis draped the older man's arm around his shoulder and waited for the deckhand to do the same. Then they lifted him.

"Where we going?" The man rallied for a moment. "I don't feel so good."

"We're taking you to the infirmary, sir. What's your name?" Travis hoped for details, but none came.

After a while, the man woke. During his short lucid periods, Travis learned his name was Caleb Wharton from Friendship, Tennessee. More importantly, before dying, Caleb Wharton had given Travis the deed to his land and offered him heaven.

Chapter 1

With a short piece of cinder, eighteen-year-old Heaven Wharton scratched another vertical line between the logs across the rough chinking. According to the marks, Pa had been gone now for almost ninety days. She set the cinder on the protruding edge of the log just over the marks and out of reach of her little sister, Angel's, hands.

"Angel, it's time to get up." Quiet from her parents' bedroom seeped into the kitchen.

Gathering the hem of her work apron, she wiped the cinder from her fingertips. She let the smudged fabric fall and settle against her black skirt. She hadn't heard from Pa since he left. Their supplies were running low, and it was four weeks until Christmas. If he didn't send for them soon, she'd have to go ___wn. She hated going there without Pa. She didn't have ___endly way about her when it came to Angel. He could ___ake a stranger change his tune about treating Angel like a broken doll. And the stranger would be friends with Pa before he moved on. Heaven just got mad, and angry words sparked from her tongue in defense of her sister. No, she didn't look forward to going into town without Pa.

Soft footsteps shuffled behind her. She felt her face tighten.

This wasn't the life she'd been brought up to live. "Go back and put on your shoes, please." Her sister's stockings would be filthy.

"I'm sorry. I forgot." Footsteps thudded against the plank floor as Angel went back for her shoes.

Heaven's fingers gripped into fists. That was Angel's last clean pair of socks. They'd have to wash this morning, even though it wasn't wash day, so she would have dry ones by tonight.

Angel returned with her feet covered. "Do you think we'll hear from Pa today?" Her eleven-year-old sister had asked that question every day since their father had left.

"I hope so, Angel. We'll keep praying for him, just like we do every night before bedtime." Pa had left them behind in Tennessee and gone to look for work at the new Union Stock Yard and Transit Company in Chicago. He promised to send money so they could join him. So far he hadn't even sent a letter.

"I wish Ma were still alive. Then we wouldn't be by ourselves." Angel's blond curls were a tangled mess, and her unfocused blue eyes still held the sleepy morning look.

Heaven stooped and gathered the small girl into her arms, attempting to hug her own sadness away with Angel's. "Me, too. But she's not, so we're going to be strong, right? The Wharton women are capable, that's what Pa says, and that's what we are—Wharton women." Heaven wished for the same confidence she'd used in her tone. Instead, her stomach looped into a knot and pulled tight. If Pa didn't come home soon, she wasn't quite sure what she would do. Thankfully, it wasn't spring, so she didn't have to worry about plowing, and her great-uncle seemed to have had an affinity for green beans. There had to be a hundred jars of them in the cellar, but without Pa around, they hadn't been able to get fresh meat. She'd tried shooting rabbits, but she always missed. There were a few pieces of smoked beef and ham in the spring cellar that would take them through another month. After that, Heaven realized she'd have to leave Angel in the cabin while she went out to hunt something bigger and slower.

And what will I do when I kill it?

Her parents had sold their beautiful home and moved into this little two-room cabin in Friendship because Pa had been fearful the battle might reach Nashville. At least that was the story they told their daughters, but Heaven found out it was because her pa had lost the house in a game of cards. Turned out moving from Nashville kept them from being killed in the war. And Heaven and Angel were safe, but not her mother. Her parents should have taken the offer of Heaven's friend, Annabelle. Annabelle's father offered to let them live in their carriage house. Her father was too proud to do that, Ma said. At least there she knew what to do and suspected she would still have her ma.

Now Heaven had been left in charge without the knowledge she needed to run a home without help. They had been to the only church in town a few times, not often enough to make any friends, at least not any close friends like she had in Nashville.

In Nashville they had floors that gleamed from wax. Here the floor was made of rough wood planks, and crawling creatures had made their way into the cabin all summer. Now that it was cold, it was the mice they had to worry about.

In Nashville, before the war, she only had to worry about small things. Would she be able to get to the Sunday social if it rained? Would Jake like her new hair ribbon?

At the thought of Jake, molasses-thick sadness filled her soul. Things would have been different if he'd returned from the war. But that was before. She had to remember that life was over because of that awful war, and she had to set it behind her.

Now they were farmers. "We are starting a new life," Ma had said as they packed a wagon a year ago with the belongings they hadn't sold. "Be thankful your great-uncle Neal left us his farm when he died, and we have a place to live."

"If Wharton women are strong, how come Ma died from typhoid last spring?" Angel tugged her fingers through her tangled curls.

"Sometimes things don't make sense." Like now. Heaven, at eighteen, should be married to Jake and living in her own home, maybe with a baby on the way and one on her knee. Instead, the war had taken her intended, the fever had taken her ma, and now it looked like Chicago had taken her pa. Her hand fluttered to her neck and she caressed the lorgnette her mother used to wear. "Did you fold up your nightdress and put it under the pillow?"

Angel shook her head no.

"Please see to it then."

While Angel did as asked, Heaven stood in front of the cookstove, thankful to her great-uncle that she didn't have to cook over an open fire, and gave their breakfast a quick stir. It would be ready soon. She gave the spoon a sharp tap on the edge of the pan to clean it and then set it to the side on a small plate that rested on the warming shelf.

"All done. I don't know why we have to be so neat about

things." Angel plopped her hands on her hips. "We don't have any visitors."

"It wouldn't do to have a messy house. Proper ladies keep their houses in order in case someone should drop by for a visit." She plucked Angel's cap off the branch their mother had hung on the wall next to the stove to hold their hats and wet things. "We need to gather the eggs, and when we come back in, the porridge will be ready." She placed the scratchy, black wool cap in her sister's hand.

With a sigh, Angel set it on top of her head and yanked on the sides. "I could do the chickens myself, you know."

"Soon."

"You say that every day." Angel's lips drew into a pout.

"And I mean it." Heaven helped her sister with her coat and wrapped a black knitted scarf around her throat. She wouldn't take a chance that Angel would get ill. Then she slipped on her own coat and looped the egg basket over her arm.

The cold end-of-November rain that threatened earlier when Heaven went to milk their cow made good on its promise. Big plops of water pelted them as the girls stepped off the porch.

Angel stretched out her hand and waited for Heaven to grasp it.

The chicken coop wasn't far, but there was still enough distance for the rain to trickle down Heaven's neck and make a trail between her shoulder blades. She shivered and wished she'd wound a scarf around her own neck even if it was that awful black. She loved her ma, but she was tired of wearing mourning clothes.

Reaching the slanted door of the chicken coop, Heaven let go of Angel's hand to yank the metal handle on the ill-fitting door. The wood, swollen from the rain, held tight to its frame. It took several strong pulls before it gave way. Inside, the small structure held little heat, and the missing chinking between some of the logs let in the only light. The wind blew rain through the doorway. A few of the chickens were on their nests clucking, still getting ready to lay eggs.

The rain intensified, pinging against the tin roof. The chickens that weren't laying scurried around Heaven's feet, pecking at her ankles, reminding her they wanted to be fed.

Angel felt along the side walls where the chickens roosted on shelves. As her hand touched fluffed feathers, a loud squawk sounded.

"I'd say she has an egg for us today. Be quick or she'll peck you." Heaven tossed dried corn kernels onto the straw-covered floor. The chickens pecked and bickered with each other as they searched for the grain. The black rooster flapped his wings and crowed and pushed aside a hen to collect his breakfast.

Her sister slid her hand under a speckled hen, pulled out an egg without getting pecked, and held it up. "Is it a golden egg?"

"Not on the outside. It's a brown one."

"Do you think we'll ever find a golden egg?"

Heaven winced. If only it were possible for that to happen. "I don't think so, Angel. Our riches come from God, remember?" Heaven nudged the handwoven gathering basket into Angel's arm.

"Then I'm going to ask Him to send us a golden egg so we can get our steamboat tickets and go where Pa is." Angel's mouth twisted while she worked her free hand through the air, finding the rim of the basket. She traced the edge then nestled the egg inside before turning back to search for more eggs.

"I don't like November. Do you, Heaven?"

"Hadn't thought about it much. I guess it's not my favorite month since the sky always seems gray and the leaves have dropped to the ground. I like October when the sun hits the leaves and they look like they're on fire."

"Ouch!" Angel's hand came away from the hen with the egg. "Got it anyway, you old meanie. Jake said your hair looks like that when the sunshine sometimes lands on it."

"You remember that?" Heaven touched her strawberry blond waves, remembering how, when the sun brought out the red, Jake would call it his special fire that warmed his heart.

"I remember lots of things."

Heaven knew her sister would soon want to talk about memories too painful to discuss if she didn't change the direction of the conversation. "What's your favorite month, Angel? I bet it's a summer one, because you like to get in the creek with a bar of fancy soap."

"No, it's not. It's December. I know that's when baby Jesus was born, but I like it 'cause we always get a stick of candy and a little gift." Angel's brow furrowed. "Is that bad, Heaven? Would Ma be mad at me for saying that?"

Heaven bent over and kissed the top of her sister's head, inhaling the scent of the woodstove that snuggled in her hair. "No, I think Ma would understand." She handed the egg basket to Angel to carry back. "This is your chore, remember?"

"I know."

The wind whistled through the cracks in the coop. Heaven shivered. Winter was pressing down on them. "I think we should go to town today. It's only going to get colder, and we need to stock up on a few things just in case Pa isn't able to send for us before Christmas."

"I like going into Friendship. Are we going to take the wagon?"

Heaven laughed. "No, I don't think we will be purchasing that much today. We'll take our basket and walk."

"We can't even ride Charlie into town? Even though it's raining?" Angel begged. "Please?"

Heaven sucked in a breath. What had she been thinking? It was raining, and Angel could catch a cold, which could lead to something more serious. "Maybe we should wait until tomorrow when the sun might be out, and it would be a more pleasant journey."

"No! Let's go today. We can take Charlie, and it's not raining that hard. We can drape Great-Uncle Neal's old overcoat on top of us to stay dry. Please, Heaven." Angel folded her hands into prayer hands, her fingertips touching her chin. "It's been forever since we've seen a single person besides ourselves."

"What if we stayed home and baked a cake instead?" Heaven was sure that bribe would work. They hadn't made a cake in a long time, and now that she'd offered to do it, she regretted it. There probably wasn't enough flour to make one since the mice had discovered it.

"I want to go to town. Please, can we go? Please!"

Heaven wished she hadn't suggested it, but once you let a horse out of a barn without a lead, it is hard to rein back inside. "We'll leave after breakfast unless—" She paused. "Unless it starts raining hard."

Angel jumped up and down with her hands clasped tight to the basket. Her blond hair floated like a cloud around her head while the eggs clacked against each other in the basket.

"Angel! The eggs!"

The spring went out of her legs. "I can't wait! I'm going to eat really fast." The small girl stepped out of the chicken coop, not waiting for her sister.

"Wait for me, Angel Claire. Remember, there is a hole in the path to the cabin. You don't want to smash those eggs. They almost didn't survive your excitement about going into town."

Angel stopped. "Are you ever going to put the rope up so I can come out here by myself?"

Heaven's body tensed. She had to let her sister do things for herself, she knew that, but it didn't mean she couldn't watch Angel's every step.

"Do you think there will be enough to make me a jump rope, too?"

"There might be a piece left. I'll string it later today. If it stops raining."

"It's a good day. I get a rope line, a jump rope, and we get to go to town!"

Heaven didn't share her sister's excitement. Too many things could go wrong. Still, she needed to go to Friendship, and if she went today, she wouldn't have to think about making the trip again.

Unless Pa didn't send for them soon.

Travis Logan passed another swamp where bald cypress trees stretched out the bottom of their trunks and dug in their roots to make their homes. He slowed his horse, Pride and Joy, to a gentle walk to cool him as he approached the town of Friendship, Tennessee. Early in the morning it drizzled, leaving the last leg of his journey damp and uncomfortable for both him and his horse. He was in search of Caleb Wharton's place and knew he was close. Still, he considered it right smart to head into the general store for clearer directions before going any further, maybe even warm up a bit.

Friendship appeared to be a good-sized town. He passed a general store, post office, and livery stable. A man wouldn't have to go far to get what he needed. Right in the middle of the main street sat a public well. With a quick pull on the reins, he halted his horse and dismounted. He looped the leather reins around the saddle horn. His boots squished in the muddy street as he led his companion to the water-filled troughs to drink. The town was quiet, only a few people on the sidewalks. He figured the earlier rain may have kept some folks home. A stagecoach pulled away from the hotel, its wheels sucking mud. The driver tipped his hat at Travis then flipped the reins to increase the speed of his team of horses.

While Pride and Joy drank his fill, Travis scratched the black's neck and looked over the other half of town. There was a second general store doing business at the end of the street. If you couldn't get what you needed at one place, you could probably get it at the other. Gathering the lead line in one hand, he walked the horse to the front of the Peacock & Co. General Store and then tethered him to the hitching post. He adjusted his black hat with a finger, raising the brim so he could see better.

Across the street, stood a boarding house with a sign swinging from a post in the yard, MISS EDNA'S PLACE OF REST. Sounded like a funeral parlor. Might be cheaper to stay a week there than at the hotel if he couldn't move into Caleb's place right away. He didn't know if Caleb had left it vacant or hired a caretaker. He didn't intend to show up unannounced and take over the farm. A person needed time to pack up his belongings and find another place to stay. Not too much time though. He wanted to get started making the place his own. His mare would be arriving in Dryersville next month.

The horse bumped his velvety muzzle against Travis's shoulder. The blue eyes, signifying the horse was a true black, seemed to question him. Travis reached up and scratched Pride and Joy's forehead. "Won't be in there long, buddy."

Three wide, worn wooden steps led to the covered sidewalk under the Peacock & Co. sign. Travis noted the toy wagon and kitchenware display in the front glass windows. He paused long enough to wonder if he'd ever have a wife and child to treat some Christmas. Maybe Friendship had a woman who would steal his heart the way his mother had stolen his father's. He wanted a marriage like theirs, built on trust and companionship. It had taken him awhile, but now he knew Mary couldn't be the one to give him that.

The wood and glass door yawned onto the porch, spilling out a blond-headed woman holding on to a younger girl's hand. At that moment, the sunlight decided to break apart the clouds, and with its touch, turned the woman's hair the color of gold and fire.

An older woman with a gray bonnet tied tightly around

her plump chin blew through the door after them. "Now, don't forget we'd like to see you in church on Sunday."

"We'll keep that in mind, Mrs. Reynolds." The golden-haired beauty didn't stop. It looked more as if she sped up her pace trying to get free of Mrs. Reynolds. "Don't imagine with the winter weather we'll make it too often."

"We will look forward to seeing you when you do come." Mrs. Reynolds turned back to enter the store and stopped the moment she spotted him. Her eyes leaped from his to the scar on his cheek.

He tipped his hat to her.

She offered a "Welcome to town, stranger," smile and then stepped back into the store.

The rustle of the pretty woman's skirt brought his attention back to her. Travis couldn't remove his eyes from the two females. Was the golden-fire-haired one married? Since she wore black, she might be a widow. The younger one was most likely a sister, too old to be the woman's child. Something didn't seem right about the younger girl. The woman had a tight grasp on the child's hand even though she was old enough to navigate the stairs on her own. He listened as she said "now" each time they stepped down.

Golden Fire Hair carried a woven basket on her arm, which she removed and placed in the younger girl's hand. She untied the horse on the opposite side of the stairs where he'd tied Pride and Joy. It was a nice-looking gelding. He was appraising its value and mentally measuring how many hands the horse stood when he realized the woman had noticed him staring. He tipped his hat, "Howdy, ma'am. Nice horse you have there."

Her face flushed, and her thank-you came out more like a warning growl.

"His name is Charlie," the younger girl said.

"Shh. Don't say anything." The woman turned back to face him, despite the scowl she wore. He sensed the hedge of protection she placed around the child. "We must be going."

He removed his hat and held it low, shielding his chest. "Be seein' you." He watched her help the child onto the horse, climb on behind her, and ride away before turning the knob and entering the store.

The warmth from the box stove sitting in the middle of the store sucked him in like a bug to a flame. The heat seeped through his damp overcoat into his skin and melted the tightness from his ride out of his shoulders and back.

He felt bad for Pride and Joy having ridden in the same cold rain. He'd order extra oats tonight if he stayed in town.

The quietness of the store settled on the back of his neck. Sure enough, he drew stares from the woman named Mrs. Reynolds and another woman holding a bolt of checked fabric. Their chatter halted as he walked past, and his hand went to the white line on his face. His scarred cheek gave him the appearance of a man with a reputation—one not well earned. He ignored the women. Walking past the barrel set up for a game of checkers, he headed straight for the counter. Once those in the store seemed to deem him no threat, several quiet conversations began behind him.

"Name's Henry. Looks like you were caught in the rain this morning."

"Travis Logan. Yes, it was a miserable ride."

"Haven't seen you in here before. Are you here to stay or just passing through?" Henry stroked his graying black whiskers with his rough hand.

"I'm looking for directions to Caleb Wharton's place." He placed his hand on the glass counter next to a jar holding stick candy and wondered about the little girl he'd just seen. Did her sister buy her one of these for the trip home? He hoped so. As a kid, he'd liked the peppermint ones.

"What do you need with Caleb?" Henry stood straighter as he lowered his hands under the counter, a move Travis knew would make it easy to draw out a rifle in case of trouble.

He withdrew his hands from the counter and took a half step back. "Caleb's passed on and left his farm to me. I thought I'd take a look to see if it will work as a place to raise horses."

"Horses?" The clerk dragged the stool next to him closer and perched. "That right? What happened to Caleb?"

"Caught something that couldn't be cured on the Mississippi."

"And he left you his place?" Henry smoothed his rough linen work apron at the chest with his hairy hand.

"Yes sir. Made me promise to come here. Said it was heaven and I'd love it."

"Sounds like Caleb." Henry tugged on his earlobe then spat in the spittoon behind the counter. "Well, ain't that something. Heaven, huh? You're not far, about a mile down the road you rode in on. There's a broken wheel half buried on the corner of his land. The lane's growed up a bit, but you can see it if you look for it. You'll find the cabin around the bend."

"I'll need a few supplies. I imagine I'll be back in town later for more, once I know what I need."

"I'll be glad to help you, but I imagine you won't be needing much as there is a. . ." Henry coughed. "Caleb's had someone looking after the place." He reached in his apron pocket and withdrew a pad of paper. He set it on the counter and pulled a pencil from behind his ear, ready to take Travis's order. "Caleb brought the missus and his family here in early spring. The place was in pretty good shape. It belonged to his wife's uncle—odd old coot, he was. Surprised us when Caleb decided to head north to look for work, but he wasn't quite the same after his wife died."

"He didn't say much about that. All he talked about was this place, so he might have changed his mind about working up north." Tension that had been riding his shoulder blades left. This must be a sign that giving up doctoring was the right thing to do. He could use a break, and a homestead in good shape with milking cows, chickens, and a nice barn seemed to be in his future. "Then I guess I'll just head out that way now, since it sounds like all I need is already there, just like Caleb said." As Travis walked out the door, Henry laughed, and Travis thought he heard him say, "I hope he has a gun."

Chapter 2

As they rode Charlie home, the warm noon sun stroked its fingers down Heaven's back, rubbing away the angst Mrs. Reynolds had caused. The horse's feet squished in the mud, making a sucking sound with each pull from the road. It wasn't a long way back to the cabin, but it was slow-going with the muddy road. She didn't want to rush Charlie and take a chance on him twisting his leg. She didn't need a lame horse, or worse, one with a broken leg. Once back in Memphis, she had wanted to surprise her pa with a picture she'd drawn and instead ended up witnessing her pa put down a sick horse. Her stomach soured at the remembrance. No, slow and steady would be best.

The horse trod past the cotton-stubble-filled pasture. Disturbed by the noise, a flock of blackbirds took to the sky and veered to the south.

"Who was that man at the store?" Angel's light voice added to the rhythm of the creaking leather of the saddle.

"I've never seen him before. That's why I didn't want you to talk to him. We don't want anyone else knowing we're out here alone." Last month three men on horseback had stopped to see if she needed any help chopping wood. They didn't want to help. They wanted her home and quite possibly her as well.

She sent them back down the road with a few rounds from the shotgun and then prayed they wouldn't return. So far they hadn't been back, so she guessed they'd moved on. She probably should have mentioned it to Preacher Reynolds, but she didn't want to be beholden to anyone. He would have made her and Angel move to town and live with them. That would have left their home unprotected. She couldn't do that. She'd promised Pa she'd take care of the place and keep it nice so they could sell it.

Heaven's disappointment in not receiving any news at the post office from her pa turned to worry. What if he was hurt and couldn't get a letter to them? Or maybe he thought it unnecessary to let them know he arrived safely and was saving every penny so he could send for them. Her free hand went to the strand of hair hanging in front of her ear and began to twist the wayward lock.

Or had something even more awful happened to him? Her lungs shriveled, and she found it difficult to breathe. She knew these were the times that were supposed to bring her closer to God, but mostly she wanted to yell at Him for the way things were turning out in her life.

"Heaven, are you twisting your hair?" Angel tipped her head back onto her sister's chest, smashing her mother's lorgnette into her skin.

She dropped the strand of hair from her fingers and moved the small magnifying glass. "Why?"

" 'Cause Ma always said you twist your hair when you're worried. I think you're worrying about Pa. Are you?"

Her sister's perception of things unseen had grown in the last month.

"I'm not twisting it right now." She wasn't since she'd let it drop the second Angel mentioned her habit. She couldn't have Angel's brain sizzling with worry, too. "Pa is fine. I'm sure of it." She wasn't positive about that either, but she didn't need Angel thinking about what might be wrong. "Besides, we're doing fine without him." She wasn't so sure of that either, since there wasn't anything but that small amount of salted meat left. But eleven-year-old Angel didn't need to be thinking about where the next meal was coming from.

"I miss his stories."

"I'll read to you tonight, or maybe we can make up a story together. We could try and piece a few of Pa's together and make a new one." Truth be told, even if she was too old for Pa's stories, she never tired of hearing him spin one.

"It won't be as good as sitting next to Pa while he tells it."

"I can't do anything about that, Angel. You will have to make do with me until he sends for us." Angel's back went board hard against Heaven's chest. Yes, she could try and protect her sister from as much as she could, but some things could only be fixed by a father.

From the movement of the leather strips, Angel could picture Charlie's powerful neck bobbing as he walked. She relaxed against her sister's chest, holding the reins. She knew she was only allowed to hold them because he knew the way home. Heaven wouldn't have let her take them otherwise. No one would ever have to lead Charlie back to the barn where he knew he'd be fed when he arrived. If anything, he had to be held back from running the entire way.

She had to find some way to make Heaven let her do things. The only thing she couldn't do was see, but Heaven kept her in the cabin like she was a drooling idiot not fit for public gatherings. "Mrs. Reynolds said we should come back to church soon."

"Uh-huh."

"Mrs. Reynolds said they are having a Sunday school Christmas play, and there is still time for me to be a part of it, but I need to go to Sunday school."

"Uh-huh."

"Mrs. Reynolds said. . ."

"I know. Angel, I was right there with you." Heaven's voice had that stone-sharp edge to it that Angel recognized as warning her that she had *almost* gone too far. Her ma had that same tone. She guessed that was where Heaven learned to use it.

"I know." She would have to approach this problem another way, because she wanted to be an angel in the play. After all, it was her name, so she should have the part. "Don't you miss seeing other people, Heaven? If we went to church more often, we could make new friends."

Heaven didn't say anything for so long, Angel thought she might have fallen asleep, which meant she drove the horse by herself. She lifted Charlie's reins higher. Her heart expanded with excitement then deflated when she felt her sister stir behind her.

"I miss my best friend, Annabelle, very much," Heaven finally replied. Heaven didn't know it, but Angel saw her sister's words as teardrops.

Angel missed her school friends in Nashville, too. They didn't even know she was blind and didn't have to go to school anymore. Wouldn't they be surprised to know that she missed learning, too? Right now she'd even be happy to see Fred Thompson, and she didn't like him, not since he tied her braids together last fall.

Friendship didn't even have a school. How would she ever make any friends if Heaven didn't take her to church?

The fire crackled in the fireplace, sucking the dampness of the day out the chimney with its smoke. Heaven gently rocked in the old blue rocking chair they'd brought with them from Nashville. The chair had sat on the back porch for as long as Heaven could remember. She and Annabelle often climbed in it together when they were small and munched lemon drop cookies the cook gave them.

Did Annabelle like being married? The wedding was set for last June, and Heaven was sick about not being able to be there, even if she didn't much care for the man her friend was marrying. Had they moved in with Annabelle's father, or were they able to move into a place of their own? Annabelle might even be with child by now. Heaven hoped for the best for her friend but wished she and her childhood friend could climb in the bed and have a night of talking like they did before Heaven's family moved.

The last few golden moments of sunlight slipped through the windowpanes and cast the cabin in a cheery glow. She needed to stop soon if she wanted to get to the barn and feed

Charlie and the other animals before dark. She liked this part of the day, putting the animals to bed. Even that tiresome goat, Mr. Jackson, was worn out by then and would leave her skirt alone.

Her knitting needles slid across each other, adding a background rhythm to the tune Angel hummed while washing her stockings. Heaven hoped that by having to wash on a day that wasn't washing day, Angel would remember to put her shoes on instead of racing across the floor that never seemed clean.

Heaven squinted in the dim light, not wanting to light the lamp until she came back from the barn. There was still time to knit a few more rows before the last bit of red faded from the sky. The scarf was a Christmas present for Pa. The one he'd taken up north was thin with wear. She'd unraveled her mother's blue wool sweater. There was enough to make two scarves for Christmas gifts. This one was for Pa. Then she'd make one for Angel. A few more inches and Pa's would be completed.

Then what? The rocker creaked faster against the plank floor. She didn't have an address to send it. She would continue to pray they would hear something soon. Just because there wasn't a letter at the post office today didn't mean they wouldn't be in St. Louis or Chicago to celebrate the Savior's birth. Not likely though. She knew how long it had taken them to travel to Friendship from Nashville, even though they came by wagon and not a train. She could only imagine how long it would take to get to one of those northern cities, especially on a steamboat. It was time to realize they would still be living in this cabin come Christmas.

Heaven's shoulders sagged. She lowered the knitting to her

lap and rubbed her forehead with her fingers. She would have to go hunting soon or go into town hanging her head and asking for help. She couldn't do that, wouldn't do that. She was a Wharton, and Whartons made their own way no matter what life planted in their path. Pa had made that clear. Whartons weren't moochers.

She longed to have her pa back in control. No longer would she have to worry about Angel's health and safety. At least she wouldn't have to do it all alone.

Maybe she ought to consider taking Angel to Sunday school. Mrs. Reynolds had said something about a Christmas social, too. Not that there were a great deal of men around here to marry, but maybe she would meet someone. Someone who wouldn't mind that her sister would have to be included in any future plans.

Maybe the man at the store today?

She had pretended to ignore him, but when he took off his hat, she couldn't escape the desire to pat those wavy dark brown curls into submission. The scar on his cheek looked fresh, but so many men these days wore scars visible and invisible from the war. Maybe he'd be at the social. They'd be properly introduced and fall in love, and then she wouldn't be alone.

Humph! Now she was dreaming. She was awful close to the age of being considered a spinster. Her chances of finding love would be better up north—if Pa would just send for them. She picked up her knitting, the needles clicked faster and no longer accompanied Angel's tune. There wasn't one.

Angel had stopped humming.

Heaven slowed the rocker. She set her knitting aside and

glanced over to see what had caused the cessation of the happy tune.

Angel stood with a back stiff at their ironing board. One hand held a dripping stocking as her head cocked to the left, listening.

Heaven's heart quickened. She dropped her knitting into the basket sitting next to the rocker. "What do you hear, Angel?"

"Pa's home!" Angel squealed. "His horse is coming down the lane!" She let the stocking she'd rinsed fall back into the bucket. Hands held in front of her, she bolted across the cabin floor toward the door.

Springing from the rocker, Heaven caught Angel by her mutton sleeve as she raced past. She pulled her to a stop and encircled her arms around her. "Wait. Let's make sure it's Pa before we go telling someone we're here alone."

With quick steps, she reached the corner where they kept the rifle. Pa told her to leave it there so she'd always know where to find it. She picked up the heavy weapon, cradling the barrel in her arms. She'd get Angel settled before getting in her shooting position. "Get up in the loft and stay there. I'll call you out if it's Pa."

Angel whirled around and faced Heaven with her hands curled into fists.

"Go, Angel!"

Her lower lip curled into a pout, but she turned and headed for the loft. She counted off each of her steps like a nail driven by a hammer until she reached the stairs.

At every number, Heaven flinched. It was Angel's way of expressing her anger. She wanted to be independent, but

Heaven knew Angel wasn't ready. When her sister's feet cleared the last step on the loft ladder, Heaven turned back to the door. She cracked open the wooden door and shoved the Spencer's barrel through the narrow opening. Her hands shook, and her mouth lost all its moisture.

She stepped onto the covered porch, aiming the rifle. One rider came trotting around the bend. One rider. Her shoulders felt lighter. Maybe Angel was right. Maybe it was Pa! She shielded her eyes from the setting sun.

Then her heart broke into chunks. It couldn't be him. This man sat taller on a horse than Pa. He wore a hat down low over his eyes, but she could see enough of his face to know it wasn't someone she knew. His clothing resembled what the man outside the store this morning wore. Someone must have told him about her being alone up here, probably Mrs. Reynolds. She didn't care how good-looking she thought he was when he tipped his hat to her. He was just another one of those marauders trying to take their place. Where grief had settled in her heart, anger now planted its boots. This time she wouldn't bother to warn the rider. No need to waste the words—they didn't seem to change any of their minds. By accident she'd learned that if she fired in the air, they turned around and left.

She set her feet like Pa trained her and brought the butt of the gun above her shoulder, aimed above the man's hat, and fired. The rifle kicked. She stumbled two steps back and slammed her elbow against the cabin door frame. She tumbled sideways, dropping the gun to the porch. The shot echoed in her ears. Then horror blossomed in her throat as the man slid from his horse to the muddy ground.

She'd killed him. Now Angel would be alone, because she was sure once the sheriff found out Heaven had murdered the man, she would hang.

Chapter 3

The rumble of stagecoaches, the blare of a train whistle, and the din of shopkeepers calling out their wares on the Nashville street pelted Jake Miles as he rode in his enclosed carriage. He kept his focus on the horses' twitching ears as they pulled the carriage. They weren't immune to the bustling noises, but they didn't flinch the way the man holding the reins did.

The team's iron shoes clanked against the cobblestone, scraping against the stone sideways as they hit a sunken place in need of repair. His raw nerves reacted, tightening each muscle like knots on a ship's rope. He concentrated on keeping the panic inside of himself. *You're home. You're safe.*

Glimpses of stores he'd frequented before the war snagged the edge of his vision. He narrowed his lids to tunnel his line of sight, not wanting to see the harsh marks etched on his city by the Union Army or the face of anyone who might know him. He didn't want to be singled out, called a hero, or asked if he had news of others who were still missing.

He had nothing to offer any of them.

After his unexpected arrival two nights ago, he had hidden in his boyhood bedroom at his parents' home. He extracted promises from them and the house staff not to let news of his return be told to anyone. He was too broken to be seen. Broken on the inside where it counted. Once again he wished for a missing limb or eye. If he had something broken to show on the outside, then maybe he wouldn't feel so much weighty guilt.

Today he'd ventured out among the living, knowing after all this time that he must release his fiancée from her promise to wait for him. She needed someone whole, not the shell of a man he had become. He pictured her golden hair and blue eyes tearing the moment she saw him. She, like the others, thought he was dead. Maybe she hadn't even waited for him. His stomach reached for his heart, and they twisted together. He hadn't thought of that possibility. His parents hadn't heard from her since the false news of his death had been confirmed. She'd been beyond consoling, they told him, hiding away in her home grieving. His own parents hadn't even lived their lives. Instead, they'd quit all aspects of societal life, including attending church. They'd turned into hermits, facilitated by the help of servants who saw to their needs for food and clothing. He found that disturbing and hoped that would change now that they knew he wasn't dead.

It would be for the best if Heaven had married someone else. Still he needed to talk to her, see her, and touch her soft hands one last time. Make sure she was all right. Then he could let her go and could get out of Tennessee. Head for the West where a man could leave behind the coward and find something decent within him. If there was any to be found.

If he hadn't run into Bradford Pickens at a market in Knoxville, he wouldn't have returned at all. Pickens kept going on and on about Jake being a hero and getting out of the war alive. Jake wanted to punch him in the mouth to stop his lies. Then Pickens said he was heading back to Nashville, and he would let the others know he'd seen Jake.

He knew he had to get back before Pickens did and tell his family he'd survived the war. And Heaven. He wanted at least that small bit of respectability left to his name.

A man waved at him from the sidewalk, and Jake fought the urge to turn the carriage about and return to his parents' home. He kept going, his last bit of courage growing smaller. His mother made him promise he would see Heaven today. Jake wished he was off to see the place and not the woman. It would be much easier to face the Almighty than the woman he was about to disappoint.

The redbrick two-story house didn't have the same appearance. The drive was overgrown, but there were fresh buggy tracks. He parked his father's carriage in front of Heaven's home, fighting the instinct to turn and run.

The big tree that had graced the yard still stood. A shaft of sunlight reflected off of something in the bark, and he walked over to inspect it. Bullets were lodged in its majestic trunk.

"Yankees shot the tree and the house, inside and out."

Jake looked up to see who was speaking. A man, one he didn't know and several years his senior, had stepped out onto the porch. Had Heaven married after all?

Jake said to the man, "They left their mark on a lot things around here." *Including me.* "Were you here then?" Maybe Heaven had been spared living through the Battle of Nashville.

"No, the other family was. They were anxious to sell and leave those memories behind. What brings you by the place?"

He hung his thumbs on his overall straps.

The other family. Did that mean the Whartons had experienced what he had not? The dark feeling of guilt swirled thick around him. "I was looking for an old friend, Heaven Wharton."

"They don't live here anymore. I heard her father lost this house in a poker game to the man I purchased it from. They were gone by the time the Yankees got here."

Relief snapped the band of tension around his chest, and he relaxed. She was safe and not married, at least not to this man. He was grateful she hadn't married an old codger. "Do you know where they moved to?"

"Heard tell they moved out west somewhere." The man's cheeks sucked in as he pursed his mouth and then spit a wad of tobacco off the porch into Mrs. Wharton's once-prized rose bushes. "Hope you find your woman."

Jake slid his hand across the rough tree bark. The last time he'd been here, he'd kissed his girl good-bye and made her a promise. She'd worn a blue dress the color of a stormy sky that brought out the jewels in her eyes. The tears in them made them sparkle. His gut clenched. If only he still deserved her, he'd have run home the moment they set him free. But he didn't, and that's what he had to remember.

"Me, too, sir. I've some things to say to her."

Heaven scrambled to retrieve the fallen rifle. She held it and aimed at the man on the ground in case he was fooling her and sprang to his feet. She waited, but he didn't move. She lowered the rifle to her side, unsure of what to do next. The world seemed to have gone silent. Maybe God had taken her hearing for this awful act of murdering a man.

Angel appeared in front of her, tugging at her sleeve. "Did you kill him? I didn't hear the horse run off, and I don't hear a voice. Shouldn't we go see if he's dead?"

Sounds of the farm joined her sister's questions. The chickens were cackling, and the rooster crowed. Heaven let out the breath that had clogged her throat. "I—I guess we'd better see. I hit him, Angel. I never hit anything."

"Where did the bullet get him? Could you tell?" Her sister's eyes were wide, and Heaven worried the images she was envisioning were more vivid than the reality.

"I aimed in the air like always and pulled the trigger. Then his hat lifted off like a blackbird in flight, and the reins slid from his hands. Without making a single sound, he slipped off his horse and hit the ground." Heaven stepped off the porch. "I'm sure I killed him."

Angel grabbed Heaven's arm. "I'm going with you."

"Stay here, Angel."

"No. I'm coming, too. If he's dead, he ain't going to hurt me."

Heaven's fingers felt numb, and her legs were as heavy as that rifle in her hand had been. She vowed she'd never shoot that thing again, at least as long as that man lying in the mud wasn't dead. Maybe she'd gone too far. Maybe she couldn't handle taking care of Angel and the farm. Maybe it was time to go to town and throw herself on the mercy of the good preacher and his wife—if the man wasn't dead. "Stay close just in case he's foolin' us."

"What are we going to do with him if he ain't dead yet?" Angel asked.

"I hope he's wounded and not badly." Heaven walked a bit faster, pulling her sister along by the hand at a pace she'd never before used. "We'll have to tend to his injuries."

"Then he'll tell the sheriff you shot him. If he is dead, we can bury him in the back field. That way no one will ever know. We'll be long gone and living with Pa before anyone finds him."

The casualness of Angel's voice sent shivers of dread through Heaven. Had they suffered so much loss that life had become trivial to her sister? She stopped, and with her free hand, she pulled her sister closer, looking into eyes that couldn't see. "Angel, I was wrong to shoot that man. I didn't even know why he was coming here. I acted out of fear, and that gets me and a lot of people in trouble. We will try and save him, and if he isn't saveable, well then, we'll just have to think of a way to save me without burying the poor man where no one will find him. He might have a family, and they'll want to know what happened to him. Think about us. We haven't heard from Pa in a long time, and that causes us concern, does it not?" *Please, God, if he is dead, don't let him have a family waiting for him the way we wait for Pa.* She took her sister's hand in hers and squeezed it. "I know you mean well, little one, but we have to live right. Come on, let's see what we can do for this fella."

Annabelle Singleton's special order for wool had come in this morning. She waited for it to be brought to the counter, excited to get it. She had plans to start her stock of fine knitted accessories. When she had enough made, she would somehow open a shop in Memphis, no matter what her father said. It had to be that far away, where her father couldn't interfere with her ideas and try to take over, keeping her his little girl. And far enough away that no one would know about her embarrassment.

She'd waited out the war for her fiancé to return, not once even casting a longing look at another man. She'd rolled bandages and thought of William, made sewing kits and wondered if one of them would get to him. She did it all, holding the love of William in her heart. Then he'd broken hers. He didn't even have the decency to tell her in person. Instead, he'd sent a letter about how sorry he was to hurt her, but you can't help love, he'd said. When it comes, it comes.

Apparently it had come in the form of a Yankee woman who now bore his name.

She'd decided then and there she would become an independent woman of means and, thanks to her grandmother leaving her some gold, the opportunity glistened in front of her.

"Here you go, Miss Singleton." The clerk placed the wool on the counter for her to inspect.

She brushed her fingers over the strands. Its softness would be perfect for her project. "Thank you. Can you wrap that for me, please?"

"Of course." The clerk drew out some brown paper and placed her precious bundle inside.

"Mrs. Kirby, I'll be right with you."

Annabelle went cold. She hadn't faced William's mother since the letter. She bit her lower lip. How could she smile and be graceful to her when her son had broken Annabelle's heart?

"That's all right. You all take your time. I'm in no hurry."

Annabelle sucked in air at the unfamiliar voice. Could *she* be here? Annabelle angled her body slightly, wanting to see the woman that attracted William enough to jilt her. Had William even mentioned Annabelle? Both Mrs. Kirbys stood behind her. The younger one offered a smile so sweet Annabelle felt like she'd eaten too much Fourth of July ice cream. William's mother ignored her.

"Miss Singleton?"

"Yes?" Did her voice shake? She'd wanted William's wife to be ugly, thinking—hoping—maybe he'd felt sorry for her and that's why he married her. But that wasn't it; the dark-haired beauty with porcelain skin could have been a china doll. Everything Annabelle wasn't.

The clerk pushed the package tied with twine across the counter. "Would there be anything else you'll be needing?"

"Not today, thank you." The package crinkled in her hand, and she clutched it tightly. Her face felt hot. She had to get out of the store away from the fiancé stealer. With a quick step, she turned and brushed past the two Mrs. Kirbys without a word, making a beeline to the door.

She had to get out of this town. Running into that woman was an impossible situation, one she couldn't have happen again. It was too painful. William had been a good catch before the war, and he returned from the war with all his limbs intact. Now there were few available men, unless she wanted to marry someone ancient.

And she didn't.

Taking care of her father had been enough of a warning of what it would be like to be married to someone his age. Hosting parties for old couples, endless dinners, and no children. No, she didn't want that kind of life. She'd rather make it on her own.

"Watch out!" A carriage went past her in a blur, coming within a horse hair of running over her.

"Whoa!" The man on the carriage bench yanked back on the reins. The horses slowed and settled with a whinny.

Annabelle, numbed and shaken by her near death, thought she had to be seeing things, because the man on the carriage seat looked just like Jake Miles, and everyone knew he was dead.

"Annabelle?"

Odd, he sounded like him, too. "Jake?"

He climbed down from the carriage. "Are you hurt?"

"Aren't you dead?" What a silly thing to ask when the man stood right in front of her. But she was so sure he was dead.

"No, that was a mistake. I'm alive."

"A mistake that you're alive?" Befuddled, that's what her brain was. Surely he didn't mean a mistake to be alive.

"Sometimes I feel that way." He looked away from her.

"Did you just get back? This is big news, and no one has mentioned it to me. What happened to you?" Had he been a deserter reported as dead? She hoped not. The Jake she knew before the war had starch.

"Been here a few days."

She waited for a buggy to rumble by. "Does Heaven know?" She wanted to be happy for her friend but found it difficult. She'd found comfort these last few weeks in knowing Heaven was unmarried, too. She'd even considered asking her to set up shop with her since it appeared they would be spinsters.

"No. I'll be telling her as soon as I can find her. I went to her house, but she's not there."

"No, her family moved to Friendship in January."

"Heaven, too? Did she marry someone?"

"No, she waited for you." And here he was, back like he said he would be, and looking for Heaven. Jake was a much better man than William.

"I'll need to get a train ticket then."

Train ticket. That's all she heard. Could this be her chance to get out of this town? "When are you leaving? I'd like to go with you. I haven't seen Heaven in so long."

"No. I need to see her alone, and I'm not planning on returning to Nashville. I'm leaving as soon as I can. Tomorrow afternoon at the latest."

"Then I'd like to send a few things with you for Heaven and Angel."

"I don't imagine I'll have time to wait for you to pack up a box of pretties for them." Jake edged toward the carriage. "If you're all right, then I need to get back home. I promised Mother I'd have lunch with her."

"I'm fine. Please give your mother my regards." A plan began to formulate in her mind. With her father away on business, she would be able to pull off her escape sooner than she thought. She wouldn't be able to ask his permission. He wouldn't let her visit Heaven. She'd asked him hundreds of times since that awful letter came, crushing her heart and her dreams. Surely he would understand she had to get away now that William and his bride had returned to Nashville.

It hurt that Heaven's dream of being married was about to be resurrected, but she soothed the pain with the knowledge her new dream was about to begin.

Chapter 4

Heaven scooped up the black hat from the drive and approached the man lying still, face down in the mud. She dropped the hat next to him as she kneeled, grimacing as her black skirt sunk in the mud. He seemed to stretch out to the next county in length, and she hoped his weight was in his legs, or she didn't stand a chance of moving him. She had to turn him before he suffocated in the mud. Sticking her hands between him and the earth, she lifted, hoping to get him high enough that he'd fall the rest of the way, landing on his back.

Her arm muscles strained against his weight. She almost had him. . .if she had a little more strength. "Angel, quick, bend down here next to me."

Angel touched Heaven's head and then brushed against her side until she knelt in the muck.

"Stick your hands straight out, and you'll feel his chest." It wasn't proper having her sister touch a stranger in such an inappropriate manner, but then she ought not be touching him either. Mrs. Reynolds wouldn't approve. Then again, she wouldn't have approved of Heaven shooting this man either. She almost laughed and would have if the situation hadn't been troublesome.

"His chest is as hard as dirt." Angel wiggled her shoulders, knocking into Heaven's. "Now what?"

"On three we push as hard as we can. One, two, three!" The man seemed to stall halfway then rolled to his back, taking them with him.

"Whoa!" Angel seemed to fly as she somersaulted over the man's body and landed with a thud.

Heaven's hands were stretched out in front of her. Her stomach lay across the man's chest. Heat flooded Heaven's face. This wasn't proper at all. She pushed off the ground and scooted on to her feet, thankful no one was there to see her sprawled across this man.

"Angel, are you okay?"

Her sister stood, brushed her hands on her skirt, and laughed. "That was fun. I'm fine. I told you I could help." Angel smirked. "So, is he dead or alive, and where did the bullet hit?"

The man on the ground moaned.

Heaven screamed. Her hands covered her mouth as she backed away.

"Guess we don't need to bury him," Angel said. "It's a good thing, too, because I don't think we could have drug him around back. We'd have had to pile dirt on him right here, and that would've looked suspicious."

"Angel, watch what you're saying!" Heaven bent over the man. "Can you tell me where you're hurt?" The brownest eyes she'd ever seen looked into hers. Her breath caught as recognition dawned. "You're the man from the store this morning."

"Hurts. Heard a gunshot. Did my horse spook and toss me?" His hand moved to the side of his head, exposing a white jagged line where there must have been dark curly hair.

Then Heaven noticed the river of blood pouring through his fingers. Her vision wavered into semidarkness. *God help me. There's blood, and lots of it.* She steadied her mind. She didn't have the luxury of being a Nashville lady right now. "We'll figure that out later. Do you think you can stand and walk into the cabin?"

Angel gasped. "We're taking him inside?"

"We can't very well leave him out here bleeding, Angel Claire. That wouldn't be polite."

"He's bleeding? So you did hit him?"

At times like this, she wished she could stare her sister quiet. "Shh." There might still be time to cover this up if Angel didn't blurt out the truth. Maybe he could be led to believe it was a stray shot from a hunter.

The man struggled to push into a sitting position. He held his head, "Dizzy, but I think I can make it. My horse—needs—"

She glanced over at the horse that seemed content to watch them while snatching bits of dried grass. "He'll be fine. I'll get him in the barn right after we get you settled and fixed up. Try standing now. Hold on to me in case you get so dizzy you start to fall." Heaven offered her hand to help steady him. Once he was upright, Heaven had a feeling that if they didn't hurry to the house, he'd be on the ground again. "Angel, take two steps to your right, and you'll be next to him. I need your help to support him. Now grab his arm and sling it around your neck. I'll do the same."

Heaven staggered under the weight as the man's knees buckled. "Hold on, Angel! Don't you dare fall, mister, or we'll leave you where you land this time."

"Do my best, ma'am."

"I appreciate that." She didn't want to talk. All of her energy went into bearing his weight. She had no idea men were so heavy.

"It's getting dark."

"Yes it is." Heaven hoped he meant the sky and not what was going on inside his head. A few more paces and they'd be at the porch steps. "We're almost there, sir. Angel, once we get him up the steps, I want you to open the door so I can get him inside."

"Where you going to put him?"

"I think Pa's bed would be best."

"Why not a chair?"

"Because I think a bed's the best place."

"I don't. I think a chair is best. He ought not be in a bed in our cabin—not without Pa being here."

Sometimes Heaven wanted to treat her sister like a turkey and wring the common sense right out of her. "You're right, but Pa isn't here, and I am. So we're going to do what I say."

"I still don't know why we can't stick him in the rocker and work on him there."

"Steps, Angel. One, two, three." Angel made it to the porch deck, skittered to the door, flung it open, and rested against the door frame.

The man moaned and grew shorter as his knees buckled. His weight pressed against Heaven's shoulder. "Can't stand much longer."

"Angel, help! We can't let him fall. Help me get him to the

bed." It wasn't far, but it seemed as if they were trying to reach Nashville by foot. As they gained momentum, the man's weight became unwieldy, and it was all Heaven could do to steer him toward the bed. She pretty much aimed his fall rather than eased him gently down.

He sat on the bed and then fell over on his side with a thump, his feet still planted on the floor.

"Now is he dead?" Angel asked.

"No, just out cold, which is good. The wound needs to be cleaned and maybe even stitched tight. Better to do that while he's out." She didn't look forward to drawing a thread through the man's scalp. Last November, when they first came to live at Great-Uncle Neal's cabin, Pa tore his arm open on a tree branch. Ma had tried to show Heaven how to stitch his skin together, but one look at that needle going through skin had sent her crashing to the floor. Now she would have to do it, because there wasn't anyone else. It wasn't right that Pa had left them. Once again her anger flared. That was at least twice today, wasn't it? Well, it wasn't fair. He should have taken them along or at least sent word to them by now. Didn't he know she was sick with worry? And now she had to sew skin together!

"What about his horse? Can I take him to the barn?"

That reminded her of her promise to hang the rope between the barn and the house. She'd convinced Angel to wait until tomorrow. *"Never put off till tomorrow what you can do today."* She heard Ma's voice as clear as summer springwater in her head.

"No, not by yourself. It's dark, and you might lose your way back."

Angel clutched her hips with hands of iron, and she stood taller. "Dark? Heaven, it's always dark for me. I have a better chance of getting back than you ever will."

"You can't leave me alone with this man. It isn't proper."

"Maybe you should have thought of that before you dragged him into Pa's bed."

"Angel!"

"It's true, and you know it. Besides, one of us has to get that horse in the barn before he runs off. Do you want me to stay with him?"

She glanced back at the man on the bed. How long would he be unconscious? He was bleeding a lot, a steady trickle running down the side of his face onto his arm. He'd landed in a way to make it easy for her to patch up. The bleeding had to be stopped now. But Angel outside alone terrified her.

"Heaven?" Angel grasped her arm. "I can do this. You have to take care of him. He's too heavy to drag out of here if he dies."

"Go. Hurry. Don't dawdle. Just stick the horse in the stall and get back here. I'll feed everyone later."

"I will."

"Watch out for that hole. Remember, it's thirty-six steps from the porch, and then step to the left. . . ."

"I know. You've been making me count it now for weeks." She turned and headed for the door faster than Heaven had seen her move in months.

Freedom, sweet freedom. Angel hated that her sister shot that man, but she almost couldn't contain her joy at the unexpected gift his injury had brought. A chance to do something on her own. She couldn't mess this up. If she did, it would be forever before Heaven let her venture out alone. At the count of thirty-six, she stepped left and continued counting in her mind. It was so easy to count and think of other things now. Like how to find the horse. She stopped short. Good thing Heaven hadn't thought of that, or she wouldn't have let Angel out of the house. Still she had to figure out how to find him.

Come on, Angel, you're smart enough to figure this out. Think it through. She cocked her head and listened. The wind blew leaves to her left. That's where the horse had been. She took two steps in that direction and listened again. She could hear tree branches swaying and clicking into each other. No horse sounds, no pawing the ground or heavy breathing through the nose. She puckered her lips and made a kissing noise.

Horse lips ruffled together in response.

Satisfaction filled her posture. She knew where that horse stood. Now all she had to do was to get his reins and lead him into the barn.

Annabelle returned to her father's home, clutching her embroidered handbag containing her freedom, a train ticket for tomorrow morning, close to her chest. With freedom less than a day away and a foolproof plan of escape in place, her heart warred with her stomach. She'd never been so daring. Did it show on her face? In her walk? She needed to appear normal and not flushed with the thrill of what was to come.

"Good afternoon, Miss Singleton." John, their manservant,

helped her out of her coat.

"John, I've made arrangements to have some things I won't need shipped to Heaven Wharton and her little sister. A porter will be here later today to pick them up."

"Will there be a large or small package, Miss Singleton?"

Annabelle attempted to appear thoughtful as if she weren't quite sure. She didn't want John to suspect anything. "It might be best to pack it all in one of those old trunks. That way everything will arrive intact. Don't you think, John?"

His eyebrows rose slightly.

Annabelle fiddled inside her purse. Did he suspect she was planning on leaving? Distraction might be a good idea. "My wool came in today. I want to get that trunk packed quickly so I can start working with it."

From her peripheral vision, she saw his eyebrows settle back into place. Good, he didn't suspect anything.

"Would you be needing any help with the packing, Miss Singleton?"

"No. No thank you." Did her voice just squeak? She faked a cough. "I do hope I'm not catching a cold. I best hurry. I know what I want to send to Heaven. I do believe I'll ask Cook for some of that jam Angel likes so well. I'll wrap it to keep the jar from breaking. Thank you, John. I'll let you know when the trunk is ready to be brought downstairs."

"Yes, Miss Singleton. And I do believe Cook would be happy to send the little one some jam. I'll request it on my way to collect the trunk you'll need upstairs to pack."

"Thank you." Annabelle scurried to the stairs. First thing she needed to do was collect her mother's wedding ring out of the box in her father's room. She'd planned on wearing it when she married last June, so if she tilted the truth a tiny bit, the ring already belonged to her.

But would it keep her safe? The trains were dangerous to ride on alone, but Jake would be with her. But what if he changed his mind and didn't board at the last minute. Maybe she should take someone along. But who? And she'd have to find them a way back to Nashville, unless they wouldn't mind going all the way to Memphis and never coming back.

Chapter 5

Heaven wrapped a cloth around the pot handle and lifted it from the stove plate. The cabin door opened, and Angel stepped in wearing a smile that had been missing for months. "Where have you been?" Heaven hauled the heated water across the room to her pa's bed. "Why did it take you so long?"

Angel's smile slipped from her face, and Heaven knew she'd wounded her sister.

"I had to find the horse, and then I took off his saddle. I fed everyone, too."

Heaven stopped abruptly, and the hot water sloshed across her chest. "Ouch!" The pot in her hand swayed from its cloth-covered handle. She tightened her grip. "You did?" Angel was outside in the dark where just last week a wolf stole a few chickens when they'd forgotten to shut the door to the coop. Fear gripped her, twisting her stomach so much she almost doubled over.

"Heaven, nothing happened. I'm okay. I didn't get eaten or attacked by anything except that dumb goat, Mr. Jackson." She tugged at her skirt. "I think he took a bite out of my skirt. I think I heard it rip."

"But how? How did you find your way to do all of that?

I never put up the ropes for you." She set the pot on the floor next to the bed. She took the cloth from the handle and dipped it into the hot water, wincing from the heat. Too late now to keep Angel contained. She'd expect to be allowed outside all the time. But she couldn't think about that now. A bigger problem lay in her pa's bed.

"You taught me how to listen and count, and that's what I did. He didn't die while I was out there, did he?" Angel rubbed her hands together to warm them. "If he did, I figured we could tie a rope to his legs and let his horse drag him out of here. It would be easier than us trying to move him since he'd be deadweight."

"He's still breathing and hasn't woken up yet. I'm praying we won't have to try your method, although it's an interesting solution." She wrung out the cloth, and the water ran into the pan. Heaven held her breath. It was just a wound. All she had to do was wash it and see if he needed stitches. *Please, God, if I have to sew him up, keep him knocked out.*

Angel tiptoed across the floor and stood next to her sister. "Sure hope he doesn't wake up and start yelling like a girl."

Heaven bit her lip. "So pray, Angel. Pray that he doesn't wake up until we have him all fixed and bandaged. God have mercy on him, 'cause if he wakes up while I have a needle in his skin, I'll most likely end up sticking it in his eye."

"As long as he still has the one eye, he'd be better off than me." Angel breathed over Heaven's shoulder.

A tidal wave of guilt rushed over her, trying to suck her under. She didn't have time for self-pity right now. "If you aren't going to commence praying, then please go retrieve Ma's sewing basket."

"I'll pray while I'm getting it. I can do two things at once just like you." Angel stepped away, "Heavenly Father, Heaven done shot that man. . . ."

"Angel, God knows what I've done. You don't need to confess my sins to Him. I'll do that later. Just pray for what I asked, please." She dabbed at the wound. The blood wasn't coming out as fast now. She glanced at the stranger's face and touched the scar, tracing it with her finger. It didn't detract the least from his handsome face. His cheekbones were chiseled, and yet the scar seemed to soften his look rather than harden it. It was still pink, so it must have happened only a short time ago. She didn't feel so bad now about shooting him. He must be a troublemaker. Someone else stitched him up not long ago. Wonder what he was after then?

Angel continued praying, "And that's all we are asking, God—keep Heaven out of jail, and make this man go away."

She should have been listening to Angel. Who knew what she'd requested from God?

"Here's the basket." Angel set the basket on the floor. A log in the fire sizzled and then popped. "Want me to thread the needle?"

Heaven's head popped up before she could stop it. Hope coursed through her. Had her prayers been answered?

Angel flashed a toothy grin. "Got you."

Heaven gritted her teeth and choked back a sob. She dropped the cloth back into the water, wiped her hand on her apron, and then picked up the basket.

"Are you mad at me, Heaven?"

"No, I just wish you could see, and for a moment, I thought you could." *Where was that silk string Ma used?* "Ouch. Found the needle."

"So you're going to stitch him up?"

"There isn't anyone else, is there?" Her fingertips brushed against the spool of silk thread. She grasped it. Now what? She tried to think. Ma had done something with the needle before she'd started to sew her pa's torn skin. What was it? "Angel, what did Ma do to the needle?"

"She stuck it in the fire."

"That's right." Heaven stood and hurried to the fireplace. She bent down where the coals were hot and placed the needle as close as she could without getting burned. The fire was hot, and she couldn't hold it there long. She just hoped it was long enough.

Her hands shook as she tried to wiggle the thread through the eye of the needle. Outside Pete the rooster crowed. He should be locked in the chicken coop away from the wolves. She couldn't think about him now. She squinted, holding the needle up to the firelight, and shoved the thread at the hole for the third time. This time it glided through.

Bending over her patient, she aimed the needle at his skin. Bile rose in her throat. She swallowed. She'd have to get closer. Her arm wasn't long enough, and it was dark. She backed away. "I need to light the lamp and bring it over here. I should have thought of that sooner."

"I could do it without a light. I make good stitches. That's what you told me—nice and small." Angel grasped her sister's elbow.

Heaven yanked her arm away. "No. I can't let you touch an unmarried man that way. You're too young." She spun around and took a few steps to the kitchen table where the oil lamp stood. She pushed the needle through the top of her apron and then lifted the chimney from the lamp and turned up the wick. She struck a match, touched it to the wick, and up shot a flame. She blew out the match and then lowered the wick and replaced the chimney.

She set it on the stool next to the bed where its graceful flame danced across the wall. She knelt on the floor and withdrew the needle from her apron. It was time. She would have to touch his face and again was grateful he wasn't awake. This was hard enough without having the man stare at her. Her palm rested against his face. Rough whiskers poked her skin. With caution she leaned over the wounded area and squeezed the skin between her thumb and index finger as tightly as she could. "Angel, sing something. Help me get my mind off what I'm doing."

"Swing low, sweet chariot, comin' for to carry me home. . . ." Angel belted out the words.

Heaven cringed. "Never mind, Angel."

"It's a good song, and it might comfort him if he can hear us."

"I think I'll do better without the song. So don't sing it." She held the needle poised to stick it through her patient's skin.

Angel continued to hum the tune.

Dear Lord, let this man remain ignorant to what went on here tonight. She plunged the needle through the skin and forced herself to think of quilting.

"Mary!"

The sound of thrashing and mumbling startled Heaven, waking her. Disoriented she shoved the blanket she had wrapped over her to the floor. Why was she in the rocking chair?

"Mary!"

Her patient. He was awake. She took a step and stumbled, falling to the floor, her feet entangled in the blanket. Righting herself, she hurried to the man's bedside. "Shh! Shh!" She tried to soothe him while feeling his brow.

His arm shot around her, pulling her close to him. Her face was within kissing distance of his. "Mary." He mumbled. "Why?"

Heaven untangled her neck from his arm. He was burning up. A fever. And Heaven knew he was as good as dead, just like her ma.

Heaven hollered up the ladder. "Angel, I need you."

She ran to the reservoir attached to the stove and ladled the lukewarm water into a bowl. She swiped a clean cloth from the shelf and hurried back to her patient. She set the bowl on the floor and dipped in the rag. She washed his face, hoping to take away the heat. Not wanting him to get chilled, she retrieved the blanket she had been using and covered him with it.

Angel clattered down the ladder. "What's wrong?"

"He's got a fever." She hoped the panic was only in her body and not in her voice.

Angel came over next to her sister. "What do you want me to do?"

"I need you to keep washing his face with this rag." She put it into her sister's hand. "I am going to get the willow bark tea brewing."

"But he ain't awake. How is he going to drink it?" Angel asked.

Heaven stopped in her tracks. How would she get him to drink it? "I'll think of something." Or at least she hoped she would.

She lit a lamp and placed it at the end of the table where the light would shine onto the cabinet. She whipped the curtain covering the lower half to the side, exposing their supplies. She pushed things aside until she uncovered the medicinal basket. She picked through the herbs and medicines her ma had brought along and grabbed the dried willow bark. Her mother's graceful handwriting danced across the brown package.

She needed to heat the water for the teakettle. While the water warmed, she crossed the cabin floor to the bedside of the man. Angel clearly had done what she could, as there were water drips blossoming across the quilt. She put her palm on his forehead. Still hot.

He thrashed in the bed again. "Mary, why?"

Who was Mary? Heaven faltered. Maybe he did have a wife. If he did, she wanted to make sure he lived.

"Is it working?" Angel nudged her elbow.

"I don't think so. He's still hot."

The teakettle whistled.

Back at the stove, she poured the hot water into a mug and placed a palmful of dried leaves into it. It would have to steep for at least a quarter of an hour. She collected a clean kitchen cloth. She would dunk it into the liquid and moisten his lips. Maybe she could squeeze drops into his mouth if he called for Mary again.

She thought it had steeped long enough; she didn't know for sure. She strained the tea into another mug to remove the bits and pieces of willow bark. Collecting the cloth and the tea, she went to her patient.

"Did you add honey?" Angel's face scrunched. "It tastes awful without it."

"No, I don't imagine he'll notice the bitterness."

"That stuff's awful. I'd notice even if I was near death."

"You were near death. Do you remember what it tasted like?" She moistened her patient's lips.

"No. I can't remember." Angel looked disappointed. "I don't remember anything about being sick. Only when I woke up, I couldn't see, and Ma was dead."

"I'm thankful you're here, Angel, or I'd be all alone trying to take care of him."

"Mary?" His eyes fluttered open.

"She's not here, sir. You need to drink this."

He closed his eyes and moaned. "Mary?"

Heaven seized the opportunity and squeezed the cloth into his mouth and prayed the willow bark would bring down the fever and that he wouldn't choke on the liquid.

He spat it out.

"Oh!" Heaven jumped back and wiped her face with the hem of her apron.

"What happened?" Angel's voice was edged in fear.

"He spit it out, and it landed on my face."

Angel snorted a donkey laugh. "Told you to put honey in it."

"I didn't think he would taste it." She stared at him. His eyes were closed. He wasn't aware of her at all.

"Guess I'd better add the honey."

"I'll get it and a spoon." Angel hopped off the stool. "Be right back."

Heaven sighed. It was going to be a long night.

Travis didn't want to open his eyes if the sunlight hurt his head this much with them closed. What he couldn't figure out is why his head hurt. Slowly he cracked them open. A finger of sunshine stabbed him in the eye. He covered his eyes with his arm against the assault. His head throbbed, or rather, one side of his head did, not both. What happened to him?

He wasn't lying on the ground, and he was warm and dry. In a bed. *In a bed?* He'd been on his way to Caleb's place. After that he couldn't remember.

Before slamming his eyelids closed, the brief glimpse of the room he'd seen had offered a view of a chinked wall and a daguerreotype on a dresser of two people he didn't recognize.

Pieces of images came to him—angels, heaven, and a choir. Had he left this earth and then returned? No, that didn't happen. It could have been a strange dream, but if felt real, and the pain in his head wasn't his imagination either.

"Sir, are you awake?" A soft hand brushed against his arm. "You had a fever, but it's gone now."

Slowly he dragged his arm away from his eyes. The sunlight kissed the hair of the woman standing next to him. The woman from the store. Holding a rifle. His heart pumped blood through his veins faster than water out of a bucket full of holes. He struggled to sit up. He had to get away from this crazy woman.

"I'm not sure you should do that yet. You have a pretty ugly head wound." She hoisted the gun, resting it on her shoulder.

He sank his head back into the pillow. He'd try it her way, at least until he was strong enough to wrestle that rifle away from her. "How'd I get that?"

Her face paled, and her stunning blue eyes rounded. "I was aiming over your head."

"You shot me?"

"I was trying to scare you away. You must be taller than the others. I'm sorry—unless you're coming here wasn't honorable." Her finger snaked into the trigger hole. "Then I won't be sorry at all."

"I was on my way to Caleb Wharton's home."

"Well, you found it, but why were you coming here? Did someone tell you we were all alone out here?" Her grip on the barrel tightened.

"Caleb told me to come here."

She withdrew her finger from the trigger and lowered the gun. "Pa? Pa sent you? Did he send passage money with you? Where is he? Did he send a letter with you? Is he okay?" Her face flushed with excitement, making her blue eyes shimmer like sapphires.

Travis had a feeling Caleb had been less than forthcoming. Considering his feverish state, he guessed he could excuse the man. "I'll tell you everything I know as soon as you put that gun over in the corner."

She spun around and headed to the corner, seemingly assured he wouldn't be a danger to her since he brought word of her father. Travis was glad she did as he asked. He didn't want her holding that gun when he told her about Caleb.

"What's your name anyway?"

She turned back and smiled. "Heaven Wharton."

In a flash, he understood what Caleb had done.

Travis wanted her far away from the corner before he gave her any information about her father. He watched her almost float across the floor with a Christmas-morning smile. Beautiful. And he was about to hand her a stocking full of nothing. That smile would disappear, and most likely, giving her the news about her father would keep that smile locked away for a long time. He hated to be the one to cause that.

"You didn't tell me your name." She stood further from the bed than before. Now that he was awake, he figured she wanted to maintain propriety.

"Travis Logan."

"Are you from around here, Mr. Logan?" She gathered the side edge of her apron, twisting it between her fingers.

"No I'm not. My family resides in the eastern part of the state in Knoxville." He could see the impatience in the jiggle of her foot. Still she seemed determined to be the gracious southern hostess.

"What county would that be, Mr. Logan? We're originally from Davidson County. Nashville."

"It's Knox County, Miss Wharton." His throat was dry. "Could I trouble you for a drink of water before I tell you about your father? I have such a bitter taste in my mouth."

"That's from the willow bark. I'll get you some water."

"Why did you give me willow bark?"

"You seemed feverish, thrashing about in the bed, and I knew that's what my ma would have done for you if she were here."

"That was a good idea. It must not have been a high fever since I'm better this morning. Except for this." He touched the side of his head and winced.

"That's going to take some time to heal. I tried stitching you up, but it's a lot different to pull a needle through skin than through cloth. My stitches aren't as pretty." She glanced away, but not before he saw her face scrunch.

"It's a bit different, that's true. Have you done that before?"

"No, I tried to watch Ma stitch my father, but I fainted. So it's a miracle from God that I was able to close your wound."

Travis knew about miracles, but that he'd been on the receiving end didn't seem fitting. God should have chosen to save Caleb, not him.

Annabelle finished with the note she'd penned for her father on her last piece of fine foolscap and blew on the ink to dry it. She hadn't written that she didn't plan to return to his home, only how much she had to get away, especially after her encounter with William's wife.

William's wife.

It galled her to write that, and it showed with the blobs of ink she'd left on the paper. Satisfied she'd given him enough information, she placed the pen back in the crystal holder. Her plan was set in motion now, the trunk sat at the station waiting, and she'd found a reliable, perfect, and unexpected chaperone.

She sipped the chamomile tea and nibbled at the small piece of toast she'd brought upstairs with her. She'd been too excited, nervous about the trip to eat her dinner. The tea had cooled and no longer held any appeal. The toast was too dry to consume. She dropped it onto the flowered china plate and pushed her chair back.

Had she forgotten anything? The few things she'd knitted, three dresses, a dress for Heaven, and the jam for Angel were at the top of the list. She'd filled in the trunk with things she needed to start her new life and some that would remind her of home—an embroidered pillowcase her mother had made and one of father's cigars so she could conjure him in her mind with a sniff.

Anticipation instead of sleep filled her thoughts as she wandered around her bedroom memorizing it, because if her plan worked, she wouldn't be returning. She stopped at her dressing table and picked up the framed daguerreotype of her mother. It might fit in her reticule. She wanted to bring it with her, but no, if she did, her father would immediately know she had no plans to return. She hoped someday he would send it to her. She hugged the frame to her chest. "I miss you, Ma."

Chapter 6

The cup Heaven carried shook against its saucer as she walked across the cabin. It was as if her body knew something wasn't right and didn't want her asking questions. She couldn't believe she'd stood there acting like a debutant, asking everyday questions, while all she wanted to do was shout like a little girl, "Where's my Pa?" Her black skirt rustled as she crossed the floor, as if whispering warnings of unpleasantness to come. She hated that skirt.

"Here you are, Mr. Logan. Do you need help, or do you feel confident that you can hold the cup?" She avoided looking at the stitched side of his head, preferring to concentrate on the curly dark hair mussed from a rough night.

He reached for the cup, brushing his fingers against hers. It caused a tingle to rush through her. How strange. That had never happened when Jake touched her hand. The tremor caused the cup and saucer to tip until it almost slid out of her grip, but she found the strength to hang on until he had a firm grasp on it. She stood at the foot of the bed while he drank. It seemed it took a lifetime for him to drink the contents. When he finished, he didn't offer her the empty cup.

She held out her hand to take it from him when small

taps echoed under the window as something walked across the porch.

"Mr. Jackson! That troublesome goat is walking on my porch again!" Her hands curled into fists. She wanted him off of there. He was always chewing on the posts. She took a step toward the door and stopped. Mr. Jackson could wait. He'd just come back again anyway. She didn't want to delay any longer. She spun around, "You were going to tell me about Pa?"

He pointed to the stool next to the bed. "It would be best if you sit, as it's a long story."

His tone made her knees weak, but she made it to the stool without embarrassing herself by tripping and landing on his chest. She took time to arrange her skirt, making sure her ankles were covered. She looked and found him staring at her. His brown eyes were warm and caring. Mary, whoever she was, should consider herself blessed.

"Who else lives here?"

"My sister, Angel, is asleep in the loft." Her sister had helped last night in ways Heaven wouldn't have thought possible. The two of them worked in harmony like a pair of well-trained horses.

"I met your father on the steamboat, not long after we left Memphis."

"You know where he is! You've brought our passage money?" She scooted to the edge of the stool. She had so much to do—lists to make, things to pack—and she needed to find someone to buy this place. Then she realized Mr. Logan hadn't answered her question. In fact, he stared at her in a sad sort of way. "You don't have the money? Were you robbed?"

"Please, Miss Wharton. Let me finish."

The bad feeling slid on like a strained pelisse. "Go ahead. I'll listen."

"While we were on the deck observing the water, your father fell. . . ."

"He went overboard? He drowned!" She sprung to her feet. Her hand caressed the back of her neck while she paced the length of the bed. "I knew he shouldn't have gone on that boat. He should have taken us with him and traveled by land. If we'd gone with him, he wouldn't have. . ." She hiccupped a sob.

"Miss Wharton. He didn't drown. Please sit down."

She sat but didn't want to. The small, dark cabin closed in on her. She forced herself to look him in the eye. "Tell me."

"He didn't drown, but he isn't alive."

Numbness crept from the roots of her hair to her toes. She worked her lips, trying to form words. A guttural sound escaped before her vocal cords could shake free of the shock. "Not alive? Dead? Pa's dead?" Her mind flew into action. She was left to take care of Angel. What would she do now? How would they survive the winter? There was no family left to run to. Maybe Annabelle's father would let them stay, but she would have to get there, and the train fare. . . And Angel! What would she tell her? Her mind pushed and pulsed against the sides of her head. She feared her skull would burst.

"Miss Wharton,"—he touched her shoulder—"I can see lots of things are worrying you. Would you like me to tell you the rest of what happened later?"

"No. No, I have to know now so I can tell my. . ." A sob

escaped. "My sister." They were alone now, just the two of them. The realization found purchase and settled into her shoulders. It was an enormous burden she wasn't sure she could carry. She dabbed her eyes with the hem of her apron. "Go ahead, tell me."

"I did everything I knew how to do, but nothing worked. I tried to save him. I couldn't. He died on September 27 from a high fever."

Fever. Icy cold formed layers around her heart, and she fought to take a breath. It wasn't possible—no not at all. Not Pa, too. The man had to be mistaken. "September?" That wasn't long after he'd left. That's why they hadn't heard from him in all these months. "What took you so long to come and tell us?"

He seemed uncomfortable, wiggling in the bed away from her, and turned his head. "I wasn't aware there was anyone to tell."

Her mouth slacked open, and she gasped. Surely Pa had mentioned them, unless he'd been too sick.

"Then how did you know to come here?" Suspicion marched into her mind. He was here because he thought the place was abandoned.

She was right about shooting him after all.

Annabelle greeted her companion with a conspiratorial smile as she climbed into the closed buggy. She'd scooted out of the house with a cheery good-bye wave to John, even though leaving without saying a proper forever farewell to him left a small knot of sadness hanging in her throat.

"Good morning, Mrs. Miles." She slid under the edge of the wool carriage blanket Mrs. Miles held up for her. A waft of attar of roses hugged her. Annabelle's own mother used to wear that fragrance. "Isn't it a great day to ride a train?"

"Isn't it though, even if it's a bit chilly? Now we must stay out of Jake's sight so he doesn't make us disembark before we've even left the station." The older woman smoothed the blanket over her lap.

"He's going to be surprised to see us, isn't he?" Annabelle hoped Jake wouldn't be furious at her for asking his mother to be her chaperone. Mrs. Miles had agreed readily, stating she'd enjoy spending time with her son. She had told Annabelle how much she had missed him. On the train he wouldn't be able to hide in his room the way he did at home, and Mrs. Miles said she had a lot she wanted to say to him.

Mrs. Miles's striking green eyes glimmered as she patted Annabelle's gloved hand. "I do hope to see him marry Heaven while we're there, too. I've been praying he'll come to his senses once he sees her and forgets that nonsense about not being good enough for her."

"That would be nice." If Jake did marry Heaven, then Mrs. Miles would have to travel back alone. Annabelle hadn't thought about that situation. Even though she'd made the decision to travel to Memphis on her own, that was her worry, one that Jake's mother shouldn't have. She'd simply convince Heaven not to get married without Jake's father present. She tugged the edge of the blanket under her hip and settled in to take in her last views of the city she'd called home.

"Pa's dead? What happened?" A young girl's voice shrieked from above.

Heaven's eyes widened. "That's my sister, Angel. Apparently she is eavesdropping. I have to go to her."

Travis tugged the blanket under his chin. "Before we continue this conversation, do you think I could—could use the, um. . . ?"

Her face flushed a delightful rose color as she understood his request. He hadn't meant to embarrass her, but he really needed a trip outside.

"Of course. Do you think you can make it alone, or. . . ?" Her throat bobbed as she swallowed. "Should I bring you a chamber pot?"

Now her face was past rose, more of a blood-red color. Come to think of it, his face was feeling a bit warm. "I'll be fine. I'll take my time getting up so the room steadies. If you'll just bring me my clothes."

"You don't need any. We didn't remove anything. That wouldn't have been proper."

Proper? Where did she think she was, in a big city where women took notes of every uncovered sneeze? "My boots?"

"Still on your feet."

"On my feet." He wiggled his toes. They bumped into leather. He peaked under the quilt. He was fully clothed right down to his muddy boots. "Guess your sheets are going to need washing."

"They were going to need it anyway after you bled all over

them." She stepped away. "I'll see to Angel while you're outside."

After she'd left him alone, he stood. His head pounded, and the room dipped and swayed. It didn't matter how weak his legs were; he would make it outside to the privy. Alone.

When he came back inside, he found Heaven next to the fireplace in a rocking chair holding her sister and stroking her golden hair. Heaven briefly raised her red-rimmed eyes and met his then rested her head against the top of her sister's. The fire had nearly died. Only a few winking embers remained.

He didn't say anything but let them grieve, knowing there was more to come. The chill of the cabin wrapped around him, sending goose bumps down his arm, and he hoped it was that and not the return of the fever. His fever must have been high for him not to remember what had occurred the night before. Gathering a few small logs from the pile next to the fireplace he knelt and placed them on the embers. With a squeeze from the bellows, air whooshed across the bed of embers. Orange and then blue flames jumped and then licked the logs until they tasted the bark. Satisfied the fire would burn, he stood, unsure of what to do next.

Heaven lifted her face. The peach tone had faded, leaving her pale. "I'll make breakfast."

Angel grabbed her sister's neck. "Not yet."

"That's okay. Can I do something?" He felt out of place. He'd seen a lot of death but hadn't experienced the womenfolk's side of it.

"There is nothing for you to do, no one to send a telegram to. It's just the two of us now." Heaven lowered her eyes and kissed the part on her sister's head.

"You have a preacher I can get for you?" He shifted his weight. "I could ride back into town."

"No!" Angel hopped off her sister's lap and slapped her hands on her hips.

Travis backed up.

"You can't tell anyone. They'll take Heaven away and lock her up." Her arms folded around her chest, and she rocked on her heels. "If that happens, I won't have anyone."

Heaven reached out her arms and encircled her sister. She pulled Angel back onto her lap, all the while glaring at him.

Travis looked at the door. He should leave and come back later when they'd had time to calm down. Then he would tell them the rest. But he couldn't. He had never been able to shrug off his need to rescue animals and humans. These two were scared and feeling hopeless. He wouldn't abandon them. "They won't lock her up. I promise. If anyone asks, I'll tell them it was an accident."

Travis found himself in the kitchen. What did he plan to do in here? He wasn't sure, but at least he was away from the scary girl who seemed even fiercer than her sister. He picked up a toy-sized china cup. It looked as if it would hold only a thimbleful of coffee, as his father would say. "Can I get anyone a cup of coffee?"

Heaven released her sister and wiggled out of the rocker, leaving Angel. "Forgive me, Mr. Logan. I've forgotten my manners of hospitality." She wiped her eyes with her hands and appeared to pull a smile from out of nowhere and apply it across her face. "I'll make you some breakfast."

"That would be nice." He didn't want to eat; he wasn't

hungry. But he wasn't about to mess with her hospitality manners, as they seemed important to her. He stood back and watched her work in silence while Angel huddled in the rocker in front of the fire.

"Sit down, Mr. Logan. Angel, come try and eat something."

"I don't want to." Angel's voice sounded dull and flat to Travis. He tried but couldn't imagine the pain the little miss felt.

"Angel, you need to come eat, too. We aren't wasting these eggs." Heaven turned from the stove and pointed a spatula at her sister. "Now."

Travis waited for Angel to find a place at the table, afraid he might take her seat and cause another outbreak of anger. "Is the chair at the end of the table all right for me to sit in?"

"It's Pa's chair, but I guess he won't be needin' it, so you can sit there." Angel scooted closer to the table.

Heaven plunked a plate on the table in front of him. Travis sat and stared at his plate of scrambled yellers. His stomach flipped and did a twist. Perhaps he wasn't quite ready for heavy food, or maybe it was the untold details of why he was at the Wharton's home. He picked up a piece of perfectly browned toast. With a knife, he shaved off a sliver of butter. "Did you make the butter here on the farm?"

"Miss Bessie did." Angel spooned a hunk of eggs into her mouth. "Heaven just churns it into butter."

"Angel, please act like a lady at the table. Don't talk with your mouth full, and take smaller bites." Heaven filled a china cup with coffee nestled in a saucer. It rattled as she set it in front of Travis.

His finger wouldn't fit through the handle of the tiny cup.

He picked it up and rested it in the palm of his hand like an egg, afraid it would crack. "Thank you for the breakfast. It seems I'm not that hungry though."

"Does it hurt much? I'm sorry I don't have anything to dull your pain. We don't keep spirits in the house."

His hand went to the wounded area and touched it without consideration of the possible contact pain. He winced. He'd have to cover that after he talked to Heaven about her father's wishes. "It's not too bad. I have some pain medication in my saddlebag. If it gets to feeling worse, I'll take some. I don't like to use it though. I've seen soldiers get to where they want more and more of it long after their pain should have been gone."

"Are you a doctor?" Angel asked.

His eyes shifted to the toast on his plate. Eating would buy him time before having to answer. He picked it up. He was unsure what to say to Angel's question. He was a doctor, still, but he didn't want to be. He no longer wanted to wake up regretting a mistake he might or might not have made that caused a man to die. "I was. During the war." No longer hungry, he dropped the toast on the plate. Crumbs broke off, scattering on the worn tabletop.

"We could have used you last night, since we didn't know what we were doing when we patched you up." Angel spider-walked her fingers across the tabletop to the right of her plate where her glass of milk sat.

Travis, sure she would knock it over, grabbed her hand and placed it on the glass.

"Stop it! Don't help me!" Angel pushed back from the

table. "I can do things. I can do lots of things if people would just let me."

Travis was taken aback by the display of anger. Then it occurred to him that Angel hadn't been blind since birth. He'd seen this same behavior in some of the soldiers with head wounds that caused them to go blind.

"How long has it been since you could see, Angel?"

"Angel, finish your breakfast. There's too much talking going on, and it's going to get cold." Heaven scrambled out of her chair. "*Dr.* Logan, I imagine that your coffee could be warmed up a bit."

Why did Heaven want to avoid his question? It seemed odd to him, or maybe they were one of those families that ignored such things.

"That would be nice." He held up his cup. "Then I need to see to my horse." He noticed the dried mud on his jacket sleeve. "I need to get a set of fresh clothes, too, one less distressing to look at."

She topped off the cup with the dark liquid. "I fed your horse when I milked the cow this morning. I fed the chickens, too, Angel. After last night, I thought you might like to sleep a little later."

"That's okay—just for today."

Heaven began to clear the table. Since it had been a small breakfast, it didn't take long to accomplish the task.

"Before you get your shirt, I want to know everything about how Pa died and why you were the one chosen to tell us."

Travis cleared his throat and ran his hand against his scruffy chin. He needed a shave. "I don't know if you want

Angel to hear all the details."

Angel wrapped her arms around her chest. "I want to know."

"You can talk in front of her. He's her pa, too."

Travis felt his shoulders tighten. "You're stubborn women. But I'll answer your questions after I get my clean clothes." Because when they found out what he had to say, he was sure Heaven would go for that rifle and usher him out of the cabin.

"Your clothes can wait. We can't." Heaven plopped in the chair across from him, next to Angel. She grasped her sister's hand. "Go on now. Tell us about our pa."

"Caleb, your father. . ."

"Quit stalling," Angel said.

He cleared his throat. "He caught something in Memphis is my best guess, and when he fell on the deck, he was sweating and feverish."

Heaven paled, and her eyes widened at the word "feverish." He wondered why.

"Did he say anything about Angel and me before. . . ?" Her eyes glistened. "Before he passed?"

Angel pulled her hand out of Heaven's. "That's all? He caught a fever and died? That's why you've been stalling? Lots of people get a fever and die. That's what happened to Ma. Might as well get him his clothes and send him back to town. He's told us what he came to say, and he promised he would tell people that you shot him by accident."

Travis glanced at the corner where the rifle seemed to sparkle. "There's a bit more."

Heaven's eyes narrowed. "More?"

Could he get to that gun before her? He scooted his chair

back and angled his body toward the door. "Before your father died, he had the ship's captain write his will." His legs tensed, readying to spring from the chair. "He left me this farm."

Heaven stood so fast her chair fell, banging on the floor.

Travis was a second behind her, ready to run for the gun.

"Why would our pa give you our home?" Heaven's lips narrowed, and her lips rolled in tight.

"I don't know. We'd been talking in between his bouts of fever about where the best place to raise horses would be. He insisted it was here." The peach had returned to her cheeks, but not the sweet blush color, more the overripe, ready-to-explode-with-juice color.

"I'll get your clothes, Dr. Logan, and then I want you out of here and on your way back to that Mary you were calling for." Heaven's frostbitten words stopped him from telling her what else her father had given him.

Chapter 7

All concern about being prim and proper fled Heaven's mind as she gathered the hem of her skirt and stormed off to the barn. She sidestepped the hole, realizing she no longer had a need to fix it. Not if what Dr. Logan said was true. He would have to take care of this place now.

Inside the barn, sunshine poked its long fingers between the boards, lighting the tack corner, making it easier to see.

Mr. Jackson butted against her thigh, smearing mud on her fresh white apron. She pushed his head. "Go away, goat."

He stepped back and then reached down to nip at her hem.

"Stop it!" Mr. Jackson irritated her on a good day. Today she looked at him and saw stew meat.

She unbuckled a saddlebag. It wasn't proper to be going through a man's personal belongings without being married. Unsettled, she rushed the chore. Her fingers touched cotton, and she pulled out a shirt. A paper fluttered to the ground.

Mr. Jackson made a dive for it.

She snatched it up. "Not for you." She was thankful she retrieved it before him and that the barn floor was dry so there wouldn't be telltale wet marks. It wouldn't do if Dr. Logan thought she'd been sneaking through his private papers.

Holding the paper with great care, she slung his clean shirt over her shoulder, wishing she didn't notice the scent of leather mixed with the smell of spice. It smelled just like him, making her feel warm and safe, and how could that be when he was taking their home from them? *Can't trust your nose, goose.* She planned to put the paper back, hoping he wouldn't notice it had been moved. Silly, really, since he would know she might have seen it, since he'd let her retrieve his shirt.

As she moved closer to the saddlebag, a ray of light snaked through the barn wall, illuminating a name she knew, and knew well. Her pa's perfect penmanship caught her unaware. She traced his name with her fingertip. He'd touched this paper. It was the last thing that she knew for sure he had written. With this new loss, her grief weighed heavier, and this one final contact with her pa overcame her good manners.

Before she knew what she was doing, she'd read the document from beginning to end.

Bile rose and burned her throat. She swallowed the thick spit. She wouldn't let her father get away with this. Not this. Anything but this. Unconcerned about how much her mother would have chastised her for unladylike behavior, she bent and gathered a large amount of her dreadful black skirt into her hand, hiking it higher than her ankles. With the other, she grasped tight the disturbing paper she'd discovered. With her head down, she charged toward the cabin.

Blinking back angry tears, she shoved the paper in her apron pocket as she ran over the bumpy ground. She was going to send Dr. Logan packing, and she didn't care if she had to shoot him again. This time she'd aim for his heart, and his Mary could wonder what happened to him forever for all Heaven cared. Angel would be amenable to helping bury him out where Pa had planned to pen the pigs last spring.

The fingers of the earth snagged her foot. In her hurry, she'd forgotten about the hole in the path. On her way to the ground, she heard an awful popping noise and felt a lightning bolt of pain. Right before she hit the dirt, she grasped the paper tighter. Then her mind took a nap.

Heaven opened her eyes. Her face felt sticky. Touching it, she found it covered in mud. Why was she on the ground? She braced herself with one hand and pulled her leg a fragment closer. Pain landed like a mule kick in her chest, taking away her breath and sending it to the Mississippi. "Why, God? Why?" As soon as life around her began to sour, it went on to curdle soon after.

She smacked the ground with a fist. "How much more pain are You planning to send my way, God? I can't take it anymore!" How would she manage now? Because she'd surely broken her leg. Could it get any worse? She'd shot a man, caused her sister to go blind, and now she'd messed up her own body.

"Angel!" Her sister's hearing had improved since losing her sight. Heaven hoped to reap the benefit. She shivered, causing waves of pain to roll through her leg.

"Angel!"

Nothing.

Maybe she should shout for Dr. Logan. No, she wouldn't ask him for anything.

"Angel! Help me! Please help!"

What was taking the woman so long to get his shirt? He paced the floor of the cabin, wondering how he was going to explain Heaven's father's will. Standing up straight in a pile of goose poop would be easier than telling her he only wanted—

Angel bumped into him, or did he bump into her? "Dr. Logan! Heaven's calling. She cried, 'Help!' Can you see what's happening?"

"I didn't hear her, but I'll go see." Apparently Angel had no intention of letting him go alone, he discovered as he followed her to the door. Stepping out on the porch, he didn't see anything, but he heard a moan. "Miss Wharton?"

"She's by the barn. I can tell." Angel headed to the steps. "Come on, she needs us."

"I'm right behind you. I see her. She's lying in a heap on the ground."

"I bet she fell in that hole she keeps telling me to watch out for."

"It looks like she did." Travis looked to the sky for a moment. *Why, God?* He couldn't seem to escape people who needed doctoring.

Angel squatted next to her sister. "Heaven, you fell in the hole, didn't you? Good thing Dr. Logan and I are here to save you."

Travis bent over. His head wound thumped. "Do you think you can walk?"

"No, I can't get up at all." Heaven's forehead was drawn tight with the pain.

"Guess I'll have to carry you inside then." He slid his arms under her and lifted.

She screamed and went limp.

Travis was thankful she didn't weigh much, since he wasn't feeling quite as strong as he did yesterday. Yesterday he'd been in good health on his way to his new life. Today he had a hole in his head and a beautiful woman in his arms. Now that she was captive, he took the chance to observe her without fear of being shot. Her face, missing the angry hue of this morning, was alabaster white. And holding her close, he noticed the tiny speck at the corner of her eye wasn't dirt but a birthmark in the shape of a teardrop.

"Angel, can you get the door?"

"Are we by the hole?"

"About two steps in front of it." He waited to see if she would cling to him or head out on her own.

"Then I'll start at three." She took a step and started counting. When she reached ten she stopped. "Will you tell me if I count wrong? I don't want to trip on the step."

"I will." He followed behind her as she made quick time across the yard.

"Seventeen. I should be at the step. Am I?" Angel looked over her shoulder. Her gaze hit his chest.

"Yes you are, and there are three. . ."

"I know. Three steps." Confidence showed in her stance as she flew up the stairs and made it to the cabin door. "Stick her on Pa's bed, I guess."

Travis's stitches pulled as he lowered Heaven. As the blood rushed to his cut, his head throbbed.

She opened her eyes and cried out with pain. "It hurts! Did I break it? My leg, is it broken?"

"I'm not sure yet, since I haven't had a chance to inspect the damage. It might be a bad sprain. I'll have to take off your boot so I can look at it."

"Angel can do that." Her face was no longer white but red.

"She could, but can she tell if your leg is broken or if it's a sprained ankle?"

He could see the waves of indecision on her face. "I'm a doctor. I've seen a lot of ankles."

"Ladies' ankles?" Horror showed in her widened eyes.

"No ma'am, just soldiers' ankles. Will you let me look at it?"

She nodded.

He unlaced her boot and pulled at the heel to remove it.

She screamed.

He stopped. "I'm going to have to cut this off of your foot."

"You can't." Her voice wavered. "Please. It's my only pair."

And she wouldn't have the money to buy another pair he guessed. "It has to come off, Miss Wharton, and if I have to pull it off, it's going to hurt so much you'll wish you could shoot me twenty more times."

"No, wait. Please. We have laudanum in the kitchen. Angel, can you show him where we keep the medical basket? I can't stand this pain."

"You have laudanum? Why didn't you use it when you were stitching me up last night?" If she had, maybe they wouldn't have had this conversation this morning. He might still be sleeping, and she wouldn't have stepped in that hole.

"I forgot we had it."

"Forgot it? Or didn't want to offer it?" Travis shook his head in disbelief.

"Please?"

"I'll get it." He chastised himself for making her think he wouldn't give it to her. Angel collected the basket while he found the medicine and grabbed a spoon. He hesitated giving it to her, having seen others take even a small amount and not be able to stop once the pain was gone. Still, he didn't think he could treat her like a soldier and set her leg without the pain being deadened. His shoulders tensed as images of the battle-field slammed against each other in his mind. Here he was taking care of someone—again. All he'd wanted to do was raise horses, and now everything was complicated. He had to treat her; he couldn't just walk out of the house and leave her there.

Soldiering forth, he sat on the stool next to the bed. He poured the liquid into the spoon. "Open up and swallow fast. This won't taste good."

He gave her the large dose and waited for the telltale haze to slide across her eyes, signaling the power of the drug. She smiled at him and then winked. Startled, he withdrew his eyes from hers while wondering if he'd given her too much. She was quite small, not like the men he'd treated. Even the youngest were larger than she was.

"Angel, I need you here, too, or rather, I would feel better if you stood close by while I treated your sister. I noticed your sister prides herself on propriety."

Angel nodded, her lips screwed up as if she were considering saying something.

"Is there something on your mind, Little Miss?"

"It's just that if something improper happened, I wouldn't see it. So how can I protect Heaven?"

He sighed. From what he'd quickly learned about the Wharton women, they were all about protecting each other from harm. "No, I suppose you can't see me, so you'll have to trust me. I'll tell you everything I'm doing as I do it so you'll be able to hear my voice and know where I am."

"Guess that's all I can do." Angel rushed past him and scooted him off the stool. "You stay by her foot. No way am I letting you kiss her, not when you've been calling for Mary."

Mary. He felt like he'd been gut shot. How had Angel known about her? He must have said her name last night while under the influence of the fever. It wasn't likely he'd ever be kissing her again. Just another failure in his life. No matter that others said, it was better this way. He didn't think so then, but now that he was looking at the beautiful woman in front of him, the pain of betrayal was beginning to fade. But he brought it back to the front and filled in the diminishing colors. He wouldn't be blinded again by a pretty face, no matter how sweet that teardrop by her eye looked or how the softness of her skin tweaked a long-forgotten feeling of wanting to be responsible for someone. No, he wouldn't be dazzled by such things. He'd take care of her long enough to see her back on her feet, and then he'd leave.

Leave? But the farm was his, wasn't it? It was a dilemma. If he left, someone else would eventually take it from Heaven and Angel. Or worse, Heaven would actually kill the next man who rode down her drive. That had to be why Caleb had given him both the farm and Heaven. As if you could give a daughter away without her knowledge. He had some cogitating to do.

"Dr. Logan." Heaven's voice was thick as honey.

Her eyes were glazing, and Travis knew the medicine was working. "Yes, Miss Wharton?"

"I don't. . ." She blinked or more like closed her eyes and opened them slowly. " 'Tis not working—the medicine."

"Yes it is, Miss Wharton. I do believe it's about time for me to slip off that boot."

"Dr. Logan. You are a beautiful man." Heaven's eyes lowered, and she stroked his hand with a finger. "You have such capable-looking hands."

His hand felt as hot as a poker just out of the fire where Heaven's finger had mapped its way across the back of his hand. He jerked it back. This was not something he'd ever experienced in the battlefield.

Angel snickered. "Maybe we should keep him, Heaven, if you like him so much."

Travis wiggled the boot free.

Heaven whimpered. "Stop. Please stop!"

"It's off now." He slowly rolled down her stocking to see if the skin had broken. He hoped not, because that would mean months of recovery.

"I'd like to keep Dr. Logan." Heaven's voice seemed thicker. He liked the way it sounded.

"Dr. Logan?" Her eyebrows couldn't seem to settle in one place as she attempted to focus on him.

"Yes, Miss Wharton?" Travis wondered how he would splint the ankle.

"I think I could love you. Could you love me, too?"

Heat crept up his face as Angel put her hand in front of her mouth to hold back the laughter. He was glad she couldn't see him, because she would likely tease him mercilessly. He wasn't a stranger to that, not with having older sisters.

"I'm sure I could, Miss Wharton. You are a mighty desirable woman." If she knew what else her pa had given him besides the land, would she still be saying that? He'd have to figure out what to do with these two soon. His plans hadn't included a wife, much less one with a precocious sister.

"Then I think we should get married soon, Dr. Logan. Pa's right. And I'm so tired of being alone. If we were married, I'd not be alone anymore."

She stared right at him; shimmering sapphires with feathery lashes pierced his heart in the lonely place, making a hole where she entered like a thief in the night. She'd make someone a beautiful wife, but not him. Then her eyes closed, and her head fell back on the pillow. From the way she was snoring, he knew she would be out for a while.

Her ankle was sprained, not broken. The tightness in Travis's neck released. Heaven's treatment wouldn't be pleasant, but not as unpleasant as it would be if she had broken a bone. She'd have to soak her foot in a bucket of cold water several times a day. He shivered again. As cold as this cabin was this morning, he wondered if a layer of ice would form across the top before she could plunk her foot into it. He felt sorry for her, but it was better than a broken ankle. The last time he'd treated a broken bone, an infection turned the foot green. He shuddered at the memory of sawing off that man's foot. At least this time the patient should retain all of her parts.

"Angel, I need some old clothes that I can cut into strips. I have to bind your sister's ankle. Do you think you could find me something to use? Something Heaven won't be angry about us taking scissors to?"

Angel stood. "I suppose we could use one of Ma's crinolines. Heaven won't be happy about that though." She twisted a curl in her fingers.

No, she probably needed her mother's things to make new clothes for her and Angel. "What about a shirt of your father's?" Caleb wouldn't be needing those anymore. A man's shirt didn't have enough fabric to make anything useful for the remaining Whartons.

"Pa left a shirt and a pair of pants behind. Sometimes Heaven wears the pants though, to clean out the barn."

Since the barn belonged to him now, he knew Heaven wouldn't need to muck it out. "I'll take the pants. They'll make long and strong strips. If Heaven complains, I'll find a way to calm her down. Can you bring me the scissors from your sister's sewing basket, too?"

Angel took a step forward and touched Heaven's arm. "Heaven? He wants me to get the scissors. I know I'm not supposed to, but if you don't wake up and tell me not to, then I'm going to do it."

Heaven remained still.

"Guess that means it's okay."

Angel's toothy grin lightened his mood, and then the dangers of a blind child handling sharp scissors occurred to him. "I imagine this one time it will be okay to break your sister's rule. Just point the sharp end to the ground. Don't run or skip on your way back here."

"I can do that. Pa's pants are hangin' on the wall peg behind you."

Light on her feet, Angel took off, seeming to forget her vow of never leaving Travis alone with her sister. He shook his head. That poor girl needed to be able to do more things on her own. He would tell Heaven about the soldiers he had worked with and how their attitudes about life got better when they were treated normally. Not that Angel acted like a spoiled invalid. Far from it, she was as sharp as a razor just run over a strap. It seemed to him Angel's problem was her sister. Maybe he could work with Heaven on that while he was here waiting for her to get strong enough to go. . .to go where? It seemed she and Angel didn't have a place to go.

Angel brought him the scissors. "Heaven never lets me touch these. I told her I could, and I would be careful. Can I cut the strips out of Pa's pants?"

Travis wanted to say yes. "If there was another pair, I would say yes. But since we only have the one, I probably need to cut them so we get straight strips."

Disappointment flashed over her face, and her little body seemed to grow smaller as he hunkered down on the stool. "I understand."

"I think you could do it, darlin', but one wrong cut, and we'd have to get into your mama's petticoats. I would rather Heaven be mad at me than at you if a mistake is made."

Angel lifted her face and beamed. "So it's not because I can't see?"

"No, Little Miss, I don't want to get your sister's ire up.

She's already shot me once this week."

Angel giggled. "That she did, Dr. Logan."

Annabelle grasped the edge of a chair as the dining car rounded a curve, sending her off balance. She would have landed on the floor if not for the gentleman who caught her.

He steadied her. "Are you all right? These trains often take you on a ride you didn't purchase a ticket for."

She touched her chignon, checking that her hair hadn't escaped its silver net. "I'm fine, sir. Thank you kindly for assisting me."

"My pleasure. Thaddeus Kincaid at your service anytime, Miss. . . ?"

"Singleton. Thank you again, Mr. Kincaid." She noticed the clipped speech and harsh ending consonants. Mr. Kincaid was not a southern man.

"Annabelle?" Mrs. Miles tapped her on the shoulder.

She turned slightly, trying to avoid knocking anything from the table they stood next to.

"Are you okay, dear?" Mrs. Miles patted Annabelle's cheek. "I saw you almost take that dreadful fall."

"Mr. Kincaid rescued me, Mrs. Miles. I'm quite all right." The dining car door opened from the other end, and Jake stepped into the aisle. He stopped and tilted his head as if to make sure he was seeing correctly. They'd been found out a little earlier than Annabelle had hoped.

"Mother? Annabelle?" Jake hovered behind Mr. Kincaid. "What are you doing here?"

Mr. Kincaid stepped aside.

Annabelle scooted past him and grasped Jake's arm. "Surprise! Your mother and I thought it would be wonderfully fun to go with you to visit Heaven."

He scowled at her. "You did, did you?"

Annabelle dropped her hand to her side. She hadn't expected him to be happy, and he wasn't. He resembled Mrs. Cooper's growling terrier that used to plague her and Heaven when they walked to school. She backed up a few steps, letting his mother get closer.

"Jake, when she asked me to escort her, I couldn't think of a better thing to do. I've not had a chance to visit with you since you came back, and now I'll get to see Heaven as well." Mrs. Miles tugged at her son's sleeve. "Have you eaten? Annabelle and I were getting ready to have lunch. Of course you haven't. That's why you're in the dining car."

"Mother. . ."

"Now, Jake, don't be angry at us. We girls need a little adventure in our lives. So come, sit and dine with us. Then you can tell us how you're going to catch Heaven when she faints at the shock of seeing you."

"Mother, I told you. . ."

"I know, Jake. You think you're going to break that girl's heart again and tell her you can't marry her. I think when you see that lovely girl again, you're going to change your mind." Mrs. Miles stopped at a table and waited for her son to pull out her chair. "Annabelle, come, sit by me."

"Yes, Annabelle, please sit by my mother. It's quite kind of you to accompany her on this unsafe journey." His face said otherwise, lips drawn in a straight line and no hint of friendliness in his eyes.

So that was why he was angry. He thought she'd endangered his mother. She hadn't. So far everyone had been kind and helpful. "I knew we'd be safe once we found you. And that didn't take long." *Just long enough to keep you from making us leave the train.*

A server placed steaming bowls of tomato soup in front of each of them. Annabelle bowed her head and silently gave thanks, pushing back the nagging feeling she shouldn't have left home without talking to her father one more time. She would have though, if he'd been home. She was right to take this opportunity, since her father wouldn't be home for two more weeks. Waiting that long wasn't possible. Not with that northern, fiancé-stealing woman in town.

Annabelle observed Jake as Mrs. Miles engaged her son in a stilted conversation in which he gave one-word responses. The Jake she knew always wore a smile, suggesting something fun was about to happen. His blond hair hung shabbily around his ears, and his face held a sharpness that wasn't there when he left. What had happened to him while he was away? Everyone said he was a hero, the only man in his regiment to make it out alive from the Battle of Shiloh. Most southern men wouldn't brag about that but would wear it like a suit of fine clothes everywhere they went.

". . .luggage, Annabelle?" Jake stared at her. "Mother said you brought luggage. How many bags?"

Around them dinner plates were kissed with the sounds of silver. The dining car steward walked the aisles refilling glasses.

"I have a trunk filled with things for Heaven." *And what I need when I leave Heaven's.* No need to fill him in on that plan just yet. For now she'd keep that secret tied up in her heart.

"With Mother's things, I'll need to arrange transportation to Friendship. I had planned to rent a horse."

"How far is it from the station to Heaven's?" She hadn't considered getting the trunk delivered.

"We'll disembark in Jackson. The rail line doesn't stretch to Friendship."

"Stagecoach then? Or can we rent a buggy?" She wondered how much extra that would cost. She had to be careful with her money if she wanted to succeed on her own.

"Something. We'll have to wait and see what's available." Jake picked up his glass and drained it. "Now if you'll excuse me, I'm going to the smoking car."

"Jacob, I had hoped we could talk more after dinner." Mrs. Miles's shoulders sagged.

"Not tonight, Mother." Jake stood and nodded at Annabelle. "Pleasant dreams, ladies."

He'd grown ungrateful as well. Annabelle reached over and squeezed Mrs. Miles's hand. She wished her mother were still alive. Jake should be more thankful. "We'll have a nice time without him. I brought a new book along, and we can take turns reading to each other."

Mrs. Miles's lips rose up gently. "I'd like that."

Chapter 8

Travis set the bucket of cold water he'd collected from the pond on the floor next to the bed. "She's going to wake up when her toes hit that water. It's likely she'll be fightin' mad. Angel, I want you to step back so she doesn't land a solid hit on you if she starts swinging her fists. Might be right nice if you'd pray she doesn't hit me."

Angel backed up against the cabin wall.

With great gentleness, Travis slid one arm under Heaven's head. Using the other hand, he maneuvered her into a sitting position.

"What are you doing? I hear the blankets moving, and I can't see you!"

"I apologize. I did say I would tell you everything. Your sister needs to be in a sitting position, so I slid her up against the wall close to the edge of the bed. That way I can dangle her leg over the edge into the bucket."

"Heaven's not going to like this—you sliding her on the bed and touching her leg, not being married. No, she won't like this at all. It's not proper, not proper at all."

"No, not for anyone, unless they are a doctor. Don't you forget that only a doctor can do this sort of procedure, and that makes it proper." God forgive him, he had no idea if the ladies of society would ever forgive Heaven for this, but they would never find out. He didn't have a choice, or at least not one that wouldn't put Angel in danger of getting hurt.

Heaven's eyes slid open one at a time. "Please, Dr. Logan, say you're going to marry me." Then, just as quickly as her plea expanded into the room, her eyes closed.

Angel was still praying when Travis heard her say, "If Heaven wants to marry Dr. Logan, that's okay with me, too. . ."

He had to get out of this house. Too many marrying-minded women for him to be around. Heaven's head lolled to one side, and then her shoulders began to follow. He bent over her and placed his hands under her arms to level her.

Heaven reached out and grabbed him with both hands and pulled him close. "Dr. Logan, you have my permission to kiss me, but just this once."

He was sorely tempted to do just that to those rose-colored lips. He grunted. It had been a long time since he'd kissed anyone. Mary had been the last. "Maybe another time, Miss Wharton, when you're not drugged. Angel, I'm propping your sister against the wall, and then I'm stuffing a blanket around her so she doesn't slide down again." After he was satisfied she wouldn't be moving, he stooped, grabbed her foot, and plunged it into the cold water.

Her shriek pierced his ears. Her fist landed on his cheek mere inches from his wound.

"Leave it there!" Travis barked. "It's sprained, and if you don't leave it, your foot will swell like a watermelon." He held her ankle with one hand and fended off her fists with the other. "Be still, please, Miss Wharton. I'll let you remove it in a few minutes."

"What happened?"

Heaven's fingers were still curled into tight fists, but at least they weren't flying at his head anymore.

"You tripped in that hole you're always warning me about." Angel sat on the bed next to her sister. "You done swinging your fists at him?"

Heaven groaned. "I did? I told you it was dangerous. Did I hit my head, too?" She ran her fingers through her hair. "Why is my mouth filled with cotton?"

"The laudanum you had stored but didn't remember to use on me? I gave you some. It makes you thirsty, gives you a head-ache, and does a few other things." He thought better of telling her the drug made her talk out of her head and say things she didn't mean. There wasn't a need to embarrass her. He looked at Angel and wondered if she would tell her sister about the marriage proposal. Right now she was stroking her sister's hand. Maybe she realized her sister wasn't in her right mind when she said those crazy things.

The cabin was getting colder. The fire had feasted on the logs he'd put in earlier. He'd tend to it and then wrap her ankle.

"Angel, can you get your sister a cloth to dry her foot? I'm going to throw another log on the fire." He turned back to Heaven. "Keep your foot in there until I get back."

"Just make that fire roar. The water is so cold. I have goose pimples."

Travis took a quilt from the end of the bed and wrapped it around her shoulders. "Maybe that will help."

She tugged the quilt tight around her shoulders. "Hurry back. I don't know how much longer I can keep my foot in here."

Travis added several more logs to the fire. Angel waited by her sister and held out the cloth to him.

"This will be fine, Angel." With his fingers, he tilted Heaven's chin, trying to ignore how soft it felt. He inspected her eyes, looking for signs of too much of the painkiller. They didn't seem overly glazed or dull. He was reluctant to give her more, but if she fought him too much, he would. "I don't want to give you any more laudanum, so this is going to hurt a bit. You can scream if you want to. Angel and I won't judge you for it."

"What are you going to do to me that will make me scream?" Her voice wavered.

He knew she wasn't as sure as she wanted to sound. She probably didn't want to cause any distress for Angel. "First, I'm going to take your foot out of the water and dry it. I don't want you to try and help me support it. If you do, it will hurt more. Let me do all the work, and the pain will be less."

Heaven nodded and sucked in her breath and held it.

Either she would yell really loud or pass out. He hoped for the latter.

Travis lifted Heaven's foot from the water. Water drops plunked back into the bucket. He resisted the urge to rub her icy foot with the towel to get the blood circulating. Instead, he gently patted the cloth over her diminutive foot. A foot he wouldn't normally ever see unless he was married to her. Especially since he had given up doctoring. "You all right?"

She let out a ragged breath. "Maybe there's still some drug working to keep the pain away."

"Maybe." He was feeling his own injury now and was a bit tired and shaky. "Angel, can you scoot the stool over here for me?

I need to sit while I do this part."

Angel did as he asked and then climbed on the bed next to her sister.

He rested Heaven's foot on his lap.

She gasped and brushed the quilt from her shoulders. "Dr. Logan!"

"Does it hurt now?"

"No, it's just my foot"—her face was flushed—"is in your lap."

"Excuse the impropriety, Miss Wharton. It's the only way I can wrap it tightly. My head is hurting, or I'd try and do this another way."

Her head lowered, and her hair fell over her face, hiding it from him. "Much obliged, Dr. Logan."

Angel couldn't see the two of them, but she found the exchange interesting. With Heaven declaring her love for Dr. Logan and him taking such good care of Heaven, Angel was thinking of possibilities. She liked Dr. Logan, and Pa had given him their home. If Dr. Logan liked Heaven, they would have a place to live.

She heard carriage wheels rambling down the lane. "Someone's coming. I'll find out who it is." She slid off the bed and headed for the door before her sister had a chance to respond.

Stepping out on the porch, she could hear voices in the distance. She grinned. God must agree with her plan, because those were the voices of Preacher and Mrs. Reynolds. She couldn't wait to bring them inside to meet Dr. Logan, who at this very moment had his hands on her sister's leg.

A rooster bickered with another one out in the yard as the

buggy creaked to a stop. Angel listened to the huff of the horses' breath and the creak of the springs on the carriage as someone stepped out. Preacher Reynolds probably, since the man always got out first and helped his lady out. Angel had no idea why that was so important. She didn't need help getting out of a carriage. Maybe that changed when you got as old as Mrs. Reynolds.

She waited, not yelling a hello as she normally would. She was practicing her lady skills just as Heaven would want her to. No shouting at the company. Company should come to the door and be asked in immediately. Company should be offered something to eat and drink. That's what she would do, with one little bend in the rules. She'd wait until they were on the porch before saying anything to Heaven about their guests.

"Come on in. We are so glad you stopped by. Heaven will be thrilled to see you. She's in here." Angel maneuvered them to the bedroom doorway. "Look who's here, Heaven. Preacher and Mrs. Reynolds came by to say hello."

Horrified couldn't be the best word to describe how Mrs. Reynolds looked, but it would have to do. She stood there with her mouth forming an O, taking in Heaven's exposed leg draped across Dr. Logan's lap. And him—he looked frightful. Still in his clothes from yesterday and the bandage around his head.

"What's the meaning of this?" Preacher Reynolds pushed past his wife. "Why is there dried blood on the sheets? Who is this man? What's he doing here?"

Heaven's mouth refused to work. Her tongue stuck to the roof of her mouth.

"I'm Travis Logan—Dr. Logan." He offered his hand to Preacher Reynolds, who stared at it and then smiled and offered his own back.

"Dr. Logan. We hadn't heard about you setting up an office in Friendship. Welcome to our town."

Heaven relaxed a bit.

"Thank you, sir. I haven't set up an office yet. Not sure I will. I planned on raising horses on what I thought was a vacant farm."

"Now why would you think that it was uninhabited?"

"He galloped down the drive like he was going to steal everything we owned. And that's when Heaven. . ." Angel stood behind the Reynolds, who seemed to be frozen between the two rooms.

"Heaven thought she and Angel were in danger yesterday, and she shot in the air to warn me away. Except she missed. That's why there's blood on my clothing and the bed." Travis finished Angel's sentence.

Mrs. Reynolds rushed into the room. Tears welled in her eyes. "Heaven, Angel, I'm so sorry. This has been an awful year for you. I'm so glad we came to see you. Preacher Reynolds heard about a man coming out here, and we wanted to check on you. It's a good idea we did. Why didn't you come and get help after you shot him?"

Heaven wanted to scream. Why wasn't that an obvious answer? "I couldn't send Angel, and I didn't want to leave her here with him. If I took her along, the man might have bled to death before we returned."

"It's not good to be this far out of town when you're alone.

I don't know what your father was thinking when he left you."

Heaven forced her brain to pay attention. She was walking on marshy ground. Soon it wouldn't only be marauders she had to worry about, but the good church people wanting to help her. She wouldn't mind some assistance, but not the kind they would want to give to her and Angel.

"Now you're hurt. I don't think you should be living out here alone. We need to find a place for you to stay."

Yes, that was the kind of help they would offer. "We have a place." Heaven flashed a quick look at Dr. Logan. *Please don't tell her, not yet.* She moved her leg, and the pain in her ankle caused her to yell.

"Heaven took a misstep on her way back from the barn and sprained her ankle. Right now I'm wrapping it. I'm grateful you're here, Mrs. Reynolds. Angel was chaperoning, but with her unable to see, it's questionable if she's suitable."

"I am suitable." Angel stormed into the tiny room overflowing with people. "You told me everything you were doing so it would be as proper as it could be. It wasn't like I could go for help."

"Humph." Mrs. Reynolds moved closer to Heaven. "Very questionable situation. Are you saying this man slept here over-night with the two of you?"

Heaven did her best to follow the conversation—the one said aloud and the unspoken one. Was the woman suggesting that she and Angel climbed under the quilts with Dr. Logan? "Not with us, Mrs. Reynolds. He was here, Angel was in the loft, and when I wasn't checking on him, I was sleeping in the rocking chair or reading my Bible."

"So your sister wasn't even downstairs? Preacher, we need to plan a wedding this weekend." Mrs. Reynolds patted Heaven's hand. "Now don't you worry. We won't let anyone know about this indiscretion. It will stay right here in this cabin, but we've got to make it right with the Lord."

"But. . ." Heaven tried to think of a response.

"It's okay. Heaven already asked him to marry her." Angel beamed brighter than the afternoon sun.

"Marry?" Heaven glared at Travis. When had she asked him to marry her? It was the last thing she wanted to do. Marry the man who stole her family farm? There was another reason she was mad, too, but her mind seemed to be loosely wrapped in cloth, allowing only a few thoughts to slip through.

"Sir, nothing improper happened here." Travis stood chest to chest with the preacher. "It was two people needing immediate care, is all. There's no need for forcing a marriage."

"I see." Preacher Reynolds didn't look like he understood, but at least he wasn't insisting on marrying her off right away.

"Would you mind stoking the fire, Preacher, while I tend to Miss Wharton?"

"Not at all. Seems like you have plenty of women now to properly chaperone."

Heaven watched as the preacher left the room. Why didn't Dr. Logan want to marry her? *Mary.* Maybe he was already married to Mary. She stifled a giggle. But what if he wasn't? He wasn't wearing a wedding ring. The laughter died in her throat. He didn't want to marry her. Why did that hurt?

Another rejection—this time brought on by a man and not caused by a bullet. *Jake.* If he were here, he would marry her, and he wouldn't wait until the weekend. She didn't even know

Dr. Logan, not like she knew Jake. Even if Dr. Logan looked good enough to sop up with a biscuit, that didn't mean she wanted to marry him. He wanted her home, but not her and Angel. This marriage business must have been Angel's solution. She would give that girl a detailed lecture on why that was not only improper but disrespectful to make up such a lie.

Dr. Logan returned to the stool and picked up her foot. "I need to get this bound. Would you like some more laudanum? I'm afraid what I gave you earlier has worn off by now."

Why did his eyes have to look so kind, comforting even? His calm manner and easy touch with her ankle even made her feel secure.

"No, I don't want any more. I still don't feel normal, so perhaps there is still some residue?"

"You are looking a bit peaked. It'd be better not to take it if you can handle the pain from the movement." He unwrapped the cloth that he'd started before the interruption of company. "I have to start over. This must be wound tightly or it won't give you enough support."

Mrs. Reynolds peered over Dr. Logan's shoulder.

"Ma'am, if you could move to the bed, I believe I could do a better job of this. If you'd hold Heaven's hand, she can squeeze it when she hurts. Then she might not have to scream, scaring all of us and keeping me from having to do this again."

Her brown hair, twisted into curls around her face, didn't correspond with her expression, which was anything but lovely, since it was screwed up with displeasure. "Yes, Dr. Logan. I can see where that would be helpful." The thick material of Mrs. Reynolds's dress rustled, unlike the soft cotton his sisters wore.

Mrs. Reynolds perched on the edge of the bed. "Give me your hand, dear."

Heaven placed her hand in the open palm. She wasn't sure if she hoped she had to squeeze hard enough to make Mrs. Reynolds squeal or not. She'd like to, but that would be just like cutting off her nose to spite someone else, as Pa would say. As if anyone would cut off their own nose. She sniffled. She missed him, missed him badly.

Dr. Logan lifted Heaven's ankle, and pain spiked straight up through to her hip. She wrapped her fingers tight around Sister Reynolds's.

"Oh my, but you have a good grip." Mrs. Reynolds peeled Heaven's fingers from hers.

Heaven wanted to smack her. Maybe she should scream next time. That would no doubt be considered the proper thing decorum necessitated, rather than being too strong.

"Are you almost done, Dr. Logan?" She would like to watch his hands wrapping her ankle so she could do it herself. Doing so would likely send Mrs. Reynolds back to the marriage discussion. Instead, she tried to imagine how those lovely locks of hair would feel in her hand. She felt the fabric of her skirt being arranged across her toes.

"Yes ma'am. I'm finished now. Mrs. Reynolds, perhaps you could get clean sheets on the bed for Heaven. I think the girls might want to sleep together tonight. Rest assured I'll be sleeping in the barn."

Clean sheets? Heaven hoped the ones in the trunk were decent. She'd been washing Pa's sheets and putting them back on the bed as soon as they dried. At least there was another set. Heaven glanced at Mrs. Reynolds. "I'd be grateful to you, ma'am. Angel can help you."

"You do look plum tuckered out. I'll do that, but I reckon you should come back home with us." Mrs. Reynolds patted Heaven's arm. "You can't stay here alone."

"I'm not alone. Angel's here."

"She can come, too, of course."

"My animals need taking care of." She wasn't leaving her cabin. Enough people and things had been taken away from her, and she wouldn't stand to lose one more. If she moved out, it was as good as giving up.

"I'll stay on awhile. They're going to need help," Travis said. "I can sleep in the barn and take care of the animals while Miss Wharton's an—. While she heals. She'll be up and around in about a week."

Why didn't he tell them he owned the land now, that Pa had given it to him, and that Pa was dead? Could he be reconsidering taking it from them? If that were true, she wouldn't leave, because if she did, she had a feeling she'd never be coming back. Once it was known her pa was dead, she and Angel would be taken care of. The church family would flock to her aid, insisting she wasn't capable of taking care of the small homestead and Angel. Then someone would find an old toothless man that could still stand and insist they marry. She didn't want a husband if it wasn't Jake—and that was impossible even for God.

"If Dr. Logan will stay in the barn for a few days, I wouldn't have to trouble anyone to help take care of my animals. Considering how he ended up with a head wound, it would be handy to have a man about the place until I can hold a gun steady." She might as well become 'that eccentric spinster' sooner rather than later.

Mrs. Reynolds stood up, all starch in her veins and her nose slightly in the air. "We'll ask Preacher Reynolds about what to do. You all keep this door cracked while I'm gone." Without waiting for a reply, head high she left the tiny room.

Angel followed the motherly Mrs. Reynolds.

"Why didn't you tell them about Pa and his will?"

"It's not for me to tell, Miss Wharton. I figured you'd let everyone know when the time is right. Now, if they'd have asked me why I was here, I would have told them, but they didn't." Dr. Logan smiled. "That might be considered lying, but in this case, I consider it a chance for you to handle your grief the way you want to."

Weariness of the day smothered her. She was tired and worried about the future, and this kind man had offered her a gift—a time to recover before her world fell like bird feathers from a cat's mouth.

Mrs. Reynolds rushed in the room, tears dripping from her eyes. "You poor soul. Angel told us about your father."

"I'm sure it was this laudanum that kept her from speaking out, and I didn't feel it my place to inform you." Dr. Logan held Heaven's eyes with his, making her feel all warm inside. "I believe they need some time alone to take in the loss."

"Dr. Logan, I mean no disrespect, but these girls need to be comforted with a woman's touch, and leaving them alone will not accomplish that."

"None taken, Mrs. Reynolds; however, it has been my experience the family needs time to grieve amongst themselves before they have to put on a brave face for others. With this recent loss, I would expect that to be most important. If they want to come into town tomorrow, I'll be happy to bring them."

"We'll need to have a service for Mr. Wharton soon. Even though there's no body, the family needs to do something to honor the dead," Preacher Reynolds said from behind his wife. "Perhaps it would be best to plan on that rather than a wedding?"

Angel buried her head in Heaven's shoulder and hiccupped a sob. Heaven gathered her closer. The poor child had been through more than enough tragedy this year. Both of them had. How would she ever help her sister to feel secure again?

"If you think that best, Preacher."

"I do, and this man is a healer, so it will be fine for him to sleep in the barn. And, Mrs. Reynolds, I know your proclivity for helping people, but I think tonight it would be best not to mention this to the other ladies in town."

"I do not gossip. I'm very careful with my choice of words, sir. I don't appreciate you disparaging my character in front of these fine people, especially the doctor." Mrs. Reynolds put a hand to her chest. "Is that what you want, Heaven? To be alone tonight? I could stay here, I suppose." She glanced around the room. "There doesn't seem to be a place for me to sleep."

"Don't make us go. I don't want to go, Heaven." Angel's muffled voice sounded far away to Heaven. Right now nothing seemed real to her.

"Yes ma'am. I want to stay in my home. Angel and I would feel closer to our pa here, and I'm tuckered out. I can't imagine a ride into town with my ankle. We'll be fine, especially with

Dr. Logan out in the barn."

"Then I'll put some dinner together for you and tidy up before we leave. Preacher, since Dr. Logan is wounded as well, you can help me by tending the animals and fixing a bed for him out in the barn."

"There's no need to fix dinner for us, Mrs. Reynolds. We have a nice stew left from yesterday that can be reheated."

"At least let me get the biscuits rolled out for you. I wish I'd have brought along one of the pies I made today. We were in such a rush, I forgot about them. We could ride back to the house and get it, maybe bring back a few other things to eat as well so we could join you for supper."

"No, really, you've done enough." Heaven was glad the woman didn't ask what she'd done other than cause Heaven distress. "I'm not hungry. Are you, Angel? Doctor?"

Dr. Logan shook his head. "I'm ready to rest more than eat."

"Not hungry," Angel said, but her face at the mention of pie had said otherwise.

Heaven wondered if Angel thought the Reynolds's might change their minds about them staying at the cabin if they had time to ride to town and back.

Preacher Reynolds carried Heaven to the rocker in front of the fire. Heaven figured it was so she could visit with Mrs. Reynolds as she worked. Heaven would rather have been stuck in the chicken coop or out in the barn with Mr. Jackson. "There, now you're settled. Dr. Logan, why don't you come with me to the barn, and we'll scout out a place for your bedroll."

Dr. Logan nodded. "I'd like to check on my horse."

"I'm coming, too." Angel bolted for the door.

"Angel." Heaven wanted Angel to stay. She didn't want to be left alone with Mrs. Reynolds. Besides, would those men be capable of watching out for her sister?

Angel halted. "Please? I want to pet Dr. Logan's horse, and Mr. Jackson needs petting."

"Be careful."

"I will."

Mrs. Reynolds came up from the root cellar with a jar of green beans and set them on the table. "I looked at your stew, and I think some of these"—she held up the jar—"would be a nice addition, and it looks like you have a lot of them to use up."

"That we do. Great-Uncle Neal apparently had a great fondness for the vegetable." Heaven hoped the woman hadn't taken the time to inspect the lack of any other kind of vegetables in the cellar.

Mrs. Reynolds took a bowl from the kitchen shelf and placed it on the table. She started adding flour, lard, and water to make the biscuits. "You're almost out of flour. Should I bring some up from the cellar?"

"No. We'll get it when it's needed." Heaven didn't want her to know there was none left.

"Your great-uncle was an interesting man, you know. He worked at the cotton gin and never missed a Sunday service. Shame he never found a good woman to marry."

"Maybe so, but if he had, we wouldn't be living here."

"The good Lord has interesting ways of carrying out a plan, doesn't He?" Mrs. Reynolds flopped the dough on the floured tabletop and rolled it with a pin. "Why don't you close your eyes and rest while you have a chance, dear?"

"Thank you, ma'am." Heaven closed her eyes. At least this way she wouldn't have to keep up her end of the conversation.

After the rumble of the Reynolds's carriage wheels faded, Heaven turned to Dr. Logan. "Thank you for giving us at least one night alone."

"They'll be back, you know." He pulled out a chair from the kitchen table and plunked down.

"I hope so." Angel hunkered down by her sister's feet close to the fire while Heaven brushed her hair. "Last time, when Ma died, they brought pie. Remember, Heaven?"

"Yes I do. You ate so much pecan pie you got sick." Responsibility burdened her shoulders. Her sister should have pie, meat, and a family. Could she ever hope to fill Angel's needs? Exhaustion filled her body. Her eyelids felt heavy, and the brush she used on Angel's hair weighed more than Mr. Jackson.

"Miss Wharton?"

Startled awake, she straightened in the chair. The brush now rested in Dr. Logan's palm. When had he taken it from her? Anxiety poked its fingernail into her heart. "Angel?"

"She's fine. I finished her hair and sent her to bed. She's waiting for you. I thought I'd carry you there before I head out to the barn."

Carry her? For a moment, she'd forgotten about her ankle. As nice as it would feel to be cradled by someone, she wouldn't allow herself that pleasure. "I can do it."

He sighed. "I thought you'd say that." He reached down and snatched her up before she could breathe in and out.

"Put me down."

"No. You're my patient now. I want you to get better. Tomorrow I'll fashion a crutch for you, and you'll be able to get around without further injury. Tonight I'm taking you to bed."

She watched his face grow red and felt the heat of her own body betraying her.

"Th–thank you." It was only a few steps to the small bedroom, and Heaven couldn't help but wish it were miles away. For one brief second, she allowed herself to feel the safety of those strong arms. Too soon she was in her pa's bed with Angel.

"I'll get the lamps extinguished and the fire banked before I head out to the barn. Is there anything else you might need?"

Her nightclothes, but she wasn't about to ask him to get them. "I can't think of a thing."

The lamplight flickered, giving the room a comforting glow that begged her to rest. Or was it the man in the room that made her feel safer than she had in a long time?

Chapter 9

Travis strolled around inside the barn, stretching his arms over his head trying to loosen the kinks that had settled in overnight. He wouldn't admit it to anyone, but he didn't think he'd ever get used to sleeping on a hard surface. He much preferred a soft bed. He should've known not to spend money on another horse to breed with Pride and Joy. At least not until he'd ridden out and checked the property Caleb had left to him.

This little complication of having to add a wife and her sister to his life didn't sit well with him. He didn't like being a pawn any more than Heaven. But he was stuck. He had to take Heaven with the farm; otherwise, he'd leave them defenseless. His hand brushed his wound. Maybe not defenseless, but not crack shots either.

Caleb's last will and testament would stick in a court of law as far as the farm went, but not the part about Heaven. And it shouldn't. Isn't that what this war had ended up changing? Owning people? Heaven's father didn't own her, and neither did he. Most likely, the old codger just wanted him to leave his daughters cared for. He hadn't mentioned Angel though, and that bothered him until he remembered Caleb's days were filled with thrashing, sweating, and convulsing. Just because he didn't mention his youngest daughter didn't mean he had no love for her. Travis knew he couldn't leave Caleb's daughters to fend for themselves. They could be hurt and forced out of their home. Not to mention the farm was in dire need of repairs. And that is why he had to marry Heaven, like Caleb wanted. Like Caleb ordered in his will. But he didn't want to. He wanted a wife and family after he had his horse farm thriving.

Travis was glad the cabin wasn't all sissified. There wasn't a doily to be seen or a cozy draped over a china teapot. He didn't mind all that stuff as long as it wasn't in his house. A good house needed a chair by the fire, a bed, and a stove big enough to heat the house. Apparently Heaven felt the same way. There might be hope for a compatible match between them. There was a spark; he knew that yesterday when their hands touched on that coffee cup. He felt it and knew she did, too, by the way that cup almost landed on his lap.

A goat bumped against Travis's hip.

Light spilled in as Angel came through the barn door.

"Good morning, Angel."

"Morning."

He scratched the goat's ear. "Friendly goat, aren't you?"

She ran her hand across the goat's back. "Mr. Jackson is my friend. Mrs. Jackson isn't as friendly. You have to be careful around her, because she'll knock you down."

He wondered whose idea it had been to name the goats like married people. He found it odd but funny to be addressing the animals like people.

"You want to meet Mrs. Jackson?"

"I'd like that."

She took his hand, and together they walked to a stall containing an all-white goat. A pregnant goat.

"We don't know why she's so mean. We keep her locked up so she doesn't hurt us."

"Has she always been ill-tempered?"

"No sir. When we got her, they both were nice, but they didn't have names and they were always together, so I named them Mr. and Mrs. Jackson. And she stopped giving milk, too. We haven't had cheese in a long time"

"Might be because she's expecting a little one. They get that way sometimes."

"A baby goat?" Angel squealed and then steepled her hands against her mouth while she bounced on her toes. "When's it going to be here?"

"I'm not sure." It was the wrong time of the year for a birthing. He wondered at God's wisdom of bringing another chance of grief for the small girl bursting with excitement. Then again, God's wisdom in this entire predicament had him wondering.

A black kitten scampered across the floor followed by a gray and white one. At least there won't be a mouse problem. That would have been easier to fix than the one waiting inside the cabin.

"Dr. Logan, I'll tell you what chores are yours. The one thing you must remember is that the chickens are my responsibility."

"Then I suppose it's quite fine with you that I've mucked the stalls and fed the animals in the barn this morning."

She scrunched her face as if she wasn't sure she should believe him. One of her eyebrows dipped. Was she frustrated because she couldn't see if he'd done them? Then she sniffed.

"Yep, it's fine. Doesn't smell as bad in here as when Heaven does it. You can go with me to the chicken coop, but don't forget. . ."

"It's your responsibility."

She turned her face his way, and he saw her toothy grin. "Good. You learn quick."

At the chicken coop, she allowed Travis to open the door that seemed to be hanging from a loose hinge. He would fix that soon. He put one foot inside the door.

"Stop. You can't come in here, remember." She had one hand perched on her hip. "Stand in the doorway and wait for me."

"Yes, Little Miss, I'll mind what you say." He watched her work, her lower lip rolled between her teeth as she'd slide her hand under a hen and scoop out the egg. Soon she had a basketful.

"We don't usually get this many. Maybe they knew you'd be here for breakfast." She cocked her head and fell silent for a moment. "I should cook breakfast this morning, because Heaven won't be able to stand without hurting herself."

He could see hope in her face, so he said he'd like that. Now he wondered if she knew how to cook eggs.

As Heaven smoothed the covers on her parents' bed, her sight landed on the small miniature of them. Her heart crumbled. She remembered Ma setting it on the chest of drawers and saying, "This is our home now, Heaven. Always remember, where we are as a family is our home. It's not four walls that make a home. It's family. So no matter where you end up, make those four walls look and feel like your home."

Ma commented on how sad it was Uncle Neal's marriage plans fell through, but if he hadn't made those plans, there probably wouldn't be the nice wood floor and kitchen stove for them to use now.

Heaven had shot back with some stinging retort about the floors not being quality and what good was a stove if there wasn't someone to cook for them? Her head dipped to her chest, and the tears flowed as she remembered how she'd acted. What she'd said to her ma. She covered her lips with her hands, but that couldn't undo words already spoken.

Not long after that, Ma had fallen ill, and she didn't get a chance to make this cabin feel like their home. Before she died, she'd extracted a promise from Heaven to make the cabin into a home for her sister and Pa.

She hadn't kept it. The cabin looked almost the same as when they moved in. Except for the branch Ma had found for them to use to hang their mittens and hats, nothing had been changed. The windows were bare. Great-Uncle Neal's old broken chair still sat in the corner. The few pieces of furniture they'd brought along hugged the walls where Pa had shoved them when they arrived. A happy thought flitted through her sorrow. She could almost hear Pa promising Ma to move them later as soon as she knew where she wanted them and the playful interchange between them.

Now she and Angel were currently without a home of their own. Unless she could convince Travis to give the farm back to her. Maybe they could come to some sort of arrangement where he could live somewhere else and raise his horses here. She'd be willing to let him do that. She never thought about staying here and making it her home, but now that she was about to lose it, she knew it was too late. The farm had become their home. They had memories here, not all good, but some of them were. She would fulfill her promise, find a way to keep this place, and let it blossom into a proper home.

Proper home? Right now it wouldn't qualify as much more than a shack. She would reread that chapter in Ma's book about what it took to make a proper home. Then she would start doing it right away, because somehow she must convince Dr. Logan to move on and find another farm for his horses.

She'd stuck the book in her sewing basket by the rocker. Eyeing the distance between the bed and the fireplace, it seemed possible to get there without too much trouble. She hopped on one leg and leaned against the wall for support. Winded, she collapsed into the rocker as the door opened.

Angel bustled through and slammed the door behind her. "Got a bunch of eggs this morning for a change. Dr. Logan says if we had more chickens, we could eat some of the hens that aren't laying."

Now why hadn't she thought of that? Ma would kill a chicken and make a nice dinner for them. Heaven hadn't ever even tried to do that. After watching her mother pluck feathers, she had no interest. Chicken with green beans would be a nice change from green beans and biscuits and green beans and potatoes.

"I'm going to make the eggs this morning, Heaven. Dr. Logan says you have to stay off of your ankle." Angel's voice was puffed with importance.

The mouse-ate-the-cat smile on her face took Heaven by surprise. She didn't even know Angel wanted to learn to cook. Maybe she did, know—a little. It was dangerous though, and she hadn't been willing to help her learn. It was much safer to have her roll out the biscuits.

"Think you can manage to roll out the dough while I cook?" Angel's words issued a challenge as she set the egg basket on the table. "I think we'll have to use all of these eggs, because Dr. Logan said he was hungry enough to eat the sides of the barn." She giggled and then slapped her hand over her mouth. "I'm sorry, Heaven, that's probably not a proper thing to say."

Angel held her breath and picked up the still-warm egg. She ran her thumb over a few tiny bumps on the larger end of the oval. She concentrated, not wanting to mess up and have Heaven take over, scolding her and making her feel like she'd never be able to make her own breakfast. She had placed the bowl on the table, and she found it now, tracing the edge closest to her with a finger. Keeping her finger on the bowl, she brought the egg in the other hand to rest next to it. It was time. All she needed to do was smack it against the side and move her hand forward an inch or two. Fast. She let out her breath and took another one.

She smacked it and reached forward. The egg left a satisfying slurp against the bottom of the bowl. She'd done it. Secure in her method, she continued cracking the rest of them in her basket.

"I'm doing it, Heaven. I'm making scrambled eggs. I'm sorry you hurt your ankle, but I'm happy, too, because now I get to make breakfast."

Her sister sat quietly. Then she heard her start patting out the biscuits. "Yes, Angel, I do believe you can make your own breakfast. I think I'm going to make a few extra biscuits, just in case there aren't enough eggs to satisfy Dr. Logan."

Angel didn't comment. She was already planning dinner.

Travis's teeth grated against a bit of shell. He looked at Heaven. She seemed to be experiencing the same problem with her breakfast. Their eyes met, and the corners of Heaven's lips began to turn up.

He shook his head, trying to discourage her from smiling. A laugh welled in his stomach, aching for release. He gnawed on his tongue to keep the mirth from bellowing into the room.

"Do you like my yellers?" Angel asked, popping a heaping forkful into her mouth.

Travis waited to see if she would say anything about the shells that had to be in her breakfast.

She chewed and swallowed. "So do you or don't you like them, Dr. Logan?"

He'd try diplomacy. "For your first try, they aren't bad. I could use a bit more salt on them."

"It's hard to hear salt, and I didn't want to put in too much." Angel pushed the saltcellar toward him.

"Thank you." He salted his eggs and began to pick through them, looking for the offending crunchy pieces. "Heaven, what are you and Angel doing today?"

"I thought you could teach me how to shoot that Spencer so I don't get knocked back into the cabin when I use it." Heaven took a long drink of her coffee.

"Seems to me you didn't have any problems when you aimed at me."

"Heaven can't hit anything with that rifle—except for you. You're the first thing she's shot, and we can't eat you, and even I know that wouldn't be proper." Angel took another bite of eggs. "I think I cooked the eggs too long. They're crunchy."

Heaven set down her cup. "It's the shells, Angel. When you cracked the eggs, a few bits of shell fell in. You'll get the hang of breaking those eggs before long. It took me awhile to learn how to break them cleanly, too."

"I'll try it again tomorrow morning, then." Angel's feet banged against the bottom rung of her chair. "So, are you going to teach her how to shoot or not, Dr. Logan?"

"I'm not sure how I can do that, Angel. You need to stay off of that sprained ankle, Heaven, so it will heal faster." He flicked another piece of shell with his fork to the side of his plate.

"Or you could show me while I'm sitting down. Lots of things we could eat are on the ground anyway, like rabbits."

"It isn't necessary for you to be shooting game." Did she think it possible to sit on the ground and shoot? No wonder she hadn't been able to hit anything.

"Why not? I have to provide for my sister, and I figured while you're here you could teach me some things." Her fork clanked against the plate. Her stare intensified, as if daring him to say that this wasn't where she would be living.

"Because I'm going to do the hunting. You're either going to marry me or move out. Either way, you won't be needing to shoot at anything."

Heaven's chair grated against the wood floor as she pushed back from the table. "I'll not marry you—you arrogant—arrogant doctor!"

"Even though it's what your father wanted?"

She stood, rested her hands on the table's edge, and leaned toward him. "He didn't know what he wanted. You said yourself he was delirious with a fever. In fact, I don't think anything written on that paper is real."

"Are you challenging me?" His stomach curdled, and not from the breakfast. What if she was right? Caleb did have a fever, and she might be able to convince the law he didn't have ownership of the farm. Now he was concerned. If he didn't have this place, what would he do with the mare he'd bought to breed?

"I think I'll see about going to the judge with Pa's will and ask him what he thinks."

"I'm pretty sure they'll take one look at you and see you're a woman and not capable of running a farm and tell you the best thing would be to marry me." He stood up and leaned across the table and met her halfway. "I'll be happy to hook Charlie up to the wagon and drive you there."

Heaven's knitting needles flew as she fumed. She wanted to stomp around the back pasture and work off her anger, but instead she was stuck inside with this ankle hampering her every move. Her emotions bubbled. Not the pretty kind of bubbles you got from fancy milled soap—more like the kind you get in your stomach before you lose your lunch. Marry him? Indeed.

After the way he spoke to her at breakfast? As if being a woman wasn't worth spit? The most he could do is offer to court her and then ask her to marry him, not assume it would happen because it was written on a piece of paper. Not even if it was signed and legal. She'd take Dr. Logan up on his offer to drive her to the courthouse and fight for this place. Being hitched to him until "death do you part," despite what her father had wanted, wasn't going to happen.

She checked her work and noticed she'd dropped a few stitches. Undoing them, she realized her anger wasn't helping her progress on Angel's Christmas gift.

It was just like Pa to try and fix a mess that never would have happened if he'd been responsible just once. Pa lived by that verse about the birds of the air and fields of flowers never worrying about what to wear. He said God took care of everything, so he didn't need to. Heaven thought that was purely bad Bible reading. It wasn't using your common sense to live like that, if you tried you went hungry and your family had no home to live in.

The rocker under her moved faster. If that verse was true, she wouldn't be sitting here with a sprained ankle, a root cellar full of nothing but green beans, and a man trying to marry her.

It didn't matter how good-looking he was or how nice he was to her and Angel. She didn't love him. But could she? Could she grow to love him? The rocker slowed. Could she marry him? Had God provided for her and Angel? If she wasn't so prideful, she'd march out to the barn where he was probably measuring for expansion and winning over Angel and tell him she would marry him.

But that wasn't right. Ma always said it's best to marry for love. And she didn't love Dr. Travis Logan.

Angel opened the door. Fresh cool air blew through the room, making the flames in the fireplace dance. "Are you still mad? 'Cause if you're not, Dr. Logan wants to know if you still want to learn how to shoot. He said if you're mad though, you shouldn't come out 'cause he doesn't want to hand you a loaded gun in his—his presents."

"Presence."

"That's what I said, but I didn't see any presents."

"Presence means being around somebody, not gifts."

Angel frowned. "That's not interesting. I thought we were going to get presents from him. He oughta give us something since he's getting our farm. Don't you think, Heaven? Why did Pa do that? Give us away like that?"

"I'm not sure." She set her knitting in the basket next to the rocker. "Come sit here with me for a bit."

Angel climbed into her lap and leaned her head against Heaven's shoulder.

Heaven wrapped her sister in a hug and began to rock. "Pa was sick. Remember how Ma was when she had the fever? She would ask us to do strange things like chase fireflies in her room."

"She asked me to bring my pony around so she could feed him a carrot, too. I didn't have a pony."

"That's right, she did. The fever made her see things that weren't real and made her say things she didn't mean."

"Did I do that, too?"

A lump formed in Heaven's throat as she remembered her

fight to keep her sister from following her ma to the grave. She didn't want to think about that week.

"Did I?"

"Yes, you asked me to get your pet rabbit and put him in bed with you."

"I didn't have a pet rabbit."

"No, you didn't, but you had a name for him."

"I did?"

"You called him Knocksbury."

Angel giggled. "That's a funny name. Why did I call him that?"

Heaven ached at the memory of the frantic feelings of not being able to bring her sister's fever down and Angel crying out for Knocksbury to help her. "I don't know."

Chapter 10

Travis cracked open the door and peeked inside. "Can I come in? Angel, you didn't come back. Are you both mad at me now?" Travis stepped inside. He'd had a long listen to what God had to say about his behavior. Not that he heard God's voice like Abraham and Moses. If a bush ever started speaking to him, he wouldn't be as brave as Moses. He'd hightail it so fast his feet would melt on the path. He had come to the realization that he had been unkind to Heaven. The verse about taking care of widows and orphans sat heavy on his heart. He was here to eat humble pie and ask for forgiveness.

"Still mad, but not angry enough to shoot you. Angel said you would teach me if I came outside."

"But you're still inside."

"Angel and I had to do some talking."

"About me?" He wouldn't blame them if they'd been tearing him apart, but when he walked up to the door, he'd heard giggles. Maybe they were making fun of him. His heart tore a bit.

"You and Pa." Heaven leveled her gaze at him. "We were wondering exactly what he said to you while he was feverish."

"Did he say funny things like me when I was sick?" Angel smiled in his direction.

"He did say one odd thing over and over. I never could figure out what he was trying to tell me." He pulled a kitchen chair over by them and straddled it.

"Tell us, please."

His eyes followed Heaven's hand as she brushed a piece of that tantalizing blond hair back behind her ear. Why did he want to touch it so much?

He weighed his words before saying them. He imagined they were hoping for words of love about them. He decided to give them the puzzling statements, hoping they wouldn't ask for more, especially Angel.

"Your Pa kept saying something about green beans—to eat enough and I would be sustained."

"Green beans?" Heaven sputtered.

"Those nasty green beans?" Angel laughed.

They broke into gales of laughter. Travis didn't understand the humor, but the sound delighted him.

Once they'd quieted, Travis decided to teach Heaven how to shoot. She was too beautiful and Angel too precious, and he wanted to see to it that Heaven could protect them both if needed. "Get out of the chair. I'll teach you how to shoot."

Angel hopped off her sister's lap, and Heaven rose.

"Angel, get the door please. Heaven, I think if you sit in a chair, we can work out the fundamentals. Stay there, Heaven, and I'll come back for you." He picked up the rocker and held it in front of him. The way her eyes narrowed when he brought the idea up suggested she didn't think it would work. He carried the chair to the yard and turned around to go get Heaven.

She stood on the porch with the front of that ugly black skirt in one hand hoisted just enough to make it easier to walk down the stairs without tripping. The other hand gripped the porch post.

"Heaven, I told you I would carry you out here." The woman was stubborn and independent. Those could be seen as good qualities, but right now he couldn't come up with when that might be.

"I'm able to walk well enough on my own." She took a step, and pain flashed like lightning across her face.

"Stay put, will you?" In a few steps, before she had time to argue, he scooped her up in his arms.

"You didn't give me a choice. Is this how it's going to be? You make all the decisions while you're here?" She squirmed in his arms. "If you'd put me down. . ."

"I will." He dropped her into the rocker.

"This isn't going to work."

"Yes it will. The rocker will give you the feel of needing to keep your balance when you shoot. You can't stand up and shoot, because as your physician I won't allow it."

She sniffed and angled her nose skyward. "I don't remember hiring you for your services."

"Guess they come free with being on my farm."

She scooted against the back of the chair and held out her hands. Her eyes were loaded bullets. "Hand me the gun."

He picked up the rifle from the ground where he'd placed it when he came outside. She still looked put out with him. He hesitated, wondering if handing her a loaded gun was a good idea.

"Are you planning on teaching me today, or do you want me to stare at you like you're one of those marble statues they have in Italy?"

He handed her the rifle. "The first thing you have to do is rest the stock against your shoulder."

She looked at him, questioning him with her eyes.

"This part." He patted the end of the rifle. "If you don't rest it there, it's going to kick back hard and knock you over, not to mention leave some ugly bruising on your shoulder."

Something passed over her face, maybe understanding? He wasn't quite sure. Perhaps she'd already found out the hard way what happens when you don't hold a rifle the right way.

Heaven placed the stock against her right shoulder.

"Now look down the barrel with one eye."

She did as he asked.

"Close the other one." Earlier he'd set up a target. He stood behind the rocker and leaned over, just above her shoulder, and made sure the rifle was snug against her tiny frame. "See that circle I whitewashed on the log?"

She nodded, bumping her head into his chest and causing his breath to flutter.

He needed to concentrate on what that gun barrel was doing, not her pretty head that smelled sweet. He suffocated the attraction. "That's where I want you to aim. Take a deep breath. When you feel you're ready—and only then—pull the trigger." He let go of the gun.

She sat there. A slight breeze lifted her hair and wafted a soft, clean smell his way.

Did she think the target was going to move? No wonder she couldn't catch any dinner if it took her this long to make up her mind to shoot a log. A rabbit would have hopped away and had a bunch of baby bunnies by now. "Anytime you're ready, just pull the trigger."

As she pulled the trigger, she sneezed. The gun popped off her shoulder.

The rocker flew back, knocking Travis right below his waist. His breath wheezed out, and his eyes burned and watered. He grabbed the back of the chair to keep it from spilling over on its back and him from collapsing onto the ground.

"I think we're done for the day." He squeezed the words out of his lungs. He took the rifle from her. "I'll be heading to the barn to spend time with my horse." And recover. It would be awhile before he'd work on teaching her to shoot again. So far, all that woman managed to do with a rifle was find some way to harm him.

Heaven didn't understand why Dr. Logan had taken off to the barn in such an abrupt manner. He had been so kind before she fired the Spencer. Perhaps the sound brought up memories of her shooting him? He appeared to be limping, and he held his midsection. Maybe he was going to be sick from Angel's shell-filled eggs? Had the hit from the rocker caused him a stomach disturbance? Still, it seemed out of character for him to roughly grab the rifle out of her hands and make off for the barn, leaving her to get back to the house on her own. She wanted to practice more than once.

"Why do you think he quit teaching you so fast?" Angel helped her sister up the stairs. "I would have thought he would have made you shoot a few more times, especially since you didn't hit the target."

At least her sister had stuck around. Funny how she found herself dependent on her sister after all the times Angel had counted on her for help. She wasn't sure how she felt about that.

"Maybe he thinks I'm hopeless." It was useless. She'd been trying for months to hit something, and so far Dr. Logan was the only living or dead thing she'd successfully struck with a bullet. And shooting people wasn't a useful skill, as she didn't intend to take up a life of robbing and killing folks.

"I don't think you are." Angel opened the door and helped Heaven to a kitchen chair. "You take care of me, and you never give up. Remember how you kept trying until you figured out how to make cheese from Mrs. Jackson's milk?"

She plunked down onto the chair. "I miss that cheese. Dr. Logan says it won't be long though, before the kid is born and we'll have goat's milk again."

Angel looped the handle of her sister's sewing basket across her arm and brought it to the kitchen table. "How long do you think we can stay here if you don't marry him?"

"We're staying on this farm forever. I don't know how yet. I'm wondering if we can buy the farm from him. If we can make cheese and sell it in town. . ."

"Do you think we could make enough money?" Angel's voice rang of hope.

"I don't know. I've heard about making soap, too. Maybe we could learn how to do that." She'd need some kind of fancy mold to form it. They could just cut bars, but she knew from living in Nashville the fancy-shaped stuff sold for more.

"We could make it smell pretty with some lavender. We still have a jar we dried this summer." Angel parked her elbow on the table and rubbed the dimple in her cheek with her finger. "I wish I could still see to draw. I could make the labels."

"You still could. If we used a potato for a stamp with a simple design etched into it and some dye, you could make the labels."

"And you could write our names on them. Heaven and Angel Fanciful Soaps." Angel sighed. "Let's try, Heaven. I don't want to leave our home."

Travis walked slowly around the barn between the stalls until the pain in his groin subsided. That woman was disaster disguised in a pretty package—at least when it came to his body.

He stopped at the pregnant goat's stall and leaned over the half wall. The long-eared white face peered at him from the corner. "How are you feeling, Mrs. Jackson?"

She ambled over and nipped at the cuff of his coat. "I need that sleeve." He pulled his hand out of her reach. "Looks like you're doing fine."

He'd climbed up into the hayloft earlier and tossed down several bales of hay. Separating it with a pitchfork, he'd then strewn it about her pen to help keep her warm. The expecting goat shouldn't be in this condition this late in the year, but it happened sometimes. Heaven was as surprised and excited as Angel had been when he told her Mrs. Jackson was going to have a kid sometime soon. They knew Mrs. Jackson kept gaining weight and accused her of stealing food from the horse and cow. They'd even tried to catch her taking it but weren't successful.

It was conversations like these that made him realize Caleb knew his womenfolk needed a man, and that's why he'd given the farm to Travis. He even saw why Caleb wanted him to have Heaven. Though the man's method was unorthodox, his heart had been in the right place. Heaven's appeal, her kindness and sweet nature along with her resistance to marrying him only made him want her more.

It might be fun to court her—if she weren't so dangerous.

"Dr. Logan!" Angel's holler came from the cabin porch followed by the sound of a bell.

At Angel's call, his heart skipped a beat then calmed as he realized it was time for supper. He went to the barn door to answer her just as she retreated back inside. He wondered if she'd shout again if he didn't come in right away the way his mother did. He didn't think he'd chance it. He was hungry.

Inside he found two women with flushed faces waiting for him. "What's the excitement about?"

"Heaven came up with a plan so we can buy the farm from you." Angel squealed.

"Sit down. Supper is ready," Heaven said.

Travis slid into what he was beginning to think of as his chair. Angel scooted her chair out and sat. "So what is the plan, Heaven?"

"Soap. We're going to get a herd of goats and make fancy soap and sell it at the general store." The spoon she held in her hand kept time with her words. "We need more goats though. I'm not sure how much milk it will take. Angel and I will have to experiment."

"Soap? Fancy goat soap? You think that's going to support

you?" Travis knew he'd said the wrong thing as the words were leaving his lips. Too late to call them back and no way to make it appear he hadn't meant it.

The spoon whacked against the inside of the pot as Heaven dished their dinner onto plates.

"Angel and I have a good plan, and while we may not make a lot of money, you should at least consider our offer." *Thwack.* Potato bits sprayed in the air as she emptied the spoon onto a dish. She turned and slapped a plate full of green beans and potatoes on the table in front of him.

How could he fix this? Fancy soaps didn't seem like a moneymaker to him. His mother's words echoed back to him from a time before the war. Her advice on women: *"Show some interest in what they are saying."* He'd give that a try. "What are you going to name your company?"

Angel slipped out of her chair and made her way to the hutch. "We made some labels. Heaven's real smart, and she figured out a way to use potatoes to stencil them. We were going to write Heaven and Angel Fancy Soaps, but that was too hard to etch. She let me stamp them."

She handed him the label and sat back in her chair. "What do you think? Do you like them? Are they pretty?"

"HA?"

"*H* for Heaven and *A* for Angel." Angel's foot tapped against the chair rung. "Are they pretty?"

He couldn't help it. Having sisters had made it impossible to ignore something so easy to make fun of. "HA. HA. HA. Could I have some of that fancy HA HA soap?" He laughed.

Heaven gasped and whirled around from the stove with

Angel's plate of food. "That's mean."

"No, listen. HA—it sounds like a laugh. Get it?"

Angel giggled. "It does, Heaven. Ha-ha-ha."

Heaven slammed Angel's dinner in front of her and then sat across the table from Travis. She narrowed her eyes, and sparks of fire seemed aimed, ready to fire at him. "We are making an effort, and it isn't nice to—to laugh."

She giggled and then broke into a hearty laugh, grabbing her stomach, which surprised him. She was so petite, he'd have thought she'd have a dainty behind-the-hand giggle. At that moment, he knew he had fallen into the depths of Heaven. And just like that, he fell in love with her.

Chapter 11

This morning Dr. Logan had wrapped her ankle tight again after making her soak it. She hated that bucket of cold water first thing in the morning. But once he wrapped the strips around her ankle, it felt better.

She leaned on the branch he had found in the woods to help her take the weight off her hurt ankle. She didn't know what she would have done if he hadn't stuck around to help her and Angel. Getting up and down the front steps took a long time. And in this cold weather, she was outside longer than she wanted to be. Crossing the yard to the chicken coop and barn seemed much farther than it had a few days ago.

Angel had taken to Dr. Logan, following him everywhere and offering such devotion to the man it made Heaven jealous.

She had taken care of her sister for a long time, and Angel had never seemed to admire Heaven the same way.

Angel popped through the door. Heaven noticed she was alone again. "Did Dr. Logan put up a rope for you?"

"No. I showed him I could count my steps and make it to the chicken coop just fine. He said I didn't need a rope, but you might since you had perfectly good eyes and stepped in that hole. Dr. Logan said he was going to teach me how to do a lot of things. He's a nice man, Heaven. I think we ought to keep him."

"He is not an animal, Angel. You don't keep humans. You should have learned that from that stupid war."

"Daddy kept Auntie and Buck." She scurried over to the fireplace and held her hands out to warm them.

"He did not keep them. They worked for us, and Daddy paid them." *Didn't he?* "When he couldn't pay them anymore, they left, remember?" Her stick clunked against the wooden floor as she walked over to her sister.

"Is that why they didn't come here with us?" Angel's bottom lip trembled. "I loved them."

"I did, too, and I would love to have Auntie here right now. I miss her cooking so much."

The door opened, and Dr. Logan came through with an armful of wood and the blustery wind.

"And if Buck were here, we would have lots of wood and fresh meat, don't you think?"

"Fresh meat? I heard that. If it's all right with you two, I might go hunting for some." He set the logs on the side of the hearth. "Think you women could manage to cook a rabbit or two?"

Heaven sputtered. "We could do that."

"What about a deer?" Travis asked as he unbuttoned his coat. He hung it on the branch as if he had every right to do so.

"I've never cooked anything that big." Heaven watched him take a seat in her rocking chair. His dark hair was tousled from the wind, and his cheeks held a red tinge. He was healing well. "I'd like to try. Do you know how?"

"I think I could manage. Might have to throw together a

smokehouse pretty quick if I get a deer."

Heaven hoped he would find a deer. That would keep her and Angel in food for a while. Visions of venison stew for Christmas dinner danced in her mind—with green beans of course.

". . .can get that stove working in the barn so it won't be so chilly."

She shook her head.

"You want me to take you to the Reynolds's so I can sleep inside?"

"No, we're not leaving." She should have been listening. What had he said before mentioning sleeping in the barn? "How long can you stay?"

"Forever. It's my farm."

"Then Angel and I should sleep in the barn and not our home?" She slapped her hand over her lips, too late to capture the words she'd spat out of her mouth.

Angel whirled around and faced her sister. "I don't want to sleep in the barn."

Dr. Logan rose from his chair and towered over Heaven. "That's not what I said. Don't untie my words and restring them so they say something else."

"So you aren't throwing us out of our home?" She wanted him to say it, needed him to reassure her and calm her worry.

"Not today." He strode past her and grabbed his coat. He turned back and cocked his head.

She waited for him to say when. Instead, he shook his head and left the cabin, leaving her stomach scrambling and her mind trying to piece together the meaning of his actions.

The next morning, the kitchen had been straightened and schoolbooks set on the table. Heaven's shoulder still ached from the unpleasant incident with the rifle. She couldn't believe she'd sneezed, once again causing herself pain. She wouldn't let that Spencer win though. After she did school lessons with Angel and implemented a few of her plans for their home, she would go back out there and shoot that log until it grew hands and surrendered.

"I don't know why I have to learn multiplication tables," Angel whined as she slumped in the chair.

"It's part of growing up. There may not be a school here, but you are going to learn whatever I can teach you. Besides, math is important, especially if we're going to be making money. Someone needs to know how to keep track of how much we have."

"I can't see. How am I supposed to do that?" Angel folded her arms in front of her on the table and laid her head on them.

"Sorry, no sympathy from me. You've been following Dr. Logan around, learning all kinds of things. You don't even need me to get in and out of the house now that he's fashioned that stick for you."

"The stick keeps me from walking into things, but I don't see how I can read numbers on paper with it."

"Dr. Logan was telling me about a way you can learn by feeling bumps on paper. I don't know how to make those, and neither does he, but someday you'll learn. And when you have to learn that, you won't have to learn your multiplication tables, because you'll already know them."

"So I can concentrate on learning what they look like on the bumpy paper?" Angel lifted her head. "Where am I going to learn how to do that?"

"Dr. Logan said there are schools that can teach you to read Braille—that's what it's called." This wasn't a conversation she wanted to have. She knew what Angel's next question would be.

"But they aren't around here, are they? Are you sending me away?"

She was right; she knew her sister. "No, not right now. I don't even know where there is a school. Or if they take children your age. But if we have to leave here, I'm going to find one, and that's where we'll move to."

"Maybe we should just go now and forget fighting for the farm." Angel chewed on her thumbnail.

Heaven stilled. Leave the farm? She hadn't considered doing what was best for her sister at all. But once she located a school, what would she do for money? And how would they survive? They had nothing, except what Pa had left on an account at the store. That wasn't enough for transportation anywhere. Where would they live?

"The farm is our home—for now."

"Maybe if you marry Dr. Logan like Pa wanted, he would send me to school."

Her heart couldn't break into more pieces, could it? How did this happen that she would have to give up so much— from her first love to her parents? But how could she refuse her sister's plea? *Please, God, help me. I don't know what to do. I know people marry for convenience, but I so wanted to be loved.*

"I'll think about it, Angel." And she would, but if she married Dr. Logan, it wouldn't be until she knew his character better. She could grow to love a decent man maybe, but not one who would harm her or her sister. So far Dr. Logan had been a gentleman, but he hadn't been here long enough to know for certain.

Travis rode Pride and Joy across the rough fields and through the tree line looking for good places to hunt. He'd found the creek, but it was too cold to fish.

He ducked as a cedar branch came close to swiping his face, and he held up his hand to push it aside. A light, cold breeze slid under his jacket collar, and he hunched his shoulders. Pride and Joy's gentle walk soothed Travis's jumbled thoughts. Riding a horse with a smooth gait like this one always did that for him.

He needed some time to think and consider the best way to court Heaven. It would take work, because he knew she was against marrying him. She didn't know him yet, and he intended to fix that starting this afternoon.

He liked her spunk. Despite yesterday's mishap with learning to shoot and the head wound—he rubbed the prickly patch on his head where the hair was beginning to grow back—he wanted to spend time with her. He wanted to find out how those lips felt under his and if she fit in his arms just right when he hugged her. The pieces of the puzzle God had placed before him were beginning to come together. God sent him here, not Caleb. God had chosen Heaven for him. Now he needed a plan to get her to see that, too.

Annabelle had grown weary of the train adventure, as had Mrs. Miles. Jake had remained aloof the entire trip. He'd rented a covered buggy at least for the remainder of the trip. He grumbled about the cost and how he should have seen Heaven by now. It was all Annabelle could do to hold her tongue. The last thing she wanted was to be abandoned by him, and she had no qualms that he would leave her behind.

He was not the Jake that went away. Annabelle didn't think it would be too difficult to convince Heaven to wait a bit before marrying him. She'd need time to reacquaint herself with this new Jake. The outside hadn't changed, but the inside of him seemed gray and disinterested in anything but his cigar.

Mrs. Miles had grown quieter and smiled less often than when they'd left Memphis on the Nashville, Chattanooga & St. Louis Railway.

"Are you warm enough, Mrs. Miles?" Annabelle wished Jake could see how much he was hurting his mother. She missed her own mother dreadfully. That was one of the reasons William's betrayal hurt the way it did. She had looked forward to having a mother, even if it would have been a mother-in-law.

"Yes, dear. I'm fine, but looking forward to warming up at Heaven's by this evening. We were rash in this, weren't we? They may not even have room for us to stay."

"We'll make do, and if it isn't possible, I believe there is a hotel in town." Annabelle knew that's where Jake and his mom would most likely stay. Heaven's description of the cabin in the letter she'd written in early spring was that it was quite small. So much so that she and Angel slept upstairs in a loft. She didn't think she should mention the Wharton accommodations now though. They'd see for themselves soon enough, and then a decision could be made. She would stay with Heaven though, even if it meant sleeping in the barn.

Chapter 12

Heaven hadn't counted on rain. A darkening sky replaced the sunlight that warmed the cabin a few minutes ago. She glanced out the front window. They'd had an awful lot of rain this fall. There had been talk of the Mississippi flooding and concerns about how far the water would reach if it did. Dark clouds were bunching up like Baptists at a potluck.

Dr. Logan was out there on his horse somewhere. Right after lunch he'd said he needed to think about some things. What did a man think about? She hoped it was about leaving. No, that wasn't truthful. She wanted her farm, but she'd come to enjoy his company.

Thunder crescendos rocked the air. There wouldn't be any practicing her marksmanship this afternoon. Lightning arched, fracturing the sky. She twisted her apron strings in her hands. How far away had he wandered?

"When's Dr. Logan coming back? If he doesn't hurry, he'll get wet." Angel sat on the tufted, black horsehair, serpentine-back sofa and hugged her doll to her chest while whispering secrets into its ear.

The regal settee against the backdrop of rough wooden walls was as out of place as she and Angel were in this cabin.

So many of the things they'd brought belonged in a fancier home. Still, she was grateful to have these bits and pieces of their old life. They'd arrived at the cabin, expecting it to be furnished. And it was, according to a bachelor's lifestyle, Ma had said. Her uncle didn't need much—a table, a chair, and a bed. Heaven thought that's probably why he never found a woman to marry him. He was an odd fellow, Ma had said. As if Heaven couldn't figure that out. All she had to do was look in the root cellar at all those canned green beans.

"I'll check the kitchen window. Maybe he's coming from that direction." She hurried across the puncheon floor, leaned across the sink, and searched through the wavy glass for a glimpse of him or his horse. When had the trees grown so thick? A movement in the grove of cedars caught her eye. Horse and rider burst through the trees. For a moment, his eyes connected with hers, and her heartbeat kicked up its rhythm. Travis was back. "He's coming."

The sky broke apart and released hail. She watched in horror as the ice dropped like eggs from the sky, striking Travis and his horse. The ground in front of them disappeared into a field of white. He angled his head down and seemed to knee the horse to a run toward the barn. Her heart slammed against her chest as she watched him hold his arm across his face in an attempt to protect it from the bruising hail. She wanted to shout at him to use his other arm, protect the wound on his head, but he wouldn't have heard her through the thick log walls. "He's going to the barn."

"That's good." Angel started humming a lullaby to her doll.

Heaven popped on her toes of her good foot to see him

better. The hail was slippery, and Pride and Joy could go down. He could roll over and crush Travis. She swallowed even though her mouth was dry. Her mouth formed the words *Be safe*. Be safe, Travis. Travis? When had she decided to call him by his name instead of his title? So informal, and yet his name felt right on her lips. A smidgen of disloyalty to Jake's memory pricked her heart. She'd loved him and promised to forever. But Jake wasn't here to love anymore—the man was dead and not coming back. But Travis was here to love.

Love? She didn't love Travis did she? Impossible. She was just worried about him, that's all. Wasn't it?

He would be wet and cold when he came inside. She reached in the reservoir and dipped out water and filled the coffeepot. She'd make some to warm him.

His footsteps thudded against the wooden porch, and Heaven threw open the door before he reached it. "Come in. You've got to be soaked. Did the hail hurt? How is Pride and Joy?"

Travis's eyes widened as he brushed past her. "He's fine."

She drew back in shock at his brusque reaction. Maybe she was overmothering. And she did not want to be his mother.

Heaven was having difficulty seeing her stitching. She'd have to use precious oil if the storm didn't move on soon. Lightning sparked light through the bare windows and caught her attention. She had planned on making this cabin a home, so why not start now?

Travis sat in her rocker with nothing to occupy him but the drying of his clothes.

Angel busied herself at the table with the abacus they'd brought with them.

Heaven narrowed her eyes and focused on Travis's strong, capable body. She wanted to move the furniture, and with his foot tapping, he became the most likely candidate. But would he willingly move the heavy pieces? Ma had a way to get Pa to do things he didn't want to do. She said all she had to do was be a lady and he'd smile while he did her bidding. Would it work for Heaven?

Angel slid the beads across the wire and softly counted.

Heaven smoothed her long hair behind her ears and remembered what Ma would say about presenting herself as a lady. She straightened her shoulders and wished for a bit of Ma's honeysuckle perfume to dab on her wrists. She could get it from the trunk, but Angel would be sure to notice the scent and ask why she wore it. She'd have to do this with just her charm. Using dainty steps, she walked toward Travis, presenting her best smile.

"Are your clothes getting dry?"

He looked up at her and blinked. "Gettin' there."

"That's good. You wouldn't want to catch your death of cold." She felt silly, like a little girl playing dress-up with her mother's finest hat perched on her head. She let her shoulders fall back to their normal position, but she kept the smile. "You must be wondering why we have our furniture arranged so oddly." She waved her hand around the small room as if it were stuffed with priceless belongings.

She waited for a response, but all she received was a raised eyebrow. "When we moved here, Pa brought our furniture inside and left it. He promised Ma he would put it where she wanted it this winter."

She tried batting her eyes at him, but he furrowed his brow and looked at her oddly.

"Are you all right?"

She covered her face with her hands and rubbed at her eyes with her fingers as if she'd caught an eyelash in one of them. She hoped it covered the heat of the blush that was surely creeping across her cheeks.

"Yes sir. I am, thank you. I'm just feeling a bit sad. It's winter, and now Ma is gone, and so is Pa. And seeing you sit by the fire like he did. . . ." A tear sprang up, surprising her and apparently scaring Travis, for he jumped from the chair as if a cinder had landed on his sock-covered foot.

She thought she'd done all the grieving she could when they buried Ma. How was it possible for a body to hurt this much in one lifetime? Her breath collapsed in her lungs as a sob fought for an exit. Dizziness slammed against her head.

"What can I do to make you feel better?" He leaned toward her with outstretched hands as if he wanted to pull her into a hug, but then he dropped his arms to his sides and backed away. "I know I can't bring them back, and I'm truly sorry about not finding a way to bring your pa here for burial."

"It's distressing not having him lie beside Ma. Not holding a graveside service makes it seem less real. I start thinking, as soon as Pa gets back. . ." She swallowed another piece of her grief. "Then I remember. He isn't coming back. We won't be together again until we're in heaven."

Angel sniffled. The abacus slid across the table.

Heaven turned, and saw her sister's tears dripping down her cheeks. The numbness she'd been feeling since she'd heard about her pa's death finished melting away, leaving behind raw pain. She hastened to Angel's side and pulled her out of her chair into an embrace. They rocked back and forth on their feet together while they expressed their grief through rivers of rain. "It's going to be okay, baby. We still have each other."

Somehow Travis had gone from trying to comfort two distraught females to shoving around furniture. All he'd intended to do was to stop the crying. Watching the two of them mourn and not being able to help them while bearing guilt for not saving their father, he'd blurted out the first thing that came to his mind. He asked Heaven if she wanted him to move the secretary desk, with its bookcase covered with glass doors, closer to the window. The tears had desert-dried in a flash.

"Just a little to the left, I think." She splayed her hands on her hips and tilted her head to the side. Happiness rode across her face. "After this we can move the sofa across from the fireplace and the hutch closer to the kitchen so we don't have to walk so far to put away the dishes. But first it would be best if you would get the carpet from the loft. It will be nice to have that piece of home under our feet again."

Where were those tears? Even Angel strutted around with her hands on her hips giving orders about not scratching the floor. Heaven's smile was as bright as the sun that had gone missing around lunch. He shoved the heavy desk an inch. He hadn't planned on decorating a house, but it was worth it to see her bustling about looking like she'd been given the title to the farm.

She hadn't given up. The little minx was making the cabin into a real home. She probably thought he wouldn't want to take it from them then. She was right, but she was wrong. He had every intention of keeping everything promised to him in Caleb's will. Especially Heaven.

"It looks like you're planning on staying around."

She swung around and faced him, her sapphire eyes sending sparks his way. "Of course we're staying. Why would you ever think we're leaving?"

"Good. That'll make Mrs. Reynolds happy. I'll ride to town tomorrow and talk to the preacher about arranging it."

The smile dimmed and disappeared. Her face hardened. "I never said I would marry you. I said we weren't leaving our home."

Chapter 13

Travis had escaped the cabin right after he set the heavy sofa in place on top of the ugliest rug he'd ever seen. Heaven clapped her hands with joy when he rolled the threadbare thing across the floor. Angel had taken off her shoes and said she needed to feel colors. The design was almost impossible to figure out. Heaven said it had belonged to their family for a long time. He wanted to say he could tell but thought better of it. Heaven's face shone with excitement, and so did Angel's. He didn't want that light to extinguish.

Feeling as if he'd come calling without a chaperone, he left them to putter around. At least in the barn he knew there would be something to do. He spent time with Mrs. Jackson. It seemed she would be dropping her kid any day. For some reason, unlike Heaven and Angel, the goat let him get next to her. As he was in the stall with her, he started thinking about Heaven's idea of making fancy soaps and cheese to sell. She'd need to get more goats to make it profitable. He could get them for her with the little money he had left over from purchasing the breeding mare. That horse would be coming in soon. He'd have to ride to Dryersville to get her.

Travis unfurled his bedroll onto the barn floor. He slipped

his suspenders from his shoulders, wincing at the soreness. . . . It was one of many places on him that had taken a beating from the hailstorm. He couldn't remember ever seeing hailstones that big. He unbuttoned his shirt and checked out the purple and green spot. It was warm to his touch; his body already doing its healing work.

It felt warmer in here tonight. He didn't know if it was because the woman had worked him so hard or because the weather was changing. Still, it was December, and that led him to the conclusion it was Heaven's doing that kept him warm.

He settled into his makeshift bed. The night sounds of the barn were comforting. Horse hooves rustled the hay. Pride and Joy might be feeling some soreness from the hail, too. He noticed a lack of livestock, guessing Caleb had planned to send for his daughters the minute he'd found a place to live. There was the one sad-looking cow, the two goats, a horse, some chickens, and no pigs. He was guessing they'd canned a lot of green beans, as it seemed they had them every day. Sometimes twice.

Fresh meat would be good. Maybe tomorrow he'd find a rabbit or two. A stew would go a long way to making those beans tolerable.

He stretched his hands over his head, and something soft swatted his fingers. A barn kitten. He wiggled them again, and a soft, furry ball pounced on his hand. He grasped it and brought it to his chest. A marmalade-orange fluff ball assessed him with wide green eyes.

"You're a young one, aren't you? Quite brave, too, to attack a defenseless man on the floor." He stroked the kitten behind the ears and was rewarded with a noisy purr. It kneaded his chest and then settled for a rest. Travis watched as the kitten's eyes opened and slowly closed a few times before staying shut.

He lay there thinking about what it would take to get Heaven to fall in love with him. If she weren't so stubborn about this being her farm, her home, her whatever she wanted to claim at the moment, she might be able to see him as someone besides the man who wanted to take it all from her.

The kitten's purr quieted. Its little body heated him as well as a woodstove would. He stroked the tiny head, and the low rumble started again. "Shh. Go back to sleep."

Maybe Travis should tell Heaven how nice the cabin looked. That it looked like a home. But he wouldn't. Not yet. He'd wait until she said she would marry him. Besides, the cabin had looked fine before he'd had to shove the sofa, haul furniture, and unfurl a carpet. At least she hadn't hung curtains or spread a cloth across the sawbuck table.

Heaven flung the cotton tablecloth across the kitchen table and then straightened it so the sides were even. She then placed the lit candlestick in the middle. Taking a step back, she surveyed the room, admiring it. "We did it, Angel. It looks like home. I wish you could see it." Heaven grasped Angel's hands, and they twirled in a circle.

"It smells like home." Angel's smile spoke of pleasant memories.

Heaven released one of her sister's hands but held on to the other. She closed her eyes and inhaled the room's scent. She could smell Ma's honeysuckle and an underlying trace of Pa's cherry tobacco. Small moments of time hugged her.

"You're right. It does smell like home and Ma and Pa. I was thinking of using one of Ma's old skirts for curtains. Would you mind?" Heaven knew the perfect one. Ma had a white damask skirt that had a grass stain across the bottom. She could trim that piece off or fold it over, and no one would see it.

"Can I help?"

She squeezed Angel's hand and let go. "Yes you can. We'll work on it tomorrow. Now it's time to blow out the candles and go to bed."

Travis smelled the biscuits burning before he opened the door. He stepped inside the smoke-filled room. "What are you doing?"

Heaven appeared out of the haze. "Leave the door open." She fanned the bottom of her apron, attempting to shoo the smoke from the cabin. "We were making breakfast and talking about the stories Pa used to tell. Then Angel. . ."

"I said we should write them down so we don't forget them." Angel came up behind Heaven with a dish towel flapping in the air.

"Anyway, we found some paper, and while Angel told the stories, I started writing them down." Heaven sighed. "And we forgot about the biscuits."

"Now our home won't smell like Ma and Pa anymore." Angel's lip trembled.

Travis had no idea why she thought it smelled like them in the first place. He scratched at the wound that was healing on his head. The stitches were probably ready to come out. He'd been looking forward to those biscuits. It was the only thing these two seemed to make with any skill. "Now it will smell like breakfast all the time." He waited for a backlash of angry retorts.

"Burnt up breakfast," Angel said.

"Bad for your belly breakfast," Heaven said.

Angel giggled.

Travis didn't understand. Why weren't they angry—if not about the biscuits—then at him? It seemed that when things like this had happened at home, his father had taken the blame. He never remembered his mother laughing about burned food.

Chapter 14

Heaven took advantage of the unusual day of warmth and opened the window and door to air out the cabin. The oil lamps needed refilling, and she collected them one at a time while balancing on her stick. She set them on the table, removed the glass chimneys, and placed them to the side, thankful they weren't blackened. They would need only a quick swipe of the cloth this morning.

"Angel, the lamps are on the table, so don't bump it."

"Won't it be nice to have something to eat besides a mess of green beans and those walnuts we found, Heaven? I hope Dr. Logan brings back a deer. I've been dreaming about roast." Angel swept the kitchen floor. She wiped her brow.

Heaven trimmed off the ragged burned edges of the wicks until they were straight. Then she filled the lamp bases with oil, stopping about a half inch from the top. "We need to be thankful Great-Uncle Neal liked green beans enough to can a mess of them. Without them we'd be living on others' charity by now."

"We can thank God for sending us Dr. Logan, too. I'm real glad you didn't kill him, Heaven. He's been right handy around here." Angel stopped sweeping and leaned on the broom. "In fact, I think you should marry him. After all, that's what Pa wanted, right? That's what was on that paper."

"Hush! You promised not to tell anyone about that."

"I didn't. You already know about it, and so does Dr. Logan. I didn't mention it to him, but I could if you don't want to. I could be your go-between and fix things between you."

"Angel Claire, you'll do no such thing." Heaven replaced the glass chimneys. Being married to Travis wouldn't be awful. He was a handsome man, and if they had children, they'd be adorable. It wouldn't happen though. Just because her pa wanted it didn't mean Travis did. She wished she still had that paper, because she wanted to see how that part was worded. Did Pa say the farm and Heaven now belonged to Travis, or did it leave any room for her to get out of the contract? Maybe if she didn't marry him, he couldn't have the farm? Where had he put that paper? Back in his saddlebag? She might have to take a walk to the barn later. Guilt of looking at things not belonging to her niggled at her conscience. But what if there was a way she and Angel could stay here and it was on that paper? If there was a chance, she wanted to know. "If we're meant to marry, God and Dr. Logan will see to it."

Angel let go of the broom, and it landed with a dull thud on the wood planked floor. "Sometimes God works a little slow around here. Sometimes I think He's forgotten all about us, what with takin' away most of our family. Sometimes, Heaven, I get real mad at Him."

Angel plunked down in the kitchen chair and lowered her head to the table. "I'm not going to cry. I'm not going to cry. I'm. . ." She sniffled.

Heaven knelt by her sister and stroked her hair, fighting off her own desire to let loose of tears fighting for an exit.

"Angel baby, it's okay to be mad at God. Pa always said God was capable of handling our anger. Everyone gets mad sometimes at people they love, don't they?"

"Uh-huh."

"You don't need to worry about us being a family. We're family, you and me. We're going to be just fine." *An awful small one, God. How are we going to survive if I don't marry Travis? And God, why him? Why, if all if this was going to happen to us, didn't You let Jake live so we could be married?*

Angel raised her head from the table. "How?"

"I'm going to ask Dr. Logan to teach me how to take care of this place as soon as I can walk without this stick. And if he won't teach me, we'll find someone who will."

"But, Heaven, this isn't our house anymore." Angel turned and sank into her sister's arms.

"I'm not giving up, Angel. I'm going to find a way to Bells or Dryersville and talk to one of those lawyers. It's not right, Pa giving our home away. And I bet since he had a fever, he wasn't right in the head when he signed that paper."

Angel sat back in the chair, releasing her grasp on Heaven. "Why do you think Pa did that?"

"If he had been thinking straight, I don't think he would have. I wonder if he was worried about us being alone and wanted to fix that before he died." Perhaps that was the answer. It would be like Pa to think about their future. At least he'd cared. What if she'd never heard about his death? What would the awful unknown of being abandoned by her pa have done to her and to Angel? As it was, she'd been limping along thinking they would be leaving any day instead of preparing for the winter. Unless Travis stayed, they'd be eating nothing but green beans and nuts until spring.

"Does that mean he liked Dr. Logan?"

"Maybe he did. I can't see him just being grateful for Dr. Logan's doctoring and then giving away his land and family."

"Well he did, and now we're stuck."

"No we're not. Somehow I'm going to fix this. I promise you, Angel, I will make a home for us, if not here, then in a better place."

"Can I have Ma's lorgnette until that happens? I know I can't use it to look at stuff, but every time I get worried, I can touch it and know you're working on making things better."

Heaven grasped the chain. It brought her a sense of security. When she touched it or noticed its weight around her neck, it was as if Ma were standing with her. Why didn't she think of giving something like this to Angel? Ma didn't have a great deal of jewelry, but there was the brooch that had been passed down several generations. Such a sentimentally valuable piece of jewelry wouldn't be appropriate for a young girl who could lose it, but she had planned on giving it to Angel when she was older.

Angel's sister went silent. No movement came from her—not even the sound of her fingers in her hair. "Heaven? Are you mad 'cause I asked for it?"

"No, I'm just thinking about it."

Quiet surrounded Angel. It was times like this that made her as nervous as a long-tailed cat in a room full of rockers. She couldn't see faces, and that left her without any information about what a person was feeling. Was Heaven angry? Sad? Angel sat still waiting for some indication from her sister.

She heard the lorgnette chain scratch against fabric. Could it be? Then she felt the chain brush her hair as her sister lowered it onto her neck. Angel reached up and touched her chest, but it wasn't there. Sliding her hand down her stomach, she found the beaded chain close to her waistline. Resting it in the palm of her hand, she traced the small metal flower at the end of the slick glass. She brought it up and brushed her lips. "Thank you, Heaven." She wiped a lone tear from her chin. "I'm going to go show Dr. Logan."

Heaven's stick thumped loudly across the floor. Her hand went to the spot on her chest where the lorgnette had rested since her ma died. She swallowed a milk pail full of tears and sunk into the rocker, letting it surround her with its comforting memories.

Chapter 15

The sun had forgotten it was winter. Not even a chill hung on the edges of the morning. Heaven didn't even need a shawl on her shoulders. It was perfect weather to walk off some of the anger she had at her father. Not all of it. She wanted to retain some of it. She'd need it to fight for their home. Her energy fizzled by the time she reached the pond. Slowing, she took in the scenery that graced her home. Friendship wasn't in the mountains, but right now she could almost pretend it was. The land dipped low beyond the pasture just past the straggly line of cedar and poplar trees. That's where she wanted to go. It wouldn't be an easy walk, but it would be an investment in her spirit if she could see beyond her own troubles.

Taking a breath, she hobbled a few steps then a few more. Winded, she stopped and sucked in the fresh air.

Mr. Jackson nudged her hip as if to egg her on. She scratched the white tuft between his large black ears. He wasn't a pet, but he thought he was. She considered how many more goats they'd need to make cheese and soap to sell. And with the extra goats, she wouldn't have to worry about the grass getting too tall where it would hide rattlesnakes.

A few more steps and the pain worsened. She'd have to turn back. She'd come farther than she'd thought, but not far enough to reach her destination. Disappointment took over her mood. She had to make a decision—press on or go back.

She took a step toward the cabin. It wasn't a choice, not when she'd have to cover so much ground to return. "Come on, Mr. Jackson. Let's go home."

"Naaa."

"I'm saying yes, Mr. Jackson. You'd best follow me with that sweet black face of yours. I don't want you taking off on an adventure. You can get lost. You're my hope for the future."

Angel stood in the yard. "Heaven!"

Yelling. She despaired of ever teaching her sister how to act like a lady. "I'm coming."

Angel met her in the yard and held out her hand. "Let's go see Mrs. Jackson. Maybe she'll be nicer to us now that we know she's going to have a baby."

Heaven took her sister's hand, and they walked to the barn. Dr. Logan was inside staring at the hayloft. "What are you looking at?"

"There should be more hay to get these animals through the winter."

"Pa thought we'd be with him by now, so he didn't store much." Heaven defended her father, even though at the time it occurred to her there might not be enough to make it a month if winter came early or the rain quit and the grass dried.

"I wonder who has some extra they would be willing to sell. Any idea?"

"You don't need to worry yourself about that."

He spun around and glared at her. "But I do. My animals need to be taken care of through the winter."

"So do *my* animals." She wasn't going to back down from claiming the animals as hers. And Angel's. They'd been taking care of them, not her pa, and she would fight to keep them, especially Mr. Jackson. "Why do you want to raise horses? It doesn't make sense to give up being a doctor. Can't you do both?"

"I could, but I'm not going to." He hung the milking pail on a nail outside the cow's stall.

"Why not?" Angel stroked Pride and Joy's nose. "It's not like you're going to make lots of money with horses or fixing people."

"Angel!" Heaven racked her brain. What did Ma's book say about tactless thoughts expressed? "That's not nice. It's not proper to talk about money, not even to your husband."

Travis's eyebrows slanted down. "Where did you learn that, Heaven?"

"Ma taught me that. It's the husband's job to take care of the family and the money. Wives don't need to be concerned about such things." She wished she believed it with the conviction her words carried. It seemed to her that Ma was much smarter when it came to taking care of things. Pa seemed to be selling things almost as soon as they got them. One of them had been that sweet little pony he'd bought her for her eighth birthday.

"Guess some families are different than others. My mother was adamant about her daughters learning how to take care of themselves in case they ended up with a good-looking man worth his weight in dirty dishwater."

He had sisters? Heaven pondered that for a moment. What

would it be like to be able to take care of herself and Angel and not be dependent on anyone? She'd have a bigger family. Could she do that? With Pa dead, she didn't have a choice unless she married Travis. If he would marry her. If he did, would he let her tell him how to spend his money?

"How many sisters you have?" Angel tugged on Travis's coat sleeve.

Heaven winced. She'd been trying for months to get Angel's speech correct. "How many sisters *do* you have?"

"*Do* you have, sir? Is one of them Mary?"

How had Heaven forgotten about the woman he'd called for when he was feverish? She watched Travis walk to the shelf where they kept the grooming supplies. Why didn't he say something? Was Mary someone he loved, and then Pa threw Heaven in with the farm? And now that he knew Heaven was a person, he didn't know what to do about Mary?

Travis picked up the currycomb and brush. "No, Mary— well, she was someone who promised to wait for me until the war was over, but she didn't. Married my best friend." He opened Pride and Joy's stall door and slipped in next to the horse. He scratched the horse's neck.

Happiness fluttered in Heaven's stomach. Mary didn't matter. Or did Travis still love her?

"I have three sisters, and all of 'em older." He tousled Angel's hair. "They were always picking on me or making me play house with them."

"I bet they miss you," Angel said. "Why don't you go home and be with them?"

Heaven grinned. She wanted him gone, too.

"They're all married and have their own kids now. It felt right to start off in a new place."

"I'm sure they miss you. Where are you from?" Heaven wanted him gone, but if he did go, what would happen to her and Angel?

"A ways past Knoxville." He stroked his chin. "They might miss me, but not likely. I haven't been around much, what with the war and all."

"Did you go home when it ended?" Heaven leaned against the barn wall. The wind blew between the boards, and she tugged her coat closer.

"Yes ma'am. I went to see my parents and stayed for a bit. I ate a lot of good dinners, and one day my father asked if I would be starting a practice in town. That started me thinking about taking care of people. I didn't want to do that anymore."

Chapter 16

Travis led his horse, Pride and Joy, out of the barn. Every day he stayed here he grew uneasier about Caleb's will. He'd been right about one thing—there was plenty of room to raise horses here. Caleb's property could be fenced in the back and would be a nice place to train horses. The barn was a bit small, but that could be fixed easily enough. It just didn't feel right to take it from Caleb's family and to take Heaven as a bride if he couldn't love her the way Christ loved him. Then again, she was a cute thing and not dull to be around.

If Heaven was capable of taking care of the place, he might consider leaving. He felt sure Caleb had sent him here for more than the land though. Two women alone were an easy mark. Was that enough reason to marry her? If he did, he could be sure she couldn't betray him like Mary. You can't betray someone you don't love.

He whispered in the horse's ear. The horse nickered back.

"Do you and your horse talk to each other often?"

Travis looked up to see Heaven grinning while holding on to the porch railing.

"Thought I'd give him a good grooming since my head is feeling better."

"I'm glad it's healing. It's awfully warm today isn't it?"

Travis tied the horse to the porch railing. "A bit unusual. Might try and catch a few fish down at the creek today since it feels like fishin' weather."

"Fish would taste good for dinner since you didn't find anything yesterday." Heaven winced.

"Ankle hurting you?"

"A bit, though it's getting better. Could you bring out my rocker? It's such a nice day, I'd like to enjoy it before it turns cold again."

He pointed at the ball of yarn in her hand. "Going to do some knitting? That's a pretty blue. Are you making it for Angel?"

"Shh, I am working on something for her for Christmas. She can hear my needles, but as long as I keep it away from her, she doesn't know what I'm doing."

Travis smiled. "I can do that." He climbed the steps and stopped next to her. "You have some flour on your cheek."

"It's from making the biscuits this morning. Sorry there isn't a cake baking." She raised her hand to wipe it off.

He stopped her with his.

"Let me. I can see where to wipe." He used the edge of his hand and gently brushed away the white dust. Her skin was as smooth as his mother's prized china but as warm as a kitten. He leaned in closer. "I do believe"—he looked into her eyes and almost drowned in the shimmering blue—"you have a speck on your eyebrow." He moved his thumb from her cheek and slowly slid it across her brow.

Her breath came a little quicker, but she didn't back away

from him. "Dr. Logan? Did you get it all?" Her soft words fell from her lips.

Lips full like ripe peaches ready to be picked and handled with great care so as not to bruise them. He might have lost his mind, but all he could think of was that Caleb might have been right. He may have found a piece of heaven on this side of the curtain. He lowered his head and brushed his lips against hers.

She gasped but did not move, so he kissed her again, brushing the back of her hair with his hand. Her lips melted into his.

"Heaven," he said, his own breath coming a bit hard. "I do believe your father was right to name you that."

"What are you all doing out here?" Angel stuck her head out the door. She appeared to be staring right at them.

At that moment, Travis was thankful the little girl couldn't see. He had surely broken every rule there was by kissing her sister.

Heaven kept her eyes connected to his as she stepped back from him. "I am waiting for Travis to bring out the rocker. It's such a beautiful day. I thought I could keep my weight off of my ankle and still be outside."

"Well, standing there looking at each other is not going to bring the rocker outside," Angel said.

Travis broke away from Heaven's magnetic eyes.

They both stared at Angel.

"How do you know we are looking at each other?" Heaven's hand went to her cheek.

"I can't see you if that is what you all are thinking." Angel grinned. "But I listened to your footsteps, and I can tell where you are, and *Travis* stopped right by yours, so I guessed you were looking at each other. Was I right?"

Heaven's face was beet red.

Her sister had caught the informal use of his name. Travis rubbed his hand over the back of his neck. "Yes, Little Miss, you're right."

"But what I don't understand is why you stopped moving and then didn't say anything. Are you mad at each other?" Angel stepped out on the porch close to her sister as if she could protect her from Travis. And Travis thought she probably just did protect her sister from a few more kisses.

"No, we aren't mad." Heaven finally spoke. "Why don't you get the Bible, and I'll read to you. Travis is going to groom his horse, so he can listen, too."

"I'll get it. Can we read about Jesus being tempted by Satan? I like that story, because I always get tempted by stuff, but Jesus always wins." Angel went back into the cabin.

Travis let out his breath. "Do you think she knows?"

"I don't know. It's one of her favorite stories, but it does seem fortuitous that she picked it for today. Maybe it would be a good one for us to pay heed." Heaven touched his arm gently.

Travis nodded and stepped away to get the chair.

"Travis?"

He turned to face her. "Thank you. It has been a long time since I was kissed. I had forgotten how wonderful it feels, but I think it best that it not happen again."

"You're welcome." Who had kissed her before? And why didn't his kisses feel better than those of whoever had kissed her before? Travis didn't care for that thought at all.

Glory be. Heaven wanted another one of those kisses. She was sure when Travis's—she could call him that now that he'd slid his lips across hers and she'd let him—lips touched hers, the whispers from the cedar trees stopped, the chickens quit cackling, and her world grew a lot warmer.

And then Angel had bounded out the door. Good thing, too, because Heaven would have gone back for more of those block-out-the-world, good-feeling kisses from that man.

Chapter 17

Annabelle hadn't been this hot since last August. She fanned her face with her hand, wishing for a real fan. Mrs. Miles's face was gleaming, and she kept dabbing it with her handkerchief. Both of them had dressed for the winter temperatures. It surprised her that the climate was so different from back home.

"Why don't you take off your coat, dear?" Mrs. Miles asked while peeling off hers. "It's so hot."

Take it off? She couldn't, not until she had a safe place to put it. "I'm fine, really. This way I can keep my traveling clothes a bit cleaner." And she wouldn't have to worry about misplacing her future.

The carriage wobbled and bobbed for hours it seemed. Jake had been silent for this part of the trip, as had his mother. Annabelle brushed her forehead with her hand. A headache edged sideways and slipped into her body the minute she climbed into the carriage, and it proceeded to swell with each mile that passed.

"Do you know how much longer, Jake? I think we could all use a break. It would be nice to get out of the carriage and walk a bit." She smiled her best save-the-next-dance-for-me smile.

He scowled at her.

Was this what it would have been like to have a brother? If so, she was glad to be an only child. When they were younger, she'd wanted Jake for a brother because he was fun and even his teasing made her feel special.

"We should be coming to the town soon." He squared his shoulders and looked straight ahead as if making sure she wouldn't continue making conversation with him.

"Are you feeling okay, Mrs. Miles?" Annabelle patted the woman's hand.

" 'Tis hot today, isn't it? So odd for this time of year." Mrs. Miles waved her hand in front of her face to stir the air.

"Do you think it's like this all the time? We are far west of Nashville." Annabelle tugged at her collar, hoping to allow a small breeze to flow into the neckline. Nothing but humidity entered. They rolled past another long line of cedar trees.

"I really don't know, dear."

Annabelle was tired of seeing cedar trees and poplar trees and cypress trees. At first she thought the cypress were interesting, with their multifingered roots rising out of the low-standing water. Now they held no interest. She wanted to see Heaven and was quite ready to get away from grumpy Jake.

"Friendship's up ahead," Jake said. "We'll need to water these horses before going much further."

"Heaven doesn't live far from here then. Her letter said she was on the west side of town." Joy fluttered through her. She needed to hug her friend, someone who understood what it was like not to have a husband and a baby on her hip.

"We'll stop in town and ask someone. You and Mother can get out for a bit."

"It would be nice to get some refreshments before we rush to the Wharton's. We don't want to embarrass her by dropping in unexpectedly and catching her unprepared for visitors." Mrs. Miles brushed her graying strands of hair with her hands. "Do I look presentable, Annabelle?"

"Yes ma'am, you do." She patted her own coif to make sure all the strands were neatly tucked inside the net. Her excitement grew as the carriage climbed the small hill. Soon her life would change for the better. She closed her eyes and envisioned her shop, but beyond a building painted yellow, she couldn't see the store's sign. She needed a name for her business. Once she had that, she was sure the vision in her mind would be complete. Heaven would help her think of a good one. She had a knack for that sort of thinking. The carriage wheels slowed, and she opened her eyes. They had arrived.

Jake stopped the carriage in the middle of the street next to the public well. "I'll water the horses. Why don't you two go inside the general store we passed on the corner and see if you can get directions to the Whartons."

The carriage swayed as Mrs. Miles stood. "I do hope they have something cool to drink."

Jake climbed down and raised his arms to help his mother to the ground. "We might need to find a café if you are wanting a snack. You can ask about that as well."

Annabelle waited for him to turn and help her disembark. When her feet hit the ground, she gave him a half smile. "Thank you, Jake, for being so considerate of us on this trip." She linked arms with Mrs. Miles, and they crossed the street to the board-walk that ran along the buildings.

The store held a slight touch of coolness between its wood walls. Not enough to cool off a man who'd been driving in the hot sun, but enough to appreciate. Jake blinked a few times to adjust his eyes. After the bright sunlight, it took a bit to adjust to the store light.

It was bigger than he'd thought from the outside. A few women stood close to the counter. They had several bolts of fabric in front of them. He didn't see Annabelle and his mother.

He glanced around at the various items offered for sale, including a selection of Christmas gifts. He supposed he should get something for his mother before he left for the West. He'd come back into town later and pick it up. Annabelle could give it to his mother for him.

He found the women at the front of the store standing in front of a china display. He almost smiled at the coat draped over Annabelle's arm. She'd finally admitted to being hot and taken it off. "Annabelle, did you ask for directions?"

"Um, not yet. We saw this pretty dish"—she held up a small china dish covered in roses—"and we were trying to decide if we should get it for Heaven."

"Doesn't look all that useful to me. Guess I'll get the directions while you two shop." To get to the counter, he scooted past the two chatting women with the fabric. He noticed they'd added lace to their selection. Jake excused himself and scooted around them so he could talk to the clerk who waited behind the counter.

"I'm looking for the Wharton place." Jake's nose twitched

at the brine odor rising from the barrel of pickles next to the counter.

The clerk's eyebrows edged up, "You are? That other fellow that went that way awhile back never came back."

One of the women at the end of the counter gasped, distracting Jake.

"Mrs. Reynolds, you didn't just leave her there?"

"She wouldn't leave. Besides, he is a doctor, and she's hurt."

Jake brought himself out of the women's gossip and back to the conversation he'd started. "Another man?"

"Yep, he was looking for Caleb's place. Told him he'd better have a gun with him."

Another gasp behind him. Really, women were so emotional, full of gossip.

"She really shot him?"

That got Jake's attention. He whipped his head toward the gossipers.

"So, son, what do you want with Caleb's place?"

Jake turned back.

"I was asking why you needed to get to Caleb's?" The clerk leaned forward on the counter, searching Jake's face for something.

"His daughter is my—my friend. I've brought her best friend and my mother along as well. For a visit."

"I'm sure she'll be glad to see her friends."

"She said she was aiming over his head and missed." The other voice piped up. Mrs. Reynolds, he guessed. She must be the town gossip.

"God was watching out for him."

"Heaven, too, and Angel. Where would that girl go if her sister went to jail?"

Jake stilled. Were they talking about his Heaven? Had she found someone else then? She'd shot him? And he was living with her? Without marrying her?

A crack of thunder rolled through the building, shaking the glass windowpanes. Jake whirled around. The widows no longer let in the hot sunlight. The sky had taken on a bruised appearance.

A man burst through the door. The wind came from behind him, banging the door against the wall, shattering the glass. "Tornado's a comin'! Everyone in the cellar!"

Chapter 18

Travis stared up at the bunching clouds. The sky had turned dark gray green. The wind whipped away the heat. A branch snapped and splashed into the creek. He didn't like the dropping temperature. He pulled the fishing line back to the shore and collected the bucket of caught fish. He'd clean them back at the cabin. He wanted to get there, just in case the weather took a turn for the worse.

He did. He wanted to be with Heaven. One kiss and she'd filled the giant hole left in him from Mary's devious behavior. *Thank You, God.* Caleb was right, heaven did wait for him here in Friendship. Now he needed to convince Heaven that being married was the best thing to do. He had a feeling she was going to fight him on this. She kept asking him questions about how to do things so she could do them when he moved on, even though he told her repeatedly he wasn't budging from this land.

The air felt heavy and thick on his face.

Lightning filled the sky, followed by a volley of thunder close enough to make a hardened soldier jump. The wind rushed around him, pushing him forward, urging him to take bigger strides. The clouds ripped open and sent driving rain so solid it felt like nails piercing his face. He dropped the fish and the pole. Thunder sounded overhead, his ears popped once, then twice, and the sky turned pea green. A loud rushing of wind buffeted his face, making it sting. It grew darker, and it seemed time had skipped ahead to midnight. Then he heard it. Wind that strong had to mean—a tornado!

He ran but gave up and dove for a gulley when the dark gray cloud spiraled just north of him. His breath caught. He wasn't in danger, but Heaven and Angel were. He struggled against the wind. He had to get to them. The wind knocked him to the ground, and in desperation he crawled toward the cabin and prayed as he'd never prayed before.

The sky had grown darker. Rain again. Heaven was sick of it. She collected her knitting and went inside. "Angel, another storm is coming. Do you think you can get the rocker back inside? It's heavy, and I don't think I can help because of my ankle."

Angel set the doll she'd been playing with on the settee. "I can try."

Heaven followed her to the porch.

Angel tried pulling, but the rocker barely moved. "It's too heavy."

"That all right. Maybe Travis will come back before it rains. I'm sure he'll notice the clouds piling up. Then he can bring it inside."

"It won't hurt it to get a little wet, since it's just wood." Angel pushed past her and went back inside and curled up on the couch with her doll.

Heaven shrugged. "I guess it would eventually dry out." She dropped her knitting basket onto the kitchen table. She touched the coffeepot on the stove to see if it was still warm. It wasn't hot but warm enough. She flipped over a china cup she left out to dry and filled it halfway. She didn't want to risk spilling a full cup while she hobbled back to sit by Angel.

She sat next to her sister and set the cup on the small table next to the settee. "Would you like me to read to you while you play?"

"Can you read the story about David killing the giant?" Angel kissed her doll's cheek. "I like that one."

"Me, too." Heaven picked up the heavy Bible from the side table and flipped it open to 1 Samuel and turned the pages until she reached chapter seventeen. "Here it is." She began reading the story and had just reached the part where David asked what the reward would be for killing Goliath when Angel grabbed her arm. "What?"

"My ears are popping. Something's wrong." Angel cocked her head.

"What do you mean?"

"I hear something different. Like the wind is going faster than I've ever heard it go before. It's noisy." Angel paced the floor, fiddling with her ears.

"It's just the storm." Heaven placed the ribbon bookmark inside the Bible and closed it. "I'm sure it is." But Angel might be right. She'd never seen the sky turn so dark in the middle of the day.

"No, Heaven. Listen. It's not just raining. The wind—it doesn't sound right. We have to get in the cellar." Angel grabbed Heaven's hand and pulled. "Please believe me. We have to go now!"

Heaven sprung to her feet and followed her sister. She pulled open the trap door to expose the wooden ladder. "Angel, you go first." Heaven feared it would take her too long and Angel wouldn't have time to get down the ladder. At least Angel would be safe in the cellar.

Heaven left the trap door open. She couldn't close it, because she would have to put more weight on her sore ankle. Just as she made it to the bottom rung, something blew through the window, and shards of glass sailed down the steps.

Heaven screamed. She grabbed Angel around the waist, and the two of them squatted against the back row of shelves holding the canned green beans. Thunder shook the shelves.

A roar rushed over the house. A high pitched screeching made them cover their ears. Then it grew quiet.

"The animals!" Angel grabbed Heaven's arm and pulled her toward the stairs. "Mr. Jackson was outside!"

"So is Travis, but we can't go yet. It might not be over." Heaven yanked Angel back from the bottom stair. They toppled to the dirt floor.

A rush of wind once again roared over their head. And then there was only the patter of rain.

"How did you know we should come down here, Angel?"

"On a walk last spring, Pa and I saw a tree pulled up by its roots. Pa said sometimes wind out here blows hard enough to do that, and if it happened, I should get in the cellar."

"I'm glad Pa told you, because I didn't know that." Heaven couldn't wait any longer. "I have to see if Travis made it back."

"I'm coming with you." Angel hopped off the floor and followed her sister upstairs.

In the kitchen, Heaven grasped Angel's arm before she went past her. "The glass windows are all broken, and. . .and nothing is in the right place."

"But we just made it a home." Angel's voice wavered.

Heaven wanted to cry, too. "The front door is gone, and the table is upside down." A chair leg impaled the glass book case and hung like an oddly shaped coatrack. Then she noticed the cold wind coming from the side where the bedroom was. Only it wasn't there anymore. The doorway led to the outside.

"Angel, this is bad. Ma and Pa's room is gone. Just gone. Hold on to my hand, and I'll tell you what's happened. I want to go outside and see if any of our things are there."

"Is Pa and Ma's picture gone?"

"Probably." And a lot more. She had left the Bible with their family records on the settee, and it was on its side. The rug under it hadn't moved, and. . . She stopped, and Angel bumped into her. "Angel, that is the oddest thing."

"What?"

"The cup of coffee I was drinking is still sitting undisturbed on the little table. If you only looked at the table and cup, you wouldn't know anything happened in here."

She stepped through the doorless opening onto the porch. "The rocker is gone, too." She'd never be able to get another rocker that brought so much comfort through memories. The sun was now shining as if there had never been a storm. Heaven gazed upon the pieces of the bedroom walls scattered across the yard. There was no sign of the bed or the quilt that had covered it. Something glimmered, and her heart raced. Could it be the photo of her ma and pa? "Wait here, Angel. I think I see something."

She hobbled down the stairs, ignoring the twinge of pain, stopping where she'd seen the sparkle of glass. She bent down. Her spirit crashed.

"What did you find?" Angel hollered.

"Nothing, just a piece of glass."

Rain hammered the store windows. Thunder crashed overhead, startling Annabelle with its intensity.

Mrs. Miles grabbed Annabelle's arm. "Hurry!"

Annabelle slid the pretty dish back on the shelf, giving it an extra push so it wouldn't sit on the edge. She looked in the direction of where she'd last seen Jake. He wasn't there. Had he left without them? She turned back as Mrs. Miles again tugged at her arm. "Where's Jake? Shouldn't we wait for him?"

Mrs. Miles shook her head and pushed Annabelle toward the front of the store. "He was at the counter conversing with the clerk."

Jake appeared at her side. "Mother, Annabelle, come on."

Mrs. Miles pulled at Annabelle's arm, dragging her forward. "We have to go."

Annabelle's mind connected with the warning in Mrs. Miles's voice. As she rushed for the stairs to the cellar, her coat slipped off her arm. She stopped and turned to go back.

"Leave it!" Jake grabbed her arm and yanked her along with him.

She stumbled forward, looking back at her future disappearing under feet.

After first herding the women into a corner of the store's cellar, Jake moved closer to the entrance and away from them. Annabelle huddled in the corner next to Mrs. Miles, who clung to her like a wet cloth while her son ignored them both. She couldn't understand his need to be alone. Except down in this hole in the earth, he couldn't really distance himself from them. Still, he had managed to remove himself as far as he could.

She must get upstairs as soon as it was safe and get her coat. She hoped everyone thought her breathlessness came from the fear of the storm and nothing else. If they knew or suspected it was more than a coat, it would disappear. The store above them creaked and groaned as the wind pushed and shoved against its wooden sides. Something fell on the floor upstairs. Annabelle jumped.

The coat had to be there. It couldn't have been caught up in the twisting winds. If it had, she would be forced to go home. Shards of fear hammered against her nerves. Why had she sewn all of her money in the hem? Her desire to get away from her ex-fiancé's new wife and lead an independent life had led her to act with foolishness.

The tight quarters and smell of fear rode Jake's bones. He hung his head and studied the dirt floor. He should help calm Annabelle and his mother, but he couldn't. His only desire was to get out of this town and move on to where no one might find out what had happened on that battlefield. He tapped his foot, eager to get above ground and complete the task he'd come this far to do. With all the prattling from his mother and Annabelle about Heaven on this trip, he'd begun to think he was making a mistake by not marrying her.

He remembered how soft and small her hands were in his and the way she laughed at his silly pranks rather than crying like the other girls. Heaven always looked at him as if he were responsible for all the good in her life. A man could get caught up in feeling like a woman's hero in moments like that. Those memories had been circulating in his mind for most of the trip.

Then the storm came. He was glad. It reminded him that his reasoning was correct. Heaven shouldn't be tied to a man like him. He couldn't even comfort his own mother in a storm. He wasn't worthy of any woman, much less Heaven. On the inside, he still wore the colors of a coward.

Chapter 19

Heart thumping, Travis slipped and slid as he ran across the wet pasture. He brushed the rain from his forehead as it dripped into his eyes. Trees were snapped and lying on their sides. A tree stuck in the ground, trunk side up, next to a section of splintered logs in the pasture. He moved faster. The tornado had touched down here, but what about the cabin? Were Heaven and Angel safe? He had no idea if they would know to go to the cellar in a storm like this.

He slipped on the wet grass and fell on the ground. Breathing hard, he stood up and bent over with his hands on his knees and sucked in a breath. His head throbbed where he'd been shot. He touched it. The stitches held, and his hand came back clean. With his breath more even, he ran for the cabin. *Please, God, let them be all right. I don't care about the cabin and barn. They can be rebuilt, but Heaven and Angel can't.* He pushed through a stand of cedar trees and saw it. The cabin stood, but the added-on bedroom was missing. The barn stood, and on the front porch, the woman he cared about waited.

"Heaven, are you and Angel all right?" He ran like a little child runs to his mother after he's had a nightmare. He stopped at the bottom step and grabbed the railing.

"I came—as—fast—as I could run."

"We're okay." Heaven rushed down the steps and hugged him. "Angel heard the wind coming and made me go to the root cellar."

"I told her so, and for once she listened to me," Angel said. "Are the animals okay, Dr. Logan?"

"The barn is intact, so I think they are. I'll check on them in a minute."

"But Mr. Jackson wasn't in the barn." Angel's voice wobbled. "Mr. Jackson! Mr. Jackson, where are you?"

Travis's heart split as he looked around and didn't see the troublesome goat anywhere.

"Can you see him, Heaven?" She trotted down the steps. "Mr. Jackson!" She turned back toward the cabin. "I don't even hear him. We have to find him. He might be hurt."

Heaven went to her sister and hugged her. "We'll find him." She turned to Travis. "Won't we, Travis?"

"If you're okay, I'll start searching right away." He brushed a hand over Angel's hair. "I'll do my best to bring him back to you, Little Miss. For now, why don't you and your sister see if the other animals are okay? Can you do that? Check on Pride and Joy for me and tell him I'll be back soon with his new pal Mr. Jackson."

"I'll pet him on the nose and scratch his ears, too, Dr. Logan. Please find Mr. Jackson. He's my favorite animal in the whole world."

Travis's eyes met Heaven's troubled eyes. What if he couldn't find the goat? Would it be too much for Angel? She'd lost so much in one year. Humans couldn't take that much pain, could they?

"When I get back, I want to ask you something, Heaven. But first I need to find a goat."

A horse thundered down the lane.

Heaven twirled around as if to run to the house. Travis grabbed her by the arm. "No need for that rifle. I'm here."

The rider was at the house in mere seconds. He didn't even dismount. Rather, he rode up next to them. "Doc, you have to come to town. Preacher sent me. There's people hurt."

His medical instinct kicked in, but he fought it. He'd given up this emergency way of living. He felt the tension of his decision rumbling through his veins. He could stay and search for a little girl's lost goat or help save lives. When he looked at it that way, there wasn't a choice.

"Heaven, Angel. . ."

"You have to go. Angel and I will look for Mr. Jackson." Heaven touched his arm. "We'll find him."

"Preacher told me to fetch you and Angel, too. He said Mrs. Reynolds was needing help at the church. She's organizing something so people will have a place to sleep and eat."

"But Mr. Jackson!" Angel's lower lip trembled.

"I think he'll find his way home, Little Miss." Travis took her hand. "He'll get hungry for your petting, and he'll find his way back. As soon as I can, I'll come home and see if he's here. If not, I'll start searching."

"You promise?"

"Promise." He hoped the goat would come home, healthy. He didn't want the responsibility of a dead goat heaped on top of all his other failures.

Heaven's mind buzzed like a hive of bees. What did Dr. Logan want to ask her? Had he changed his mind about taking the farm? Maybe he wanted to know if he could buy it from her. The more she thought about him and the kiss, the lighter her step. At least thinking about it and Travis was taking her mind off the cruel reality that half of her home was possibly in some other county. She wanted to change before going into town. She opened her mother' trunk. Her perfume sat on top. She pulled out the stopper and dabbed the honeysuckle scent behind her ears and then set it aside. She'd wear one of Ma's skirts, maybe that pretty gray blouse with the black trim and ruffles on the cuff as well.

"What are you singing about—Travis?" Angel said. "Are you in love with him?"

"Certainly not, and why are you calling him Travis? And I wasn't singing."

"If you aren't in love, why did you put on some of Ma's honeysuckle perfume?"

"I was missing her, that's all."

"Well, I miss her, too. How come I don't get to wear any?"

"You aren't old enough." Angel should change, too. After landing on the dirt floor, the back of her dress was filthy.

"You need to wait here while I run down to the cellar. Don't move around in here, or you might get hurt."

"I'll just stand here and make up songs about Travis for you." Angel leaned against the doorway where the door used to be hinged.

"I wasn't singing about him," Heaven said under her breath. She picked up the small vial of perfume and walked over to her sister. "Angel, you're right. Hold still, and I'll put a little bit of Ma's scent on your neck."

Angel took a deep breath. "It smells just like her."

"Yes it does." Heaven replaced the bottle's stopper. "Now stay here while I run and get the green beans."

Down in the earthen cellar, Heaven gathered several jars of green beans in a basket to take to the church, glad the exchange with Angel had stopped for now.

"It's time to go. Travis will have Charlie at the door in a minute." She nudged Angel out the door and then set the basket on the porch. The temperature had plummeted. It was hard to remember the brilliant sunshine and warmth of the morning. She slipped her coat over her shoulders.

"I don't understand why I can't stay here," Angel whined. "Please let me stay on the porch and call Mr. Jackson. He might hear me and find his way home."

Heaven tried to focus on the fact that Angel was younger and had lost so much, but then so had she, and her sister was wearing her thin. "I'm not leaving you here alone. Button your coat. It's getting colder."

"Is it because I'm blind? Is that why you won't let me stay here? 'Cause I can see, you know."

Heaven spun around, wincing at the pain in her still tender ankle. She grabbed her sister by the shoulders and pulled her close.

"What do you see, Angel? Can you tell me what color Dr. Logan's eyes are? Or show me where the stain is on my skirt?

Can you see if someone with a gun is standing in front of you threatening to take our home? No you can't. You're coming with me, and not because you're blind but because you're eleven and you're all I have left."

"Mr. Jackson is all I have." Angel shoved Heaven's hands away from her and stomped to the porch railing. She hung over it and bellowed. "Mr. Jackson! Mr. Jackson, please come home!"

That stung. The goat was the only thing her sister had? She took a breath, ready to respond with her own hurtful words, when Charlie's nose edged out of the barn door followed by the wagon. Travis stopped the horse at the porch steps and hopped to the ground. "You ladies ready?"

Angel stormed down the porch steps. "If I have to be. It's not like anyone is going to let me help. I'd be more useful here calling for Mr. Jackson."

Heaven snatched up the basket of canned green beans from the porch floor. "Thank you, for taking us to town with you. I'm sure you wanted to ride off immediately to see to the people in town."

"I couldn't leave you here. You're my first responsibility. How would you get on Charlie to ride to town when your ankle isn't quite healed?" He bent down and scooped her off the porch and carried her to the wagon.

Yes, indeed, how could she? She'd have managed, but she doubted anyone from town would have ridden out to tell her they needed help if she didn't have a doctor sleeping in her barn. She settled on the bench next to Angel, who hugged the outer edge. That meant Heaven would have to ride shoulder to shoulder with Travis. She smiled.

Travis climbed into the wagon and signaled Charlie to get moving with a jiggle of the reins.

Angel leaned into her sister and pulled Heaven's head close to her ear and whispered, "His eyes are brown. You don't have a stain on your skirt, because you changed into one of Ma's skirts right after the tornado. And if the sun hits a man's gun just right, I can see a light. So I can do all those things you think I can't." Angel turned her body away from her sister, scooting as far away as she could.

Shock waves ricocheted through Heaven. Was it possible? She wrapped her arm around her sister and pulled her tight and leaned close to her ear. "How do you know his eyes are brown, Angel? Can you really see them?" Heaven hoped it was true. Could her sister's sight be returning? *Please, God.*

"I know, because I heard you singing to yourself about his lovely puppy-brown eyes."

Travis couldn't help the grin on his face. She'd been making up songs about his eyes? Sure, it had only been a week, but he could see why her father thought she was Heaven. Except when she didn't get what she wanted. Then she was like an old rooster that ought to be put in a pot and boiled. If she had her way, he'd have taught her everything he knew about guns, horses, and doctoring in one day so she could send him packing. He hoped that kiss changed some of her mind about that. It changed his.

But he had no plan to marry the woman if there wasn't love between them. He'd watched his parents' marriage, and that's the kind he wanted. A partnership so full of love that he and his sisters were always complaining about the quick kisses by the stove if they happened to walk in while his parents were so engaged. Kissing Heaven by the stove sounded good to him. He snuck a glance at her. She did have on a nice skirt, still black but a softer material. He knew from picking her up that it wasn't a work-on-the-farm skirt, more like what his sister would wear to church. Even her blouse had lace on it—black, but it was lace.

Angel hadn't changed though. He'd heard the arguing all the way in the barn. From what he'd learned about Heaven this week, she'd be upset about Angel choosing to keep on her old clothes. He'd keep that to himself, but it was nice to know she wasn't all prim, proper, and perfect.

"How long do you think we'll need to stay in town?" Heaven caught him staring at her, and her cheeks turned a pretty pink.

Charlie splashed through a puddle, sending dirty water up his leg. He'd need a good brushing tonight. The wagon creaked though the same hole in the lane, tilting enough that Heaven leaned against him.

She put distance between them fast.

He bit his lip to keep from smiling. He'd kissed her, but leaning against him in a tipping wagon must be against some rule.

"Not sure. It depends on what kind of injuries. If no one is seriously hurt, it won't take long; otherwise I might need to stay overnight."

"Overnight?" Her eyes widened. "I planned to be back before dark. I have animals to take care of, including your horse."

"Don't fret. I can always take you home, or someone else

can drive you and then ride Pride and Joy back to town for me if I can't take you."

"That's good. I don't want to stay in town. Like I said, I have a farm and. . ."

"And we have to find Mr. Jackson. Don't forget. You said, Heaven, that we would leave as soon as we helped get the dinner served." Angel's voice rose on each word. "You promised!"

"I did, but I didn't think about Travis not being able to return right away." She sighed. "We're going to find Mr. Jackson perched on the porch when we get home. He's making you worry for nothing."

"You know how to drive the wagon. You can take us home."

Travis scratched the side of his head. They sounded like his sisters getting ready to go into battle. "Angel, your sister is capable of driving the wagon home. She cannot jump out of it though, because her ankle could be reinjured. Unless you'd like to continue doing her chores?"

"I could, you know. I'm capable, too." Angel slapped her arms around her middle and tucked her hands under her arms. "But you probably don't want to keep eating my cooking. Heaven says I have a lot to learn."

She was right about that, but he had learned from his experience with his sisters about speaking the real truth. "I think you scramble eggs better than anyone." He just didn't have a desire to eat them again for every meal next week.

Heaven rotated the basket of green beans on her lap. She tapped her fingers on the lid of one of them. "I hope they weren't expecting something baked."

"I'm sure the beans will be appreciated. Mrs. Reynolds has

probably mentioned your ankle being sprained to a few people, so they wouldn't expect you to be baking pies and bread this week."

He couldn't read the expression on her face, but he thought it might be relief. Maybe she couldn't bake any better than Angel scrambled eggs.

"I'm sure you're right, since they knew to ride out to my farm and ask you for help."

Chapter 20

Heaven concentrated on the bobbing jar lids riding in the basket on her lap. They were screwed on tight, holding in those green beans, just like she was trying to keep her fears from getting loose and making a mess. When she went back into the cellar, the first few jars she'd picked up where heavy, and she worried that their one never-ending supply of food was going bad. What would Travis do once he figured out there wasn't much else to eat?

She should have stayed home with Angel. They could have searched for more of their belongings, maybe found a way to block off the open doorway and the windows. In town she would be subjected to questions about her father and the man that brought the news. Questions she didn't have answers to give that she liked. If they knew Pa had given Travis the farm, she wouldn't stand a chance at getting it back. They thought women shouldn't be in charge of their own lives, even though they'd proved themselves as a whole for generations and through this last mess when their men took off to fight. She'd watched as some of them returned and shooed their wives back into the parlors, as if they didn't have an ounce of wisdom about what to do without their husbands telling them what to do.

She did not want to be one of those women—ever.

The cedar trees thinned as they reached town. From the distress in the messenger's verbal demands about getting the doctor to town quickly, she'd expected to find everything flattened. Instead, she could see a path were the tornado had touched down. The tops of some of the trees were snapped in half, while those around them bent as if trying to bow to those untouched by the wind.

"What's it look like? Is the store still there? The post office?" Angel bounced on the seat next to her as the wagon dipped in and out of the low spots on the road.

"We aren't quite there yet," Travis said. "I can see rooftops though."

Heaven straightened her back and lifted her head, trying to see what he could see, but couldn't. He was much taller. "I hope it skipped most of the town—all of the town would be even better."

"It might have; tornados are odd like that. Taking a house and leaving the barn or. . ."

"Do you think it took Mr. Jackson?" Angel's voice, no longer demanding, had faded to one without hope.

Heaven squeezed her sister's hand. "I'm praying that didn't happen."

"Me, too," Travis said as he reached over Heaven's lap and covered their hands with his.

Heaven didn't know what surprised her most—that he was praying to find Mr. Jackson or the warmth and security flowing through his touch. That he cared about her sister woke something in her heart she'd thought long gone.

As the wagon reached the crest of the hill, Heaven gasped as a man darted across the street and climbed into a buggy.

"What? Tell me, is it all gone?" Angel squeezed her sister's arm with both hands.

She watched the buggy pull away from the hitching rail and head out of town.

"Why'd your arm go all stiff? What aren't you telling me? Are there dead bodies on the street?" Angel tugged hard on Heaven's sleeve. "Were you two doing something naughty 'cuz you think I can't see? Did he sneak a kiss?"

"Hush, Angel. There aren't any dead bodies, and no kisses have been exchanged. Please be still. All that bouncing around you're doing hurts my ankle when you bump it, that's all."

Could there still be some of that laudanum in her brain causing her to see things? Maybe she was tired. Sleep hadn't come easily this week. Jake was dead, right? Or had his death been a mistake? She'd heard of that happening, but the war had ended last year. If he was alive, he would have come to her by now. Wouldn't he? And if it was Jake, why wasn't her heart singing love songs?

Annabelle snuggled in her coat, secure in the knowledge she still had her money and her plan was intact. She had left Mrs. Miles behind as she raced upstairs. The coat wasn't where it had fallen from her arms, and prickles of fear had raced through her. Then she noticed it draped across the store counter. Some kind soul had placed it there, and he or she hadn't discovered the secret in the hem. She wouldn't take it off again until they reached the farm. She was glad it was cold again. Now there would be no need to pretend it necessary to wear it.

"We'll be there soon." Jake put the horses in motion. "When I exchanged the carriage for the buggy, I asked the livery man where the Wharton's farm was located. He said it's about a mile out of town."

Annabelle tapped Jake's arm. "Did he think the tornado hit their farm?"

"I asked, but he didn't know. He said a few homes on the west side of the town got hit hard. He hadn't heard about the outlying farms."

"Jake, maybe we should stay and help these people." Mrs. Miles twisted her gloved hands in her lap.

"No, we need to get to the Wharton's farm. If they're fine, I'll leave you as soon as I speak to Heaven and then come back to help."

Annabelle wondered if he would come back to the Wharton's if he went into town. She needed to talk to him. It was time to tell him she wouldn't be returning to Nashville either.

Heaven waited for Travis to help her down from the wagon in front of the church. His strong hands surrounded her in security. Except there was no secure place or person. She knew that now. The cabin hadn't been flattened by the tornado but might as well have been. With the back room ripped off and an open wall exposing them to the elements, she knew there wasn't a way she could repair it. She didn't have the funds or the skills. Her father was right to leave the farm to Travis. But to leave her and

Angel without means was unthinkable.

Travis carried her over the small muddy stream that had formed in front of the church and placed her on the wooden porch. He waited until she was steady on her feet. "I'll get Angel."

Her heart was turning to Travis, but she was afraid. Did she want to love him because he could save her and Angel? Or was she truly falling in love with him as Angel had suggested on the drive into town? She watched him carry her sister to her as gently as he'd carried her. She touched her lips and remembered this morning's kiss. It had been more than pleasant. It had warmed her in places that never before felt heated. Not even with Jake.

Dear Jake. She did miss him, and when she thought she'd seen him, she'd been glad. But not in a way that shouted love. It didn't matter anyway; the only man she had to choose was Travis. Things had changed much since she'd had her coming out party in Nashville.

"Thank you, Dr. Logan." Angel slid from his arms and stood next to her sister. "Don't forget we have to go back soon to find Mr. Jackson. You promised."

"I'll not forget, Little Miss." He tipped his hat to them and climbed back on the wagon. "I'll tie Charlie up by the post office, since that looks like the only place where the wagon won't sink in the mud. I'll come back here to find out where they need me."

Heaven stiffened. She didn't consider answering all the questions alone, without Travis. "We can wait for you." She shifted the basket to her other arm.

He cocked his head and grinned. "I'd like that, Miss Wharton, but don't you think that would fuel the gossip about us?"

She bit her bottom lip. He was right. It wouldn't help matters if she walked into the church holding onto his arm. She nodded and touched her sister's shoulder and turned away from him. "Are you ready, Angel?"

"Of course. Why, shouldn't I be?" Angel held her hand up for her sister to grasp. "I like being at church. You're the one who gets upset."

"You didn't like it when the Rush boys were pulling your pigtails and making fun of you not being able to see." She held tightly to her sister's hand, directing her to the door.

"They're stupid boys. Dr. Logan says when boys make fun of you, that means they like you."

Heaven looked at her sister's smiling face and wanted to hug Travis. She wished she had remembered that from her youth. "When did he tell you that?"

"The other night when we were checking on Mrs. Jackson."

Heaven pushed open the heavy door. The enchanting smell of fried chicken made her mouth water. How long had it been since she'd had some? She could taste the crunchy skin mixed with the salt and pepper. Her stomach begged for a piece.

"Do you smell that, Heaven?" Angel inhaled. "It smells like the best part of church."

"I think God is the best part, Angel."

"I know. But doesn't it smell like church—the dinners on Sundays and all the starched, clean clothes?"

She took a deep breath. "Yes, you're right, it does." The sanctuary was full of apron-wearing women. The high-pitched voices seemed overwhelming after the quiet of her home. She glanced about the room for someone she might know.

Mrs. Reynolds caught her eye. With a load-bearing smile, she squeezed through a group of women to get to them.

"You came! I'm so glad you did." Mrs. Reynolds cut off any more discussion Heaven might have had with her sister.

Heaven thrust out her basket of green beans. "I hope this is okay. We didn't have anything baked, and then the tornado took off part of the cabin."

"It did? And you came to help anyway? Thank you." Mrs. Reynolds gathered Heaven in a hug. "You two have been through so much this year. You're such very strong—yes, strong—women."

Heaven felt the moisture in her eyes gathering reinforcements. "Ma used to say that to us."

"I hope it didn't make you sadder to hear it from me then." Mrs. Reynolds stepped back. Concern crinkled around her eyes.

"No, it's a nice memory. Thank you."

"Is your ankle better?"

Angel piped up. "Heaven's better, but she's going to get tired fast. We'll have to go back to our farm soon because Mr. Jackson is lost."

"Mr. Jackson? You have another man at the farm?" Worry worked the preacher's wife's brow.

"He's my best friend, and he's going to be a daddy soon, so he needs to get on home," Angel continued.

Mrs. Reynolds's lips pursed, and her glance shot from Angel to Heaven.

"Mr. Jackson is our goat." Heaven stifled a laugh. Had the

woman really thought they had another man hanging around the place?

"My goodness, Angel! Bless your heart. You had me worried that there was a missing man out there at your farm."

Angel giggled. "I'm sorry."

"If you two will help me and the others, we can get this noon meal together. I have some of the older boys assigned to set up some chairs along the walkways. It's a bit too wet to have people sitting on the ground. As you can see, they've already moved the pews around. My husband won't like that, though I suspect God wouldn't mind."

"There isn't much choice is there, since there isn't a school building?" Heaven said as she followed Mrs. Reynolds.

"Not yet, but there has been plenty of talk about getting one started."

"Angel!" A bouncing blond girl about Angel's age wove through the women. "Remember me? I'm Cassie."

Angel straightened. "I do."

"Come help me cover the tables. It'll be fun." Cassie grasped Angel by the hand. "Say you will. Please."

"Heaven?" Angel tipped her head, waiting for her sister's answer.

"Yes, of course." She listened to the girls' lively chatter as they moved away. Guilt slammed her. They should have been coming to church. Angel had friends here, and maybe Heaven did, too.

Mrs. Reynolds held out her hands. "Let's get those green beans heated up. I bet you are getting tired of eating these."

"Great-Uncle Neal seemed to enjoy them more than we do.

I am grateful to have them, especially now that we won't be leaving Friendship."

"Neal was a bit odd, but our church family loved him and still misses him. Do you know why there are so many green beans?"

"No, do you? Angel and I have been wondering why he didn't can anything else." Heaven picked up her steps to match Mrs. Reynolds's quick ones.

"He was a funny man. He loved those green beans, and one day he announced that's all he was planting since he couldn't find a wife to make him anything else. He said they were a life-sustaining vegetable. We never could figure that out. They must not have been, since he died not long after canning his crop."

"Maybe not for him, but they've been keeping Angel and me alive. Pa, in his grief, didn't plant a good garden last spring, and what he did plant, I didn't know how to can." Heaven wanted to slap a hand over her mouth. Why was she telling this woman about their lack of food? Maybe it was the motherly way Mrs. Reynolds had about her.

"Goodness, child! We'll have to see what we can do for you. Might be some people willing to trade green beans for peaches and such."

"That would be lovely. Thank you so much for thinking of that. Angel and I don't want to take help from others, but trading would work out right nice." Her gaze landed on a basket of fried chicken. She wanted some of that, and Angel needed to get her hands on a leg or two as well. Her stomach growled.

Mrs. Robinson stopped. "Dear, why don't you find your sister and get something to eat and then come help us? I imagine what with the tornado hitting your place, you didn't have time for eatin' before you came here to help."

Heaven hoped the relief didn't shine like a full moon on her face.

A tiny hand escaped the tightly wrapped bundle and brushed Travis's cheek as he handed it over to Mrs. Shaw. "She's a pretty one, and looks healthy, too." This was the best part of being a doctor. A healthy newborn baby fresh from God always made him happy. That perfection could be formed unseen in the womb was something only the great Creator could do.

Mrs. Shaw rubbed a thumb across the baby girl's cheek. "I'm so glad you came, Dr. Logan. She wasn't supposed to be here for two more weeks. I don't know what we would have done." She looked at him for a second, then her attention fixated on her daughter.

"I'm sure Mr. Shaw would have figured out how to get you some help. Babies seem to pick to be born during the oddest times." Travis stood back. "You take care now. Let the others do the work around here while you get your strength back. I'll ride over later and check on you unless you'd rather your doctor come."

Mr. Shaw patted his wife's hand. "We don't have a doctor in town. There's a midwife that helps with birthing and minor cuts. The town's been trying to get a doctor to hang his shingle. Trying to get a school started for all these little ones we have running around town, too. It's time to get on with living now that the war is over."

Travis slipped his coat over his shoulders. "A school's a sure sign of a prospering town." He slid his arms in and buttoned two buttons. "I need to head back to the church and see if there's anyone else needing help."

"I'll walk you out." Mr. Shaw gently touched his wife's hand. "Be right back."

Travis took note of the sparsely furnished cabin. It didn't hold near what Heaven's cabin did, but he could see touches of love sprinkled in the room. A hand-carved cradle waited next to the hearth, and a quilt of blue and yellow squares rested in the rocker. That's what Heaven and Angel had been missing. He understood their need for moving that furniture around and saving their father's stories. Even that ugly threadbare rug made sense to him. And now their home was ravaged by the storm. He'd see to fixing that right away. For tonight he wasn't sure they should sleep there, but he had a feeling he wouldn't be able to keep Heaven in town. Or Angel, at least not until that rascal Mr. Jackson was found.

Mr. Shaw held out his hand.

Travis took it in his and shook it.

"Thank you again for coming for my Etta. We were both unnerved when she started having those pains. And this being the first one. . .well. . ." Mr. Shaw's Adam's apple bobbed. "Helping your wife is not the same as helping a cow along. You wouldn't be thinking of settling down here, would you? You'd have plenty of patients."

"We'll see, although my heart is leaning toward raising horses rather than doctoring."

"Me and the missus are going to be praying that you'll stay

and take care of our little girl as she grows up."

Travis hopped on Charlie, glad he'd left the wagon in town. He'd be able to get back to the church faster. His work for the town folk was done, and the sun was still shining. He'd pick up Heaven and her sister and begin the process of finding pieces of their home.

Angel hadn't been this excited in quite a while. Cassie introduced her to Debbie and Luanne. They didn't treat her like she couldn't see, and they made sure to tell her where to be careful. Not that there had been a lot of opportunities for making friends with Heaven hovering close by.

"I'm sure you could still be in the play. We have to ask Mrs. Reynolds. You could be the angel that doesn't speak," Debbie said. "That's what I'm doing. I get to wear wings, and I don't have to say any lines. Mrs. Reynolds said my role is to look angelic and smile."

A tablecloth flapped, and Angel heard it swoosh across the smooth tabletop.

"Robert Rush is going to be Joseph. Can you imagine?" Luanne giggled. "He's been swaggering around town like he has the most important role in the play."

Angel took in all of the back-and-forth conversation, cherishing the closeness of her new friends.

"So do you want to be an angel?" Debbie touched her arm. "It would be fun."

"I'll have to ask my sister."

"Go with me, Debbie, to get the rest of the cloths," Luanne

said. "Angel, if Mrs. Reynolds isn't busy, we'll ask her if you can still be in the play. We'll be right back."

Angel listened to their footsteps and giggles fade.

"I think Robert's brother is cute," Cassie whispered to Angel. "But they say he's even meaner than Robert."

"Thomas was mean to me. He didn't even know my name, and he pulled my hair. Then he called me a dumb blind girl."

"Then I'm not going to like him."

Angel covered her lips with her hand and leaned close to where Cassie was sitting. "It's okay. It means he likes you if he's mean."

"Then you can have him, since he's been nice to me. I guess he doesn't care for me."

Angel didn't know what to say to her new friend. Dr. Logan didn't say anything about what to do if a boy likes you. "Maybe when a boy really likes you, he starts being sweet to you."

"Do you think so?" Cassie's voice trilled with hope.

"Guess we'll have to wait and see." Angel didn't have any answers about boys except what Travis had told her, and she had never cared before, but now she had a flaming interest in finding out about these brothers and how she could get them to like her.

And she knew just who she would ask. Dr. Logan would give her answers her sister wouldn't.

Chapter 21

Angel squished in between Heaven and Travis. Heaven tried to conceal her disappointment, but the upturned corners on Travis's face led her to believe she'd failed miserably.

Angel tugged on Travis's coat sleeve. "What kind of baby did you get?"

"A human one."

"I mean, boy or girl?"

"A tiny perfect little rosebud of a girl. Looks like her mother."

Travis looked at Heaven and winked. Her stomach flipped. Was he thinking of having babies with her? She ran down that path with him, picturing not one but three little ones.

"Did they name her yet?" Heaven tried to focus on the scar on Travis's cheek, because if she looked him in the eye, she was afraid he would read her thoughts and see those three little ones.

"No, not yet. When I go back next week, I'll find out."

The wagon didn't sway as much as it did on the trip into town. Heaven noticed a roll of canvas in the back and some—could it be; had he bought flour and sugar? Her spirits lifted. "What's the stuff in the back for?"

"Thought we'd close up that hole in the cabin so you won't be so cold tonight. I was hoping if I bought some flour and sugar you might be convinced to make me a cake. It's been a long time, and I'm hankerin' for something sweet."

"I'll make it for you. I can cook now." Angel nudged him with an elbow.

Travis coughed. Panic widened his eyes. "I'm sure you can, Little Miss, but I was thinkin' it was time for your sister to start doing some of the kitchen work again. Her ankle is much better."

"Maybe I can help?" Eagerness trickled through her words.

"You can lick the spoon. I won't fight you for it—this time." Travis ruffled Angel's hair. "Next time though, look out. I'll be first in line for that spoon licking."

Next time? Heaven added that to her tangled thoughts. She draped an arm around her sister. "I'd appreciate your help. We'll make it tomorrow. We'll have a treat after we clean up from the storm. Thank you, Travis. We'd both be happy to make your cake for you."

"Heaven, do you know how to mix a cake?" Angel whispered.

"I have Ma's recipe box. There has to be a recipe in there that's good. I'm sure it will turn out fine." Just like going to the church had turned out better than she'd expected. Angel had been accepted by a group of girls her age and managed to convince Heaven that her sister had to be in the play. To her surprise, she'd agreed.

And she'd learned some things about her great-uncle.

"Do you think Mr. Jackson came back home?" Angel twisted her hands together, let them go, and then did it again.

"If he's as smart as you say he is, then I think he'll be waiting." Travis pulled up on the reins. "No need to run home,

Charlie. We'll get there soon."

"He always does that—tries to run home. It ain't even time for him to eat," Angel said. "I made a lot of new friends today. They didn't even care that I couldn't see them, Dr. Logan."

"A true friend won't care if you see the same way they do. There's more to a person than sight."

Heaven glanced up and got hooked by Travis's eyes. So full of compassion for her sister. And she wanted him to kiss her again. And the way he was looking back made her think he wanted the same. She had never felt this way about Jake. Maybe this was what love was like. It stole your heart when you weren't willing to let it go, and gave it away.

The sun poked through the clouds but didn't give up any of its warmth. Heaven shivered. The night would be cold even with the exposed places covered. She and Angel would have to sleep on the floor in front of the fire.

Charlie turned down the cedar-lined drive.

Angel scooted to the edge of the bench seat. "Can you see Mr. Jackson yet?"

"We can tell in just a minute. Be patient." The right side of the wagon dipped into a gulley, jarring Heaven. She grabbed the side of the wagon to steady herself.

"I see him. On top of the wood pile." Travis laughed. "Looks like he didn't wait on us for dinner. He's chewing on something. Looks like paper."

Heaven abruptly lifted her head. A piece of paper fluttered from Mr. Jackson's mouth to the middle of the logs. "It's a book. Hurry, Travis, hurry. That might be our family Bible."

Travis clicked his tongue.

Charlie needed little urging, and he lunged ahead.

Heaven chewed her lip. *Please don't let it be the Bible unless it's the only way we're going to find it. And if it is the Bible, please don't let him be eating the page with our family history.*

Travis stopped the horse close to the woodpile and jumped from the wagon. "I'll get it."

"I'm coming, too." Angel climbed to the ground and stood. "Which way do I go, Heaven?"

"Got it." Travis called. "It's not the Bible." He walked over to the wagon. "I'm sorry, Angel. I didn't mean to leave you here. I wanted to rescue the book before any more damage was done to it."

Heaven scooted across the bench and waited for Travis to help her down. "What is it?"

Travis smoothed out the paper and held it up, "I'm not sure."

Heaven recognized the illustration on the back side. Her heartbeat picked up.

He flipped over the paper and chuckled. "Seems to be from a book or magazine—*A Guide to Raising Proper Ladies.*"

Mortification numbed Heaven. She wanted to reach out and grab it from him, but Angel stood between them.

" 'Important rules to always remember. A proper lady never speaks with—' " he read.

" 'Her mouth full of food, lest she resemble a pig at the table.' " Angel finished the rule. "That's Ma's book. Heaven's been teaching me from it. I know lots of rules, but they're hard to follow. There's one about not asking to go to the outhouse."

"Angel Claire Wharton!" Heaven wished the tornado had

swallowed her sister instead of her Bible. She pushed Angel aside and tore the book, or what was left of it, out of Travis's hand. "Give it to me."

He held on to it for a second.

She tugged again.

He released it. "Heaven, I'm sorry."

She limped off to pick up the other pages that were scattered across the yard, not wanting to hear an apology from him.

"Heaven, my mother has the same book," Travis yelled. "She's used it to teach my sisters. Why, I bet I could quote a few of those rules myself."

She wouldn't answer him. How dare he laugh. Ma had only tried to make her a desirable bride for Jake. And she would have been a proper wife for him, too, knowing all that she did, unlike what you needed to know to be a farmer's wife. She knew what fork to use but not how to clean a chicken. Ma's little book would have worked for her if Jake hadn't died. Jake was somebody. The only son, destined to take over his father's business. She'd have been hosting afternoon teas and soirées instead of feeding farm animals and mucking stalls.

"I'm going to put Charlie back in the barn and unload the wagon since you're not ready to speak to me. Just don't forget you promised to make me a cake."

"I'm going with him," Angel yelled.

Traitor. Even Angel didn't understand the injustice of Heaven's life. She continued to ignore the two of them, even though they were laughing and seemed to be having a good time. Once she heard the wagon roll inside the barn, she stopped and sat on a log. She pulled her knees under her chin and encircled her legs with her arms as she'd done when she was small. A tear trickled down her face, and she let it slide to her skirt. She didn't care, not anymore. God had abandoned her and her sister, left her to some man who thought her previous life was amusing. How brazen of him to think that.

She scooted off the log, landing on her bad leg first. Her ankle screamed, but she didn't. There was no need to bring that man out of the barn to help or lecture her. She was not in the mood to be appeased.

Annabelle's patience had been stretched slingshot tight, and she was about to fire. "I do hope this time you got the right directions, Jake Miles." She held out her arm and let him help her into the rented coal-box buggy.

"Everything has turned out fine. Mother was able to freshen up at the hotel, and we unloaded the luggage she brought."

He didn't mention they'd toured the countryside going east instead of west, which is why his mother needed time to freshen up. "Jake, I'm not returning to Nashville."

"You have to go back. I'm not going, and Mother needs a chaperone to get home." Jake scowled at her.

"Here I am," Mrs. Miles called from the steps. "It takes me a little longer than you young people to navigate those steep stairs."

Jake rushed forward to take his mother's arm. "That's fine. Annabelle and I were conversing about travel arrangements."

"I don't want to talk about traveling anywhere for a while. I need to rest before I take that journey back home." The buggy sagged as Mrs. Miles stepped into it. She slid across the leather bench next to Annabelle.

Jake climbed in after her and took the driver's seat without a word. His sullen slouch let Annabelle know this discussion hadn't ended.

She wouldn't let him convince her to return. Not when she'd made it this far. And besides, she'd left her father that good-bye note. If she returned now, she'd never be able to leave. Her father would make sure she never got the chance. All of her freedom would disappear faster than Cook's special tea cakes on a Sunday afternoon.

"It's quite pretty out here, isn't it?" Mrs. Miles peered out the buggy.

Annabelle watched the cedars—some standing tall and others bent in half—and wondered what Jake's mother found so pretty. The cedars weren't even a pretty green this time of year. More of a green mixed with mud.

"It's nice, Mother, but it's not Nashville. I'm sure you would be fighting boredom without your ladies' societies."

"You would be surprised, Jake. Since we lost you"—she leaned forward and grasped her son's shoulder as if to remind herself he was still there—"or thought you were. . .gone, your father and I didn't see a need to keep socializing with people. We told you that at dinner, remember?"

"You mentioned it."

"It didn't seem right to try and advance ourselves in the social circle without a son to carry on the business or the family name." She squeezed her son's shoulder and let go.

Annabelle ached at the motherliness of that touch. Her eyes

burned with tears for what she didn't have.

"There, that's the broken wheel up ahead. The one the clerk at the store mentioned." Jake pointed.

"And the split rail fence!" Annabelle wanted to stand up and shout, but instead, she tightly folded her hands and settled them on her lap. "Hurry, Jake. It's been so long since I've seen my friend."

"Or my son's fiancée." Mrs. Miles leaned back and smiled. "I cannot wait until you have children, Jake. Imagine! I had lost hope, and now it seems God has blessed me with a future."

Annabelle cringed. Jake's mother was going to be powerfully disappointed when her son told his fiancée he no longer wanted to marry her.

Travis hopped back onto the wagon, disengaged the brake, flipped the reins, and directed Charlie back into the barn.

Angel was waiting for him. "Now Mrs. Jackson is missing."

Travis jumped off the wagon and tied Charlie to a post. "Wonder how she got out." He strode over to the goat's empty pen. The hay was pushed about in small piles, some of them flatter than others, as if the top layers were tastier to the pregnant goat. "Looks like she managed to work open the latch, or maybe the wind jiggled it loose."

"I have to unhitch Charlie, and I'd like to get some of this sweat off of him before I head out and look for her."

"I hope she's okay. Mr. Jackson would be sad if she isn't." Angel rubbed Pride and Joy's nose.

"She's probably out looking for a snack. There's a lot of

tempting goat treats out in the woods." Like Heaven's Bible and an apron or two, he suspected. "I don't think she'll wander far. She'll tire out quickly."

"Do you think she'll have the kid before we find her?"

"I'm not sure. I don't know when it's due. It will come when it's time. Could you get me the brush and currycomb, Little Miss?" Travis tied Charlie to the barn post.

Angel showed a tooth-filled smile. "I sure will, Dr. Logan."

"I bet you wish you didn't laugh at my sister." Angel headed for the corner where the tack was stored.

"She doesn't scare me." Her eagerness to please and do something on her own warmed his heart. She had that same no-nonsense face her sister seemed to wear often. He wondered if their children would acquire that look from Heaven. *Humph. Children.* First, he had to get the woman in front of a preacher.

"Why not? She makes me want to hide in the chicken coop sometimes."

"Is that why you came in here with me?" The little orange cat scampered across the floor and rubbed her body against Travis's leg. He bent down, picked her up, and cradled her to his chest. Her purr rumbled bigger than her body.

"Yes. Sometimes she needs to work things out all by herself without anyone to boss while she does it." Angel spun around and headed for the tools he'd asked for.

"Why don't you just call me Travis?"

"Wouldn't be proper. Heaven calls you Travis though, so maybe she won't be mad if I do, too." Her answer fluttered back to him as she scooted things around on the shelf.

Of course not. Wasn't that the reason he was in here hiding

from Heaven? The usage of proper manners and behavior? He should have paid more attention to what his mother was teaching his sisters.

"Here." Angel thrust the tools out in front of her.

He grabbed them with one hand. "Little Miss, I've got something for you." Travis handed her the kitten.

"Oooh."

"She needs a name, since she's decided to sleep on my chest at night."

"She's so soft." She put the kitty next to her nose. "Hi there."

The kitten responded with a soft meow and more purring.

"What color is she?" She stroked the kitten's back.

"Reddish orange, with a few stripes of cream licking her face. More like a fresh-picked persimmon now that I look at her. Do you remember what they look like?" Travis whipped the currycomb and brush in an easy rhythm across Charlie's withers.

"Um-hum, they taste good in cookies. I think I'll call her Miss Simmons, because she's too little to get a husband. Not like my sister."

Travis's hand stilled. "Do you want your sister to get married, Angel?"

"I wouldn't be opposed to her marrying you. You're nice. Jake was always mean to me. I was sorry he got killed, and that made Heaven cry a lot, but I wasn't sad that they weren't getting married."

Travis decided he didn't much care for Jake—even if the man was dead, God rest his soul. Angel was too precious not to show kindness to.

"Do you hear that? I hear a buggy coming down the drive."

"We'd better get out there, or Heaven will be going for the rifle."

"If she can find it in all that mess." The kitten in Angel's hand wiggled, its thin, sharp claws connected to her sleeve. "Time for you to get down and explore, Miss Simmons. Come on, Travis, we'd better hurry just in case." She took three confident steps and then stopped. "Don't tell Heaven I called you by your given name, please."

"I won't. We'll keep that between ourselves." He smacked the horse on the rump, and into the stall he went. "I'll toss him a bit of hay and be right there. And don't worry, she can't shoot anyone, because I took the gun."

Chapter 22

Heaven heard wheels rumbling down the road. Where was that rifle? Did she have time to run inside for it? She gave a frantic look at the barn. Where was Travis? Why didn't he rush out here and make sure the company a-comin' wasn't coming to harm them?

Through the cedar trees, she caught flashes of the black buggy. Then it came into view. Intrigued, she stopped in her tracks. She'd seen this one for rent at the livery. Who would have rented a buggy to come see her? Not someone who wanted to trade peaches for green beans.

The driver wore his hat low over his eyes, but that wasn't unusual for a hired driver. She waited for him to stop the horses. Then he climbed down and helped a familiar-looking woman step down.

Could it be? Was it? The red hair, the way the woman stood. Unfamiliar feelings sprung up, and then she recognized them as joy. The woman turned, and Heaven felt her anger at Travis fly away, and the corners of her mouth lifted as if strung by string. She didn't care about manners or being a proper lady. This was her friend. Her best friend.

"Annabelle!" She tried to hurry, but her ankle kept her at a slow walk. "Is it really you?"

"It is!" Annabelle's feet made quick time across the trampled grass drive and gathered her friend into a hug. "Heaven! What happened to you? You're limping."

"I fell in a hole. I'm much better."

"Annabelle!" Angel hollered from the barn door. "Is that Annabelle? Did you bring any jam?"

Heaven felt her face flush. "I'm sorry. I've been trying to teach her better manners. She just doesn't want to learn."

"Neither did we, if I remember correctly." Annabelle's laugh fit her name with its gentle, rolling peals.

"We don't need to inform her of that though, do we?" Heaven couldn't stop looking at her friend. God had provided her with the best gifts today, even if He didn't stop the destruction of her home. "Annabelle, did you get caught in the tornado?"

"We were in town at the store. They had us all go down into the root cellar." She waved her hand at the front of Heaven's home. "It looks like it hit you."

"It did, but we're okay, and we'll get it back together. Although I don't know that you'll want to stay with us. There's not much to eat unless you like green beans. We do have plenty of those. And sleeping conditions might be a bit cold tonight, what with the windows, door, and part of the house out in the yard."

Angel charged forward with her hands out. She reached Annabelle and touched her skirt. "It is you!" She threw her arms around Annabelle.

Heaven understood that need. Annabelle represented home

and all of its memories. Her eyes burned from salty tears, and she wiped them away with the back of her hand.

"Angel, I know how much you like Cook's jam, so I brought you some. I'm glad you didn't change your mind about liking it."

Angel let go. "Never. It's the best, and all we've been eatin' is green beans."

Annabelle grinned, but her eyebrows twisted in confusion.

"Angel!" Heaven wanted to yank those words out of the air before Annabelle understood the truth behind them.

"Did you come alone? Without your husband?"

Annabelle's toothy grin slid to the ground. "No, I'll explain later. But I did bring you a surprise."

"You shouldn't have. Having you here for a visit is surprise enough."

"I think you'll love this one, better than seeing me." Annabelle pointed at the driver.

Heaven looked away from Annabelle's smiling face. "A surprise?" She went cold all over. Her eyes were deceiving her, not once but twice today. *Jake is dead. He's not coming back. That is not him.* "The driver looks like Jake, but that can't be."

The man walked closer. "It is me, Heaven."

Heaven's good leg gave away. Her eyes strained, almost popping out of her head. She swayed. Annabelle steadied her.

"It's a shock, I know. That is why I made him bring me along. When he showed up in Nashville looking for you, I didn't believe it either."

Jake and his mother stood in front of her. "I am so sorry, Heaven. I know they told you I was dead. I was captured and put in prison up North. I was so sick I did not even know who

I was. I guess someone saw me go down and wrote home to tell everyone I was dead."

Heaven reached with her fingertips and stroked his cheek. "Jake."

He reached his arms out and pulled her into them. "Heaven, I have missed you so much. Thinking about you got me through the terrible times. I could not wait to get home to you."

"Hi, Jake. 'Member me?" Angel tugged on his sleeve.

He let go of Heaven and turned to her sister. "This can't be little Angel. You're all growed up. I bet you got beaus lining up at the socials out here."

"No, Heaven says I'm too young." Angel spoke as if he were standing a further distance from Heaven instead of right next to her.

Jake quirked an eyebrow. "Something wrong with her?"

"Jake!" his mother warned.

"I'm right here. I can hear you; I just can't see you." Angel stomped her foot. "Why do people think that?" She went back toward the barn.

"Sorry, Heaven, I didn't know she was so sensitive."

"Annabelle, why didn't you write me and tell me Jake was alive and you were coming to see me?"

"Heaven, I've been wanting to come since your letter came saying your papa had left for Chicago. Then Jake turned up in town, and I couldn't wait for letters to be written and sent. Jake wanted to come out right away." Annabelle smiled at Jake. "He's a hero. Did you know that?" Her face glowed.

"A hero?" The pain on Jake's face hurt Heaven. All this time, she'd thought he was dead. Thought about marrying another man, even kissed one. That wasn't her fault though, not when she thought he was dead. But why didn't he write her himself?

"I am not a hero. Far from it." Jake dropped his gaze to the ground. "Sometimes you just do things without thinking, and the ending turns out for the good. I don't like to talk about it, but since you want to know, I was supposed to be on guard duty, but I had a cramp in my leg and was moving slow. If I hadn't been, I wouldn't have seen the band of blue coats. I sounded the alarm, and there was a lot of shooting, but most of my unit survived. Then later that day, we ran into another band. When I woke up, I was in a transport to a Yankee hospital. I didn't know my name, only that I was a rebel, because I had on a gray uniform."

Annabelle reached over and patted his arm. "It's okay, Jake."

"How about a kiss for a returning soldier?" Mrs. Miles tweaked Heaven's cheek. "I've been waiting to watch this reunion."

This was too much for Heaven. Jake was alive, a hero, and now his mother was demanding kisses for him just when she was thinking about Travis and how she wanted him to kiss her.

"Mother, it might be too soon." Jake raked his eyes over Heaven. "Then again, it's been a long time since I've had a kiss from this pretty woman."

Before she could stop him, he pulled her into his arms and smashed his lips into hers.

That man was kissing Heaven. Resentments from the past clouded Travis's judgment as he remembered another woman, another man, and another kiss. He captured his anger, caging it until it proved useful. He stepped quietly next to her ear and whispered, "You okay, Miss Wharton?"

Heaven stumbled back, lost her balance, and landed in Travis's arms.

"Nothing wrong here, mister. Just getting my welcome home kiss from my intended," Jake said.

Intended? Travis did not like the sound of that. Nor did he like the way Jake held on to his woman. Not until he saw Heaven being held by another man was he positive he would fight for her.

"So, Heaven, who is this? You should be resting that foot. Here, let me help you inside, and you can rest while I get our guests some refreshments." He snaked his arm through hers.

Jake stepped back, confusion on his face. "Jake Miles." He stuck out his hand. "Heaven's intended, unless. . ." He looked at Heaven. "Unless you got married."

Heaven shook her head no.

Travis took Jake's hand in his and gave it a good pump. "Travis Logan. No, she is not married to me—not yet. She proposed. I just haven't answered—yet."

Heaven gasped. Her eyes widened as she stared at him as if a wild animal had walked across her path.

"Well, you did ask me the night you sprained your ankle."

Angel hung out the door, "Yes you did, Heaven. You said you loved him and asked him to marry you soon."

Travis scooped her up in his arms. "Let's get the weight off that foot and get inside where it's warmer."

"Put me down, Dr. Logan."

He noticed the lack of the friendly address of Travis and the return of the proper Dr. Logan. "I will in just a moment. You'll be snug as a bug in your rocking chair. Then you can introduce me to these beautiful women who came with Mr. Miles."

"My rocker is gone; the tornado took it. Mrs. Miles is Jake's mother. And Annabelle is my best friend."

Heaven didn't put up a fight about him carrying her. He considered that a good sign. "If you all will kindly follow me to the cabin, I'll see what I can do about righting the place so you can talk."

Travis led the group to the house. With the door blown off by the tornado, the cabin stood exposed. He'd need to do a bit of work before he'd feel comfortable about Angel and Heaven sleeping in here tonight.

He stepped inside.

Heaven screamed.

He almost dropped her. Then he saw why she was upset. Mrs. Jackson had decided the most beautiful rug in the world, according to Heaven, was the perfect place to drop her kid. He didn't know whether to laugh or offer thanks to God. He decided to offer thanks, silently.

There was nothing in her mother's book that could have ever prepared her for the mortifying moment Heaven was now living. Mrs. Jackson, her all-white goat, had given birth on Heaven's rug. No, not just a rug, but the one her great-grandmother had treasured and passed down.

As if the tornado wasn't enough, God? He brought Jake back alive, and that was good, but why did he have to arrive with his etiquette expert mother when that goat had tromped up the front steps into her cabin and given birth on her carpet? She let her head rest against Travis's chest. If only she could stay here in his arms and sleep—make it all go away. She was so tired.

"Heaven?" Travis's breath whispered across her head. "Are you going to be okay?"

She tipped her head back and tried to say something.

"Too much today? You're white as a sheet." He squeezed her more tightly against him. "Cold, too."

"Why'd you stop, Dr. Logan?" Angel pushed against his back. "Why'd Heaven scream? What's in there?"

"Step back, child." Jake jerked her away.

"Ow." Angel pulled her arm out of Jake's grasp and rubbed it.

"There's no need to be rough with her," Travis growled.

Heaven was grateful he'd stepped in to correct Jake.

Angel wiggled past Travis. "What is it, sissie?"

Her sister hadn't called her that since their Ma had died. "Set me down, please, Travis."

He did, but he took his time about it and didn't let go of her completely, wrapping an arm around her shoulder.

"Angel, Mrs. Jackson had her kid." Heaven swallowed. "On Great-Grandma's rug."

"That's the problem? There's a goat in the cabin?" Jake stepped past Travis and Heaven. "Let's get it out of here and clean up this mess." He strode over to the rug and looked back, his lips curled. "Good thing this was old; it will have to be burned."

"But it belonged to. . ." Angel stepped forward. Travis grabbed her with his other hand.

"Don't move, Little Miss. It's still a mess. Nothing is the

same as before the tornado. It wouldn't be a good thing to get hurt." Travis squeezed Heaven's shoulder.

He was looking out for Angel, smoothing Heaven's protective side, giving her a measure of peace.

Mrs. Miles and Annabelle piled into the cabin.

"There really is a goat in here. And a baby one. It's so sweet." Annabelle inspected the ruined rug. "It's bad, Heaven. I don't know if it we can get it clean."

Mrs. Miles nodded. "Time to get a new one and start passing it down. Although you won't need to get one, not once you and Jake get married."

Angel stomped a foot. "She ain't marrying Jake."

"Angel, now is not the time. There's a lot of discussing to be done with Jake and Travis," Heaven admonished. Her home was in shambles. What the tornado hadn't accomplished, the goat managed to take care of. Muddy hoofprints decorated the upside-down table, and even her apron had been snacked on. "As you can see, it would be best if the three of you returned to town tonight. If you could come back tomorrow for a visit, then Angel and I will have taken care of this mess and we'd be happy to serve you a nice lunch." She'd found her voice, but it sounded thread thin in her ears.

"Nonsense, child. We're going to get this place back together right now." Mrs. Miles glanced around the room. "It won't take long."

"No, no thank you!" Had she shouted those words? It didn't matter. She didn't want Mrs. Miles putting her home together piece by piece and commenting on how her life would be with Jake. "I'm sorry, Mrs. Miles. I do appreciate your offer, but I can see that the trip has tired you. Why don't you allow Jake to take you back into town? I'm sure there will be room at the hotel."

"We've already taken care of that. We acquired rooms before we came this way." Mrs. Miles searched for a place to sit. "I don't mind getting my hands dirty, Heaven, but I can see this has been a bit too much for you already. We'll head back into Friendship. Are you sure you won't come and stay with us, where it's warm and the critters can't come in?"

Angel squared her shoulders. "She said we will be staying in our home tonight. We'll be just fine."

"Heaven, will you at least let me stay? I'd like to help. It's been so long since we've talked." Annabelle's sincerity spoke to Heaven's heart.

"It's going to be cold, and we'll have to sleep on the floor."

"I don't mind."

"Say yes, Heaven. Please," Angel pleaded.

She found it harder than ever to say no to her sister. "It will almost be like old times."

"Except you never let me stay with you and Annabelle. This time you will though, right?" Angel's face shone with eagerness.

Heaven smiled, and her shoulders relaxed. It would be good to share stories with her best friend in front of the fire. "This time you can stay."

"Guess that means you don't want me to stay either?" Jake wore a stormy look. "It looks like most of the work is women's work anyway. Where does he sleep?"

"In the barn." Travis answered before Heaven could. "You're welcome to come back after you drop off Mrs. Miles and sleep there with me. I'm not one for gabbin' before bedtime though."

"I'll stay at the hotel with Mother. That way I'll be able to bring her back earlier." Jake stepped over to Heaven. "I'll bid you goodnight." He grasped her hand and brought it to his lips.

Her glance shot across the room and locked on Travis stoking the fire. Compared to Jake, he'd been kind and concerned for her. Jake had changed from the man she remembered.

"Perhaps we'll get a chance to speak alone tomorrow?"

Heaven shivered, and not from desire. What was wrong with her? She should be overjoyed to spend time with Jake. Maybe Annabelle could help her make sense of it all.

Travis's fingers curled into his palms. He shoved his hands in his pockets. "Let me walk you to the door."

Angel snorted. "You said there isn't a door."

"He's being polite, dear. That's how things are done." Mrs. Miles picked up the hem of her silk dress and stepped over a shattered teacup.

"Something else you've forgotten, Angel." Heaven frowned, one more thing for Mrs. Miles to take note of—her inability to teach her sister how to behave.

As soon as the buggy noise quieted, signaling the departure of Jake and his mother, Heaven breathed. Not that she'd been holding her breath, but it seemed to be such hard work to make the air go in and out of her lungs.

"Heaven, I know this is a mess in here, but if you can wait for me, I'll take care of dragging out the rug." Travis stood in front of her.

Why wasn't it hard to breathe around him?

"Angel and I will get Mrs. Jackson and her kid settled in the barn. That is, Angel, if you don't mind helping me."

"Yes sir." Angel made her way to the door and stepped out onto the porch. "You shoo them this way."

"Will do in a minute. That's a great idea. Wait there." He started to turn the kitchen table over.

"Stop, Travis. First, I need to wash off those muddy footprints. It will be easier if the table is upside down."

"Don't move anything heavy. Once I get the goats bedded down, I want to get the canvas over these openings. Then I'll be back in to help you get your home back together."

Heaven hunted in the kitchen for two clean aprons. She handed one to Annabelle. "At least Mrs. Jackson didn't get to these."

Chapter 23

The buggy rocked and swayed down the drive. Jake mulled over his feelings about Heaven and that Dr. Logan who seemed to have claimed her. She'd even called him Travis and hadn't bothered to blush. Funny—wasn't that what he had been hoping for? That Heaven wouldn't care, and she would release him from his promise to her?

"I don't like that man staying on Heaven's farm. Jake, you should go back after you drop me off. She's your fiancée." Mrs. Miles wrapped her cloak tighter around her chin. "I would have thought you'd feel a need to stay and protect her, if not from the elements, then from the good doctor."

Jake flicked the reins. The sooner he got his mother back to the hotel the sooner he could find a place to dull his senses. His mother thought all was right with her world, now that her son was living. He supposed it was—for her.

Holding Heaven in his arms almost made him feel whole again. The quick kiss on those soft lips reminded him of who he used to be. Could he still let her go? He hadn't liked leaving Heaven with Dr. Logan sleeping in the barn either.

Maybe he couldn't let her go without making sure she would be all right. Or was it more than that? Could she heal him, fix his hidden injuries? Could they still marry and have that life they'd talked about before he'd left for the war and become a coward? The question crawled into his mind and tangled itself around his emotions.

He'd puzzle it out tonight. He would reconsider letting her go. She was worth fighting for, and he knew that doctor would challenge him for her. It wouldn't be hard to knock Dr. Logan out of the competition. Jake knew her better, knew her secrets. He also knew winning her meant returning to Nashville with her on his arm. Could he do that? Could he face those who called him a hero? No, he'd have to convince her to head west and start a new life.

Jake Miles irritated Travis worse than an infected blister on his foot. He'd wanted to help Jake on his way the moment he'd commented about Angel. Then when the man kissed Heaven, Travis would have volunteered to stick him in a cannon and shoot him back to where he'd come from. But his mother had raised him to keep such instincts under control.

What had Heaven seen in Jake to make her fall in love with the man? Did she still see it? This was a woman he professed to love, and he was ready to ride off and leave her without a door and her belongings scattered about? Something wasn't right.

He closed the gate to the goats' pen and shook it to make sure it held.

"Do you think Heaven has to marry Jake still? Heaven didn't read anything about that to me from the book. Seems like the promise she made him wouldn't be bona fide anymore since he was supposed to be dead. Why, she could have even already married someone else by now." Angel paused, took a breath. "And why doesn't he want to help get our house fixed?"

He looked to see if she was finished talking. Her mouth was closed, and her eyebrows held a question mark. She must be done. "I don't think your sister has to marry Jake or me, but she needs to marry one of us."

"Then I pick you."

"You don't get to pick, Little Miss. It doesn't work that way." He needed to get the flour and sugar in the house. He guessed it could wait until he made the temporary repairs to the cabin.

"I don't want to live with Mrs. Miles and Jake. They aren't fun like you."

"You'd be back in Nashville with your friends." He pulled the roll of canvas from the back of the wagon.

"Don't need them now. I got new ones today at church. Cassie and I are going to be best friends. We even have the same color hair."

"Is that how you choose a best friend?" He hoisted the canvas to his shoulder.

"No. We like a lot of the same things. That's why we're going to be best friends. Now if Heaven could find a friend here, she would be happy, too. It's too bad Annabelle won't be staying. She makes Heaven smile."

"That she does, Little Miss."

Chapter 24

Annabelle and Heaven snuggled under the blankets, and it was almost like when they were younger. Except for Angel was asleep in the middle and they were on the floor, not a soft bed.

"Good-looking man, even with that scar. . . . I've been thinking, Heaven, that it's not a good idea for you to be staying out here with that man by yourself."

"What?" Annabelle had been talking while Heaven was thinking about kissing Travis again. Daydreaming could be a dangerous thing or a delicious one. She just wasn't sure which it was when it came to Travis.

"With Travis?"

"But what will people say? It's so improper." Annabelle stuck her cold feet against Heaven's leg.

"Annabelle, your feet!"

"Sorry." She pulled them back. "Have you thought about that?"

"Of course I have. No one really knows us here, and things have changed since the war."

"Not that much, Heaven. What about the people in church?"

"The preacher was okay with him staying in the barn since

he's a doctor. He's been helping around here because of my ankle." Heaven squirmed, trying to get comfortable. Then she turned on her stomach and squished her straw pillow. It just was not as comfortable as the down-filled pillows she had grown up with. She flipped back on her back. "As for church, we haven't been going. It's a long walk, and with Angel not able to see. . ."

"That is just an excuse. It seems to me that Angel is handling her lack of sight just fine." She propped her head up on one hand.

"I realized that today. While we were there setting up for the lunch, Angel made some friends. She wants to be in the Sunday school play."

"As who?"

"An angel."

"Of course, that makes sense. Who else would she play?"

They giggled some more then settled as their bodies warmed and they relaxed. The fire popped and crackled.

"Angel, are you asleep?" Heaven touched her sister. No response. "We're getting out the jam and biscuits. Do you want some?"

Angel's breathing pattern didn't change.

"I think she's out." Heaven sat up. "Now, tell me why you didn't get married this summer."

"Oh, that." Annabelle waved her hand in the air as if to push the experience away from their conversation.

"Annabelle, it's a big deal, even if you make it sound like it wasn't. What happened?"

"He sent a letter. He wrote he didn't love me and he'd married a—a Yankee. I could have stood the pain, but he brought her back to Nashville."

"That's awful! How're you going to reside in the same town?"

"I'm not. Once I found out Jake was coming to see you, I figured I'd leave with him and never go back."

"Never? But your father."

"I left him a note explaining my intentions to go to Memphis and open a store. I aim to never have to answer to another man the rest of my life." Annabelle lay back on her pillow. "I'm on my own now, and that's the way it is. This world is changing, and some day getting married won't be a requirement. Instead of babies, I'll—I'll just get cats. Don't you to want to marry Jake anymore?"

"Maybe. It's just that I have thought him dead for so long. He seems different. I have to get to know the new Jake." And there was Travis and the fact that her father wanted him to have her. And the kiss.

"I think the grown-up Jake is dreamy." Annabelle sighed. "I am so tired of this place."

"Already? You just arrived." A hole in Heaven's soul opened and leaked sadness. "I had hoped you would stay for a while."

"I'll stay here for a while, at least until you get married. I meant Nashville. It isn't at all like you remember it, Heaven. There are bullet holes in some of the houses, and everyone wears clothes that are old and tattered. Food is scarce. Everyone seems angry or blank like they have no expression or they no longer live in their own bodies.

"And there are no suitors left. Either they're dead or they came back in such a state that to marry one of them would mean nursing them forever. I've had that life with Father. That isn't how I want to be married."

"There have to be some men who weren't wounded that you could consider."

"There are, but they're engaged or married. I guess I could marry some old coot, but I want a young buck."

"How young?" Heaven said. "Surely there are some boys in town. Maybe you could wait until they grow up?"

"Heaven, be serious. The prospects of finding a decent husband in the South have dissipated. Then here in your own home you have two good candidates."

"Do you want one of them?"

"No, not really. Jake is fun, but he's from our past, and I don't think he'll ever be happy if he's not living in a big house with someone to wait on him. That's not what I want. That's supposed to be you."

"Like I said, I'm not sure about Jake, and Travis seems so much older than me."

"Pshaw, he can't be that much older than us. Why don't you ask him?" Annabelle said. "He seems to care for Angel a great deal."

"He's been very good to her. Better than me for sure. He's encouraged her to do things I was afraid to let her do."

"That has to have been frightening for you. Losing your ma, and then Angel losing her sight. I don't know how you coped afterwards. Then, with your papa taking off and dying." She reached over and patted her friend's arm. "It's too much, Heaven."

"Yes, well one good thing has happened. Jake Miles is alive, and he still intends to marry me." But it wasn't Jake's face that came to her in her dreams. Instead, it was the face of Travis Logan with his coffee-colored eyes, dark brown hair, and the scar on his cheek.

Heaven's eyes flittered open. She blew out, and her breath turned to steam. Getting out from under toasty blankets seemed daunting. Staying on the hard floor made it less so. She glanced at her sister and Annabelle. They were still asleep. From the glow through the canvas-covered door, she knew it was sunny. She hoped it would be a warm day.

She wiggled out of the blanket, attempting to keep any cold air from floating under and disturbing her sister. This would be a good time to have a few moments alone to think about what she needed to say to Jake and to Travis. Angel muttered something then rolled over, anchoring Annabelle with her arm.

Heaven dragged her fingers through her hair to loosen the tangles. She yawned and then stretched. Her back crackled and popped. Sleeping on a floor was something for children.

She should start the coffee, but if she did, the racket from tending the stove would likely wake her guest. For just a few minutes, she craved to talk to God. Then she'd get back to being a proper hostess.

She slipped on her shoes and her skirt and the gray drop-sleeved shirt over her chemise. She'd lost the ribbon she'd tied in her hair yesterday. If it was outside, by now Mr. Jackson had most likely ingested it.

She peeked over at the two curled up by the fire. Seeing

no movement, she tiptoed to the makeshift door. She slipped through the edge of the canvas covering. The sun shone bright, blinding her as she tripped over something, wrenching her ankle. She popped her hand over her mouth to smother her voice, "Ow, ow, ow."

A loud groan emitted from a dirty bedroll. "What's wrong?"

She knelt and spoke low, "Travis Logan, what are you doing on my porch?"

He covered his eyes with his elbow. "It's my porch, and I'm protecting my property."

She stood. She wanted to kick him, but her ankle hurt too much. "Why are you sleeping out here?" Her hands went to her hips. She bent over and stared in his face. "Were you spying on us last night?"

He threw back the blankets and sat up. "Too many questions without coffee."

"Doesn't matter. I want an answer anyway."

He stood.

Even without his boots, he towered over her. The top two buttons on his shirt were loose, exposing chestnut hair. Quickly she lowered her eyes and noticed his suspenders rested at his waist. Realizing she'd made another mistake, she inspected the porch. Her rifle rested next to his discarded bedroll. "You have my gun?"

"Easier to shoot a predator that might try to wander in the cabin that way." He rubbed the corner of his eye.

Her head jerked up to see if he was serious. The whiskers on his chin and face intrigued Heaven, along with the way his hair was mashed flat, covering his wound. She wanted to lift it with her fingers and put it to rights. "How'd you get that scar on your cheek?"

He blinked as if he wasn't sure what she was asking about, then nodded. "That." He stroked his cheek. "Trying to help someone that was dying. I didn't know they had a knife. I think the man thought I was trying to kill him instead of help him. He lashed out and drew the blade across my cheek."

"Did that happen often? Soldiers trying to hurt you while you saved them?"

"More often than not." He touched her arm, let his hand rest a moment, then slid his fingers down her arm. "Don't trouble yourself about it."

"I'm not sure I could sleep if I'd been to war."

"Some men don't." He bent down and bundled up his bedroll and scooped up his boots. "I'll be out of your way here in a minute. Don't worry about tending the animals. I'll take care of them this morning."

"Travis?"

He turned, with a raised eyebrow.

"About Jake. . ."

"Guess you have a dilemma on your hands now, don't you? You have to pick one of us, Heaven. Guess time will tell which one it will be." He gave her a long look, as if waiting for her to choose that moment. When she didn't answer, his shoulders slumped, and then he slowly turned away.

Travis didn't bother plunking his feet into boots. He grasped the bedroll and boots close to his chest and kept the rifle in his hands. He wouldn't even stop and put on his shoes.

He crossed the frosty ground, ignoring the sharp bits of frozen dirt nipping at his soles. Inside the barn, he tossed the bedroll into the hay where he'd been sleeping last night before Miss Simmons had pounced on him, waking him. He started thinking about the women in the house and the idea that anyone or any animal wouldn't find the canvas over the door a very big deterrent. He'd rolled over and tried to ignore the thought. He couldn't. So he'd carted his bedding and himself to the porch to sleep. And that was the thanks he got from the woman he'd been protecting. Accusing him of spying on her.

True, he'd heard them talking and giggling like schoolgirls, but he couldn't make out the words. He did hear his name and Jake's, but that's all he could understand, all he wanted to understand.

He'd told Heaven she had a dilemma on her hands, and so did he. He loved that woman, but he was man enough to step out of the way for the man she'd promised to marry.

If that's what she wanted.

He wouldn't make it easy for Jake though. He planned on quietly courting that woman, in subtle ways that would make her notice the difference between the two men. It might work, unless Jake's attitude changed from yesterday. If he didn't start treating Angel right, Heaven would have nothing to do with Jake. That would be an easy way to win Heaven, but Travis didn't work that way. Angel was already special to him, and he wouldn't use her as a pawn for marriage.

The rooster in the yard crowed, pulling him back to the chores he said he'd take care of this morning. First, he wanted to check on Mrs. Jackson and Junior, as Angel had named him last night.

He picked up a boot and slid his foot in, stomping down on the heel to set it in place. Once he had them both on, he put feed in a bucket from the barrel in the corner. Pride and Joy nickered as Travis passed by his stall. "Be back with yours in a little bit. Yours, too, Charlie."

It occurred to him he needed to tell Jake that the farm no longer belonged to Heaven's family. After that, he planned on staying out of Jake's way. Travis would explore the woods and see if he could find any of Heaven's things that had been scattered by the tornado. That is, after he patched up the house so he didn't have to sleep on the porch again tonight.

Chapter 25

All through breakfast, Annabelle watched the interplay between Travis and Heaven. Last night she thought it was the warmth of the fire that caused the flush in her friend's face when she talked about Travis. Now that she saw the shy glances Heaven offered Travis, she knew differently. There was a spark between them. When Jake kissed Heaven yesterday, Annabelle hadn't seen that fire.

Could it be that Heaven wouldn't be heartbroken when Jake told her he wanted to be released from the betrothal?

Annabelle rested her fork on her plate. If that were true, Jake would be a free man. He didn't want to go back to Nashville, and neither did she. Maybe he'd allow her to accompany him further south. Or could it be possible she might entice him to marry her and return home? She examined the reasons for leaving, and the most important one was that she was on her way to becoming a spinster. She didn't love Jake, but that didn't matter to her. She'd been in love with William, and look where that got her. But if Jake were to marry her, she could return to Nashville and hold her head high. She wouldn't have to follow her father's directives; she'd be a Miles. She had some thinking to do.

Travis collected his emotions and stuffed them in his chest. He'd made it through breakfast with his feelings for Heaven somewhat challenged, thanks to Annabelle. It seemed she favored Jake, but at times he wondered if it was for herself rather than Heaven. He chewed on a piece of hay.

The tiny kid, Junior, appeared to be nursing well and was healthy despite being born the wrong time of year. When the cold winter settled in, they might have to move him inside to keep him warm enough. "What do you think, Mrs. Jackson? Maybe Annabelle and Jake are meant to be together." Realizing he'd spoken his thoughts, he looked over his shoulder, hoping he wouldn't spot Angel standing in the door. She wasn't. He let his breath break free from his lungs.

He rummaged around the barn until he located a hammer and a few other tools that would be useful for repairing the cabin. He wished he could get the bedroom back on the house, but working alone, he didn't think it possible.

Hoofbeats rounded the corner of the lane. Travis straightened. It sounded like more than one horse. Had Jake brought a bigger buggy back with him? Maybe, if he was bringing Annabelle's luggage.

"Dr. Logan!" A loud voice called again. "Dr. Logan!"

Someone needed him. He dropped the tools to the barn floor and rushed outside. He stopped short when he saw Mr. Shaw and another man. "What's wrong? Is it your wife or the baby?"

The man dismounted. "Neither. They're both doing fine.

My wife's sister is with her this morning. Dr. Logan, this is my brother-in-law, Harold Brown."

"Nice to meet you, Harold."

Harold nodded and climbed off his horse.

"So, if they're okay, what can I do for you?"

"My family owes their thanks to you for coming yesterday. Thought we'd ride over and help you put your house back together. There are a few others coming from town. Once word got out that there was a doctor thinking about setting up a practice here, everyone wanted to pitch in and help."

"But. . ."

"Nothing to say, Doc. A few women will be coming by later with the lunch meal, too. You might want to warn Miss Wharton. My wife said I was to tell you that. So I have."

This was sure to stir up a nest of hornets with Heaven. "I'll do that. Right now. You gentleman can tie your horses up by the barn, or put them in the pen if you like. I do appreciate your coming to help." He wasn't so sure Miss Proper would feel the same when he told her about more company coming with lunch.

Heaven met him on the porch. "What are those men doing here?"

"They've come to put your bedroom back on the cabin."

"Why?"

"Because folks around here are right nice if you give them a chance. Mr. Shaw said there are more coming to help. Some women are bringing lunch. Might want to grab some green beans to serve."

Her face went white. "Women from town? Here? By dinnertime?"

He nodded.

"But I'm not set up for company."

"No, I don't suppose anyone that's had their home ripped apart by a tornado would be, do you?"

"I guess not." She frowned. "But I can sure try and make it look better with Annabelle's help."

"How's your ankle? I saw you trying to hold that scream inside when you tripped over me."

"It's fine, a bit tender is all." She looked past him and brightened. "Looks like Jake and his mother are here. He can help, too."

He stepped down from the porch.

She brushed past him, rendering him invisible, as she rushed to the arrival of her intended.

She hadn't asked him if he'd slept well. She didn't seem to care that he'd had a miserable night sleeping out in the open watching over her. He should have known better than to believe she would ever marry him. She wasn't exactly like Mary. She wasn't betraying him outright, though it felt that way. Jake had claimed her first, and it appeared that he intended to keep his promise to Heaven, unlike Mary's to Travis. His stomach soured at the memory of finding his fiancée with Mort, his best friend. Mort's arm wrapped around her shoulders and their lips mashed together.

Heaven hoped her face wasn't flaming red as she raced past Travis. She had to get away from him and his ability to make her want to throw herself into his arms. Again the memory of him carrying her into the cabin yesterday sent tingles throughout her—and they weren't undesirable.

But there was Jake and his mother standing in front of her. She'd made a promise, and she would keep it. It was what both families had wanted since she and Jake were small. No matter that Ma and Pa could no longer make those choices for her. A promise was a promise. But what was she going to do with these feelings for Travis?

"Morning, Mrs. Miles, Jake. Glad you're here, Jake. A few men from town are here to help put the bedroom back on the cabin today." Travis stood behind her, close enough that if he were a cattle brand, he'd burn his initials into her back.

Needing less heat, she stepped forward. "Mrs. Miles, it won't take long to get some tea ready. Would you like to go inside?"

Mrs. Miles nodded. "The tea in town was dreadful, very weak. I hope yours is stronger. It has been so long since we've had good tea."

"It's passable, but not like we used to have. I pray someday soon the prices will come down and we'll be able to make it sweet and dark like before."

"I can swing a hammer, though I'm not dressed properly to be pounding nails," Jake said.

"I'm sure I can find something of Pa's for you to wear, Jake. He didn't take everything with him."

"I had hoped to spend time speaking with you, Heaven."

"There will be time for that later." She offered her best southern girl smile. "I would feel much safer having the cabin put back together." She shot a look at Travis. "Then I'd know for sure there wouldn't be any way for predators of any kind to get inside."

"Then I'll be happy to assist in what ways I can."

"Mrs. Miles, would you mind if I held your arm to help to steady myself? I reinjured my ankle this morning, not seriously, but I'd rather not take a chance on twisting it on the rough ground."

"My dear, that's understandable." She took Heaven by the arm, and they started a slow walk to the porch.

"Heaven, you're favoring that leg. Do you still have the ankle wrapped?" Travis asked.

"No, it was loose last night, so I slipped it off."

"Then that's the first thing I'll do this morning. It should be rewrapped to give you support and contain the swelling."

Her eyes locked onto his. Mercy, what was she going to do with these feelings? She was still engaged to Jake. Why didn't she have the same bacon-sizzling excitement when he looked at her? If Jake hadn't been standing there at that moment, she shamelessly would have felt disappointed if Travis didn't carry her to the cabin.

"Now, sir, you don't mean to be touching my fiancée's. . . um. . .personal—?" Jake stopped and faced Travis.

"I'm a doctor, and it needs to be done." Travis took a step closer to Jake. "Do you have any medical experience, sir?"

"No I have not. But Mother will be watching." Jake strode toward the cabin, his feet striking the ground and sending up shards of mud.

"Really, Jake, I wouldn't have it any other way. Mrs. Reynolds, the preacher's wife, was here the last time, and so was Angel."

Jake's jaw clenched. "Then I suppose it will be fine." He yanked the canvas covering to the side and waited for the women to pass through.

Heaven stopped, let go of Mrs. Miles, and glared at Jake. "Dr. Logan has done nothing improper." *Except for kiss me.* "He's treated me like a lady." *Except doctors ought not make a lady stir up embers of feelings inside.* "He was very gentle and didn't hurt me in the least." *Except he's taking my home from me.*

His eyes narrowed. "I'm glad he was here to help you, Heaven. It must have been a terrifying experience for you."

Annabelle and Angel were busy in the kitchen. "Heaven, we wondered where you took off to. I see you've found the Mileses. Good morning." Annabelle bent down and opened the oven door. "I'm reheating some biscuits. Would you like some?"

"We have tea, too," Angel said. "Why don't you have a seat, Mrs. Miles, and let us serve you this morning."

Heaven wanted to hug her sister. She was using her hospitality skills well. "Travis, would you mind asking the men outside to come in for some as well, before they get started. It will take a bit of time to apply the wrap."

Travis nodded. "I'll be right back. It might be best to do that out on the porch steps, with Mrs. Miles in attendance, while the men are inside."

"I'll get the bandage strips and meet you there."

"Mrs. Miles, would you like some tea, or maybe some milk?" Angel offered.

"I'll have mine as soon as Heaven is medically attended to. Jake will be honored to have his now." Mrs. Miles turned then stopped. "Then Jake is going to work on the cabin with Dr. Logan."

"Are we getting it put back together?" Angel slid into a chair.

"Yes, Angel, isn't that wonderful? God is providing us with men to help Jake and Travis with the rebuilding. They said there'll be women coming around noon with lunch." Heaven could feel the tightness of her pasted smile. God had provided for them. But why did her free will seem to be stripped away as decisions were made without her saying a word?

"Annabelle, would you mind helping me get ready for them after Travis is finished with me?"

"Of course I will help you."

Chapter 26

Heaven surveyed the cabin, which was overflowing with the men who came to help and the women serving food. Mrs. Reynolds had brought Mrs. Tate. They hadn't come empty-handed either. There would be enough food for Heaven to feed her guests for a few days.

Mrs. Reynolds had requested a trade of green beans in exchange for canned pumpkin and orange marmalade. Heaven felt awful about her first judgment of the woman. She truly had a kind heart.

The men had finished their afternoon meal, and Heaven was collecting plates from the table. "What I don't understand is how you came to be at the Wharton's, Travis," Jake said.

"I was with Heaven's father when he died en route to Chicago. He sent me out here. Made me promise."

"Promise what?"

"Caleb wanted me to take his home, said it would be a good place to raise horses."

"Just like that? He gave you the place?" Jake stared at him. "So this is *your* cabin we've been putting back together today, not Heaven's?"

Travis sent Heaven a glance she didn't quite understand.

"That, and he told me he wanted me to have Heaven." The log behind him popped.

"He what?" Jake's face was full of fire.

"I imagine he was concerned about his daughters being left alone. He shouldn't have been, since Heaven shot me before I had a chance to explain my arrival." His boot tapped loudly under the table.

Mrs. Miles gasped. "Oh Lord have mercy!"

Annabelle squealed. "You shot a man?"

"He was the first one I hit. Not the first I shot at."

Angel sat eating her warm bread with the jam Annabelle had brought. She had made herself a sandwich and hoped to enjoy the bursting blackberry flavor alone. A chair scooted out from under the table. She knew it wasn't Travis, because he took great care not to scrape the floor. She could hear her sister's voice and then Annabelle's soft laugh along with Mrs. Miles's throaty one. It had to be Jake, and he hadn't said a word to her. She hated that. He was probably staring at her, trying to look at her eyes. She lowered her head so he couldn't see them. Heaven said sometimes blind people put patches over their eyes. She didn't want to do that. Heaven said she didn't have to because her eyes were still pretty. She wondered if they would stay that way or if they would fade. Did eyes need to work for the color to stay?

Jake touched her arm as if she couldn't hear him sit down at the table like a bear in the general store. "How did you go blind, Angel?"

The bread stuck in her throat, and she coughed.

"Are you all right?" her sister called, panic in her voice.

"Fine." She cleared her throat. "I'm okay. Just went down the wrong pipe is all."

She jutted her chin toward the direction Jake's voice had come. "I got real sick the same time as Ma. Heaven saved me, but the fever made me blind. At least that is what me and Heaven think happened."

"So do you see anything, or is it just all black behind those eyes?" Jake snickered.

Angel's shoulders tightened. He was like those town boys. She could just feel it. She remembered him pulling her pigtails a time or two, and she didn't like that. He had called her pipsqueak when her sister was not around.

Once he had offered her a stick of candy to leave him and Heaven alone in the parlor, but she wouldn't take it. She didn't trust him then, and she decided she wouldn't trust him now. Dr. Logan was going to marry Heaven, so the sooner they sent Jake Miles packing, the happier Angel would be. But first she would finish this delicious jam sandwich. She wouldn't even answer his dumb question.

"So, Monkey, your mama and your papa took sick and died. You Whartons don't have much luck do you?"

"We don't need luck. We have God. Our family is better off in heaven than living here. But now that Travis is here, it is much better. He brings us rabbit meat for stew." She took another bite of her sandwich. It wasn't blackberry jam but blueberry, and it was almost as good as blackberry jam. She wished Jake would go so she could enjoy her treat without his sour attitude wafting across the table at her. And she really wished he wouldn't call her Monkey like he did when she was four.

"Hmm, seems to me like God's forgotten about the Wharton family. Here you two are stranded out here. God has to know Heaven isn't worth anything in the kitchen. Why she probably never even used a stove before coming out here, much less chopped wood."

Angel stiffened her back. "My sister can do more than you know." She put her jam sandwich down on her plate. It no longer appealed to her. She knew one thing, and that was she didn't like Jake and she planned to do what she could to send him back to Nashville, away from her sister. And she decided to start right now.

She fluttered her hand in front of her as if trying to find her glass of milk. She knew where it was. Dr. Logan had placed it at two o'clock from the top of her plate. Satisfaction almost made her smile when her hand hit the side of the glass, sending it sailing across the tabletop. She could imagine the white liquid pooling in the middle.

Jake scooted his chair back. "Watch what you're doing! You almost doused me with your drink."

She heard Dr. Logan's heavy footsteps and Heaven's lighter ones. Dr. Logan reached her first. "How did that happen, Little Miss?"

"I don't really know. I thought the glass was where it always is, but maybe Jake moved it." That was a lie, and she would have to ask forgiveness for saying it, but it had snuck out across her lips before she had barely thought it. But it did help move her plan along to make Jake look bad.

She heard the towel swish the liquid across the table. Her

sister said, "It's okay, Angel. It wasn't a lot of milk spilt. Did any of it get on your dress?"

Angel patted her skirt. It was dry. She hadn't even considered she might have made a mess of herself. Angel felt guilty then for making her sister clean up, especially when her ankle hurt so much. "I'm sorry, Heaven. Let me finish cleaning the table."

"You didn't finish your jam sandwich, and you were so excited about it." Dr. Logan stood next to her with his hand on her shoulder. "I'll get you another glass of milk and make sure it doesn't get moved."

"Will you sit next to me?" Angel asked. "Then I know it won't happen again."

"I didn't move the monkey's glass. Maybe she ought not be living out here, but in a home where they can take care of her and she can learn some skills." Jake sputtered. "Really, it is uncivilized to have someone who can't see try to feed themselves."

Angel hadn't considered that she might be viewed that way. She would have to be careful so Heaven didn't come to the same conclusion as Jake.

Heaven sucked in her breath, and the sound made Angel feel secure. She would never put her in a home for blind children.

"Jake Miles, her name is Angel, not Monkey. In fact, I think she is old enough to be addressed as Miss Wharton, so please do so. It seems the war has erased some of your fine gentlemanly manners."

"Pardon me, Miss Wharton. Your sister surprised me is all. It seems that I may have misspoken."

Annabelle giggled. "Jake, you sprung up awfully fast. One

would never know you've been shot at the way you were trying to skedaddle away from that river of milk."

Angel laughed. "Milk doesn't hurt anyone, Jake, I promise."

It was quiet for a moment, and then Jake laughed. "I supposed when you look at it that way, it was rather funny. I do apologize, Miss Wharton. I seem to remember you being such a sport when you were younger, never minding my teasing. I've grown fond of thinking of you as my little sister."

"I accept your apology, sir. While you thought the teasing was fun, I never enjoyed it." She heard the plunk of the glass on the table and knew that Travis had refilled it for her. He whispered in her ear, "It is in its usual place; let's make sure it doesn't get moved from there." She heard the creak of his knees as he bent and lifted the chair from the end of the table and set it next to her. "I will be right beside you from now on when you eat."

"Thank you, Travis."

"My pleasure, Little Miss."

Angel took another bite of her sandwich followed by a long drink of milk. Yes, she had some work to do. Jake Miles had to go.

Jake brushed away the line of sweat on his forehead that threatened to drip into his eye. He picked up another log and gave it a whack with the ax. He'd been trying to get Heaven alone all afternoon. After that embarrassment with Angel, he wanted to assure Heaven that he cared for her sister. As his mother had pointed out to him later, Heaven and Angel had become more than sisters during these trying times. He wasn't quite sure what that meant, but he didn't have a desire to have her explain it to him. He had figured out enough to know that from the way Heaven treated Angel, she wouldn't hold his past against him.

He lifted his chin and stood taller than he had in months. Heaven would help him find his way back to being a man, not a coward. Though he didn't think he'd tell her about that until after they were married, just in case.

Choosing to chop wood rather than put Travis Logan's house back together seemed childish to him, but he couldn't see his way to putting the cabin to rights. He'd come outside and discovered the low wood pile. Chopping wood would help Heaven stay warm and cook if she refused to marry him right away. And if she decided to marry him, then Travis was welcome to the wood, because Jake would have won the prize.

On the chopping block, he set a log on the cut edge, balanced it, and then swung the ax against it. The sharp split of the wood filled him with strength. This was something he could do well while avoiding conversation with the other men about his war experience.

He reset the log and let the ax fall again. What was Heaven doing now? Earlier she'd been mixed up in the middle of the women who'd come to help. He was feeling a bit thirsty. Maybe he'd see if she was available to talk to him while he satiated his thirst.

He set the ax next to the pile of split logs and ran a hand through his sweaty hair. Not much he could do about his mussed appearance; it wasn't what he'd ever consider a desirable courting look. But with Logan around, he didn't want to waste time preening. He had a feeling he might have already lost Heaven, but he wouldn't quit without trying. She'd meant a lot to him before the war, and someday—if he ever felt whole again—he'd want her with him.

Determined to speak to her, he headed for the cabin.

In the root cellar, the candle flickered and spat. The light cast a warm yellow over the multitude of jars of green beans. The color didn't add appeal to the vegetable. Heaven picked up another jar of canned green beans. It was the third one that had an odd color and weight about it.

She held it to the candlelight. It was more than the hue from the candlelight. The color seemed sickly. She set it to the side with the other two she'd found the day of the tornado. She'd meant to discard them. While not sure they had gone bad, the likelihood was they had. She still had plenty of beans to trade. She thanked God again and asked for forgiveness for her worry about not having food. God had certainly provided through the good women of the Baptist church.

She plucked another can from the shelf and wiped the dusty top with her apron. It didn't have the dull green look and felt the right weight, so she placed it with the others in her basket.

"Heaven, are you down there?" Jake's face appeared at the top of the ladder.

Her breath sucked in as she backed up. "Jake, I almost dropped my basket. Good thing it was looped on my arm, or there would have been another mess to clean up. What do you need?"

"Can I come down and talk to you?"

"In the root cellar?" The man had lost his mind. Why would he want to converse with her amid rows of beans? "I'm on my way up." His face retreated, and she climbed the ladder.

Jake waited for her. "Let me take those for you." He slipped the basket from her arm and set it on the dry sink.

"I came in for a drink of water and wondered where you disappeared to."

"Just gathering a few things to trade before the women leave. Did you get your water?"

"No." He shook his head.

"Mercy, let me get you a glass then. One of the other women would have been happy to serve you." She slid a loose lock of hair behind her ear.

Jake grasped her arm. "I didn't want anyone else to serve me. Heaven, I—can, will you take a short walk with me for a moment?"

She glanced around the cabin. Most of the women were outside helping where they could. Only Mrs. Miles remained seated by the fire. "No. I can't. There's too much to do before everyone leaves."

"Just a short walk."

She didn't want to be alone with Jake. Despite her responsibility to the promise she made him, she wasn't ready for the conversation she knew he wanted to have. "I don't want to be lollygagging while the others are working on my home."

Jake grimaced.

"It's my home, as long as I'm in it, and so far Travis hasn't mentioned me moving out."

But he hadn't asked her to stay either.

"I understand. If it will ease your mind, why not help me carry some of the split wood to the porch while we converse?" He held out his arm for her.

She shifted her weight from side to side, for a moment undecided, and then she noticed him—the Jake that had returned. Gone was the quick wit that made her hold her stomach in laughter, the sureness he carried himself with, as if the world would grow a rose path for him to walk on wherever he went. She sought the memory of him in his eyes and saw a depth they'd once lacked—worry, hurt, fear? She grasped his arm and remembered the man he was, the one who made her smile, the man her mother said would give her the world. The one she should be grateful to God for, for providing such a fine specimen for her to marry.

"Let's get the wood on the porch."

Outside Heaven piled the split wood into Jake's arms and waited for him to say something. They'd made two trips to the porch with the wood, and he'd been as silent as the wind today.

"Guess you're wondering about what I wanted to say?"

"Yes I am. If you want to talk without the others, you'd better start. Angel will be looking for me soon."

"I doubt that, as she seems to have attached herself to Logan."

She slapped a piece of wood on top of the others.

"Sorry. It's just that I came up here to release you from marrying me, but now that I've seen you, I can't let you go. I still love you, Heaven. I want to marry you, but not in Nashville."

He'd said it, what she didn't want to hear. She swallowed and tears burned. "It's been so long. I thought you were dead."

"I know, and I'm sorry about that. I should have written the moment I could. I thought it would be better this way. You could find someone whole to marry. That's not me, not right now."

"I don't know what to say, Jake. I feel like I need to get to know you again. And then there's Angel—where I go she goes. You need to find a way to get along with her."

"I understand. Do I still have a chance at winning your heart?"

She placed one more piece of wood on the stack, covering most of his face.

He let the stacked wood roll out of his arms to the ground.

She jumped back. "Why did you do that?"

"Stop. Don't stay anything else. I need you to know that I'm not going back to Nashville. I'm leaving Tennessee."

"Where are you going?"

"West, maybe to Colorado, stake out a claim at one of those gold mines. I want to start a new life with you as my wife."

"But your mother and father expect you to go back and work in their business."

"I can't do that, not anymore." He grasped her hands in his.

She never noticed before how her hand didn't seem to fit in his, not like Travis's. And now that Jake held her hand, where were the spitting sparks of fire that happened when Travis's hand touched hers?

"So will you think about it? Will you give Logan this house your father wanted him to have and marry the man your mother wanted for you?"

She withdrew her hands and hugged her arms around her chest. "Jake, I don't—"

Annabelle ran up to them out of breath. "There you are, Heaven. Travis found something, and he's looking for you."

"Think about it. Will you, Heaven? Leave with me, next week?" Jake turned to collect the wood he'd dropped.

"Leave where?" Annabelle tugged on Heaven's shawl. "Where are you going?"

Heaven didn't reply. She just shook her head and put up her hand to stop Annabelle from asking more questions. Clutching her shawl tightly in one hand, she went to find out what Travis discovered that was so important. Meanwhile, she had so much to think about. Should she marry the boy her ma wanted her to have or the man Pa had sent for her?

Annabelle watched her friend walk away. Jake still gathered wood in his arms. "Here, let me help you." She bent down and with care picked up a wood chunk hairy with splinter offerings. "It's always easier when you have someone to help you put the last pieces together."

"Sometimes it is." Jake straightened. "Thanks."

She searched his face. "Did you tell her you weren't going to marry her?"

"The opposite. I asked her to marry me and leave next week."

"You'll go back to Nashville then?" If Heaven went back, it could be bearable to go home to her father's house.

"No, not Nashville. Never back there. I asked her to go west, leave this life that's happened to us far behind."

"Next week? That won't work, Jake. I told you I'm not

going home. You have to return with your mother. I have other plans." She let the wood she held roll back to the ground and turned away from him. Why had she thought he was adorable or would be if he could change his attitude? Her lips burned as she remembered the kiss he'd stolen from her a week after getting betrothed to her best friend. Jake didn't deserve Heaven, and she would do what she could to help her see the truth.

Chapter 27

The hammering continued as Heaven rounded the corner of the cabin. The noise echoed Jake's question: marry-him-go-west. It wasn't exactly what Ma had in mind when she orchestrated the engagement. When Heaven accepted Jake's betrothal, Ma's face had beamed as if she were the bride to be; she praised God that her daughter would be living in comfort and be a part of society. Heaven shivered. Why hadn't she been as excited? She liked Jake, thought she loved him, and when she'd lost him, she'd cried herself to sleep for months.

But now? If Travis hadn't kissed her and woke feelings inside of her she didn't even know existed, she'd be accepting Jake's offer of a new life. But Travis did kiss her. And she liked it. A lot.

The side of the cabin seemed different. The logs appeared lighter than the ones on the front. She hadn't realized how much work it would have been for Travis to repair the cabin alone. How would he have even lifted those heavy logs into place?

Her steps halted. The room they were adding on was bigger than before. She tilted her head to get a better angle. It was larger. Too big for just one room, now it would be a fancy two-bedroom cabin. Angel could have her own room if they didn't leave with Jake. *God, I need direction. You've placed two good men in my life, and I don't know who You want me to choose. I'm so tired of worrying about taking care of Angel and where the next meal might come from, and yet You keep blessing me with gifts from You. But which of these men is the gift?*

She shielded her eyes from the sun, trying to locate Travis among the men working. She didn't see his dark hair at first. Then he turned and saw her. His smile blazed across the distance, and she responded.

He scampered down a newly made ladder and trotted over to a pile of coats abandoned as the men grew warm from the sun and the work.

She hurried over, not wanting to squander any of his working time. "Annabelle said you found something?"

"I did."

Light bounced off something in his hand. She blinked.

"While we were looking for fallen trees to use, I found this. Does it belong to you?" He held it out to her.

Rubbing her arm, she stepped back. Grief hammered her heart as her mind recognized what precious memory Travis held. Could it be? Her fingers trembled as she reached for the frame. With great care, she traced the crack that ran between the people in the photo. There wasn't any water damage. Other than the broken glass, it had survived. She looked up, and her eyes melded with his. Warmth filled her, soothing the pain. "It's my ma and pa."

She couldn't look away.

He took a step closer. "Heaven, you don't have to go through this alone."

Their connection snapped. Unsettled, she hugged the picture to her chest. "We've never been alone, Dr. Logan. God has always been with us."

"That is true." He pulled a hammer from his back pocket. "I guess I'd better get back to work."

"You made it bigger."

"Is that all right with you?"

"Does it matter? This doesn't belong to me anymore, as you like to remind me as often as you can."

Travis rubbed the wooden handle. He took a breath and looked as if he were going to say something. Instead, he glanced over at the grove of cedar trees. "I'll be working out here until supper if you need anything. We should have the logs pinned by then. The chinking will have to wait."

"Heaven!" Angel called out from the porch. "Mrs. Reynolds wants to know if we have any salt. We're making pie. Never mind. She said she found it."

Heaven raised her hand in acknowledgment and then slowly lowered it as she remembered her sister couldn't see her. It didn't matter anyway, since Angel had scampered back into the cabin, not waiting for her sister's response. "I'll take this inside. Again, thank you for finding it."

Travis watched her walk away clutching that photo with her shoulders sunk lower than rock in a river. He cherished her reaction when he'd given her the photo. What would it be like to lose almost everyone you loved? Then have the things that reminded you of them swept away? He'd left home by choice, no room for him there and a strong desire to be his own man. And to get away from the painful memories of Mary. He couldn't watch her marry and raise kids that weren't his. He'd made his peace with that and forgiven the both of him, but he didn't have to stick around and watch their future unfold. It no longer mattered. What did was finishing this cabin and winning Heaven's love.

"Travis." Heaven called. "Wait."

He turned back and waited until she walked across the dead weeds to him.

"Can I ask you something? It's about doctoring."

Her face was pinched tight enough to cause him pain. Was something wrong with her? "What do you want to know?"

"You know how my ma died? The fever? And then Angel got sick but she lived but lost her sight?"

"Yes, you mentioned that."

"I know you didn't have any luck saving Pa from the same fate, but I'm wondering if I could have done anything to save Ma, and maybe Angel's sight?"

She might as well have mule-kicked him in the stomach. How did she know his most vulnerable weakness? How could he answer her, tell her there was never hope, at least when it came to him saving people who contracted a fever? He had to say something, offer her a bit of hope that the next time the ending wouldn't be the same. "Why don't you tell me how you tried to get the fever down."

Annabelle meant to go back inside and help the church women prepare the meal, but instead she found herself leaning against the railing feeling all warm and happy as she watched Heaven and Travis. They stood close to each other, a bit closer than necessary. Annabelle rubbed her hands together. Heaven surely had feelings for the handsome doctor.

She knew right then she had to keep Jake from marrying Heaven and hauling her out west somewhere. Her friend had suffered more than enough this year. To marry Jake, a ladies' man at his best and a broken man at his worst, would likely bring Heaven even more grief.

Annabelle leaned over the porch railing, trying to get a better view of her friend's face. She couldn't, but she did see Heaven's posture shrink, like her spine wasn't capable of being straight despite years of training. Then she hustled away from Travis toward the woods. What had he said to upset her? Maybe Annabelle had made a mistake, and Travis wasn't as good as she thought.

She grasped the fold of her skirt to lift her hem and took off at a quick trot to follow her friend and offer her comfort.

Heaven had numbly thanked Travis and then headed to the woods. She couldn't go inside, not right now. He hadn't said it was her fault, but when she'd said she'd kept Ma and Angel tightly covered and kept the fire stoked, his eyebrows shot heavenward. Right then, she'd known it was the wrong thing to do. They were so cold, shivering so hard their teeth were clattering. She'd made them sicker by piling on more blankets. Why hadn't her ma taught her how to nurse someone? Most likely her ma never thought Heaven would have to since she'd be married to a Miles. As Jake's wife, she'd have access to a doctor anytime one was needed.

"Heaven. . .wait." Annabelle huffed behind her. Heaven wiped her shirt sleeve across her eyes and spun around.

"I saw you. . .talking. . .to Travis." Annabelle's cheeks were pink from exertion.

"Were you running?"

"No, walking fast." She dropped the skirt fabric from her hands. "It would have been easier to run."

"It is. When we moved here, Angel and I would sneak off to the back pasture and run. We knew Ma wouldn't catch us and Pa wouldn't care." She angled the photo for Annabelle to see. "Travis found this and brought it back to me. He wasn't even sure if it belonged to me."

"He's nice. Thoughtful, too." Annabelle extended her hand. "Can I see?"

Heaven, reluctant to let it out of her grasp, held on to it a second longer then gave it to her. Annabelle wouldn't harm it, and she knew Heaven's parents. She was the only person as close as her sister was to her. "The glass is cracked. But the picture is okay." She hovered next to Annabelle. "I wonder how old they were? I never thought to ask Ma."

"You look like her. You both have that wavy hair and penetrating gaze." Annabelle handed it back.

"I'm sorry that I didn't share Ma with you more. I never knew how hard it was without one." She'd been mean more than once to Annabelle when she'd asked if Heaven's mom would fix her hair, too, or show her how to arrange flowers. Jealousy had risen like the flooded Mississippi, causing her to say things she now regretted.

"I forgive you. We were kids." Annabelle pushed aside a branch that crossed in their path. She held it back for Heaven. "If I could have told you in words what I was missing, then you would have shared her." She let go, and the cedar branch shivered back into place. "I know your heart. Back then you probably saw me taking away from you precious time with your mother."

A broken branch crunched under Heaven's foot. "Ma was gone often, doing things for the church and the poorer families. The time she spent with me often felt limited. And when Angel came, there was even less." A small brown bird flew overhead and landed on a bare tree limb, making it sway.

"So, do you know what you're going to do? Are you going to marry Jake?"

"He asked me to marry him again this morning."

"I know. I'm sorry. I wasn't trying to eavesdrop. Travis sent me to find you, and then I overheard Jake ask if you would go out west with him. Does he have a plan for when he gets there?"

"I don't think so, other than finding gold." She tried to picture what the West might be like. She'd heard stories, and that life seemed even harder than the one she was living now. Even with Jake by her side, there would be a lot of difficult days. Not that she minded times like that. It made the good days seem so much better. But somehow when she pictured living out west, Jake's face did not come to mind; Travis's did.

She looked up as another bird flew overhead. It came to a stop by the other one. *That's nice. They must be family.*

"You have other options. You could marry Travis." Annabelle's red curls bounced as she rose up and down on her toes in front of Heaven. "Or come with me to Memphis! And we'll open a shop together. That would be so much fun! And of course Angel can come, too. We'll teach her all the special knitting patterns, and she can help keep the shelves filled." Annabelle grabbed Heaven and pulled her into a hug. "Please, it would be delightful to be together."

Holding the photo in one hand, Heaven embraced her friend while considering the possibilities. Starting a knitting shop with Annabelle sounded like fun, but also irresponsible. She had to consider Angel in her plans. How long would it take to find a place to live? Did Annabelle even have enough money for all three of them to live and pay rent on a shop? Most of all, was she ready to say good-bye to being a wife and mother now that it was truly possible?

Chapter 28

Angel listened to the footsteps, heel, toe, heel, toe, as Travis headed for the cabin door. "Are you going to the barn?"

"I thought I'd walk out and check on Junior. I find the little babies entertaining. Want to go with me?"

She liked the way he asked her to do things with him, just like Pa used to. She scratched at a spot behind her ear. Mosquitoes must not die off here as early as they did in Nashville, 'cause it seemed she'd wandered into a pack of them. "Yes sir." She scrambled off the floor to her feet. "Do you want me to lead you since it's getting dark?"

"I'd like to escort you, Miss Wharton, if your cute button nose wouldn't be offended by the rankness of my work shirt."

Angel coughed several times. "I'd be honored, Dr. Logan." She dipped in a mock curtsey. Her throat tickled, causing her to cough again.

"Pffft. It's not dark."

Jake. Ready retorts climbed onto her tongue, waiting for her to fire them from her mouth, but she packed them into the "proper lady basket" and shut the lid with reluctance.

Someone cracked his knuckles.

"Please don't do that, Jake." Heaven's tone was as sharp as their rooster's beak.

Step, swish, step. Heaven was wearing one of Ma's gowns. She wasn't as tall as Ma, and the skirt dragged across the floor. Whose attention was she trying to get? She hoped not Jake's. The light steps grew louder as she came near. "Are you feeling all right, Angel?"

"Peachy." She wouldn't tell Heaven her throat hurt, or she'd be tucked in bed with a warm brick before she could protest.

"Jake, I think we should see the baby goat as well. It's been a long time since I've been around farm animals, and the little ones are adorable." Mrs. Miles brushed past her, leaving behind a flower bed of roses.

Angel's fingers made their way to the itchy spot again, and she dug in. Those two were as annoying as the bug bite. She didn't want to spend time with them. She wanted Travis to herself, or at least to have only Heaven with them. "Then let's get going. Annabelle and Heaven, are you coming, too?"

"I'd love to. Thank you, Angel, for inviting me," Annabelle said.

"I think I'll stay here and heat the coffee. When you come back, it will be hot, and we'll have another piece of that pie you made this afternoon." Heaven hugged her. "It's a really good pie." She whispered in Angel's ear and sent her out the door.

Today had been a tornado of emotions for Heaven. The coffeepot clanked against the stove burner plate as she replaced it on the stove to keep warm for the others. The china cup warmed her hands as she took a sip of the dark brown brew. The silence fed her soul. Before today she'd missed the hustle and bustle of friends coming and going, having forgotten how wearying it could be to have your company face stuck in place all day like dried molasses.

The canvas-covered windows took on a reddish glow from the setting sun while the evening chill snaked through the fibers. Travis said he'd ordered shutters as glass was still too costly, but they wouldn't be in for a week, maybe longer. But with the wood Jake chopped and split, she and Angel would stay warm through the winter. She set her cup on the table and stuck her hand into her apron pocket. She pulled out her parent's daguerreotype. Someday she would get the glass fixed. For now she wanted a safe place for it where Angel wouldn't knock it over by accident. One more fall and the glass would likely crumble.

The bookcases had been righted, and there was an empty spot where books used to sit. She'd place it there until the bedroom was weathertight. She held it up for another good look. Her parents weren't smiling, but then no one did, Ma said. Back then it took so long to take a picture that smiles often drooped. But Ma's eyes seemed to sparkle, and the way Pa stood proud behind her with his hand on her shoulder, she knew they were in love. She wanted that, had begged God for it, and the only one to ask her to marry was a man she didn't love. The frame went on the newly waxed shelf. The women from church had cleaned everything. The marks on the wall she'd made to measure the passing of days since her father left were still there. They hadn't touched them. She brushed them with the hem of her apron, but they smeared. If she stayed, she'd cover them with new chinking when they did the new room.

She had to give Jake an answer soon. Angel had found a lot of motherly love in the cabin's kitchen today. The church women had treated her like one of their own—on a special day. They had her sister laughing.

Laughing. Not the laugh Angel had been offering since their ma passed. This was the belly laugh that started with a throaty chuckle and ended with tears sprinkling Angel's cheeks.

How could she take that away from her sister? Move to some unknown place where they might not even have a home? With Jake hunting gold, they'd be living in some miner's shack. She wouldn't marry him. Besides, something had changed. She liked him still. And that was the problem. She *liked* him, not *loved* him. She wanted to marry for love. She knew that now. Like Annabelle, she'd rather live as a spinster—if she could find a way to support herself. If not on this farm, maybe there would be a place in town she and Angel could afford. Maybe the Shaws would let them live on their farm and help with their baby and clean. They could bring Mr. and Mrs. Jackson and Junior and start their soap-making business.

In her heart, she knew that wouldn't happen. Times were still difficult, and it was doubtful Mr. Shaw could afford to hire her or even feed them long enough for HA to bring in enough money.

Jake was no longer a choice, but that left her staying in Friendship and marrying Travis—just because Pa said so. That rankled her, despite the knowledge she liked Travis a lot, even loved him if she weren't afraid to admit it.

And then there was Annabelle's offer to consider. Heaven knew that was a bad idea, romantic and adventurous, but not something she should do, and neither should Annabelle. Without a husband or true means of support, it was craziness to think they could move to a new town and open a shop.

The rain-sodden door shuddered against the threshold as it was thrust open. The door had been found in the woods, and one of the men reattached it, assuring her it would work fine once it dried. Annabelle came in leading Angel by the hand. "Heaven, something is wrong with her."

The light in the cabin wasn't sufficient for an examination. Travis had Heaven light the lamps along with the candles so he could examine Angel. Red spots dotted her hairline, and now she scratched her side. He glanced away from his patient to her hovering sister. "Heaven, have you had the measles?"

"When I was five. Is that what Angel has?" Heaven placed a trembling hand on Angel's cheek. "She's burning up."

The pie in Travis's stomach soured. The spots, the fever, and the cough she'd had yesterday were clear signs that she had the dreaded disease. The town needed to be notified, quarantined. The sourness turned to acidic bubbles. People in this town would die.

"The child has the measles?" Shards of panic sliced through the cabin as Mrs. Miles backed away. "Jake, we need to leave now. Neither of us has had them."

"Mother, we need to stay and help." Jake took a step closer to his mother and away from Heaven.

Travis noticed. If the man loved Heaven, why wasn't he offering her comfort?

"Annabelle,"—Heaven's face leached to the color of porcelain as she spun around and faced her friend—"did you have them when I did?"

Annabelle shook her head in denial. "No, Mother kept me locked in the house every time there was a threat so I wouldn't catch them. It worked, because I didn't catch them."

"Then you have to leave. With Jake and Mrs. Miles." Heaven pushed her friend toward the door. "Jake, get the buggy."

Annabelle whipped away from Heaven and backed up against the wall. "I'm not leaving. You need help. I wasn't here before, but I am now."

Angel scratched at her face.

"Don't." Travis grabbed her hand. "If you do that, you might get scars on that pretty face."

"But—I—can't—help—it. It itches." Angel whined and tried to pull her hand back.

"I'll make a plaster for you. Heaven will smear it on the spots, and it won't itch as much." Travis struggled to talk like a comforting doctor. "The rest of you all need to go back to town. Stay in your rooms. Jake, you need to find Preacher Reynolds and ask him to get the word out. Everyone should stay home. Maybe we can keep the town"—he remembered Angel's presence—"safe."

"Heaven, when you were at church the other day, did anyone mention not feeling well?"

"No, not that I remember." Her wide eyes didn't even blink at him. He knew she was thinking about what had happened the last time a fever came to this cabin. He wanted to reassure her that this was different, but he couldn't. And if he tried, she would know he was lying to her.

"Cassie was coughing. She coughed a bunch." Angel's hand went back to her scalp. Her fingers went walking.

"So it's probably making its way through town now." Travis knew he couldn't turn his back on the town. He would be called, and most likely some would die. He didn't want to look Heaven in the eye and tell her that her sister might be one of them.

Jake took Annabelle's hand. "You need to come with us, Bella. Dr. Logan knows what is best, and that's for us to be in town. It won't help Heaven if Angel gets better and then you get ill."

Bella? So now that Heaven wasn't jumping into Jake's arms, it looked as if he was setting his sights on her best friend. Annabelle seemed to be a smart woman though and would see through him.

Mrs. Miles gathered the stitching she'd brought along. "He's right, dear. Your mother protected you when you were young, and now that she's gone, I feel I should do so in her place. Get your things together. It's a good thing we didn't bring that trunk of stuff along."

"Angel, I'm going out to the barn to get what I need to mix up that plaster for you. Say your good-byes to your friends."

Travis left the cabin with Jake thumping down the porch steps behind him.

"Logan, think she'll survive?"

Travis halted. He stared at the barn and saw army tents in his mind. "I don't know, Jake. A lot of people don't." His flesh crawled as if he'd been ordered back to the front. Devastation of families awaited him wherever he went. Beads of sweat rolled down his neck as the tents turned into Heaven sobbing over the death of Angel.

Chapter 29

Heaven pinned the last cloth on the line to dry. There had been more washing to do with Angel getting sick to her stomach. Heaven saw Travis running toward her from the woods, holding something. She smiled. He'd been out all day searching for anything belonging to them that might have been dropped in the woods by the tornado. Before lunch he'd found her rocking chair, the paint scratched and the wood dented.

What had he found this time? She met up with him by the porch. He held his treasure behind his back like a little boy. "What is it?"

He gave her a found-a-hundred-dollar-bill grin and brought his arms around front. His hands held the Wharton family Bible. "It got a little wet. Some of the pages are stuck together. Might even be few of them missing. Here." He thrust it into her hands. "I know how much you mourned the loss of it."

"Where did you find it?" She ran her hand across the dark brown leather cover. She never thought to see it again.

"I was walking and searching the ground when a mocking bird let out a screech, and I looked up and saw something catch the light up in a tall tree. The more I stared at it, the more it seemed to call to me. So I climbed and found it wedged tight between two branches. The sun was bouncing off those gilt-edged pages like a beacon so I could find it."

"You climbed the tree for me?" She hugged the Bible to her chest and wished she were brave enough to hug him, too. "For me and Angel? You saved our family history, Travis. Thank you."

A horse came barreling down the drive. Travis pushed Heaven behind him.

"Dr. Logan!" The rider called out.

"I'm here." Travis shouted back.

The man brought the horse to a stop in front of them. "Obadiah sent me. Mrs. Shaw's turned sick, real bad. He wants you to come right away."

Heaven grabbed Travis by the arm. Fear grabbed her by the throat. "You can't go. What if Angel gets worse?"

He pulled away from her, not answering her question. "Ride on back and tell them I'll be there right away."

The messenger nodded and pulled on the reins to turn his horse, giving it a nudge. It took off on a run back to the Shaw's farm.

"I'll be back as quick as I can." Travis walked toward the barn. "You know what to do for Angel. I told you, and I believe you can do this."

Being left alone with Angel sick terrified her, and her body shook with anger. "No, I can't do it." She followed him into the barn.

"I'm taking Charlie if that's okay. He's not as high strung, and I won't have time to baby him when I get there." He saddled the horse.

Heaven clutched the Bible tighter and watched Travis

tighten the girth strap on Charlie's saddle. He gave it another quick tug and then buckled it.

"You can't mean to ride off and leave us here."

"She's ill, Heaven. I may be able to help."

"He didn't say she has the measles. Maybe it's just a cold."

"Maybe, or maybe it's something worse. I have to go." He slung the saddlebags over the horse's back.

In between the post and the stall gate, a spider had at one time anchored its web. Some of the threads were broken and quivered in the breeze that snaked through the barn walls. What had made that spider leave its home? She raked her fingers through her hair, stopping at a knot. When had it gotten tangled? "Angel needs you here." *I need you.*

"I took an oath, Heaven. To help people." He gripped his hat tightly in one hand. "You can take care of Angel. I've told you what I would do if I were here. None of it's difficult." He popped his hat on his head.

He was going to leave. She searched for some way to reach him. He had to understand why she couldn't be left. People she loved died or became blind when she took care of them. Guilt joined with fear and braided in anger. Her fingers curled into a fist, her thumbnail worried the top of her index fingers. "Where was that oath when you took care of Pa? Where was it when you decided to raise horses instead of helping people? Why does it have to be important to you now?" Behind her, Mrs. Jackson butted her head against the door. Heaven wanted to do the same. She might as well. The man wouldn't listen to her pleas.

Travis took a step toward her with his arms outstretched. Did he mean to embrace her? Comfort her? She backed away.

Her breath clawed the sides of her throat as it came in and back out at a rapid pace. "Didn't Pa tell you to take care of us? That's what you wanted, right—the farm, me? Well you can have it. All of it. Including me. Just don't leave me here alone to take care of my sister." *Or there is no deal.* She slid the Bible under her arm and wiped her moist hands on her apron then folded them as if in prayer. She rested her chin on her folded knuckles and refused to let him see her tears.

Travis mounted Charlie and tipped his hat. "Miss Wharton, I would never accept a woman in that manner." He kneed the horse and left the barn.

Heaven watched the twitch of Charlie's tail as Travis's back grew smaller. She waited for him to look over his shoulder, even turn around and say he was sorry. He didn't. She wouldn't call after him, beg him to come back, even though the words were tugging at her throat, begging to be said.

She could not allow herself to panic. But how could she stop the ice from taking root in her veins? *Get busy.* Yes, that's what she needed—to do something, follow the directions Travis left.

Her stomach felt pecked full of holes. She stumbled back into the cabin. She'd start supper. Maybe Mrs. Shaw wasn't that sick and Travis would return in time to eat with her. He'd apologize, and she'd forgive him, and he'd promise never to leave her like that again. She clung to the back of the chair where he'd sat since he'd arrived. Why did it seem she could never hold on to a man? Why did they always pick someone or something else instead of her?

Angel. Check on her first. She might have taken a turn for

the worse while Heaven had been in the barn pleading with Travis to no avail.

He'd said he didn't want her. Not the way she was offering herself. The disgust dripped off his lips when he said it as if she where one of those poor girls without mothers who worked in the saloons. Is that what she'd lowered her standards to? She didn't have a mother, and she had just offered herself in a most undignified way.

"Heaven?" Angel called out from the straw bed they'd put together for her yesterday.

"I'm right here." She hustled to her sister's side. "Are you ready for a drink of tea?"

"No. Will you scratch me?"

"I can't do that. I can draw a bath and wash you with lye soap. That seems to help."

Angel rolled away from her. "No. Go away."

"Ah sweetheart. You'll be better soon. Travis said in a few days the rash will all but disappear, and so will the itching."

"Go. Away."

She didn't reprimand her sister for her tone. Truth was she wanted to go away. She didn't want to take care of Angel again. What would happen to her sister this time?

Cook. Get busy. Peel the potatoes and boil them. Open some beans and spoon them into the pan. She operated from memory, not feeling. She even made a plate for Travis and set it in front of his chair. Then she made the fork go in her mouth. *Chew. Swallow. Repeat.* She listened for Charlie's hoofbeats. None came. She finished what was on her plate, scooted out of her chair, and checked on Angel.

"I said go away."

"I'll leave you alone for now. I'll be back as soon as I clean up the kitchen." She picked up Travis's full plate and set it on the stove for later. She shouldn't be angry at him. God had made it apparent that healing was His gift to Travis. But what did He give to her?

As she washed the few plates, she remembered the barn chores would need to be done. It hadn't taken her long to acclimate to Travis doing them for her. She set a dried plate on the hutch and picked up the other to wipe. How did he expect her to milk the cow and feed the horse and the goats while watching Angel every second in case her fever rose? The dishcloth in Heaven's hand whipped across the plate and then over her shoulder as she settled the last dish on top of the other. One pot remained to be cleaned.

He didn't even say he'd be back. He would come back though, wouldn't he? Even though he said he didn't want her? And now that he seemed to want to be a doctor again, did he still want her farm? A dishwater bubble sparkled in the glow of the lamp and expanded from her furious pot scrubbing. *But did that mean he really didn't want her either?* Her hands stilled, and the iridescent beauty exploded.

Travis felt the pace of the last few days. He hoped this was his last stop before getting back to Heaven. And Angel, she had to be better. If she'd turned for the worse, he wouldn't know, because Heaven wouldn't have left her sister to find him. Guilt gnawed at his stomach. He should have at least sent someone to the farm.

"You have to keep the baby away from Mrs. Shaw." Travis stared at Mr. Shaw's eyes until the man blinked.

"I'm sure it's difficult for all of you. I'll explain it to her again. Will you tell her I'm here, please?" Travis stripped off his coat and hung it over the back of a wooden chair. He turned back. "It looks like the town escaped a major epidemic. The mayor is considering lifting the quarantine."

"How many did we lose?"

"One was too many, but the five we lost could have been much higher."

"She won't quit crying for the baby." The man swayed the infant in his arms. "I don't know how much longer I can keep Etta away from her."

Instead of placing the baby in the hand-carved cradle, Mr. Shaw plunked the infant into Travis's arms. "Here, as long she's held, she won't cry. And if she's not making noise, it's easier for me to keep Etta calm."

Before Travis could protest, the anxious husband raced past him to the bedroom. The door closed with a solid clunk.

He eyed the small cabin, looking for a pitcher of water. It would have been good to have at least washed his hands before holding the baby. Perhaps he could lay her down for a second. He made soothing baby sounds and leaned over the cradle. The baby's eyelids sprang open, and her mouth formed an O. Her little chest rose as she sucked in air. Her face turned red. Travis scooped her up and cradled her in his arms before a sound could escape her tiny body. At least he'd washed his hands well before leaving the last sick family.

What was taking so long? He glanced at the door and

swayed from side to side. One more look at the bedroom, and he realized he would be holding the baby a little longer. He was so tired, and that rocker by the cradle beckoned him. Maybe Mr. Shaw was having some success at convincing Mrs. Shaw to be patient. He yawned.

He decided to take a chance on the baby not liking the rocker. He'd still be holding her, so maybe she'd remain quiet. He would ease into the chair. He dropped, sinking a few inches at a time until his thighs burned. The baby didn't seem discombobulated, so he sat.

This was nice; babies were nice. Babies with Heaven would be even nicer. He rocked and relaxed. He wanted to get home and talk to Heaven. The way they had left each other sawed at him. Why couldn't she just admit she loved him and would marry him? Instead, she threw the marriage sacrament at him as if it didn't mean anything. He knew she was hurt and scared when she said it, and if he were a lesser man, he would have said, "Fine, let's get it done. Get the preacher and say the words."

But he wanted a home like his parents' home, like the Shaw family's home, and he would wait until she was ready, even if he had to spend the entire winter in the barn.

Etta Shaw's voice rose to a crescendo, and Travis heard her pleading to see the little girl. He wouldn't allow it, not when the mother was this ill. So far the baby seemed healthy. The goat's milk was keeping her body strong, and he wanted her to stay that way. But he couldn't stop Mr. Shaw from taking the baby to her mother. He hoped for the baby's sake Mr. Shaw would be strong enough to make his wife wait.

Mrs. Shaw wailed. Travis's back stiffened. He gripped the

tiny baby to his chest and rocked harder. *Please God, heal her mother and protect this little one.* He'd wanted to ask for so much more, but he knew God didn't answer many of Travis's prayers, at least not when it came to healing people. The sun that had shined through the window dimmed, and its yellow fingers on the floor turned to gray.

The baby reached out a tiny hand and slid it across his chin. She was too young to have sensed his sadness and reacted to it with a caress of care, but for Travis it felt as if God had reached out and offered him hope.

Heaven wanted to get the morning chores done quickly, so she crept out of the house before the sun came out. Angel was sleeping. The poor child had worn both of them out with her whining. With a lantern to light the way and the egg basket in hand, she headed for the chicken coop. She'd start there and then feed the rest of the animals. She'd have to come back later and muck the stalls. She'd really hoped Travis would have returned by now, since that was a chore she hadn't minded handing over to him.

Angry squawks blasted from inside the coop. Something was wrong. The chickens shouldn't even be awake. She broke into a run. As the lantern swung from her hand, it cast ghostly shadows across the yard. She reached the door. It was open a crack. She'd shut it last night, hadn't she?

She yanked it the rest of the way open.

Yellow eyes glared at her, and her blood chilled as she took in the scattered feathers and a half-dead chicken clutched between sharp teeth.

A fox—and she hadn't brought the gun. She was armed with a basket and fire.

The fox growled, and she took a step back. She had to get him out of there. They needed those chickens. Without them they would surely starve. Maybe if she opened the door all the way so he'd have a clean exit, he would leave. She eased the basket to the ground but not the lantern. As long as she had that, the fox wouldn't come after her, would it? Putting all of her strength into her one arm, she dragged the lopsided door across the dirt until the opening to the coop was much wider.

Her heart thumping, she picked up the basket, and she banged it against the side of the building. "Get out!"

The stubborn fox didn't move. Just blinked at her. A red feather floated from his mouth.

She stepped to the opening and hurled the basket at him, knocking him squarely between the ears.

He shook his head and feathers flew, but he didn't release the chicken.

She yelled again, stomping her foot. This time he seemed to understand he might be in danger and ran from the building still grasping her chicken. She let him go.

The vim and vigor she had directed at the fox drained away faster than money in a gambler's hand, and hard shivers took their place. Why had she come out without her gun? She could have been attacked, and then Angel would have been all alone. She wanted to collapse onto the damp ground and have a good cry. But if she did, the fox might return.

She set the lantern on the ground and inspected the door. The fox must have tugged on the bottom of the door and worked the hinge loose from the frame. She didn't have the means to repair it or the time. She ran her hand through her hair. If she didn't fix the door, the fox would have another free meal tonight. And he might tell his friends.

She could put the chickens in the barn, but it wasn't as secure as the chicken coop had been. She slid a hank of her hair through her fingers and worried the ends. Was there something in the barn she could easily move back and forth as a temporary door? That wouldn't work, because if she could move it, then so could the fox. It would have to be heavy.

She counted the chickens in the coop. Not many were left. One seemed to be struggling for air. She plucked it off the dirt floor and wrung its neck. She could use it to make broth this morning for Angel. Maybe even have enough meat for a small meal. She took the dead chicken outside, found the bucket to stick it in, and placed it on the porch. After she finished the barn chores, she'd take care of pulling out the feathers.

As for the chickens that were still living, it seemed they would be roosting in her cabin come evening.

Chapter 30

Heaven stood at the stove, eyes burning. Sleep was something she didn't remember. She stirred the chicken broth, hoping that this time it would stay down in Angel's stomach instead of erupting all over her. She rubbed the back of her neck where the knots had settled. She took a small sip of the broth to test the flavor. She had plucked the meat off the bone earlier and set it aside on a plate. She would have some for lunch along with the dreaded green beans. And maybe, just maybe Travis would come home and she would have a meal for him.

She regretted the words she shouted at him before he left. Her embarrassment of throwing herself at him and being rejected clung like the fog clung to the cedar trees outside. She wanted to clear that fog like the sun would clear a foggy day. *Did he feel the same?* She had no way to find out until he returned. She didn't even know how Annabelle and Jake and his mother were doing. Had they come down with the measles as well?

She tasted the broth. It was the right temperature, so she dipped it into a cup and took it to Angel. "Can you sit up for me, sweetheart?"

"I don't want any." Angel rolled away from her.

"Angel, you have to try. You won't get better if you don't eat."

"Chicken broth will not cure the measles. Everybody knows that."

"Angel Claire, you sit up right now and try to drink this." Maybe if she'd barked at her like a ferocious dog, her sister would obey.

Using her elbows, Angel scooted herself up into a half-sitting position. She glared at her sister with her red-rimmed eyes. "You know what's going to happen don't you?"

"Until you drink it, we won't know, will we?" She placed the cup in her sister's hand and waited for her to take a sip. She felt her teeth move over her bottom lip as she chewed on it waiting for the results she figured would happen a moment after the broth hit her sister's stomach. But she had to try to get Angel to eat. Heaven didn't have to wait long, as Angel leaned over the edge of the bed and let the contents of her stomach flow into a pan on the floor.

"I told you so." Angel was too tired to even wipe her face before falling back onto her pillow and closing her eyes.

Heaven reached into the other bucket on the floor that held cold water and a rag. She wrung out the rag and with great care wiped her sister's face. "We had to try, sweetie. Next time I will listen to you. I hope you feel better soon, because we have a whole chicken to eat."

Angel groaned. "I don't want to talk about chicken. Or green beans either."

By afternoon Angel no longer complained, as her fever went from a slow-burning ember to a roaring fire. Heaven stroked her sister's face with a cool washcloth and prayed, begging God to save Angel, to bring her back from this rising fever that attacked her. Unlike the broken dishes–patterned quilt on the edge of the bed, if Angel died, Heaven didn't think her life could be pieced back together.

She had no hope of saving her sister. It was like before, with Ma. Only this time she was doing what Travis told her to do, and it wasn't working. She'd lost track of time between emptying sick buckets and wiping cool rags across Angel. Had it been three or four days since Annabelle had left? And Travis hadn't returned since the night he left. Heaven couldn't remember all of the days. Hours and minutes swirled together since Angel got sick.

Unidentifiable stains splashed across the bottom of her apron. She hadn't even changed her clothes for days. And when was the last time she'd combed her hair? Or even ate? None of it mattered now. She dropped the cloth back into the bucket.

Heaven stood and stretched. Washing her sister down wasn't helping, and Heaven felt blackness slipping into her soul. Maybe if she read a few chapters of the Bible, some of God's promises, she'd feel better. She fetched it from the small table next to the fireplace and brought it to the kitchen chair she'd dragged over next to Angel's bedside.

"Angel, I don't know if you can hear me, but I think reading some of God's words will make us both feel better." The weighty book offered the presence of her father and mother almost as if they sat next to her. When Travis had brought it to her, she'd cried, having thought it was lost forever. She realized he'd taken the time to look for the things that meant the most to her, the daguerreotype, the family Bible, and even that silly book on manners. He hadn't found it—Mr. Jackson did—but Travis rescued it for her. He'd been putting her home back together, not just the cabin her father had given to him. Her home.

"Angel, I'm going to read about the little girl that Jesus healed. Do you remember that story? Everyone thought she had died, and they were on the streets mourning her, but Jesus came and said she wasn't dead but merely sleeping." Her sister didn't move, not even a twitch of an eyelid.

Heaven couldn't remember exactly where to look in the Bible for the miraculous story of Jesus healing the girl before he even arrived at her father's home. As she turned the fragile pages, now water-stained and some even creased from the storm, she thought about how many people in her mother's family had turned these same pages. Had they, too, come here when all seemed lost? There weren't any papers or notes stored in it from those relatives. Perhaps they had only seen the book as something to own and not as a way to grow closer to God, as Ma had taught her and Angel.

Pa began to read from its pages only after Ma had passed on. He'd changed a lot after they moved here from Nashville. He no longer stayed away all hours of the night and came home smelling of cigars and whiskey.

She turned another thin page, and her hand stilled. She saw a passage underlined and something written in small letters next to it. She traced the inked line, Matthew 6:34, with her finger as she read. *"Take therefore no thought for the morrow: for the morrow shall take thought for the things of itself. Sufficient unto the day is the evil thereof."*

Underlined. And a note. No one ever wrote in the Holy Book. Was that her pa's handwriting? She turned the book sideways and pulled it closer to the lamplight. The print was so tiny she had to squint to read it: This is the way I want my daughters to live.

She closed the book. The way he wanted her and Angel to live? Without worry? She wanted that, too, but how was that possible when her sister could die? Her head clogged with burning tears straining for release. She swallowed them. Even though her emotions warred with her exhaustion, she wanted to think about this message.

She stood and placed the Bible back on the mantel where she'd been storing it since Travis returned it. She tugged the chair a little closer to the fire and picked up the quilt draped across the back. She sat back between the arms of the battered blue rocker and covered her lap with her grandmother's quilt.

What else didn't she know about Pa? The warmth of the fire melded with the weight of the blanket, and her eyelids shuttered. She wasn't going to fall asleep; she needed to make sure Angel's fever didn't climb higher. She rocked a little bit harder in the chair, hoping the action would help her stay awake. She entered into conversation with God, begging Him to heal Angel from the sickness and to bring Travis back to the cabin soon so they could talk. She had many things to say to him. . . .

Startled, Heaven sprung from the rocking chair. What woke her? Was Travis back? A quick glance at the mantel clock and her heartbeat jumped. She'd slept for almost three hours instead of the few minutes she'd intended.

Angel moaned and thrashed in her bed. Her hand smacked against the wall.

Heaven rubbed her eyes as she sped across the floor to her patient. She bent over and pressed the palm of her hand against her sister's rosy cheek. She yanked it back, gasped, and covered her mouth. Angel's fever was higher than ever. She had to lower it. She knew if she didn't, her sister would die. *Cold water this time, not hot, and no blankets piled to keep Angel warm.* Heaven thanked God for bringing her this knowledge through Travis as she rushed with her bucket to fill it with cold pond water. *Please, God, don't take her away from me.*

Travis wondered how Heaven could go on living after losing so many people she loved. Being a doctor at times like this made him feel inadequate. He was supposed to be a healer, and that's what he had wanted to be. When he chose to be a physician, he thought he would be saving people, making their lives better, bringing joy to the world through babies. Not this. Never this.

He straightened the sheets around the small girl, placing her little hands on top of the sheet. Carefully and artfully he arranged her golden hair and closed her eyes. *Cassie, Angel is going to miss you.* This could be Angel lying here instead of her new friend from church. The memory of Angel's face radiating happiness that day in the barn caught him off guard. He knew she would be heartsick, which meant that Heaven would be as well. Once again he would be the bearer of bad news. He was thankful this wasn't Angel, but she would be devastated. *If she lived.* He took a moment to adjust his expression before turning to the parents and saying the words they didn't want to hear. "I'm sorry. There wasn't anything I could do."

The mother's face collapsed like a melting candle, and her husband held tightly to her waist to keep her from dripping to the floor. But from where did the father pull his strength? Travis couldn't imagine being that strong if it were Angel lying there.

They knew she was dying. They'd caught him before leaving the Shaws'. He'd warned them the minute he'd seen her, but the reality that she really did die hit hard. He supposed parents hold on to hope until the bitter end. He thought about Heaven and wondered how Angel was doing. *Please, God, please let her live. Don't let the measles take her as well.* He excused himself and stumbled out of the bedroom, not wanting the parents to see the grief on his own face. Along with the fear that he might be losing someone he had come to love as a daughter.

The stillness of the room woke Heaven. It was too still. *Angel.* Ice sheathed her veins. Her own heart beat in her ears. She threw aside the quilt. It landed in a puddle on top of her feet. She took a step, but the quilt clung to her feet like lint to cotton, slowing her.

She crossed the room to the bed. Angel lay there still, her hair around her like an angel's halo. *Was she?* Heaven's hand went to her throat. *Please, God.* She bit her bottom lip to keep the cry of anguish from bolting. She laid her palm against her sister's head, expecting to feel the ice cold of the dead.

It was cool, normal cool. No fever remained, and her sister was alive. As the joy of life expanded in her, laughter exploded. "Angel, wake up!"

Her sister stretched her legs under the quilt and then opened one eye. "What's wrong?"

"Nothing's wrong! Everything is right, wonderful! Your fever is gone! You're going to be okay!" Heaven couldn't stop the happy tears—and the snot that came with them. She tugged a hanky from her apron pocket and blew.

"Ew. That's not very proper." Angel sat up in the bed.

"I don't care. I don't care if we are ever proper again as long as you are alive." Heaven crawled into bed next to her sister and gathered her in a hug. "I love you, Angel. Don't you ever scare me with another fever as long as you live. Promise me."

"Okay, but I don't know how to keep that. I'm hungry. Can I have some green beans and taters? I don't want any chicken broth ever again."

"Yes, I'll run down into the root cellar right now."

Angel was awake, and her fever had broken. Heaven couldn't sing enough praises to God for weathering the storm of sickness with her. She'd come out stronger, and she could take care of Angel no matter the circumstances. As soon as she could, she would tell Annabelle that she and Angel would go with her. She loved Travis, but unless he loved her, she couldn't marry him. Despite his kind ways toward her sister, it wouldn't be enough for her. She wanted to be loved the way God loved her. And she had His love now and for always.

She climbed down the ladder to the root cellar. Maybe she should take what was left of the green beans with them to Memphis, because, as her uncle had said, they were life-sustaining even if they weren't appealing after so many days of eating them.

The lamplight flickered and illuminated the jars she'd set aside when the women came the day after the tornado. She might as well take those upstairs and empty them before someone ended up eating them by mistake. She slipped them into the basket she carried.

Once upstairs, she took the jar of beans she would cook and placed it on the table. "Angel, I'll be right back. I want to dump out the jars with the spoiled beans outside."

"Don't take forever. I'm really hungry."

Right now Heaven didn't mind her sister's orders. She was grateful Angel was giving them.

Mr. Jackson waited on the porch. He'd been there since Travis left. Her very own guard goat. "Stay here, and come get me if Angel calls." She laughed. "Now I'm talking to a goat as if he were a living breathing person!"

At the back of the cabin, she popped the lid of the first jar and poured it out. Something chunky landed in the middle of the beans. She held back a gag. The beans were rotten. She opened the second jar and poured. Again something fell out, only this time it clinked against the other thing in the pile. It sounded like metal on metal. What had Great-Uncle put in these beans? She scooted the pile with the edge of her boot. The sunlight streamed into the gray-green mess of beans and sent shots of light back at her. Gold? Could it be? Is that what the message her father had left her meant? What Great-Uncle joked about? She dropped to her knees and slid her hands through the slimy beans and plucked up several gold pieces. Her heart beat rapidly as she opened the other jar and more pieces fell to the ground.

Here was her answer to all of her worries. She might have the means to stay on the farm. If the gold weighed enough, she could buy back her home from Travis.

Or she could take Angel to Missouri to the school.

With the hem of her apron, she wiped the pieces one by one and dropped them into her apron pocket. Sure she had found them all, she stood. The world around her looked fuzzy, as if she were dropped into a fairy-tale land. Even the colors looked brighter to her. Is this what it was like to live in the moment free of worry? Is that what Pa had discovered at some point? It must be why he wrote that message in the Bible. He had no idea that one day she would read it. But God did.

Something nudged her behind. Mr. Jackson tilted his head to her and back to the green beans. "You're right. It's not about the money; it's about what is life-sustaining. I need to remember what I read. Worry will not change anything. God knows my troubles and my happiness."

She turned and ran into the house to tell Angel about the find in the green beans they'd grown to detest. She'd never look at green beans the same way again.

Chapter 31

Travis let Charlie have his head as they rode toward the farm. The horse was as tired as his rider and didn't race to the barn. Travis wasn't sure how he was going to tell Angel about her friend's death. He hadn't been home since the night he told Heaven he didn't want her in the manner she'd offered herself. He hoped that Angel was okay. He should have come sooner or at least sent someone to check on Heaven and Angel.

His head nodded to his chin. He jerked awake just as Charlie entered through the barn door. Pride and Joy nickered when he saw Charlie. Travis dismounted and unbuckled the saddle. He slid it from the horse's back and tossed it over his shoulder. He carried it to the vacant sawhorse next to the one holding Pride and Joy's saddle and plopped it down.

He wished there was someone else who could take care of Charlie for him tonight. As much as he loved brushing horses, it was the last thing he wanted to do. He made quick but careful work of it, put Charlie in his stall, and gave him some grain. The kitten, Miss Simmons, wove between his legs as he walked to the door of the barn. He bent down and picked her up and scratched behind her ears. "Did you miss me? I'll be back as soon as I check on Heaven and Angel, and you can sleep on my chest." He set the kitten gently down on the ground and pulled the barn door shut just far enough that he could squeeze through it when he came back to sleep.

There was one light flickering through the shutter cracks, creating dancing shadows across the porch as he walked the beaten path. At the door, he knocked gently. He waited. No one came. Scared, he flung open the door, hoping that Heaven wouldn't be aiming her father's rifle at him.

The door shuddered against the floorboards, but he didn't hear anything. No cries of alarm. No shouts of "Get out!" Only quiet. He tiptoed inside, and by the firelight, he could see that Angel lay very still on her bed. Heaven was surrounded by chickens on the floor, and her head was resting on Angel's chest. Travis's heart lifted at the sweet scene and then plummeted. Had Angel died?

"Heaven!" His feet propelled him across the room, and he dropped to the floor next to the woman he loved. He touched her hair softly, stroking it so he wouldn't scare her as she woke. Her eyes fluttered for a second and then opened wide as she realized Travis knelt beside her.

"Travis, Angel is fine." She hastened to stand while putting her finger to her lips. He followed her to the door, and they went to the porch. "I thought she was going to die. I really did. But I remembered what you told me, and I did my best to keep her cool despite her asking for more covers. And then this morning—early this morning—she opened her eyes and she wanted to eat something. Green beans! It was a miracle, Travis. God blessed us—He let me keep Angel."

Travis pulled her into his arms, and she nestled into them.

She felt like home. He hugged her tighter, wanting to tell her how much he loved her and missed her. "I am so sorry that I couldn't get back here to help you. I wanted to. Every time I tried to leave, someone else came needing me, asking me, pleading with me to help them save their family members."

"How many died?" Heaven peered at him with eyes of blue. *Could she read that in his face?* "Not as many as I feared. But one death nearly broke me." The words that tried to follow clogged in his throat.

"Who was it?" Heaven brushed the side of his arm with her hand. Her touch comforted him. "You can tell me."

He shook his head and then realized she would find out anyway. "Cassie, Angel's new friend. I tried so hard to save her, but there wasn't anything I could do." He drew from his professional doctor attitude and pasted a calmness he didn't feel across his face. Right now, he didn't want to be a doctor. He was on the edge of shouting he only wanted to be the husband that held her and comforted her.

Heaven wavered like cotton in the wind in front of him, and he noticed the circles the color of eggplant under her eyes. Concerned, he reached out and steadied her. "Have you slept at all since I left?"

"Only a little. Every time I drifted off, it seemed her fever spiked higher, so I began to stay awake to make sure I didn't miss an opportunity to cool her with a washcloth. I am not sure how much longer I could have continued. At one point. . .I thought. . .I'd lost her."

"But you didn't, Heaven. You saved your sister." He took her by the elbow and directed her toward the rocking chair.

"You need to sit and rest. I'll take over watching her tonight."

"But, Travis, you look as tired as I feel. You need to rest in case someone needs you."

"I'm not leaving. Not again."

"Really? I–I'm hoping you're not going to give up doctoring because of what I said before you left. I need to talk to you. Travis, some things have changed. I've changed."

"I can see that. Why are the chickens in the house?"

"The door won't close, and there was a fox inside killing the chickens. I had it trapped, but I didn't have my gun. I couldn't leave Angel alone or I would have waited for it to return so I could kill it. I decided rather than lose what little food we have left, I'd bring the critters inside." She wrinkled her nose. "It wasn't my best decision. They make a mess, and it smells in here."

"I'll fix the door tomorrow, and then I'll help you clean this up. I have some things I need to tell you as well. If you're not going to go to sleep, maybe we should make some coffee and talk." He let go of her but held on to her hand and walked her to the rocking chair. Once she was settled, he snatched up the quilt that lay on the floor and draped it over her lap.

"The stove should still be warm. I made dinner for us."

"Good, then it won't take as long to make the coffee." He headed to the stove to put on a pot. During his absence, he couldn't wait to get home to her, reinforcing the feeling of love in his heart. He was going to ask her to marry him. He touched his pocket where his great-grandmother's small gold ring rested. His mother had insisted that he bring it along with him even though Travis was reluctant. His mother was confident God would provide the perfect mate for him, and it seemed He had. But first Travis wanted to be sure Heaven no longer had feelings for Jake.

Travis knelt in front of the chair and looked into Heaven's eyes. Was this the right time ask her? No. She was exhausted. He would give her the news that he brought from town and then make sure she went to sleep upstairs in the loft while he looked after her sister. Tomorrow would be better. That's when he would ask her. Things always looked better in the light of day, and he didn't want to follow bad news with a marriage proposal.

"Heaven, I saw Jake and Annabelle in town. They didn't stay at the hotel. Jake acquired tickets for Nashville."

"But, Travis, you told them to stay to make sure they didn't get sick. I need to send a telegram and see how they are." She threw back the quilt from her lap.

Travis put both hands on her arms and stared at her eyes. "Not tonight. Besides, Annabelle sent you a letter. I have it in my pocket. And Jake asked me to tell you something." He looked away from her. He didn't want to see the pain in her eyes when he told her—if there was pain.

"What did Jake say?" Heaven's voice held a hint of sorrow.

"He said. . ." Travis could feel the tension mounting across his shoulder blades as he worked for the right words to leave his lips. "He asked me to tell you that he hoped you would understand, but he was releasing you from his marriage promise. He wanted to tell you in person, but he never got the chance and didn't want to wait until it was safe to come back to the cabin." Travis thought the man a coward. He didn't like to say that about another man, but in this case, he felt justified. It wasn't right not to tell Heaven in person that he wouldn't marry her.

She didn't say anything. She sat there quiet for a moment. He looked at her, afraid he'd see tears spiraling down her face. Instead, she had no expression at all. "Heaven? Are you okay?"

She blinked. "Yes. I didn't think marrying Jake felt right anymore. He wanted me to go west with him and look for gold. And leave Angel with his mother. I couldn't do that, especially now that I almost lost her again. She will always be a part of my life and will always live with me. No man is going to take her away from me."

She stared at him as if he were the one who suggested Angel live somewhere else.

The fire crackled and sent a spark in the air. Angel rolled over in the bed, and Heaven's eyes went to her immediately. Travis jumped to his feet. "I'll check on her. Stay here and rest."

He felt her presence behind him so close he could feel her breath on his neck. He should have known she wouldn't stay, but he wouldn't send her back. He knelt down next to Angel and whispered her name. "Angel? Are you awake? I've come back to see you. How are you feeling?"

Angel rolled over and faced him. Her face was gaunt and white even with the yellow lamplight. She looked so much smaller than when he left, as if she had lost ten pounds even.

"Hi. You were gone a long time. Heaven had to bring the chickens in the house. It smells funny. Are you going to fix the chicken coop door so they can leave?" She rubbed her eyes and yawned. "I'm glad you're back. Heaven missed you, and so did I. I hope you won't leave again."

"I'm not going anywhere, Angel." He bent over and whispered in her ear so Heaven couldn't hear him. "Nothing can make me leave you two ever again."

"Heaven?" Angel's eyes fluttered open. "I'm hungry. Did you tell Travis about the green beans yet?"

Travis whipped his head around and looked at Heaven. Was Angel falling back into another fever?

"No. I'll tell him later. First I will get you something to eat. How about a little chicken broth?"

"No! Please, can't I have something else?"

"Heaven, I think that she could try a little food."

"I ate the green beans, and they stayed down, but I don't want any more of those."

"What about a piece of toast? Would you like that Angel? Does that sound good?" Travis stroked the little girl's arm.

"Can I have some jam Annabelle brought on it?"

"Of course you can," Heaven said. "I'll make it right now."

"No. You sit with your sister, and I will make it."

Angel gave a weak laugh. "Men don't cook."

"This one does." He fished in his pocket and withdrew Annabelle's letter. "You read this while I make a mess of what's left clean in your kitchen. Those chickens have made themselves at home in there."

She smiled at him. The sadness he'd experienced in the past days melted away.

"Thank you." She tore open the envelope and read aloud.

Dear Heaven and Angel,

I hope you recover quickly. Jake has arranged for us to leave by carriage in a few moments. He thinks I am going back with them to Nashville. I am not. I am going to continue on with the plans I discussed with you, providing I can find a way to exchange my ticket for Memphis. I'll write to you as soon as I am settled. You and Angel are welcome to come to Memphis and live with me. There we can be our own little family and take care of ourselves, answering to no man. Affectionately,

Annabelle

She folded the letter and stuck it in her apron pocket.

"I hope Jake is able to stop her." Travis feared for the young woman, thinking she could travel alone and not be accosted in these times of restless recovery.

"I'm afraid Annabelle is headstrong, and Jake doesn't seem to have much strength to fight anything right now. She may get her way unless Mrs. Miles manages to change Annabelle's mind, and that is very likely. I shall pray that is what happens."

"You wouldn't want to go with her?" Travis asked.

"We could. But I don't think it's the right thing to do for Angel."

"Is anyone going to bring me toast with jam?" Angel wrinkled her nose. "Heaven, we really need to get these chickens out of here."

"Yes, of course. I'll start making that toast right away, Little Miss. And it's good to see you feeling better and ordering us around."

"You see, Travis, Angel is back to being a sweet young lady with all the rules memorized from our book." Heaven slid a hand over her mouth. Her laugh snuck past her fingers.

Angel fell back against the pillow. "The proper Angel is gone. And she is never coming back." She struggled back up on her elbows, "Did I miss Christmas?"

Heaven turned and looked at Travis. "What day is it?"

"Tomorrow is Christmas. It's Christmas Eve." The crestfallen look on her face told him she wasn't prepared. "Don't worry, I'm pretty sure Christmas will be wonderful. We will celebrate Angel being healthy." And while they were sleeping, he planned to do a little decorating of his own to bring Christmas joy to the house. And as tired as Heaven looked, he was sure she would sleep through the entire process. He only hoped that Angel would as well, since she was downstairs. Unless now that she was feeling better he could convince her to go upstairs in the loft and sleep with her sister.

Travis had worked through the night quietly carrying out chickens and putting them back into the coop after fixing the door by lantern light. Neither Heaven nor Angel had put up much of a fight about sleeping in the loft once he said he wanted to clean up the mess made by the chickens. Angel thought it was good to sleep somewhere else besides a bed of hay, and Heaven was happy just to lie down with her sister.

Once the chickens were out of the house, he made quick work of scrubbing the floor by candlelight. Then he went outside and cut down a very small cedar to use as a Christmas tree. He set it up in the corner of the living room and wondered what he could use to decorate it. Scratching his head, he could not come up with any ideas. There might be decorations somewhere in the cabin, but he didn't know where to look and probably shouldn't. Instead, he folded up a sheet of paper and wrote Heaven's name on the back and put it under the tree. He then went to the barn to retrieve from his saddlebag the new toy he had bought for Angel for Christmas. By then it was time to do the morning chores. When he came back inside, the two of them were still sleeping, which made his plan all that much better. He banked the fire, poking it until it blazed with warmth. Then he filled the coffeepot with water and ground the beans before placing the pot on the stove.

Upstairs he could hear Heaven and Angel waking up. There were some whispers and giggles, and finally he heard feet coming down the stairs. He turned to greet them, "Merry Christmas!"

They returned the greeting, both wearing huge smiles.

Heaven looked around the room with wonder. "Angel, there's a tree. Travis put up a tree for us. And the chickens are gone."

"I thought it smelled better." Angel touched her sister's hand, "Where is the tree?"

Heaven wound her fingers through her sister's hand. "Come with me. It's in the corner." She led Angel to the tree. "Travis, this is the most special tree we've ever had."

"What does it look like? What decorations are on it? Are there candles?" Angel reached out and brushed the branches in front of her.

"I'm sorry there aren't any. I didn't want to wake you up

trying to find something to decorate the tree with. I thought maybe we could do it together today." Travis stood behind the girls. "If we have it decorated by this afternoon, we could make a very special Christmas dinner with some of the things that I brought back from town."

Angel popped a hand over her open mouth and squealed. "Did you bring back good food? Like candy?"

"You will just have to wait and see."

"I have a few things I want to put under the tree to open this evening, too." Heaven's nose crinkled up as she noticed there was something under the tree with her name on it. Her hand snaked out to reach for the paper. "Is this for me?"

"Yes it is, but you have to wait." Travis loved this part of Christmas. He had missed the past few Christmases while he was away at war. Memories of teasing his sisters and his sisters teasing him about packages that were hidden and what they might contain filled him with happiness. As did this package he left under the tree. It would make Heaven smile.

Later that evening the three of them gathered around the tree. At Travis's request they sang Christmas songs.

"Can we open the gifts now?" Angel bounced on tiptoes.

He hadn't told her about her friend yet. That sad news could wait a day. "Yes, Angel, let's open the presents." He reached under the tree and withdrew the doll he'd bought for her at the general store and placed it in her waiting hands.

Carefully she pulled the paper away. Her hand moved over the porcelain face and the hair. "Heaven, it's a doll! What does she look like? Are her eyes blue like mine?"

"Yes they are, and when you tip her as if you were putting

her to bed, they close. Her hair is the color of sunshine on hay."

Heaven's voice seemed thick with emotion. Travis hoped he hadn't made her sad. He reached over and withdrew the paper from under the tree. "This is for you."

Her sapphire eyes gazed at him, questioning.

"Open it."

She unfolded the paper and read it. "Travis, are you sure?"

"Yes I am. This place should belong to you and Angel, not me. I don't know why your father gave it to me."

"Because he knew you, Travis. He knew you would come here and find us and make sure we were okay."

"That's not all, Heaven. There's something. . ." He gave a quick glance at Angel who seemed to be involved in figuring out how to unbutton her doll's dress. "Can you step out on the porch with me?"

She nodded, but he noticed she kept a tight grip on the deed to the farm.

Outside he grasped her hand in his. "I never wanted to marry someone because it's what people do. I wanted to fall in love and have a marriage like my parents. When your father *gave* you to me, it bothered me sorely."

She tried to pull her hand back, but he held tight.

"Wait, I'm not done."

Her hand stilled in his, and he could feel her pulse in her fingertips.

"I'm sure by now you realize how much I care for you. I love you. I love Angel as well. And while I know your father gave you to me in his will, I want you to want me." He bent down on one knee. "Miss Heaven Wharton, would you please do me the honor of becoming Mrs. Travis Logan?"

He watched her eyes widen, and tears pooled, creating a sapphire lake.

"I will."

Travis hopped to his feet and gathered her in an embrace, kissed her like a man in love, and then let out a whoop of joy.

"You must of told him about the gold," Angel said.

"Gold?"

"No, not yet, Angel. He asked me to marry him, and I said yes. Travis, I discovered why there were so many green beans. Great-Uncle used them instead of the bank to deposit his gold. So I'd like to give you some of it for Christmas. With that you can achieve your dream of raising horses on the Logan Farm."

"How about we call it the WL for Wharton and Logan?" Travis wanted to hug her again.

"I like it," Angel said from the doorway. "I'm going back inside to play with my doll so you can kiss each other again."

"Travis, don't give up being a doctor. You can do both. This town needs you. God gave you the gift of healing and teaching. You taught me how to care for Angel, and I'm sure there are other things I—as well as the people of Friendship—can learn. I'd give you all of the money, but"—she looked to see if Angel was really inside—"I'd like to send Angel to school someday to learn to read Braille."

Heaven stroked his arm, starting a fire the size of a barn. He backed away. "Honey, I'll do what you ask if you will do this one thing for me."

"What?" Her eyes narrowed as her head tilted.

"Ride into town with me right now and marry me so

I don't have to spend another night without you by my side."

She smiled, and her eyes sparkled with joy. "I'd be honored. I'll get Angel, and you get the wagon."

"I'll get the wagon"—he pulled her to him—"after I kiss you one last time as Miss Wharton."

Angel stuck her head out the door. "Does that mean once she's Mrs. Logan you won't be wastin' time kissin' anymore?"

"No, Little Miss, that's never going to stop. You'll have to get used to it."

A BRIDE'S FLIGHT FROM VIRGINIA CITY, MONTANA

by Murray Pura

Dedication

For Lyyndae
My wife & my friend & the first reader of all my stories

Chapter 1

Charlotte Spence lay in her comfortable down bed with the big goose-feather pillows a few minutes longer and listened to the grandfather clock downstairs strike the hour— one, two, three, four, five. Not for the first time, she wondered how she was able to sleep through those loud gongs in the dead of night. She closed her eyes again and whispered a quick prayer.

Lord, it's Your day. Give me the strength and wisdom I need. Open the gates You want opened, close the ones You don't. In Christ's name. Amen.

She stepped out of bed in her blue flannel nightgown and went to the washstand. Lighting an oil lamp and setting it on a nearby table, she washed her face and hands then crossed over to the dresser where she sat down and began to brush out her long blond hair while she read from the Bible. She was working her way through Psalm 119.

My soul is continually in my hand:
    yet do I not forget thy law.
The wicked have laid a snare for me:
    yet I erred not from thy precepts.

Thy testimonies have I taken as an heritage for ever:
  for they are the rejoicing of my heart.
I have inclined mine heart to perform thy statutes alway,
  even unto the end.

"There's a thought, Lord," she said out loud. "Your words and promises as my heritage—not beef cattle and acres of land and abundant water. Those are wonderful. But to think of You as my heritage! That's something that goes beyond horses and ranching and wide open spaces." She suddenly recalled a verse she'd read the morning before: *"I have seen an end of all perfection: but thy commandment is exceeding broad."*

Going to the closet, she glanced at the calendar on the wall with its engraving of a cowboy on a wildly bucking horse. It was Tuesday, February 2, 1875. She would be riding, not going to church, so she looked to her thick woolen riding skirts with leggings and her heavy jackets and sweaters. Above zero or not, she picked out warm gear and her blue woolen coat. After she had finished dressing, she crossed to the window and glanced out. It was still dark and would be for several more hours, but she could see by the stars it promised to be a clear morning. A thermometer was fastened to the outside of the window frame, and she squinted at it—ten above. An unexpected warm spell in the dead of winter. *The west wind brought the mild weather,* she thought to herself as she went back to the dresser and mirror to pin up her hair. *It shook the house all night.*

She left her room and went down the stairs, holding the lamp in her hand. The rich smell of fresh coffee brought her into the kitchen. It was empty at this hour, but by six o'clock all her hands would be trooping through the back door and sitting down at the large table for breakfast. Most of them had already been on the range for an hour or more. She poured herself a cup of coffee from a big pot on the woodstove. As she drank it, standing close to the stove's heat, she caught the scent of eggs and bacon and beans from the warming oven. Pete always made good, strong coffee, but his meals were even better. And his biscuits were legendary. Turning this over in her mind, she opened the small door of the warming oven and plucked two buttermilk biscuits from a plate heaped high, dropping them into a pocket. *Filching,* her mother would say. She smiled and put the coffee cup in the sink. On the way out of the kitchen, she took a red apple from a basket. Then paused and went back to the warming oven to filch two more biscuits.

"It will be a long morning's ride," she said to the empty kitchen.

She brought a Winchester 1873 carbine down from a gun rack in the hall and checked to make sure it was loaded, then opened a drawer under the rack and put a box of .44-40 cartridges in her jacket pocket. A light brown Stetson was hanging from a peg by the front door, and she placed it on her head. Two high leather boots were standing on the floor beneath the hat. She sat in a chair and tugged them on. Then she took a black scarf and wound it about her neck. It might be ten above, but a stiff breeze could still cut like a bowie knife.

She stepped onto the porch, pulling on a pair of leather gloves, and two of her men swept off their hats as they stood talking with the cook.

"Miss Spence," the three men said at the same time.

"Mr. Laycock. Mr. Martin. Pete. Are you about ready to ring that piece of scrap iron for breakfast?"

"We are," grinned Pete. "I hope you grabbed a bite before the boys ride in. They won't leave a crumb."

"I don't need anything, Pete, thanks," she said, the biscuits still warm in her skirt pocket.

"Save you a plate for when you get back in?"

"That's kind of you. Yes, please." She turned to Laycock and Martin. "May I?"

"Why sure." Laycock handed her the striker.

"I hardly ever get to do it anymore."

The iron she was going to hit was the rim off a wheel from one of the first wagons her brother Ricky had used on the Spence ranch. It was still sturdy as a rock. She bent her arm and banged the iron bar against it. The rim rang clear and sharp through the star-nicked air. The shock went right up her arm to her shoulder, but she knew one blow wasn't enough. She swung the striker back and forth inside the wheel rim as fast as she could so that the ringing was loud and unmistakable no matter where her hands might be. Then she handed the striker back to Layton.

"That's certainly enough to raise the dead," she said with a laugh.

"The boys will come pelting in from all four corners," agreed Laycock.

"So how are things?" she asked the men. "Anything I should know about?"

"We're getting some early calves," replied Laycock. "This mild spell sure helps us out on that score."

"I'll keep an eye out for the young ones then. I'm going to do my monthly ride over the ranch this morning."

"Yes ma'am, you look like you're loaded for bear."

"Anything else?" she asked.

"There's been predators," Martin spoke up. "We haven't found anything that's been killed yet, but the tracks are plentiful. Fox. Coyote. Maybe a cat. Can't tell for sure; the tracks were messed up."

"By what?"

"Horse hooves."

"Whose horse hooves?"

Laycock and Martin glanced at each other.

"We don't rightly know, Miss Spence," Martin finally responded. "But we do know one thing. It's none of our boys."

"How many riders?"

"Half a dozen. Maybe a few more. Traveling fast. Headin' north. The tracks are a couple of days old."

Charlotte stared at him. "Are any cattle missing?"

"Boys are doing a head count. So far, so good. But we ain't got to every part of the herd."

"Where are these tracks?"

"Couple miles west. By Lookoff."

"The marshal hasn't sent us word about rustlers in the vicinity, has he?"

"No ma'am."

"Let the men get a hot meal in their stomachs before they do anymore of that counting. The sun will be up soon, and that will make their job a lot easier." She smiled brightly. "Well, perhaps my ride won't be uneventful."

Laycock and Martin glanced at each other a second time. This time Laycock spoke up, Stetson still in his hands.

"Miss Spence, perhaps it'd be best if one of the boys was to ride with you. Gallagher, say, or Scotty."

"Ride with me?" Charlotte looked at him in surprise, her eyes opening wide. "Whatever for?"

"Well, there could be the panther; that's reason enough. But a group of riders belting out across our land headed for who knows where? Sounds like outlaws."

Charlotte made a face. "You don't really think so."

"Me and Martin and the rest of the hands think it's a pretty safe bet. There's been talk."

"What kind of talk?"

"About marauders in the neighborhood. About squatters being burned out down on the flats."

Charlotte's eyebrows came together sharply. "Were people killed?"

"Some say no. Others say it was bad."

"But the marshal hasn't said anything about it?"

"It's just rumors, ma'am. I expect we'll hear something, one way or the other, when Marshal Parker gets to the bottom of it."

"'The west wind carries blue skies and blue skies carry lies,'" Charlotte recited. "My mother again. It seems I'm always quoting her."

Martin smiled. "Wish we'd had a chance to meet her."

"So do I, Mr. Martin." She tugged on the brim of her Stetson. "I'd better be on my way. If things are as bad as you say, the men will never let me out of sight of the ranch house."

"You should reconsider," urged Laycock.

"I am twenty-five years old. I've been riding this land since I was a teenage girl. Even Jesse James and his barbarians couldn't keep me off God's good gift to the Spence family and its hands. I'll be back by noon." She glanced at the cook. "I hope the food will be hot, Pete."

"Hot, thick, and three plates full," he responded.

Charlotte was striding across the yard to the stables. "Three plates? Are you trying to fatten me up for the kill?"

Her saddle was hanging clean and dry from a brass hook on the wall. She lit an oil lamp by the door and carried it close to where Daybreak stood in her stall, watching her mistress with large dark eyes. Charlotte brought out the apple.

"Here's a treat, girl. Let's have a good ride together, all right?"

The palomino mare chewed and slobbered over the red apple before taking it into her mouth and working over what was left of it. Charlotte came into the stall and put a saddle blanket and saddle on its back, tightening the cinch under the horse's stomach. Then she slid the carbine into a scabbard. Leading Daybreak out of her stall, she spoke to the other horses that stood watching everything carefully and nickering their comments. At the door to the stable, Charlotte paused and looked out.

Men were riding up to the ranch house, hitching their horses to the rail, then walking around to the back where they'd head in, wash their hands, and sit at the kitchen table for the morning meal. Even those who'd been too far off to hear her striking the wheel rim knew to be at the table by six. The ranch house shone like a star, with oil lamps burning in all its ground-floor windows, drawing the cowboys in from miles around. She smiled as she listened to their banter.

"What you been doing all morning, Scotty? Grabbing some more shut-eye in the hills back yonder?"

"Billy, I could be asleep in the saddle and still work more cattle, and work 'em better, than you sitting wide-awake and ramrod stiff on that half-pint pony of yours."

"Pony? You say Bill's got a pony? Here all along I could have sworn it was a mule."

"Oh, he's got both. Rides the pony on Tuesdays and Thursdays and the mule the rest of the time."

"Glad you cleared that up, Scotty. I thought Billy Gallagher was two different men on two different nags and drawing two different paychecks from the Spence outfit."

"So I am, you worn-out old cowpokes. Why, Charlotte Spence has made Billy number one foreman and Billy number two head wrangler—I aim to retire a rich man in a few more months."

"You fellahs can stand here and spin your yarns right through breakfast if that's what pleases you. But me, I'll take bacon and beans over a cowboy's dreams. Adios."

Charlotte waited a bit longer, until she was sure all the men had ridden in and were seated at the table. Then she led Daybreak from the stable and swung up into the saddle. Urging the mare into a trot, she went across the yard and headed for the eastern end of the ranch. She was pretty sure Laycock and Martin would tell the hands she was headed west to Lookoff and send a few of them out that way to keep an eye on her. Charlotte had every intention of having a look at the panther tracks herself, as well as the trail of the riders her foremen thought might be outlaws, but not until she was sure she could be up there on her own. Her ranch hands were all good men, but she had to make sure they understood she could handle things without their help. Otherwise, how could she command their obedience and respect? Picking up the fence line, she followed it north under the winter stars. Yes, it was mild out for early February, but she still felt a sting on her cheeks.

For two hours she crossed streams that were running or partly frozen in the dark, found healthy calves with their mothers, and spotted knots and clusters of her herd happy to find good grass where the snow had melted back. Eventually she made her way up a ridge where there was a tall pinnacle of rock she called the Sentinel. She hardly ever mentioned the place to others, even though it was one of her favorite spots on the ranch, simply because she wanted to have it to herself. Her foremen wouldn't think to send Scotty or Gallagher here.

She sat back in her saddle and brought two buttermilk biscuits from her pocket. Cold as ice, they still tasted pretty good. As she chewed and swallowed, the sun rose like a great yellow and orange ball over the valley and hurled bright light at the Rocky Mountains to the west. The sight made her stop eating and hold in her breath. The white snow on the peaks burned like a world on fire. Was there any part of America more overflowing with grandeur, more rugged, and more beautiful than the Montana Territory?

"And God said, 'Let there be light' and plenty of it!" she called, her words echoing back twice over. "And so there was light! Light that had no end! Light that could not be stopped!"

She laughed in sheer delight and went back to her biscuits while she looked over the land that was spread out beneath her. Sweet Blue Meadows. Two Back Valley. The Shining Mountains. What a location her brother Ricky had found to build the Spence ranch. What a gift. It was impossible to get tired of gazing out over heartland that was God's land, land He had shared with the creatures made in His image, the human race. All kinds of people loved Montana—Indian, white, black, Chinese, Spanish. Sometimes they fought, sometimes they lived in peace. But they held in common their respect and passion for the rocks, grass, earth, and boundless sky.

Then, as the sun fully emerged, bringing the blue sky with it and making everything gleam, a feeling of deep sadness rushed through Charlotte. The sensation was so strong it made her wince. Her father and mother were dead. All her brothers and sisters were dead. No one sat on his horse beside her, loving God and God's land as she did, loving her, gazing at her with a fascination that told her he cared more for her beauty than that of the great mountains themselves. The big ranch house was empty except when her hired hands rode in for their three squares a day—no children slid down its banisters or chased each other through its halls or hollered through its windows and doorways. For a few minutes she let tears streak over her face. So much to enjoy and no man, no family, to enjoy it with.

For a few moments she let the faces of various men drift through her thoughts. Many of them had been handsome but were not men of faith. Others followed God but did not know their way around a lasso or branding iron or beef cattle. Still others seemed to love the idea of being connected to Charlotte

Spence and the Spence ranch but did not know how to love her.

She leaned into the saddle horn with her gloved hands. No, nothing had worked out. Well, she'd had her cry. She flicked the mare's reins. There was no use in carrying on like this. She was a woman alone and had to get used to it.

To make her way to Lookoff she had to come down from the Sentinel and the ridge, so she coaxed Daybreak along a trail that led to the valley bottom. Then she walked the palomino through thickets and scattered boulders. There was still snow on the highlands, so she didn't think all the tracks would have disappeared with the thaw. Her brother had taught her how to read signs, and she was curious to see what she would come up with when she examined the pugmarks—mountain lion, panther, something that wasn't even remotely like a cat?

The crying of a calf jolted her out of her thoughts. She put her horse into a trot and saw the calf standing by a large rock, its young eyes wide in terror, bawling for help. Without even thinking about it, Charlotte slid the Winchester from its scabbard and walked the horse closer. Now she saw the body of a cow just beyond where the calf was tottering on its thin legs. Instinctively she knew it was the calf's mother. Then a head lifted from the far side of the carcass. A mountain lion.

Charlotte barely had time to take it all in before the big cat growled deep in its chest and sprang, bounding over the dead body and making for the horse. Daybreak reared just as Charlotte fired, and the shot went wild. The mare kicked out at the lion with her front hooves. The cat darted around to the horse's back, and Daybreak whirled and struck with her hind legs, missing the mountain lion but throwing Charlotte to the ground. Just missing a pile of rocks, she rolled and took dirt and grass into her mouth. The palomino ran off, squealing loudly, and the lion turned to Charlotte, its eyes spitting fury. She had trouble bringing the Winchester to bear, the barrel sticking into the soft soil. The cat was going to pounce.

Jesus, help me. Help me.

The lion was on top of her, roaring and trying to bite through her neck and head. She yanked the barrel clear and shoved it into the cat's snarling mouth. Her finger was outside the trigger guard, and she wasn't able to fire. The cat thrust claws at her face, and Charlotte twisted her head and shoulders. This movement jerked her finger onto the trigger. She squeezed. The blast made her ears sting. She was able to work the lever and fire again. Then the weight and hot breath of the lion were on her face, and she almost passed out.

The lion was not biting or moving. Charlotte tried to push herself out from underneath, but it took some time. Finally she was free and sat back, trying to get a lungful of air and staring at the animal, her carbine still in her hands. As frightened as she was, she could not help but marvel at the mountain lion's strong body and long tail, at its wild and powerful beauty. She bent her head and leaned it against the warm Winchester barrel.

I wish it had never hunted my cattle. I wish it had never strayed onto our range. But thank You, God, that I'm alive. Thank You.

Finally she climbed to her feet and glanced around for Daybreak. The mare was about a hundred feet away, her head turned toward her mistress and the cat. Charlotte slowly walked to her, speaking softly.

"It's all right, girl. The lion won't bother you anymore. Don't run. You're safe. Yes, it's me."

The mare didn't move, but rubbed its nose on Charlotte's arm and snuffled against the sleeve of her thick winter jacket. Charlotte put her head against the mare's and closed her eyes. "We're both alive. We made it. Rest easy, girl. Thank God, we're both okay."

The crying of the calf made her look up.

"That's enough excitement for today," she said to Daybreak. "Let's get the calf back to the ranch and get it some milk. Keep it alive. It's all about life, girl, all about keeping things alive."

Not wanting to take the mare close to the cat's body, she tied the horse's reins to a nearby aspen and then walked over to get the calf. It was happy to be picked up and comforted, burying its little head in Charlotte's chest. Then she came back to Daybreak, took the reins in her hand while holding the calf tightly with the other, and after a couple of tries, got up into the saddle. The calf cried out at this but once the horse started moving, the rocking motion seemed to comfort it. Charlotte kept to the valley floor and moved the palomino along at a slow trot. It would take a couple of hours to reach the main ranch.

"You hold on, young one," Charlotte whispered to the calf. "I intend to take good care of a little orphan like you."

The calf was asleep but alive when Charlotte walked Daybreak into the yard in front of the house. It was about ten o'clock, she reckoned. She never used a watch while out on horseback but preferred to estimate time by the position of the sun. Billy Gallagher was sitting on his horse and gulping down a mug full of coffee Pete had just handed up to him when they both saw her. Billy was off his horse and at her side in an instant.

"What happened to you?" he asked, reaching up for the calf.

Charlotte placed it in his arms. "I guess I ran into that panther of yours."

"Where?"

"Just below the Sentinel. It killed the calf's mother."

"What happened to the cat?"

"It's dead."

"Are you cut? Are you bleeding anywhere?"

"I don't know."

"You look like you took a tumble down a mountain slope." Pete helped her down from the mare. "Better let me look you over. Come inside."

She looked at Billy. "The calf needs warm milk."

"Did it have a few days to feed off its mother?"

"I think so. She's pretty sturdy."

Billy nodded. "I'll take care of it." He headed toward the barn.

"What about Daybreak?" called Charlotte.

"I'll take care of her, too. Don't fret. Let Pete clean you up."

It didn't take long for word to get around the ranch that the Spence outfit's ramrod had tangled with a mountain lion, and the mountain lion had come up short. Not only that, but Charlotte Spence hardly had a nick on her despite firing off two rounds with the lion pretty much sitting on her head. Charlotte lay down for an hour in her room but heard the ruckus when the hands came in for lunch. Scotty had brought in the cat, and most of the men would have seen it when they rode up. She could tell that the talk around the table was louder than usual and pushed herself off the bed.

I had plans to do chores in town this afternoon. A brush with a mountain lion shouldn't change that. And the boys will want to see me.

She put on a blue dress with lace at the collar, pinned up her hair, and headed down the staircase. The men all stood up when she entered the kitchen, dropping their forks and knives and asking after her health. She smiled. They treated her like one of their sisters.

"Boys, I'm fine. It was a good bit of excitement, I can tell you that, but I'm none the worse for wear. Pete has given me a clean bill of health, haven't you, Pete?"

Pete was wearing a large apron and placing another pot of coffee on the table. "A few thumps and bumps, but she's sturdy as an oak."

"There you are. So thank you all for your concern, but please, sit down and finish your meals. How is the calf, Mr. Gallagher?"

"Top notch, Miss Spence. Drank her fill and more. She'll be all right."

"That's good news. And Daybreak?"

"Not a scratch on her, Miss Spence. I rubbed her down and gave her some oats, and she's resting in her stall."

"Thank you very much. You're a good man." She looked around the table. "You're all good men. I'm blessed to have such a solid outfit to keep the Spence ranch up and running."

"Our pleasure, ma'am," said Laycock.

"And now, if you don't mind, I'll need the black hitched up to my Philadelphia buggy, Mr. Martin, for I have some matters in town to attend to."

"Miss Spence," Martin protested, "are you sure you're fit for that?"

"I certainly am. After all, the excitement only lasted a minute or two. I'm rested up. Pete stood over me and forced me to eat hot buttermilk biscuits with gravy to restore my strength, and now I need to get into Iron Springs before this lovely February day is gone forever. I assure you, gentlemen, that considering the morning I had, an afternoon in town is going to prove most uneventful."

She was on her way in ten minutes, the black stepping smartly along the road into Iron Springs, the dark buggy rolling smoothly through the puddles and mud behind it. Charlotte was wearing a bonnet and leaning back, comfortably holding the traces in her hands. She thought about her work at the library, some sewing items and fabric she meant to purchase at the general store, and whether today was a good time to discuss some issues with her attorney, Mr. King.

A bird burst across her path and startled her. For some reason, a face popped into her head immediately afterwards. A man she had been interested in once. Zephaniah Parker. A kind man. A strong man. A young man about her age, who had his own small ranch and ran it well. A man who honored God. She bit her lower lip and thought about him for a few minutes. Then she shook her head in annoyance and flicked the reins. She had hardly seen him more than once or twice over the past year, and for all she knew, he didn't even live in the region anymore. She might never see him again and that was that.

"God's will be done," she murmured to herself and turned her mind back to the sorts of fabrics she needed to pick out at the store and which sorts of buttons would go best with what colors.

Chapter 2

Zeph eased his horse over the ridge and down the slope. Cricket was making a lot of noise and grumbling into her bit. She didn't like the slush, and she liked the ice even less.

"I know it," Zeph said to her as she blew loudly through her nostrils. "But I'm keeping us off the trail because it's even worse. We'll be into some open grass in a bit."

The sky was so blue and so bright it hurt Zeph's eyes. It was February and ought to have been colder, but a thaw had come in with the west wind and melted all the snow back. Zeph liked the break from below zero, and so did his cattle, but when it cooled off at night you wound up with too many patches of ice—bad for horses, bad for the cows.

Cricket snapped her head back.

"Whoa!" called Zeph. "What was that for? You got grass under your hooves now."

She reared. Zeph stared all around, trying to find out what was spooking her. All he saw was a thin line of smoke off to the left, coming from behind a clump of gray cottonwoods with their bare branches all tangled. That's where some of the new homesteaders from out east had settled in back before Christmas. That wouldn't be it. He looked down—there weren't any snakes out in February, even during a thaw. What was going on with his mare?

She balked, didn't want to go any farther. Zeph swung down and held her reins while he inspected the ground in front of them. Just dead winter grasses, brown as dust. Wet some from snowmelt, but that was about it. He got down on one knee—and saw the bloody footprint.

Not large. No boot. High arch. The wound seemed to be in the back by the heel. He squinted ahead. There were more of them, crossing over the grass and soft snow. Cricket protested, but he tugged her forward as he followed the prints.

"Two of 'em," he said out loud.

The two sets of tracks were obvious in the snow. The blood was pretty fresh. He kept walking, pulling Cricket along. The prints went into a gully. Cricket snorted. She had seen the two heads first.

"Hello!" Zeph called. "You all right?"

The heads ducked out of sight.

Zeph tilted his brown Stetson back and scratched at his head.

"One of you looks to have a cut. I have some bandage in my saddlebag. Good clean cloth."

Still no answer. He rubbed his jaw and thought for a moment.

"I'm Zephaniah Parker. I own the Bar Zee, just a few miles west of here in the Two Back Valley. I'm out looking for strays. Been living by the mountains for five or six years. My brother's the preacher at the church in town. And my other brother's the federal marshal. You can come out. I'm not gonna hurt you."

After a moment a boy stood up, tall and skinny, about twelve, Zeph figured. He seemed to totter on one leg. He didn't say anything. Then a girl stood up and clutched the boy's hand. She was half a foot shorter, straw-blond hair, maybe ten or eleven. Neither of them smiled.

"Can I come closer?" asked Zeph. "Take a look at that foot?"

The boy nodded. "All right."

Cricket had calmed down, and Zeph brought her over to the gully and wrapped her reins around some thick scrub. He smiled at the girl and boy. Up close now, he could see their faces were scratched, their cheeks hollow; they looked tired and gaunt. He rummaged around in one of his saddlebags while Cricket munched grass. He finally held up some strips of white cotton cloth.

"Told you I had some."

He knelt by the boy.

"You wanna show me your sore foot?"

The boy lifted his left foot, and Zeph saw the cut on the heel. It was pretty clean from all the melted snow, but he wiped some mud and grass away before he started wrapping.

"Neither of you have shoes?"

"No," said the boy.

"What happened to 'em?"

"I don't know."

Zeph shrugged, finished the wrapping, and stood up.

"The next thing is to get you home. Where are your parents? They'll likely be worried about you, won't they?"

The two kids stared right through Zeph. He'd seen that look before on ten- or twelve-year-olds, but that was back during the war and coming through a town that had been fought over by both sides. He glanced at the pencil line of gray smoke.

"That your place over there? Your mom and dad with the new settlers?"

Still neither of them spoke. Zeph looked more closely at the girl. Her eyes were bluer than the sky. But the skin around them was swollen and red. She'd been crying, a lot.

"You don't need to be scared," he said to her gently. "I'll get you back to your folks just as soon as you tell me where they are."

"We hain't got folks," she said. "We hain't got a home."

Zeph smiled as warmly as he could. "Now, what do you mean by that? Everybody's got folks and a home."

"We hain't."

Her voice had a trace of an accent. From another country. One part of Zeph's mind worked on that while another part tried to figure out what to do next.

"Well, look, I tell you what, let's go to that farm over there behind the cottonwoods, and maybe they can help us out. Do you know them?"

The girl began to cry. She buried her head in the boy's arm. *Now what did I say?* Zeph asked himself.

"Mister Parker," said the boy, "we can't go there."

"Why not?"

"We can't."

Zeph looked up at the sun. It was about three o'clock.

"The sun'll be down in a few hours. We've got to get to someplace. Now Cricket here'll take you both easy. How about we go into town and get you some food and a safe place to stay, and then we'll figure out the rest of it?"

"Don't leave us!" the girl suddenly blurted, tears running muddy down her cheeks.

Zeph shook his head. "I won't leave you. I'll stick right with you. Now let's get you up on Cricket and into town. You hungry?"

"Yah sir," she answered.

"What would you like to eat?"

"Potatoes and meat."

"I guess it'll be easy enough to rustle up some of that. You got a name, young lady?"

She didn't answer. He held out his hand to help her onto Cricket, and she slowly stepped forward and took it. He hoisted her into the saddle. She was as light as a snowflake.

"No name?" he asked again.

But she just sat on the horse and clung to its mane.

The boy came up and put one hand on the pommel. "I can get up myself, Mister Parker."

"Help yourself."

The boy winced when his left foot touched the stirrup, but he swung his leg over Cricket as if he'd been born to the saddle. *He has that accent, too,* thought Zeph. *What is it?*

Zeph started leading Cricket cross-country and to their right.

"You like horses, boy?"

"Yes."

"Have any of your own at your place?"

The boy didn't answer.

Zeph walked for a while in silence. The sun dipped lower.

"We're not far from the town," he told them. "We cut across the fields like this, and we'll be there in another hour. You seen it yet? Not a bad little place. Iron Springs. For the iron ore the miners been pulling out of the earth. Used to be a lot of gold here in the '60s. I think we're making more money now off the iron and the beef. You'll catch sight of it in a little while."

"Thank you, Mister Parker."

"You're welcome, son. How about you? Your folks drop you into this world without a name, too?"

But the boy didn't say anything. Zeph looked at his dark hair and green eyes a moment and then glanced ahead.

"Well, I got to call you something. How about I give you each a nickname? So I don't have to say, 'hey boy' or 'hey girl' the whole time?"

They didn't respond.

"I come from out of Wyoming. They've got some nice towns there. I grew up just north of what's now Cheyenne, the Magic City of the Plains. If you don't mind, young lady, I'll call you Cheyenne Wyoming. That'll be your name just for this trip. Is that all right with you?"

She stared straight ahead.

Zeph nodded. "Glad you like it. Now, son, do you want a town name, too?"

"It doesn't matter."

That accent again. Zeph had his head down while they plowed through a snowdrift.

"There's a man I greatly admire that I met in Wyoming a few years ago. Cody was his name. He rode for the Pony Express when he was hardly older than you. Then he was a scout. They gave him the Medal of Honor for the work he did. How about we hang his name on you until we reach town?"

"All right."

"Well, there we have it then. Cody Wyoming and Cheyenne Wyoming. Brother and sister. I guess I should have asked—you are brother and sister, aren't you?"

But no one spoke. And Zeph did not open his mouth again until the three of them spotted the riders coming at them over the snow and the dead grass. There looked to be six or seven men, and they were riding hard. Zeph was sure he recognized the lead horse.

Cricket reared. Zeph glanced behind him. Both the kids had jumped off the horse and were running away as fast as they could.

Chapter 3

H ey! Wait! What are you doing?" Zeph shouted.
But they didn't stop. Zeph dropped Cricket's reins
and lit out after them. The boy was already staggering because
of his wounded foot, yet he showed no signs of stopping. The
girl was racing ahead of him, blond hair flying.

Zeph got to the boy first, because he had collapsed in the
snow, blood all over his foot.

"What are you running for?"

"They'll kill us!"

"Who's gonna kill you?"

"Those riders killed our families, and they're going to kill
us, too! They said they would!"

"No one's gonna kill anybody, boy. Those are men from
town, and the lead rider is my own brother, the federal marshal.
They won't hurt you. Now stay put before that foot of yours
falls off."

Zeph went after the girl as the riders bore down on them.
He caught her and wrapped his arms around her as she kicked
and screamed.

"Nay! Nay! Nay!" She shrieked and sobbed.

"Settle down!" snapped Zeph, struggling to hold on to her.

"Nobody's gonna hurt you. Those are men from town. It's the marshal and a bunch of others, all good men who have kids of their own."

"They'll shoot us!"

"No, they won't!"

She broke free and ran a few yards before Zeph grabbed her around the waist again and picked her up off the ground, legs and arms swinging. The riders reined up right in front of them.

"Looks like you got a handful there, Z," said his brother the marshal.

"You could say that."

"What's going on?"

"Matt, I don't know what's going on. I found these kids over by the new homesteads a couple of hours ago, and nothing's made sense since."

"The new homesteads?"

"Yeah. Down in the flats by the river."

"Young lady," said Matt kindly, "I am the federal marshal, and I am here to help you. All of us are. We rode out to give you as much help as we can. That's why I'm here talking to you right now."

She had stopped squirming and was looking up at him through the blond hair that had fallen down over her face. The marshal took off his hat.

"I am Matthew Parker, but you can call me Matt. The man that's got ahold of you is my younger brother, Zephaniah T. Parker. Now this here"—the marshal swept his hat back toward the men sitting on their horses behind him—"this here with the long black coat is another one of my brothers, Jude, and he is the preacher in town, and these other three are all brothers, too. We got a special on brothers today. This is William King, and Samuel and Wyatt."

The man with the thick black beard smiled with a big row of white teeth and lifted his black Stetson. "Billy King," he said, "barrister and solicitor and attorney-at-law for the Montana Territory. I have long sticks of peppermint candy in my coat pocket. Would you like one? Or are you too old for that sort of stuff? I usually keep 'em for myself; it's my belief they make me smarter, but sometimes I share if I run into someone special."

He swung down off his large black horse and stood by the little girl. He took a long red-and-white stick of candy from inside his sheepskin jacket and offered it to her in his gloved hand. Zeph had set her down. Slowly she reached out and took the candy.

"Thank you, sir," she said.

"You're very welcome, young lady. Would you like to walk with me and give one to your brother?"

She nodded, and they headed back across the snow to where two other men were off their horses and looking at the boy's foot. The marshal watched them for a moment then tilted his Stetson back and scratched at his head and sandy-blond hair.

"We got news by telegraph that some marauders were in our neck of the woods. Then Abe Whittaker came in and told us he'd heard shooting down in the flats the day before yesterday. So I got some of the boys together, and we were heading out there to take a look. You see anything?"

Zeph shook his head. "Just these two kids."

Matt glanced over at them. "They say much?"

"They don't say anything at all, not where they live or who their folks are, nothin'."

Matt rubbed his jaw. "See any smoke?"

"No. Well, a bit from a chimney, I guess; that's all."

"Abe figured the homesteaders were burned out."

"Did he see that?"

Matt shrugged. "You know Abe. He tells you what he wants when he wants. I don't know what else he knows. But he's got that dugout by the river, so he must've seen something." He pulled his hat down again. "Now, look, we got to get out there before it's dark. We brought along three extra horses, so why don't you take the gray here and put the kids on it? Then you can get back on Cricket and all ride into Iron Springs and get warmed up."

"That's where I was heading, Matt."

"Well, now you can do it faster."

"Why'd you need all those extra horses anyway?"

"Why do you think? The telegram said it was Seraph Raber's crew."

"Raber. The Angel of Death. They sure?"

"Whoever they are, they've left a trail of dead bodies between here and Dakota. Looks like Raber's work. No one likes killing as much as him." Matt glanced down at Zeph's waist. "No gun, I see."

"No need, brother."

"Suppose Raber jumped you while you were taking care of the kids? How would you have saved them then? The war's been over a long time, Z."

"Not long enough."

"Just get 'em into town."

Matt pulled away with the others. Only Jude held back.

"You all right?" asked Jude.

"My boots are wet, and my feet are cold and sore. Getting back on my horse will make a world of a difference."

"You given any thought about where you'll put the kids up?"

"Some."

Jude suddenly smiled. The silver conchas on his black Stetson winked in the falling sun. "What about a good church woman like Charlotte Spence?"

Zeph reddened. "Charlotte. I guess she'd do. The kids had better mind their p's and q's."

"Are you telling me she never crossed your mind?"

"Not much has been crossing my mind lately. The ranch is a lot of work."

Jude turned his horse to join the others. "She's out and around. Saw her on Main Street before we left. I guess you know what she looks like. Take the kids to Miss Charlotte Spence, brother."

Ten minutes later they walked the two horses into Iron Springs, the boy and the girl on the gray mare, Zeph back on Cricket. There was maybe an hour of sunlight left, Zeph figured. The town was hopping—wagons, men on horseback, people heading back and forth across Main Street from one shop to another.

"I guess the good weather's brought everybody out of hibernation," Zeph said.

The boy and girl rode silently on their horse, but at least,

Zeph thought, they didn't act as scared as they'd been. He saw them taking in all the activity and doubted they'd even been in the town before. If they were with the new homesteaders they may not have had the chance yet.

"Pferdewagen!" shouted the girl, pointing.

"What?" Zeph looked at her and then looked where she was pointing. There was a cluster of wagons. He didn't see anything unusual. But the boy was excited, too.

"Pferdewagen, yah," he said, rising up in the stirrups, even with his sore foot.

"What are you two talking about?" demanded Zeph.

They both pointed—and smiled for the first time. Emerging from the knot of wagons came a shiny black horse stepping smartly and pulling a black buggy. Zeph knew the horse and buggy well.

"Charlotte Spence," he said under his breath.

And then it hit him. The accent under some of the kids' words was the same accent Charlotte had under some of her words. It was a little like the Germans he'd heard speaking English in Wyoming. And this "Pferde" whatever they were squawking about, that sure sounded like the real thing, the way cattleman Wolfgang Mueller used to talk when he was with his buddies from overseas.

"Zephaniah Truett Parker, what on earth are you doing sitting in the middle of the street with those two children?"

Charlotte Spence, in a blue dress with lace at the collar and a matching lace-trimmed blue bonnet, pulled her buggy up in front of them, smiling. She leaned out from under the roof of the carriage. The sun struck her golden eyebrows and sky-blue eyes. Zeph looked down at the ground.

"Well? Isn't anyone going to speak to me?"

Zeph sat up and lifted his hat off his head and gave her a crooked smile. "Miss Spence."

"Who are the children, Zephaniah? Aren't you going to introduce me?"

"This is Miss Charlotte Spence. She has a spread outside of town. She is also Iron Springs's librarian. You can say hello."

The girl poked her head out from behind the boy's shoulders.

"Pferdewagen," she said and nodded. *Vorsintflutlich.*"

The woman's eyes widened. "What did you say?"

But the girl ducked behind the boy's back again.

"What did she say, Zephaniah?"

"I don't know, Miss Spence—"

"Oh, stop that. My name is Charlotte."

"It seems to me she's talking like a cattleman I knew in Wyoming, a gentleman from Germany by the name of Mueller."

"Who are these children? Where are they from?"

"It's hard to say, Miss Spence. I found them wandering in the scrub not far from the river and the new homesteads."

"Well, where are their parents?"

"I don't know. They won't tell me."

Charlotte Spence placed one high, black, tightly laced boot into a puddle of mud and melted snow and then the other. She came up to the children on their horse and stood stroking the gray's neck. Part of her face was in shadow and part in the light. Zeph tried to keep himself from looking at the small freckles sprinkled across her nose and just under her eyes.

"I am Miss Spence, and you may call me Miss Charlotte," she said to the boy and girl, with her brightest smile. "I know the words you are using very well. Would you like to have a ride in the horse and buggy?"

The boy shrugged, but the girl smiled and nodded.

"Well then, you must tell me your names and where you are from. That's only polite."

Neither of the children spoke for a moment. Then the boy said, "I am Cody Wyoming. And this is Cheyenne, my sister."

Miss Spence blinked. "Pardon me?"

"We are Cody and Cheyenne Wyoming."

Miss Spence looked up at Zeph and he looked away. A smile curled her lips once again.

"Very well, Cody and Cheyenne, it's a pleasure to meet you. And where did you say you were from?"

The boy and girl said nothing.

"Where did you learn those words you just used?"

Silence.

"Well, let me tell you a secret. I learned those words from my grandmother. Did you learn them from your grandmother?"

"I learned them from my aunt Rosa," the boy said.

"And where is your aunt Rosa?"

"Pennsylvania."

Miss Spence nodded. "I know the words because I am from Pennsylvania, too. I grew up there. And I rode in the horse and buggies like you did all the time."

She looked at Zeph. "Until you find their parents, these children are staying with me."

Chapter 4

The sun was just coming up, the weather was still mild, and Zeph let Cricket plod slowly through the mud and puddles back to town. His ranch was only about two miles out. It used to be five miles, but things had started changing again in the last three years, especially with talk of the Union Pacific putting a branch line through. That hadn't happened yet, but the town was prospering just the same.

He'd left Byrd and Holly, his ranch hands, to take care of the day's chores. He needed to see his brother Matt and find out what was going on with the homesteaders and what they'd found out. Were the kids' parents alive? Were any of the homesteaders alive? Then he'd need to swing by Sweet Blue Meadows and the Spence ranch to see how Charlotte was making out. It was the polite thing to do.

So she'd been born and raised in Pennsylvania. He'd always thought her family had hailed from Texas. Did that mean her father and brothers had been Pennsylvanians, too? They'd fought on the side of the Union. All of them killed except the one brother who made his way to the Montana Territory and started the Spence ranching operation—and finally died of his wounds and left it all to Charlotte. Who now ran the whole thing with a ten-man crew as if she were the legendary brother himself. Ricky Spence, who could handle Indians and outlaws and hard men with one hand, and cows and bulls and beef shipments with the other.

He'd met Ricky twice. Once at a meeting to press the Union Pacific into building the connection to Iron Springs they'd always said they would, the other time when they were both part of a posse hunting down a gang that had robbed a gold shipment out of Virginia City, just south of them. Ricky coughed up a lot of blood on that ride. Zeph had made sure he got back to the Spence homestead all right. That was four years ago. Ricky never left the house again.

Zeph remembered how Charlotte stood with the lamp while he walked with Ricky up the steps to the porch. Blood was running down the front of Ricky's jacket. Zeph got him in the door, but no farther. Charlotte blocked his path.

"I'll take it from here, Mister Parker." Her voice had been like iron. But as he turned to go back down the steps she grasped his arm. Her eyes were a soft blue and gold, the lamp just inches from her face. In almost a whisper she said, "Thank you, Z."

Only his brothers called him Z. And she'd never called him that again. He shrugged. It had been the kind of sweet moment that got a man's hopes up. But after Ricky's death, she was a stranger. He saw her at the library, where he only went to take out books he thought might impress her, and at meetings of the Stock Growers Association, but he was Mister Parker or Zephaniah Truett Parker from then on, and they hardly said more than two words to each other.

Until yesterday. That was the most time they'd spent with

one another in years. He guessed he could thank the kids for that. She loved kids. People in town wondered why she hadn't applied for the position of schoolteacher. But she loved horses and cattle and her homestead, too. She could only do so much and do it well. She knew where to draw the line.

Cricket had stopped in front of the marshal's office. Matt's horse Union was already there.

"How'd you know I wanted to go here?" asked Zeph.

Cricket let him wind her reins around the hitching post, and then she nuzzled the roan gelding. Zeph stretched and walked in the door. He hoped Matt had a fresh pot of coffee.

He did, but it was almost empty. Zeph squeezed one small cup out of it. Better than nothing. Matt looked like he'd barely slept.

"How's Sally?" asked Zeph.

"Worried."

"About what?"

"Me setting up a posse to go after Raber."

"Is that what you're doing?"

"Not much choice." Matt leaned back in the chair behind his desk and looked at the ceiling. "Three families were in there, Z. Billy King did all the deeds, all legit. From Pennsylvania. They got this far without a scratch. And then Raber comes through. Killed everyone—women, men, children. Lots of hooves cutting up the mud and snow. Five or six riders. The kids said they were in the thick brush. They saw the outlaws, but the outlaws never spotted them. And that's about all they said."

"So they saw most of the killings?"

"I believe they did." Matt sat up. "I've sent out telegrams trying to locate next of kin. I expect we'll hear back later today or tomorrow. King had their names: Kauffman, Troyer, Miller. Bird in Hand. Lancaster County. Funny handle for a town. Heard of it?"

Zeph shook his head. "Did he have the kids' names?"

"No, none of that. Just the adults'." Matt got to his feet. "Trail'll be cold. I could use a decent tracker."

"I'm in—you know that."

Matt nodded. "We've got to bury them first. Jude'll do a service this afternoon. In the town cemetery. Least we can do. We'll head out at first light tomorrow. Pack for a couple of weeks. If they've left the Montana Territory, we can leave it up to someone else. I telegraphed the federal marshal who's at Lewiston in the Idaho Territory."

"Who's gonna watch the town?"

"Leaving my deputy here. You know, Luke, the new man."

Zeph put down his cup.

"Want me to brew another pot?" asked Matt.

"No, I'm heading up to Spence's."

"Yeah. I should head up there myself and look in on them. Doc Brainerd's been in to see the kids."

"When was that?"

"Last night."

"What'd he tell you?"

"They're doing fine, considering what they went through. Charlotte Spence couldn't be happier, Doc says. Treating them like her own."

The ranch was three miles north. Two of the hired men,

Laycock and Martin, met them at the main house.

"Was it Raber?" asked Laycock.

"Yeah," said Matt. "You know his trademark. No one left alive."

"How'd these kids get out then?"

"The gang never saw them. They were hiding in the bushes. You think they'd talk about what they saw?"

"I don't think Miss Spence will let you ask them," said Martin. "She wants to get their minds off all that."

"Fair enough. But no one's ever seen Seraph Raber's face. He could've stayed at the Ten Gallon Hat last night, and nobody would've been the wiser. Would be something if the kids could tell us what he looks like."

"Matt," said Laycock, "Miss Spence was wondering if Raber knows those two kids are alive."

"Who knows?"

"Because if he did, he might come back for them."

Matt looked hard at Laycock.

"Especially if he thinks the kids saw his face," Laycock finished.

Matt nodded. "Yeah. She's right. He could. You got your boys ready for that?"

"Ever since she brought 'em home."

"Sometimes I think she should be marshal."

The men smiled. Matt and Zeph headed up the steps and knocked on the door.

Charlotte had been watching Zephaniah and Matt ride in from a window. She was glad to see both of them but, she admitted to herself, if Matt had come alone, it wouldn't have been good enough. Pausing to check her hair in the hall mirror, she answered the door in her yellow cotton skirt and white blouse. Her hair was pulled back and she wore silver earrings. She gave them a smile.

"Marshal. Zephaniah Parker. Please come in."

They took off their hats and stepped into the hall then paused a moment to glance around at the large front room with its massive fireplace and rugs. She knew Zeph hadn't been inside for a long time and watched him marvel at the high ceilings and oak walls and floors, the chandeliers, the couches, and the huge buffalo head over the mantel.

"It's beautiful, Miss Spence," he said to her.

Zephaniah Parker and his polite manners that went far and beyond the call of duty!

"Matt," she teased, "can I get you to arrest him if he calls me Miss Spence once more?"

"I'll ask Judge Skinner. There could be something on the books."

"I'm Charlotte, Zephaniah Parker. Especially to you."

As she turned her back to lead the way into another room, she saw Matt raise his eyebrows at his brother, and Zeph shrug. *Well, Zeph,* she thought, *it's still the season to keep you guessing, because I'm not sure of how I feel about you myself.*

The children were sitting and eating a breakfast the cook, Pete Sampson, had served up: ham, eggs, bacon, toast, big jars of jam, a pitcher of milk. They both smiled at Zeph. She could see right away that he approved of the transformation she'd wrought in them—they'd both had baths, their hair was clean and combed, and the girl had blue ribbons in hers and was wearing a blue dress. Looking at the boy in the shirt and denim pants she'd purchased in town, she realized there was quite a change from the bedraggled young man Zeph had brought into Iron Springs the day before.

"Marshal," she said with a playful curtsy, "may I introduce to you Cody and Cheyenne Wyoming?"

Matt inclined his head. "We've met. First time I've heard their names though."

"Oh, their names are a surprise to everyone," she said, "but they insist on using them." She glanced at Zeph. "You both know Pete? Would you men like some of his excellent food or magnificent coffee?"

"That's kind of you, Charlotte," said Matt, "but I'd appreciate a word with you alone, if I may. Perhaps Z could spend some time with Cody and Cheyenne while we talk?"

"Fine with me," said Zeph, pulling a chair up to the table. "Take all the time you want. Fill me up a plate, Pete. I'm starved. You starved, Cody?"

"I was once." The boy smiled. "But not anymore."

"How about you, Cheyenne?"

"The men keep us safe here, Mister Parker, don't they?"

Zeph looked at her and nodded. "You bet. Miss Spence hires only the bravest and the best."

Pete leaned over Zeph's shoulder with a plate heaped with pancakes and sausages. "How's that, Zeph?"

"Why thank you, Pete, that'll do for a start. Any maple syrup around here, Cody?"

Charlotte led the marshal into the parlor with its antelope heads on the walls and dark brown sofa and chairs and piano. She closed the door firmly and then leaned her back against it.

"What do you have to tell me, Marshal?"

"The kids were part of a group of families that came here from Pennsylvania, town named Bird in Hand. Their folks were all killed."

"Indians?"

"White men, Charlotte. The Raber Gang."

She felt ice in her chest when he used the name. "The Angel of Death."

"Yes ma'am. I'm getting a posse together, and we'll be going after them at first light. Zeph will be my tracker."

"Is he any good at that?"

She saw Matt's eyes narrow. "Yes he is, Charlotte. Any better, and I'd swear he's got Sioux or Apache in his veins."

"Why aren't you going after them today?"

"We'll do the funeral for the families this afternoon. Set everything else to rights before we head out. Could be gone for weeks."

"I see. Anything else?"

"Well, we're trying to get ahold of the children's kin, so we've sent out a telegram. The families were the Millers, Troyers, and Kauffmans."

Charlotte passed a hand over her face. But she forced herself to speak up. "I hope you are successful, Marshal."

"Are you feeling all right, Charlotte?"

She lifted her head. "I'm perfectly fine, Matt. Is there anything else?"

"I was wondering if you would be attending the funeral with the children—"

She shook her head. "No, Matt, they've been through so much already. Next week will be soon enough for them to pay their respects."

"I understand. There is also the possibility of the Raber Gang coming for the children. We don't know if the kids saw any of their faces. It might be best if we moved them into Iron Springs for the time being, so we can offer them better protection."

Charlotte stopped leaning against the door and stood straight. She felt a strange knot of anger in her stomach, what friends and family called "Charlotte getting her Spence up." "We can take care of them perfectly fine here. There's no need to disturb them further by running them into town. They're just getting settled in."

"Yes ma'am. I don't suppose you'd let me have a chance to ask them what they saw and if they can identify any of the outlaws?"

The anger was in Charlotte's head now. "Certainly not, Matt. You should know me better than to ask. The children need to recover from their ordeal, not keep being reminded of it. You do your job and find the killers and leave those children alone."

"Yes, Miss Spence."

Charlotte led the way back to the kitchen. Her face was set like stone. Matt stood awkwardly behind her, his face looking like a hat someone had crumpled in their hands.

"Best we be moving on, Z," Matt said.

"All right," responded Zeph, getting to his feet. "I'll be back, you two, so make sure you have plenty of adventures to tell me about next time I come around."

"We will!" said Cheyenne.

Charlotte walked the men to the door.

"Thank you for coming, gentlemen. Zephaniah, I hope you will make your way here again tomorrow. I think it's important for the children's recovery to see you."

"It will be my pleasure—"

"Charlotte," she said.

"Miss Spence."

She smiled sadly and shook her head. "You're incorrigible."

"Will we see you this afternoon?" asked Zeph.

"No, your brother and I have discussed that. I think it's best the children stay here and keep putting all that behind them. A day will come when they can say a proper good-bye to their parents and relatives. But not today. Thank you again."

She shut the door firmly. Zeph could hear it being locked and then double-locked from inside.

"Well?" he asked his brother as they walked their horses back into town.

"That woman," answered Matt, "isn't afraid of anything,

and she's sure not afraid of Seraphim Raber. She wouldn't budge from that house if a whole army was coming after her."

"That doesn't surprise me. Pete Sampson told me she shot and killed a mountain lion yesterday."

"What?"

"Yes sir. Right after her horse had thrown her."

Matt whistled. "I guess that about says it all when it comes to Miss Charlotte Spence."

Zeph squinted ahead. "There's someone riding this way, Matt. They're in a lot of hurry."

Matt stared. "It's my deputy."

They spurred their horses forward. When the three reined up in the middle of the road, Zeph could see the young deputy's face was gray and tight.

"What is it, Luke?" demanded Matt.

"I've got bad news and worse news. Which do you want?"

"Dish it all out."

"We got three telegrams since you went to Spence's. Heard back from the law in Lancaster County. Those three families were excommunicated or something, kicked out of their church, but the relatives told the sheriff they'd take the kids back."

"Not so bad. What else?"

"Raber hit settlements near Copper Creek, three days' ride north. Burned two out, took some cattle, killed seven settlers. And Marshal Baker and his deputy, Ned Green."

Zeph glanced quickly at his brother. Matt had counted both those men as two of his closest friends. Ned had stood as best man when he married Sally. Matt clenched his teeth, and Zeph saw his knuckles whiten on his reins.

"Go on," Matt whispered.

"Witnesses said Raber had five riders with him. And tracks have them headed back this way."

Matt nodded. Zeph could see his mind was working fast.

"You said there were three telegrams."

"Billy King and me didn't believe the third was genuine, so we cabled back to the station at Copper Creek. They said it was the real article. Some of Raber's men had put guns to their heads."

"All right. What'd it say?"

"Short and sweet. 'Give us the two kids, or we kill the woman and anybody else we can get our hands on in Iron Springs.'"

Chapter 5

The sun was slanting through the Colorado blue spruce that lined one side of the cemetery. As Jude spoke, Zeph looked over the crowd. He figured there were about a hundred and fifty people or more. Carriages were lined up on the road. He could remember a time when Charlotte Spence was the only one with a carriage. Not any more. He guessed Iron Springs was getting sophisticated. Not so bad a thing, maybe. What were they at now, five hundred, six hundred? In the '60s, when he'd first come out, there'd been two thousand, on account of the gold strikes in the region. Lots of tents and lean-tos. Now there was less gold and more iron, and people had gone north to Helena. Virginia City had lost a lot of people, too. The difference was, Iron Springs wasn't all built on gold, so folks were trickling back in. He knew for a fact that Matt was still getting run off his feet and had requested the town increase his budget to allow him to hire more deputies like he'd had during the gold rush. His brother had kind of hinted Zeph should be one of them this time around. But Zeph was happy with the Bar Zee for now and hoped Matt wouldn't ask, at least not right away.

Matt had deputized about a dozen citizens because of the danger from Seraphim Raber, and the town council had agreed to pay them a dollar a day if they supplied their own firearms and ammunition. Zeph saw them standing at various places at the edge of the crowd: three-piece black suits and derbies, every one of them, with shiny new badges on their lapels. They all had Winchesters, too, most of them brand-new 1873s, some with the octagonal barrel; but others had carbines with the 20-inch round barrel that had just come out the year before. There were a couple of 1866 Yellow Boys, too, with their distinctive brassy looking gunmetal frames.

"Hey," he whispered to Matt, as they stood together with their Stetsons in their hands, "I thought they were supposed to supply their own firearms?"

Matt kept staring at Jude. "I had a couple of crates in the cellar."

"What about the duds?"

"Nobody said I couldn't give 'em uniforms. The tailor donated the suits. Had spares."

"In all the right sizes? Are you playing politics with this Raber thing?"

"Just want the citizens of Iron Springs to see how good it looks and feels to have their own police force."

"Anything in it for the tailor?"

"Shhh. Your brother's praying."

Zeph dropped his head and prayed, too. It was the way they'd been raised in Wyoming—not to believe in God and church and prayer for show, like some people, but to mean it and to live it.

"Lord, we believe these people would have made good neighbors," Jude prayed, "and good citizens. We believe their children would have made good playmates for our children. Now let their bodies rest under these beautiful blue mountains that You made for our joy, and may their souls rest with You in heaven until the day comes when You wed body and soul once again in a new earth and a new heaven. And, Lord, deliver us from the evil that harmed them. We ask this in the name of Jesus our Savior, amen."

"Amen" rumbled through the large mass of people as if distant thunder had pealed through the hills. Eleven pine coffins sat ready next to mounds of earth. Zeph had helped dig two of the graves and then raced back to the Bar Zee for a change of clothes. The earth had softened up, so the work hadn't been too hard.

Matt slapped him in the stomach with his hat. "You're looking like a deputy today yourself, except for the Stetson."

"Black suit's all I got."

"Where you headed now? Your ranch?"

"Not mine. Guess I'll pay Miss Spence an extra visit today and explain about those telegrams."

"No need to go there. She's here. She watched the whole thing from Lincoln Creek Ridge."

Zeph glanced up at the grassy hill that overlooked the cemetery and the town, high and sharp and away to the east. Matt's eagle eye hadn't missed a thing. Charlotte was up there, so were the horse and buggy, so were the kids; but so were two deputies, one on horseback, another in back of a clump of bushes.

"She changed her mind," said Zeph in genuine surprise.

Matt smiled. "Free country."

Zeph walked past the usual cluster that gathered around

a popular minister and shook Jude's hand—"Thank you, brother"—then made his way through the tangle of townspeople and carriages to Cricket, hitched back and away, behind a tall blue spruce. He swung into the saddle and walked her up the bridle path to the top of the ridge, passing the two deputies who were making their way down, both mounted now. He reined in by the buggy.

Charlotte and Cheyenne were in black dresses with black bonnets and no lace. Cody was in a black suit that looked like it had come from the scissors of the same tailor who made the outfits for the deputies, except he wore a black Stetson with a simple silver band. Where did she come up with all these clothes? Zeph removed his hat.

"Miss Spence."

She inclined her head. "Mister Parker."

"Cody. Cheyenne. I am sorry for today. God bless you."

"They are alive in heaven," said Cheyenne, looking up at him.

Zeph nodded. "I believe that."

Charlotte put her arms around Cody and Cheyenne. "We decided to come, but to have our own private ceremony up here."

"A good plan."

"We listened to your brother's words. He has always been a fine preacher."

"Yes, he has."

She studied Zeph's face. He noticed that her eyes looked violet.

"Do you have something to tell me?" she asked.

"I do."

"Well, climb down and we can step over there. You children don't mind if Mister Parker and I have a short chat, do you?"

"No ma'am," said Cody.

"Miss Charlotte," she corrected.

"Miss Charlotte, ma'am."

She waited for Zeph by a large boulder with a bronze plate embedded in it which he'd never bothered to read. The sun poured down over her and caught a wisp of blond hair that had escaped the edge of her bonnet, igniting it like a match. The mountains were blue and white behind her, a perfect backdrop, he thought, for her granite strength and her striking blue eyes.

She smiled as he approached, squaring his hat on his head. "What do you think of the view?"

"It's beautiful up here," he said, but he did not take his eyes off her.

She shook her head. "I meant the mountains."

"I've seen the mountains."

She averted her face quickly and began to walk. "I used to come up here with Ricky. We both liked it so much, especially at sunset when the snow turns so many bright colors: pink, scarlet, gold, green. He'd say, 'Char, you have to bring your beau up here some day,' and I'd tell him, 'Ricky, you have to bring your bride.' But he never had that chance."

"Well, Miss Spence, I'm sure you will have yours."

"Miss Spence. I suppose it's too much to ask that up here on Lincoln Creek Ridge you might use my Christian name?"

"Matt asked me to talk to you."

"Matt? You mean you can't decide to talk to me on your own?"

Zeph caught the edge in her voice. "I didn't mean it that way. I would have come out to the ranch to see you and the kids tomorrow like you wanted."

"Like I wanted? Do you want it?"

Zeph swallowed. *Okay,* he thought, *here goes.*

"Any excuse to get out to the Spence Ranch and see you is a good excuse, Miss Spence."

She lifted her head. Then her voice and the stiffness in her body gentled. "Thank you, Z."

The blood started roaring in his head, but he knew he had to stay calm and not blurt something foolish. If anything was to come of Miss Charlotte Spence and Mister Zephaniah T. Parker, there was still a long way to go. And there were other matters that had to be attended to right now.

"Miss Spence, three telegrams came in this morning. One of them was from Lancaster County. The sheriff there told us the three families were part of a church in that county, at a place called Bird in Hand, but that they'd been asked to leave the church—excommunicated, I guess, was the high-grade Wells Fargo word he used."

Her face and eyes darkened again. "Yes. I know the word. And they weren't asked. They were ordered." There was that sharp steel in her voice again.

"They did say they'd take the children back," he added.

"Did they? Did it ever occur to them the children might not want to go back to such people? That they might find more love and a better life out here?"

"There was another telegram, too. It was from Seraph Raber—"

"I'm not afraid of Seraphim Raber!"

"He said he wanted us to turn over the two kids, or he'd kill you—"

"I am not afraid of Seraphim Raber!"

Zeph thought she was going to start shouting and pummeling him with her fists. "And that he'd kill as many citizens of Iron Springs as he could."

She was silent. They stopped walking.

"We figure he has about five in his gang, Miss Spence, six counting himself. If he comes against us, there'll be a lot of bloodshed, his and ours. He telegraphed from Copper Creek. It'll take them three days to get back here. Four or five if the weather turns nasty."

Her voice was cold, and her blue eyes like new ice. "What are you suggesting I do with the children, Mister Parker?"

"We can get you safe to the railhead in Ogden, Utah in less than three days. Why don't you take the children east to their kin and stay with them for a spell?"

"He thinks the children have seen his face?"

"I'll bet he doesn't know for sure. But he's never left anyone alive, ever. He doesn't want them drawing a picture and having it plastered all over the West."

"What's to stop them from drawing a picture in Pennsylvania? What's to stop him from following those children all the way to Lancaster County with a gun in his pocket?"

"I don't believe he'll take it that far."

"You don't believe he will? Do you know him well enough to say that with a certainty? Do you know what's in a man's heart?"

"I don't, Miss Spence, but it's a chance we have to take."

"A chance you have to take? Or a chance the children and I will have to take? I notice you don't even wear a gun!"

The blood was roaring in his head again, but it was different this time. Zeph clenched and unclenched his fingers. *Lord, help me,* he prayed. He knew he shouldn't say anything. He knew he should bite his tongue and swallow his anger. But she'd pushed him too far.

"Miss Spence," he said, struggling to keep his voice down, mindful that the children were only a little ways behind them, "if it came down to fighting for a woman like you, I'd take on the state of Texas and all of Wyoming and Montana Territory and the entire Lakota nation, if I had to, and not think twice. The only way Seraphim Raber would get to you is through my dead body. The trouble is, I can't protect you and Cody and Cheyenne and five hundred people from Raber's gunmen and neither can Matt, no matter how many men he deputizes. If you're here three days from now, they'll burn your ranch and shoot up the town, kill decent folk and settlers and little old grandmothers and all your hired men, whatever it takes to get to the kids and make sure they don't make a sketch of Raber's face. Now you may not like it, but we're gonna save lives by putting you on the Union Pacific to Pennsylvania, and you're gonna stay out east until we telegraph you that it's safe. And you know that it won't ever be safe for you or the kids until Raber's locked up or hung, and that's what I'm gonna work on next. But first, I'm putting you on that eastbound train if I have to tie you to my saddle like a sack of white flour. Do you hear me, Charlotte?"

Zeph blew out his breath, and his eyes and hands were

twitching. *You fool,* his head was raving, *you crazy fool, you've done it now. You've lost Miss Charlotte Spence for sure, and there's nothing you're ever going to be able to say or do that'll win her back.*

Charlotte's eyes were fixed on him. Zeph couldn't tell what color they were—in fact, he couldn't see any color.

"Well, Mister Parker," she said quietly, "it took an awful lot to get you to say my Christian name, didn't it? Seraph Raber and his five guns, the state of Texas, Wyoming, Montana, the Sioux nation. . . I guess I needed a little bit of help."

She reached up and touched his face with one black-gloved hand. "It was wrong of me to mention the gun you never wear. The truth is, I'm proud of you for that. Forgive me. I will take you up on your proposition, and if you give me one hour, the children and I will be packed and ready for the Union Pacific Railroad. But, Z, there is just one small thing you'll have to agree to."

Zeph's head was spinning from the play-out of his anger, from her quiet words, and from her gloved hand pressing against his cheek. "What's that?" he managed to get out.

"You have to come with me to Pennsylvania. And you have to come as my husband."

Chapter 6

Charlotte laughed as she looked at his face. "Z, I don't think your body knows whether to leap for joy or run and hide. Oh, forgive me, I have a mischievous streak I haven't been able to do much with since my brother died, but I just had to put it out that way to see how you'd feel about getting hitched. It's all right, Z, I didn't mean we had to get married for real. I just meant it's going to have to look that way to others, and Cheyenne and Cody are going to have to act like they're our children. Isn't that the safest way to get to Pennsylvania?"

She could see that a lot of things were going through Zeph's head, and she let him take a moment to let them settle down. She knew she'd shown a side of herself he'd never seen before and that he wasn't sure how to deal with it. Finally he spoke up.

"A family of four wouldn't get any second looks, you're right about that."

"Is that a yes?"

"A yes to what?"

"A yes to my proposal."

Zeph took a good look at her face instead of looking down or away or over her shoulder. She made up her mind to hold his gaze. It felt different and it felt strange, but she found she also liked the sensation it gave her. She watched him muster up the words to respond to her.

"It's a yes to your plan as far as it goes."

"And do you have a plan that takes it further?"

"I got a plan that takes us to Ogden, Utah, and tickets on the transcontinental railroad."

"What do you propose?"

"The stage doesn't come into Iron Springs until noon tomorrow, and it's a milk run. Goes north for two or three more hours to Picture Butte and Nine Forks. It doesn't turn around till it's had a supper stop at Purple Springs. It's too slow. Now if we can get into Virginia City at six tomorrow morning, there's an express taking gold out. It won't stop except to change horses and drivers until it reaches Ogden. It'll have extra guards, and all of them armed to the teeth. I say we make sure we're on it."

"The four of us are going to ride down to Virginia City tonight?"

"No, there'll be six or seven of us. Matt won't let us head south on our own. Ninety minutes we'll be there, and we'll make ourselves comfortable. Once we're on the stage, the deputies will head back here."

Charlotte looked at the sun on the mountain peaks. "How long to Ogden?"

"It's an express. We go all day and night. A couple of days. We should be on the train before Raber reaches Iron Springs. By that time his people will know we're gone."

"What people?"

"Raber's got to have some friends in Iron Springs. How

else would he know those two kids are alive and staying with a woman?"

Charlotte frowned and crossed her arms over her chest to rub her shoulders. "That God's earth should have such kind of people." She looked at Zeph. "Are we going to make it, Z?"

She saw him swallow hard. "You can depend on it, Charlotte."

She gave a little smile and glanced down to the cemetery. "The graves are filled in. I told the children I would take them down there once everyone had left." She turned to Cody and Cheyenne, who were standing about fifty feet behind her and Zeph and just waiting. "We can head down now. Please get in the buggy."

Zeph rode alongside as they wound down to the town and pulled up by the cemetery's black iron gates. Charlotte brought a bag with her as they climbed out. Zeph walked with them.

The wooden marker for each of the graves was the same: KAUFFMAN, TROYER, MILLER, FEBRUARY 1875, WITH JESUS. On two of them were the additional words: A CHILD. Zeph removed his hat.

Charlotte took Cheyenne and Cody to each grave, where they placed a hand-sewn cross made out of quilt material they had stiffened with wood. When the children were bent down by one marker and planting a cross in the earth, Charlotte stood by Zeph and whispered, "They could not tell one person from another?"

"There was no one that could identify the bodies. Who knew them? And some had no faces."

Charlotte bit her lip. "That there should be such people who would do that to others."

A loud rumble made them glance toward Main Street. Freight wagons carrying iron ore thundered past on their way to the railroad spur at Vermillion. Zeph and Charlotte looked at one another. Zeph shook his head.

"The train can only handle ore and cattle. There's no room for people."

"I know," she said.

"And it's slow. Very slow."

"I know."

The children had taken a cross to one of the child markers.

"I don't know when's a good time to ask this," said Zeph.

"Ask what?"

"Do you think—is Cody—is Cheyenne—did they see the men's faces? Could they—would they—try to draw any of them for Matt?"

She stared up at him. "Oh Zephaniah, you know they're not up to that. It's enough to say a quiet good-bye without upsetting them about making drawings of those horrible beasts."

"I know, Charlotte. I hate to ask. But those men will be riding in here in a few days, and they could walk their horses bold as brass down Main Street, and nobody would know a thing. They could place men with rifles in doorways and rooftops and back alleys, and not a person would look twice until the shooting started. I know the kids have been through something no boy or girl should have to see. I don't want them to keep reliving it. But I don't want more good people to die on account of Seraphim Raber either."

Charlotte looked at the children coming back toward them and blew out her breath. "I will talk to them about it when we're alone at the ranch. I haven't asked them if the men were masked. It's not something I wish to bring up. But you're right. Others deserve a chance to live."

The children's eyes were wet. Charlotte put her arms around their thin shoulders. "You have been very kind to them all. They look down and see that. The crosses are as beautiful as flowers. Wouldn't you agree, Mister Parker?"

"They are handsome. I don't know too many resting places that have such special colors by them."

"Thank you, Mister Parker. Would you children like a prayer to be said?"

"Yah, please," said Cheyenne softly.

Cody hesitated and then nodded.

"Mister Parker, would you?" asked Charlotte.

He bowed his head. The others bowed their heads with him. "Lord, thank You for Cody and Cheyenne. Thank You that they were spared. Thank You that their family and friends are at peace and with You. Thank You for the beauty of this resting place. Thank You that tomorrow's sun will come up for Cheyenne and Cody and their good friend, Miss Spence. The Lord is our Shepherd. Amen."

As they climbed into the buggy, Charlotte said, "I will need time to speak with the children about all the plans, time to pack some food and clothing."

Zeph nodded. "We'll come by at eight tonight. Pack some winter clothes. I'm sure this warm spell won't last forever."

"No, it certainly won't. Well, I'll look for you in a few hours then. Make sure you book us some seats on the stage."

"That's done."

"Pardon me?"

"I said, that's done."

Charlotte had the reins in her hand and was about to move into the roadway. She felt a mixture of surprise, delight, and anger flow over her features. "How did you manage that?"

"Matt set it up, Charlotte, not me, so don't get excited—"

"I am not getting excited."

"He had it so two deputies would be going with you all the way to Pennsylvania—there was never any talk of me."

"So he purchased five tickets?"

"The town did, yes."

Charlotte thought for a moment. "You think you can take the place of two men?" The corners of her mouth moved upward ever so slightly.

"Dunning and Doede are all right."

She laughed. "Strange sounding name—Dough Dee."

"Strange name, good man. But I guess I can do the work of ten of him when it comes to Charlotte Spence and her brood."

Charlotte called out to her horse and pulled into the street. "We'll take you up on that, Mister Parker."

He watched them roll between wagons and men on horseback and disappear around a bend of stone buildings and tall roofs. Then he walked Cricket over to Matt's and tied her next to Union. He stood a moment, looking at the pieces of rock that made up Matt's office and jail—it had been one of seven banks in Iron Springs during the gold rush of the '60s and was built like a fort—then he opened the door.

Matt was standing by his rack of rifles and levering each one to make sure they were loaded and the action was smooth. Two deputies sat drinking coffee in their black suits and derby hats.

"Zeph," they both said at once.

"Mister Dunning. Mister Doede."

Matt glanced over at him. "Well?"

"She's never even talked with them about what happened. Doesn't know if the gang wore masks or if the kids could tell who the leader was. Hard stuff to bring up, Matt."

"I know it."

"She said she'd try and go over it with them tonight before we showed up. Maybe there'll be drawings, maybe not."

Matt nodded. "So how does she feel about going to Ogden?"

"She's okay with it. I told her eight o'clock. Who's coming?"

Matt inclined his head. "My two men here of course, Dunning and Doede. Jude. Billy King."

Zeph coughed. "There's been something of a change in plans, Matt."

"What change?"

"She wants me to go with her to Pennsylvania. Wants us to act like we're a family of four. She thought that would be better."

Matt looked at him. "She did, did she? And what do you think?"

"I think she's hit on a good idea."

"Is that right? Tell me, Z, did you put up much of an argument?"

Zeph shrugged and looked at a new wanted poster on the wall behind the desk. From the corner of his eye, he saw Dunning and Doede exchange glances and sip their coffee. For the first time he noticed how huge their handlebar mustaches were. "Sorry to disappoint you two gents," he said.

They both smiled at the same time and raised their cups. "She is a handsome woman," said Dunning, "and I had a hankering to see Pittsburgh."

"On the other hand," said Doede, "we didn't want to miss the show here either."

"No we didn't."

"Good luck, Zeph," they both said at the same time.

"Thank you, boys."

Matt had his hands on his hips. "So it's all settled. Charlotte Spence travels a few thousand miles with my kid brother—"

"Jude's younger."

"—and a gang of cutthroats hunting them down, and this kid brother is going to protect them without the benefit of a badge, a pistol, or even a slingshot."

Dunning and Doede laughed.

Zeph glared. "I'll make out all right."

"Will you?"

"I came through the war without a scratch, didn't I?"

Matt was thinking. "I can't go with you. And I guess I got to thank you for freeing me up two more guns"—he nodded toward the two deputies—"but there is a thing or two I can do."

He opened a drawer in his desk and pulled out a badge.

"Oh no—" Zeph started to protest.

"Oh yes," said Matt, pinning the badge to Zeph's black suit. "You either go as the law, or you don't go at all. I mean it."

"All right," Zeph grunted.

Matt picked up a black book off his desk. "Put your hand on this Bible and swear to uphold the laws of Iron Springs and the Montana Territory."

Zeph placed his right hand on the leather Bible. "I swear."

"And the laws of the United States and every federal jurisdiction."

"I swear."

"So help you God."

"What, am I on trial or something?"

"So help you God."

"So help me God."

Dunning and Doede raised their coffee cups in salute.

Matt opened another drawer with a key. He pulled out a holster with a six-gun.

"No!" Zeph almost shouted and backed toward the door.

Matt ignored him. "You don't have to wear it. You can leave it in your luggage until you need it; I don't care. Heck, maybe you'll never need it. It'd be nice to live in your kind of world, where there's never a villain and no one ever gets hurt or killed."

"I'm not taking it, Matt."

"You will. You're a peace officer now. It's the law." He thrust it at Zeph. "Take it. Maybe you didn't notice. It's Dad's. The 1858 Remington he always swore by. You don't think he'd want you to have it if he knew the sort of journey you're setting out on tonight?"

Zeph took the gun from Matt's hands and looked at it—the long dark octagonal barrel, eight inches, some engraving on the frame and cylinder, the grips white elk horn. It was Remington's New Army, and it had been converted from a pistol that fired lead balls, like a Civil War musket, to one that fired six .44 caliber cartridges. He caught a whiff of burnt powder and new leather and his dad's rich pipe tobacco, and saw him smiling at the dinner table and teasing Mom about something with the Remington in its holster hanging off the back of his chair. "I remember. He used to plink tin cans when he wanted to relax."

"Yeah." Matt smiled. "You shove it in your bedroll and I'll relax, too."

Zeph held on to the gun and holster. "I'll keep it because it's Dad's. But I ain't going to use it. Not ever."

"Tell me your stories when you're back in Iron Springs safe and sound." Matt snatched a piece of telegram paper off his desk. "I forgot. We heard back from Fort Abraham Lincoln."

"They're too far."

"I know they're too far. But Custer's keen. If Raber sets foot in Dakota again, they'll send a platoon of troopers to run him down. A personal guarantee."

Zeph shrugged. "He'll cut straight down to Utah and the railroad once he knows the kids aren't in Iron Springs."

"Or try to head you off through Wyoming." Matt pulled another scrap of telegram paper from his shirt pocket. "We heard back from Fort Laramie. They keep an eye on the railway anyhow. Said they'll be ready to respond if they hear from us. They're harboring a grudge against Raber. Appears he shot down two of their troopers last fall."

"Good to know the bluecoats'll be out and around. Thank you, brother."

"I guess you'd better have a talk with Byrd and Holly about the Bar Zee. No telling when you'll be back from Pennsylvania. See you at Spence's at eight?"

"Yeah. I'll be there. Gentlemen."

Dunning and Doede both raised a hand.

When Zeph had Cricket a mile out of town and headed for Two Back Valley, he reined up, twisted his body around, and dug into the saddlebag on his left. He came up with his dad's pistol and holster. Pulling the gun, he flipped open the cylinder gate and pushed against the ejector rod under the barrel. One, two, three, four, five rounds. That was all his dad loaded into the Remington. The hammer was always on an empty chamber, so he didn't shoot his foot off when he tugged the gun free. He stuck the Remington back in its holster and shoved both into the saddlebag as deep as they would go. Then he cinched the bag down tight.

He kept riding toward the Bar Zee. Behind him the bullets were scattered in a circle and sinking into the mud and snow-melt and hoofprints. The sun was going down red. He'd see Charlotte Spence in two or three hours and then spend maybe three or four months with her if he was lucky. Or blessed. *Now that would be a mighty nice way to spend the winter and spring, if it's okay with You, Lord.* Zeph began to whistle as Cricket jogged toward the mountains.

Chapter 7

Charlotte pulled aside one of the drapes at her third-floor bedroom window and looked down into the yard at the front of her house. Several men were riding up. Laycock held a lantern toward their faces. His other hand held a shotgun. She wasn't alarmed. She had spotted Zeph right away.

He was taller than Matt, but Jude had a few inches on him. His teeth were whiter and straighter than either of his brothers and his shoulders broader. His hair was a nicer shade of brown. She made a face. His shoulders and teeth and height weren't the important things. She liked his spirit. All the brothers had nice smiles and easy voices and pleasant personalities, but Zeph was something special.

She'd known it from the time he'd helped her brother Ricky on that posse. No, she'd known it before that. And when Cody and Cheyenne told her how he'd rescued them, how gentle he'd been, how he'd named them, it only confirmed what she already believed—that Zeph was strong, gentle, and caring, a true man. She had thanked God in her prayers that evening that he was the one accompanying her to Lancaster County and not a pair of strangers with badges and guns.

Years ago she had hoped to spend more time with him. But

Ricky's long illness and death had made that impossible. So had all the years since then she'd spent running the ranch from dawn to dusk. There had been no opportunity for long evening rides and talks; she could only dream about such things.

Until now. Circumstances had combined to bring Zeph and her together in such a way they would have plenty of time not only to talk, but to see what the other person was like under all sorts of conditions and in all kinds of moods. Now she would truly get to know him and find out if he was the man she thought he was. What Raber had done to Cody and Cheyenne's family was unspeakable. But the good that God was starting to bring out of it was a gift.

Still, there was the promise she had made, a promise she could not break. There was a war going on inside her, and it had been going on for years. She had always liked Zephaniah. One moment she desperately wanted something to happen between them. The next she knew they could never be a couple, ever. It was why she had always kept Zephaniah at arm's length. She had to. A promise had been made at her brother's deathbed. Yet she still wanted to be close to Zephaniah. She shook her head. There was no easy way to solve her dilemma.

She fixed a bonnet on her head, her long blond hair already pinned up. The luggage was by the front door with Martin who, to all appearances, was guarding it with an old buffalo gun his grandfather had owned. She carried a lamp into Cheyenne's room. The girl was sitting on her bed in a charcoal dress and bonnet like Charlotte's, no ribbons. Together they knocked on Cody's door. He opened it, dressed in the same clothes he had worn to the funeral that afternoon, but the hat on his head was not a Stetson; it was flat-crowned and broad-brimmed, not nearly as interesting to look at. Charlotte nodded and smiled even though Cody was pouting about the hat. *I don't want people to find you or your clothing interesting,* she thought. *I don't want any of them to notice you at all.*

"Miss Spence?" Martin called up the staircase.

"We're coming!"

"They're here."

The three of them descended the staircase. Marshal Parker stood just inside the open door, hat in his hands.

"How are you, Charlotte?"

"Perfectly fine, Marshal."

"We have the girl riding with you. We can fit a side saddle if—"

"Not at all. I'm dressed for riding under my skirts. Perhaps I'll be mistaken for a man by anyone who's out looking for us."

"Maybe. The bonnet will be a giveaway though, even in the dark."

"Then I'll take mine off. And Cheyenne's."

"That's fine. We also have a couple of packhorses to carry your luggage."

"Thank you, Matt. There is a good amount of it. But I *am* thinking of three or four months. My, it's getting chilly."

"There's a cold front moving in from the northeast. I brought some sheep-fleece jackets along. It might make the ride more comfortable for the three of you."

She laughed. "And I'll look even more like a man."

Matt smiled. "It'll help."

They came down the front steps. Zeph had the jackets

ready for her and the children. He helped Cheyenne with hers and then held Charlotte's open. She liked his touch as he tugged the sleeves over her arms. Cody had already pulled his on over his suit.

"Cody," said Zeph, "Cheyenne, you know Mister King, and these two deputies are Mister Dunning and Mister Doede. They'll be riding with us tonight."

The deputies raised their derby hats.

"You two have handsome mustaches," said Charlotte.

"Thank you, ma'am," they responded, one after the other.

"And this is Pastor Jude," continued Zeph. "He's also riding with us to Virginia City. You remember him?"

"He prayed for everyone," said Cheyenne.

"That's right. Cody, this is your horse over here, Raincloud. Think you can handle him?"

In the lantern light all of them could see Cody's pleasure at being given the tall dapple gray. "Yes sir."

"Charlotte, this is your buckskin. What do you think, Cheyenne? Isn't she a beauty?"

Cheyenne nodded and smiled. "Yah sir."

"Her name's Marigold." He helped Cheyenne into the saddle. "There you go, m'lady."

Charlotte put her left boot into the stirrup. "Will you ride beside us, Mister Parker? Or should I say Deputy Marshal Parker?" She had caught sight of the badge.

"Matt's idea," he muttered, "and only temporary."

Charlotte looked down from Marigold at Laycock and Martin. "Tell the men I appreciate all they are doing for the Spence Ranch. But I do not wish that to include getting themselves shot. If Raber's men show up, I don't want any of you to stand in the way. Let Raber do what he wants, so long as no one is hurt."

They touched the brims of their hats.

"Yes ma'am," said Laycock. "We'll look forward to the day you return."

"As will I."

She walked Marigold over to Matt. "Marshal, I have spoken with the children. They are looking forward to seeing their aunt Rosa again, so this long trip is something they are glad to take. As for drawing likenesses of the men, well, that is not something they feel they are able to do right now. But they understand how it might help you, and they are going to try and remember what some of them looked like and put charcoal to paper. When that happens, and I believe it will, I shall have the sketches sent to you by the fastest means at my disposal."

Matt nodded.

As Charlotte turned her horse toward the road, she said in a quiet voice, "None of the men were masked, Matt, and neither was the leader that they called Angel."

As she headed out with the others, Charlotte wondered if her ranch hands would listen to what she had told Martin and Laycock. Somehow she doubted it. She prayed they would make it through the next few days without a scratch. Then she wondered if that was too much to ask of God under the circumstances, given the kind of men who worked for her—loyal to a fault, hardworking, proud and brave—and the kind of men they would be facing—vicious, treacherous, and bloodthirsty. She shook her head and wished, not for the first time, that God would scour evil from the earth the way she scoured grime from her pots and pans. Then a place like Sweet Blue Meadows, already a jewel, would be a paradise without end.

But that's heaven, Charlotte, she said to herself, *and you're not in heaven yet.*

A mile from her ranch, they veered west toward the Rockies and a stretch of forest, taking a little-used track left over from the gold rush days. This route would bypass the town and any of its citizens who might be up and watching the main roads. *Who would be watching for us?* she wondered again. *Who would help a man like Seraph Raber harm two innocent children?*

She felt someone's eyes on her. It was not an unpleasant sensation, as sometimes it could be, so she let the feeling linger a moment before she turned her head. She hoped it would be Zephaniah Parker, and she was rewarded with his concerned face and smile.

"Are you worried about me, Mister Parker?" she asked.

"No more than usual, considering what we're going through right now," Zeph answered, "but you did seem awfully far away."

"Did I? Perhaps I'm missing Sweet Blue already and wishing we were to Pennsylvania and back again. Do you recall the day you first came to this place?"

They spoke softly in the dark, and their horses trotted quietly through the rocks and pines alongside the others.

She saw Zeph nod slightly. "It was '69. Thousands of people living up and down the valleys here then. Some had gone up to Helena when they had their strike in '64, but men were still pulling a decent amount of gold out of the hills in Iron Springs and Virginia City. Matt was already here. He had dreams of making it rich and buying a big spread in Texas. When Jude and I showed up, he was a deputy, and it's been the law for him ever since."

"What about you?"

"Jude was talking about being a circuit rider with the Methodist Church, and I guess I just wanted to make enough gold to get my own place in California. We hit pay dirt all right, not a lot, but Jude decided to start a church with his cut. He put that whole building up on his own, and I bought the land I turned into the Bar Zee. Funny, I never thought about California again, and he never thought about circuit riding. This place got ahold of all three of us and never let go. Maybe it's the water."

She was sure he was smiling in the dark; she could *feel* him smiling in the dark. "Your mother and father never wanted to join their sons?"

"Well, Mom passed away just after the war—at least she got to see us home to our little ranch safe and sound, and Dad, it seemed as if he never wanted to leave her side. So we'd visit him once a year, stage and train, we never could talk him into leaving Wyoming. Died in '73. I believe he would have loved all the mountains here and the valleys and the streams. He was always one for hunting and getting away from the crowds."

He glanced up at the stars, and she knew he was wondering how the view would have made his father feel.

"I guess I'm talking too much," he apologized.

"Not at all," she responded. "It makes the time pass. Please, go on."

"Well, Cheyenne was growing too cramped for Dad. They started her up in '67, just south of our place. He liked going into town at first, but he must've seen where it was heading, four thousand people in the first few months." *Now,* she thought, *he is shrugging his shoulders in that cute way he has.* "Couldn't get him out here though. Matt got married in Cheyenne for Dad's sake, and Sally didn't mind. I would like for Dad to have seen the Bar Zee, and he would have been proud to watch Jude preach at his own pulpit in his own church. These things don't always work out, do they?"

"No," she said, and she thought of her father and brothers never coming home from the war, never stepping through the door again, only Ricky making it out with a bullet in his lung, a bullet that wouldn't let him alone until it had finished what it started.

"I hate war," she said suddenly and more loudly than she meant.

Zeph was silent for a bit, and then he said to her, "I'm sorry, Charlotte. I believe your family would have liked the Sweet Blue."

Charlotte wrestled with all kinds of memories and feelings that usually she would just hold inside. But this was the ride she'd wanted to take with Zeph for years, this was the time God had given her, and she felt she needed to make as much use of it as she could.

"You warm enough, Cheyenne?" she suddenly asked the girl snuggled up against her.

"Yah, Miss Charlotte."

"All this grown-up talk isn't boring you?"

"I don't listen to much of it."

Charlotte laughed. "The perfect audience, Z."

They rode for a while without talking. She glanced around her and finally found Cody riding with Billy King. King was leading one of the packhorses, and she spotted Jude leading the other. Then she returned to the thoughts she'd thrust away a few minutes before and decided it was time to offer them to Zephaniah Parker to see what he would make of them, and of her, once she'd finished.

"Do you know what Amish is?" she asked him.

"No, I don't," he answered.

"Mennonite?"

He seemed to hesitate. "A fellow in our platoon during the war said he had Mennonite roots. Said they didn't believe in wars and violence and that his family had been real disappointed in him for joining up."

She nodded. "It's like that. The Amish broke away from the Mennonites because they wanted to be even more strict. Jacob Amman felt people should be shunned if they broke the rules of the church. Ignored. Not spoken to. Cut off. Until they repented of what they'd done wrong, and then they could be brought back into fellowship again."

She looked over at him. He had brought Cricket in closer. She took a deep breath. "I'm Amish, Z, Amish born and raised. You said once I had a sweet accent. I grew up speaking Pennsylvania Dutch. English was my second language. We were part of an Amish community in Bird in Hand in Lancaster County, the same community Cody and Cheyenne are from. I had a happy childhood, Z. There is a great deal of gentleness and love among the Amish. But my father felt it was wrong for the South to force slavery on other people. So he joined the Union army to resist them. And my brothers did, too."

She rode in silence for several minutes. All of a sudden she felt a reluctance to continue talking about her family. It was more painful to bring it up than she'd thought it would be.

"I suppose I'm boring you," she said, with an irritability she didn't mean to direct at him.

"No ma'am. Nothing that interests you could be boring to me."

"Is that right?" she snapped. *Calm down, Charlotte,* she told herself, *there's no need to get your Spence up.* "Please do not call me ma'am again."

He was quiet for a moment and then said, "I won't."

Still irritable, she decided to plunge on in defiance of her misgivings for starting the conversation at all.

"Perhaps it wasn't all about the South bullying people. My father did not feel there should be two countries. He was very much against that. But the church was against war and warned Father that if he left to fight he would be shunned, our whole family would be shunned. He was a proud man and was convinced that God had told him to take up arms against slavery. Told the elders he was done with being Amish and being part of the colony. Took steps to make sure his family would be taken care of if the elders really did turn the church against his family. Then he and my brothers went to Philadelphia to enlist."

Again she grew silent, struggling with her memories.

Zephaniah thought she was done. "Did the church turn its back on you?"

Charlotte flared. "I will tell this in my own way and my own time. I am not a rush ahead, restless spirit like you."

"I'm sorry—"

"Just stop. Yes, the church turned its back on us. Satisfied? From that time on, my mother and I and my sister, Mary, were shunned by the other Amish. No one would even say hello to us. We still lived among them—Mother wouldn't leave the house Father had built—but there was no friendship, no sense of family or community or love. Mother might have taken us to Virginia if Virginia hadn't been one great battlefield during those years. She had family there. I saw a few acts of kindness from the Amish, usually from the family Father had asked to keep an eye on us. But even when my sister, Mary, grew ill and died, there was little support."

Charlotte had been telling her story without looking at Zeph. Now she stole a glance to see if he was even listening. His eyes were locked onto her. It was obvious he was taking in every word she spoke.

"I watched Mother wither. When we received the news that Father had been killed, and then the same terrible news about each of my brothers, it was just as if the Confederate army had plunged a bayonet into her own chest. She gave up and lay down, and would not rise. An Amish family took me in after her death. These were the people Father had asked to help us. I was thirteen, and I remember how very lonely I felt, and frightened, but they were kind to me and did not seem to care that my family was excommunicated."

She was angry that she felt tears on her face. Crying was not a luxury she afforded herself. Looking up at the night sky, she swiped at her eyes with the palm of her hand. *Oh, you've come this far,* she said to herself impatiently, *you might as well be done with it.*

"We did not know Ricky had survived," she went on, "but he came one day to our door and took me in his arms and thanked the Amish family; then he said we were leaving Pennsylvania and going west and starting fresh. We came here in '66, and Ricky struck gold. He poured it all into me and the ranch at Sweet Blue. So, you see, I understand something of what the parents of these children have gone through, how awful the shunning must have been to make them pick up and leave the Amish community and travel here by wagon to start again. The only reason I am taking them to Lancaster County is because Seraph Raber will kill them if I don't.

"When this is over, I pray they will want to come back and live on the Sweet Blue. To tell you the truth, if it were just about me, I would prefer to stay here and face Raber and his savages than travel to Pennsylvania and face the people who destroyed my family. But there are others to think of. Cheyenne here, asleep against my chest. Cody. The women and men and children of Iron Springs. That's why I'm going to Ogden with you, Z, and for no other reason. I swore to God I'd never return to Lancaster County. Never."

I will not look him in the face, she said as she stared straight ahead at the winding gold rush trail, *I will not let him see my tears and my pain.* But she did turn to him in the hope that he could do something, anything, about the anguish she had locked in her heart for a lifetime and buried in beef cattle and stock prices and horses and fencing. His face was a pale blur, and she could not read his eyes through her tears.

Suddenly she hated herself for having told him, for letting him see her weakness. With a small cry that was a mix of anger and despair, she spurred her horse into a fast gallop into the night.

Chapter 8

"What's going on?" snapped Matt. His pistol was out of his holster in a flash.

But Zeph had dug in his heels and was pounding after the buckskin. He was worried about rocks, potholes, and low branches. Cricket's breath came in white spurts. Charlotte might have been upset, but she had not lost her head and panicked. He saw her bent over her horse's neck as if she were on a racetrack.

"Let's fly, Crick," he said into his horse's left ear.

Cricket surged and was at Charlotte's side in moments.

"Charlotte!" he called.

But she would not look up.

"Charlotte! Slow up before you and the girl take a tree limb in the head! Slow up! I admire you for the courage it took to tell me the things you did!"

He reached over and grabbed her reins and started hauling back on Cricket's. The buckskin fought the bit, but Cricket's weight began to throw her backward, and she slid to a stop, breath tumbling like pent-up steam from her nostrils. Cheyenne was crying. Charlotte held her. "It's been hard; it's been very hard, Z."

"I know that."

"I've prayed so many times for strength—"

"You have the strength of mountains."

Horses galloped around the bend toward them. Charlotte sat upright and kissed Cheyenne. Matt reined up in front of her.

"What's wrong?" he demanded, his pistol still in his hand. "You two gone loco? They'll hear you for miles!"

Zeph held up a hand to Matt's anger. "Easy, brother. Her horse got spooked. That's all. It was a mountain cat."

"I didn't hear any cat."

"It didn't make a sound. Went across the track right in front of her."

"I never saw a thing."

"It moved fast, and it was so low to the ground it looked like a snake."

Matt stared at him. Zeph glanced away and looked at Charlotte. He could see her eyes were swollen, but he could also see heart and strength pouring back into them. Matt holstered his gun and touched his hat brim.

"Sorry, Charlotte. I don't like running the packhorses. And that whole episode made me near jump out of my skin."

"Me, too," she said.

There were a few chuckles. Zeph let out his breath softly.

"No harm done," announced Matt. "We're miles past Iron Springs and in the middle of nowhere. In fact, that little run bought us some time. I reckon we'll be into Virginia City a lot sooner than we thought. That's what we call good news in the Montana Territory."

They counted heads and moved on, walking their horses. Zeph stayed close to Charlotte. She pulled away from the group, and he followed her. Cheyenne had her head on Charlotte's chest and was looking up at the stars glittering between the evergreen boughs.

"Thank you, Z," Charlotte said.

"No need to thank me for saying what was right."

"A mountain lion?" He saw her small smile.

"Well, there was something there."

She shook her head. A few pins came loose, and some of her hair tumbled and got wrapped up in moonlight. It took Zeph's breath away. She didn't notice. Cricket and Marigold plodded side by side. Zeph started to whistle quietly and looked up.

"I see those stars, too, Cheyenne."

"I'm looking for the Big Dipper."

"Hard to spot when so many branches get in the way. Hey now, did you see that?"

"Yah, a shooting star."

"Make a wish on it, and everything'll turn out all right."

Charlotte glanced at him. "You believe that?"

Zeph shrugged. "A wish can be a prayer. Prayer moves mountain peaks, a preacher once told me."

She smiled and looked up, too. "I used to think summer in Pennsylvania was crowded with stars. The first night Ricky took me to Sweet Blue and said he'd bought it for me, there were so many stars it was like gold dust. I swear I could hardly see any dark patches in between. It made me dizzy. I laughed and spun and fell down in the grass and mountain flowers like a schoolgirl."

"I'd like to have seen that."

"It wasn't so long ago. I think I could do it again. In the right place."

The words "with the right man" weren't spoken, but they floated in the night air between them like snowflakes. They gazed at each other. Her eyes and face gleamed in the silver light that fell down through the crisscross pattern of branches and twigs.

"There she is," one of the men said.

Matt trotted ahead of them into Virginia City. They saw a lot of light and heard a lot of noise farther down the street, but where they came in was dark and silent. One lamp burned in one window. The sign on the building read: Wells, Fargo & Co., Overland Mail Express. Next to it was SR Buford & Co. All their windows black and unlit.

Dunning and Doede swung down, Winchesters at the ready, and Dunning opened the Wells Fargo door. He leaned in and said a few words. A man with a smaller mustache than Dunning's came out. He was thin and dressed in a white shirt and gray flannel pants. He spotted Matt and reached up to shake his hand.

"Marshal. Welcome to the capital of the Montana Territory."

"Mister Wilson. These are my brothers, Jude and Zephaniah. And this is Miss Charlotte Spence and the two children, Cheyenne and Cody. Behind me is Mister William King. The men on the ground with you are two of my special deputies, Mister Doede and Mister Dunning."

"It's good to have you here safe and sound," said Wilson. "I'm the assistant to Mister H. B. Parsons, who is the Wells

Fargo agent for Virginia City. Everything is ready to roll for six sharp, so I'll just show you to your beds, and you can get settled in for the night. I've got a room set up in back for Miss Spence and her wards and another for the men. Are you staying over, Marshal?"

"I'm afraid not. Neither is Mister King. But I believe Jude and my two deputies will be with you until the stage leaves in the morning."

"Capital. I only have two cots for the men, however."

Dunning and Doede shook their heads.

"We'll be up all night, Mister Wilson," said Dunning.

"No rest for the wicked," grinned Doede.

"You do have the fixings for black coffee?" asked Dunning, looking a bit worried.

"All in there on the stove, Deputy."

"Coffee," said Doede with a smile, slinging his Winchester over his shoulder.

Matt looked at Zeph. "Need anything?"

"I'm all right."

"Charlotte?"

"I feel like I'm in good hands, thank you, Matt."

"Then we'll see you back in Iron Springs."

Matt wheeled his horse and headed back into the night, leading Cricket and Marigold. Billy King had the two pack-horses that had been unloaded of their baggage. He raised his hat—"God bless you, folks. God bless you, Cody, Cheyenne. I pray time flows like a fast river for us all while we're apart"—and followed Matt north on the gold rush trail.

Zeph walked into the station and helped everyone get

settled in. It didn't take long. Dunning parked himself outside Charlotte and Cheyenne's door, tipped back in a broad oak chair Zeph had found, Winchester in his lap, coffee mug in one fist. Doede sat in a rocker by the other door, sipping at his coffee and watching Jude put his feet up on the express agent's desk and place a nickel-plated six-gun on the large green blotter.

"Pistol-packin' preacher?" asked Doede, surprised.

Jude smiled, his hat with the silver conchas tilted forward over his eyes. "Only in the Montana Territory. And it's never loaded. Sometimes looks are enough."

Doede and Dunning glanced at each other and shrugged.

Zeph watched Wilson stoke the stove and put on a fresh pot of coffee. He wiped his hands on a cloth.

"Anything else I can do for you gentlemen?"

Jude said nothing. Dunning and Doede shook their heads.

"I'm all right," said Zeph.

Wilson rapped lightly on Charlotte's door.

"Miss Spence?"

"Yes?"

"Is there anything else I can do for you?"

"I'm quite comfortable, Mister Wilson, thank you."

"Good night, then."

Wilson turned to Zeph. "Is the boy comfortable?"

Zeph carefully opened the door and poked his head into Cody's room. "Half asleep already."

"Then I'll be locking all of you in the building for the night," said Wilson.

"Fine."

"There is one thing, Mister Parker."

"What's that?"

Wilson pulled a telegram out of his pants pocket. "This came addressed to you this evening."

The telegram was folded once. Zeph opened it.

PARKER
II KINGS 19:35
ANGEL

Zeph looked up. "Do you happen to have a Bible handy, Mister Wilson?"

Wilson nodded. "Of course. But I took the trouble to find the reference and write it out for you."

Zeph took the note Wilson handed to him. It was printed in clear dark letters.

And it came to pass that night, that the angel of the
LORD went out, and smote in the camp of the
Assyrians an hundred fourscore and five thousand:
and when they arose early in the morning, behold,
they were all dead corpses.

Zeph felt a crawling in his stomach. "When did this come in, Mister Wilson?"

"Two hours ago."

"From which telegraph station?"

"Mister Parker," Wilson said quietly, "it came from Iron Springs."

Chapter 9

*T*he man had taken a stained pillowcase and cut one hole for an eye and another for a mouth. He thrust the barrel of his pistol into Zeph's ribs and said, *"It is the Lord's will you die and all those with you. You know that."*

"I need to see your face to be sure it's you," Zeph answered calmly.

The man nodded. "All right. Then you will know for certain this is the work of the Lord."

He drew off his hood, and Zeph expected hair and teeth and bulging eyes. What he saw was a face as handsome as the dawn. The man smiled, "No, I'm not a monster, am I? Are you convinced now that your death is ordained by the hand of God?"

Zeph didn't know what to say, he was so surprised by the man's beauty. Then the gun barrel dug into his body once again, and the roar of a gun blast filled his head.

Zeph jerked upright as the stagecoach lurched and banged. Charlotte was asleep across from him in the dark, Cheyenne snuggled with her, thick quilts pulled up to their chins. Cody snored softly, with his head against Zeph's left shoulder. The guard on the other side of Cody caught Zeph's eye.

"A nasty bump, sir," he said in a low voice. "Lots of stones on the road between Virginia City and Eagle Rock. Hard to avoid them all when you're trying to make time."

Zeph grunted. He opened the wooden shutter over the stage window on his right. Trees and rocky slopes rushed past. Snow was swirling down in circles, white spots against the gray and the green.

"How far to Taylor's Crossing?"

"We're doing well, sir. Eagle Rock is only a few hours. Then a change of horses. New driver. They'll replace us as well."

Zeph closed the shutter to keep out the cold air.

"Does the snow slow us down?" he asked.

"Not much. A bit. It's the ice that causes the wrecks."

Zeph slid farther down into the blue point blanket that covered him and Cody. The stage rattled and jolted through the Idaho Territory.

If it slows us down, it will slow them down, he thought. *And even if the stage is hauling us and our luggage and a gold shipment, the four horses can make better time than a crowd of riders.*

He did not believe the gang had already reached Iron Springs. Raber couldn't be in Copper Creek one day, hundreds of miles north, and Iron Springs the next. It was someone in Iron Springs, Raber's accomplice, sending a telegram on ahead and trying to unnerve him.

It couldn't be Dunning or Doede. Or Billy King. Or Matt or Jude.

As if it would be one of my brothers.

There was hardly any way to narrow it down. It could be virtually anybody. Raber was probably paying him in gold. Why else would someone take the risk of getting his neck stretched on the end of a rope? Who did he know that needed the money that badly?

But what if there was more than one person involved? What if there were two or three?

That was a game Zeph didn't want to play. Once he thought there might be more than one, any of the people he knew and trusted could be guilty. Then Dunning and Doede could be in on it. Or Billy King and his brothers, Sam and Wyatt. Or Martin and Laycock. Or Byrd and Holly. He could go crazy trying to figure it out, and he'd be suspicious of everyone that crossed his path.

He tried to sleep again, but the stage banged and thumped and shook, and sleep would not come.

He was tired enough. Once he'd read the Bible passage the night before, he'd known it would eat at him for hours, just as the person who sent the telegram intended it should. He'd tossed and turned all night and never found a comfortable position for his body. A part of his mind expected the splintering of wood and the crash of firearms as Raber's killers forced their way into the Wells Fargo office. Suppose Raber did have hired guns that he'd telegraphed in this neck of the woods? More than once, Zeph's thoughts had turned to his father's Remington New Army buried in his saddlebag. But he knew it was empty, and the threat of a gun would not stop Raber's madmen, it would just incite them to shoot.

Before dawn Wilson had woken them up, cooked a breakfast of ham and eggs, and made sure their luggage was packed into the leather boot at the rear of the stage. The driver and three guards had been booked into one of the quieter hotels and shown up around five thirty. The driver had downed a cup of coffee with Dunning and Doede, and then they'd helped him hitch up the team of four chestnut horses. Tipping their derbies, the deputies had ridden off with two mugs of fresh coffee and Wilson's blessing.

Jude had pulled a small Bible out of one of the pockets in his long black coat and given it to Zeph. "One for the road, brother."

Zeph saw right away it was the one Jude had carried with him during the war, the Bible he'd seen Jude reading by the campfires at night. "I can't take this," he'd argued. "This is your talisman, your keepsake."

Jude had laughed. "God's my talisman, brother. This is just a book of paper and ink. It's the taking into yourself of what it talks about that's key. Open it now and then. I pray you'll find the words you need when the ride gets the roughest."

They'd shaken hands.

"I'll read it, brother," Zeph had said.

Now Zeph dug under the point blanket as he sat inside the stage and came up with his brother's war Bible. It was well-worn around the edges, and some of the binding was loose. It smelled of black powder and woodsmoke and gun grease. It naturally fell open to a number of different passages that Jude had obviously read several times over. He picked one. *"Fret not thyself because of evildoers, neither be thou envious against the workers of iniquity. For they shall soon be cut down like the grass, and wither as the green herb."*

"What are you reading, Z?"

Charlotte was smiling at him in the dimness, a crack of white light from the window shutter drawing a pale line down one side of her face.

"Nothing," he said.

"It's something. Isn't that the little Bible your brother gave you?"

He nodded.

"Read it to me."

He read her the first two verses from Psalm 37.

She stared at him. "Are you fretting because of evildoers?"

"No," he lied.

She looked skeptical, but chose to let it go. "Would you look up something for me?"

"Sure."

"Can you read Psalm 91 to me?"

It was marked with dark powder smudges that held forever Jude's fingerprints.

"'Thou shalt not be afraid for the terror by night; nor for the arrow that flieth by day,'" he read out loud, speaking in a soft voice that he hoped would not wake Cody or Cheyenne. "'Only with thine eyes shalt thou behold and see the reward of the wicked. Because thou hast made the Lord, which is my refuge, even the most High, thy habitation; There shall no evil befall thee, neither shall any plague come nigh thy dwelling. For he shall give his angels charge over thee, to keep thee in all thy ways.'"

"You see, Z," Charlotte spoke up, "there are the good angels, too, and I believe they're stronger than the evil ones."

Zeph suddenly remembered his dream. "Do you think the

people that do evil deeds actually start to look evil?"

Charlotte gazed at him a few moments before answering. "You mean do I think Seraphim Raber must be an ugly man because of all the wicked things he has done? Well, he might look like the handsomest man in the world if you saw him fishing off a bridge in his straw hat and brown boots with the sun setting just over his shoulder. But if you looked into his eyes and down into his heart, you would see nothing but filth and corruption. By their fruits you shall know them. The apples from his tree are covered with worms and wasps."

A sudden venom had come into Charlotte's voice. She turned her face away. "Still, even men like that, they say, we need to pray for. Resist their evil, but pray for their souls."

Before Zeph could think of a response, the driver bawled out, "Eagle Rock, formerly Taylor's Crossing," and the stage thundered over a wooden bridge.

While the team was being changed, Zeph and Charlotte and the children stepped out of the stage and stretched their legs. The sky was the color of lead, and a cool wind was blowing from the north, but no one was anxious to sit back down anytime soon and get jolted and tossed about for another twelve or fourteen hours. Yet the changeover of the horses and the men would be swift.

"Where's your badge, Mister Parker?" asked Cody.

"In my pocket for now."

"I thought it was great."

"Did you? Tell me, what do you think of the stagecoach ride so far?"

"It's like the Conestoga wagons we used to come here

from Pennsylvania," the boy grumbled. "You feel like a sack of apples getting bounced up and down."

"Well, in the summer," Zeph responded, "there'd be heat and dust and mosquitoes and horseflies. This is probably a little bit better."

Cody was remembering, Zeph could see, the Conestogas rumbling through the heat and flies of the plains. Then the light went out of his eyes as his remembering took him too far.

"I'm sorry," Zeph said.

"I slept very well." Cheyenne suddenly spoke up. "I felt like I was being rocked in a cradle."

Zeph put one hand on her shoulder, smiling. "You would make a good advertisement for the company that builds the Concord coaches. 'Travel across the most rugged roads in America and sleep like a baby the whole way.'"

"I was sleeping the whole way, wasn't I?"

"You were."

Charlotte had been tugging at their luggage, which was stored in the boot at the back of the coach, grunting and complaining as she dug past item after item. Finally she found what she wanted and brought over a parcel wrapped in white paper and tied with twine. She put it into Zeph's hands.

"Here."

"What is it?"

"In another day or so we'll be in Utah and boarding the train for Chicago. We have to look like a family."

"We do look like a family."

"No, the children and I look like a family, because we are dressed the same and look very plain. You look like a cowboy—"

"I am a cowboy!"

"—and your scarf and boots and Levi Strauss waist overalls will have to be stored away until we return. Until then, we must look ordinary."

Zeph stared at the package as if it might jump up and bite him. "What's in it?"

"Go inside the Wells Fargo office and find a room to change in. We will wait for you here."

Zeph returned in ten minutes, just as the guards were clambering up onto the coach and the driver was asking Charlotte to get the children inside. Gone was his brown Stetson. In its place was a flat, black, broad-brimmed hat, exactly like Cody's. A baggy jacket over a gray shirt and baggy pants and black shoes completed his outfit. He looked sadly at his cowboy boots and shirt and Levi Strauss pants.

"I've only had the pants for a year," he protested. "They're the new ones with the rivets, and I've broken them in. They fit like a glove."

"Well," said Charlotte, "the pants I made for you fit like a glove, too, just a very big glove."

Cody laughed. They so rarely heard him laugh that Zeph and Charlotte stopped talking to look at him and watch his green eyes flash.

"Where do you think she gets all these clothes?" Zeph asked him.

Cody was still smiling. "The Hunkpapa Sioux."

"I told you," Charlotte said, taking Zeph's cowboy clothing from him, "I made them for you."

"You sew?"

"And even bake. And break broncs. And sing in the church choir."

She walked back over to the coach boot and tucked Zeph's hat and clothing inside and refastened the leather cover and straps. It was beginning to snow again, and she opened the door to the stage with a flourish. "Let's carry on with the show."

They squeezed in next to a new guard, who had already made himself comfortable. He lifted his derby hat to Charlotte and Cheyenne. "Ladies, I am Slick, and I will keep you safe until we reach Ogden."

"Hello, Slick!" beamed Cheyenne.

"Hullo, my girl. How has your trip been so far?"

"It's been like traveling across America in a cradle."

Slick looked at her in astonishment. "Is that so? Well, I hope your presence will bring a little of that cradle into the coach for my poor bones. Not that I'm allowed to sleep. But a guard should always be relaxed right up until the very moment he's needed. He functions better that way."

The stage began to move, and the horses trotted more and more briskly and finally started to run. The five of them began to sway and bounce.

"You see, sir?" grinned Cheyenne.

"You're right, I feel like I am six weeks old once again."

"This is my brother, Cody. And my mother and father. We are the Wyomings."

My, my, thought Charlotte, *look who is bursting out of her shell.*

"The Wyomings? They name the territory after your family?"

"Maybe, sir."

"Well, I am Slick Doolan. That's my whole handle. Pleased to meet y'all."

He leaned over to shake Zeph's hand. Before Zeph could open his mouth to introduce himself, Charlotte reached between them, and took Slick's hand.

"Mister Doolan. My husband, Fremont, and I are very glad to have such a pleasant personality as yourself for our guard."

"Why, thank you. . ."

"Conner."

"Missus Conner. That's something different."

"My parents wanted a boy," she said with a playful pout. "When I came out they'd put so much work into planning for a little man they were reluctant to backtrack. So I got the name, a blue crib, and a blue set of pajamas."

"Well, you seem to have done all right by it all. If you don't mind my saying, Mister Wyoming."

"Fremont," Zeph grunted.

"Fremont, if you don't mind my saying, she is purtier than the blue Wyoming Rockies in the springtime. You're a lucky man."

"Oh, he knows it," said Charlotte, lightly slapping Zeph's hand.

"I do know it," said Zeph.

"And, young lady," said Slick to Cheyenne, "I guess you will grow up to be as beautiful as your mother."

"Thank you, sir."

Suddenly the stage lurched and swerved and came to a dead stop. Charlotte was pitched into Zeph and Cheyenne into Cody. Slick banged open his window shutter with his shotgun barrel and took a look. It was getting dark, and the snow was pouring down. He blew out his breath in a sudden burst.

"Well," he said slowly, "I guess we got trouble."

Chapter 10

Zeph felt his whole body tense. "What kind of trouble?"

Slick leaned back in his seat and closed the shutter. "You can't see more than a foot in front of you. We're locked in a bad squall, and it could blow for hours. I been in 'em before on this stretch. Either we sit tight, or somebody gets out and walks the horses forward. If we were on a straight run through the plains, he'd keep 'em moving slow. But here we got to worry about dropoffs and cliffs. He wouldn't be able to spot them in time."

"Will we be all right if we just stay put?" asked Charlotte.

"Maybe. Blows too long and the temperature drops out of sight, different story." Slick didn't look too happy.

"So one of you can lead the team on foot?" asked Zeph. He doubted Raber was being held up by a snowstorm.

Slick groaned. "That's the problem. Tess and Marble hate me. Always try and take bites out of me. So that won't work. Bert and Stoner up top, well, they hate horses to begin with, and the horses know it. They get down there with 'em and the team'll either kick 'em both to death, or bolt, or both. Stan's great with horses, but he's the driver. We gotta have him on the reins." He closed his eyes. "Lord above, we are stuck and we're stuck bad."

"You ever walked out of one of these squalls?" Zeph's mind was racing, looking for a solution.

"Sure, sure. You get the right person walking ahead with the team. A lot of times these storms are, you know, locals, you're out of 'em in one or two miles. But you got to have the walker. Try and run the team without someone checking what's ahead, and you'll have a wreck. I picked up the pieces of one that went right over a riverbank and another that went into a rock wall when the team panicked. You got to take it slow and sure and steady."

"I'll do it," said Zeph. He pulled on his sheepskin coat and opened the coach door.

The snow and wind caught him full in the face and took his breath away. His broad-brimmed hat vanished. He hunched over and stumbled to the front of the coach and glanced up at the guard sitting next to the driver. He was wrapped in a blanket and looked like a snowdrift.

"I'm a rancher in the Montana Territory," he called up. "Got about a hundred horses. I'll be your walker."

The guard didn't even turn his head. But the driver leaned over. "Go easy. Take the harness of the lead horse on the right. Gelding named Marble. But you got to go easy. I'll work with you best I can. Name's Stan."

"Fremont."

"You need something for your head, or you'll lose your ears. Here."

He took off his hat and threw it down. It was so heavy with snow the wind couldn't catch it.

Zeph planted it firmly on his head. "What about you?" he shouted.

"I got another under my feet."

It was completely dark now. The only brightness was the snow and the horses' breath. Zeph got up beside Sweetwater, who stood rigid. He was talking softly the whole time he approached the horse from behind. He kept using the same subdued tone once he was beside Sweetwater and didn't touch her.

After about five minutes the guard beside the driver began to get impatient, and Zeph heard him mutter, "Get him outta there, he don't know what he's doing."

Stan snapped, "Shut up, Stoner. This'll likely be the farmer that saves your dude hide from becoming winterkill."

Zeph waited until Marble was interested in what was in his jacket pocket. When the gelding began to nuzzle the pocket, Zeph pulled out an apple and let the horse take a big bite. When it had finished the apple off, there was another. Then Zeph began to walk forward. The horse moved with him and, after some reluctance, so did the whole team.

He did not do anything more than place his hand on Marble's shoulder. He could see that Stan held the reins loosely. Zeph put his head up to squint into the snow-blown night, then down to blink his eyes clear and look at the roadway. It was only a walking pace, but Marble took longer and longer strides, and Zeph had to work harder to keep up. After a few minutes he was warmer due to the extra exertion, so he didn't complain or urge the team to slow down. After about half an hour, he gave Marble another apple. Now he had a friend for life.

Zeph had taken gloves out of his coat pocket and pulled them onto his hands using his teeth. He wished he had a scarf to wrap over his face, but he found that Marble would let him lean his head gently against his neck. The warmth of the horse's flesh and breath did wonders to relieve the stabs and pinches of pain he felt on his nose and cheeks and forehead.

Think of hot things, he said to himself, *think of the Utah desert in summer or a dry August wind in Wyoming or the hot springs at Yellowstone melting back the snow and ice. Think of thick woolen blankets and heated bricks at the foot of your bed and patchwork quilts as heavy as iron ore. Warm spiced milk. Hot coffee. Apple pie and raisin pie just pulled out of the oven. A wood fire and venison roasting on it.*

Marble snorted and reared. Zeph's right foot went into nothing. He began to fall and grasped desperately at the horse's traces. Marble didn't fight his grip or panic, but pulled slowly, snorting the whole time, and dragged Zeph back over the edge. Zeph got to his feet, head spinning, and embraced the horse, who permitted it. He had a final apple and gave it to the large sorrel with a whispered, "Thank you."

They moved forward again, except that Zeph swung left to avoid the drop-off, and the team swung with him. Snow that had gone up his sleeves, down his neck, and into his loose pants chilled him until it melted and dried against his skin. Marble began to walk more briskly, and Zeph half-ran for ten minutes to get his blood pumping. His eyelashes started to collect ice, and he had to rub his gloved hands over them to keep his eyes from freezing shut. He touched a gloved hand to his mouth and came away with spots of blood—his lips were chapped and torn. *One foot in front of the other,* he said to himself. The wind shrieked and bit.

He stumbled. Hung on to Marble's traces. Felt an arm go through his. Caught a scent that made him think of oranges and cinnamon and chocolate.

"Fremont?" he asked through chapped lips. "Why that for my name?"

"Fremont's Peak," Charlotte answered.

They walked together and the team kept pace.

"Conner?"

"Fort Conner."

"I know Fort Conner. Guess I should be happy you didn't take all your names from Yellowstone Park: Elephant Back, Fire Hole, Lower Geyser Basin."

"How about Stinking Fork?"

"If you knew Charlotte Spence's wicked sense of humor, you'd thank the Lord for small mercies."

He glanced over and saw her laugh to herself at that. The snow was already thick on her clothing.

"What's this about a hundred horses?" she teased.

"If I have a good spring there'll be eleven. I guess a hundred sounded better."

"Are there any apples left in my travel bag?"

"Not sure about that."

"I thought you were having trouble tying your shoes in the stage. I didn't know you were helping yourself to apples from my luggage."

"I was having trouble tying my shoes."

"Oh."

"I never wear shoes."

"One day I'd like to be married—"

"Amazing what a snowstorm and shoelaces will bring to mind."

"—and for my honeymoon, I want to spend a whole month, maybe a whole spring, summer, and fall, just riding and camping in Yellowstone. That would be the best wedding gift a husband could give me. Other than himself, that is."

Zeph blinked his eyes several times to clear the snow and get a look at her face as she said all this. Did she mean it? Or was she passing the time? And why was she telling him?

"Doesn't sound like a difficult honeymoon to make happen," he responded. "Be sure your wishes are clear to the gentleman who wins your hand."

"Oh, they will be. There is a problem, however."

"What's that?"

"I'm married to a man already."

"You are?" Zeph couldn't tell if she was still joking.

"I am. Fremont Wyoming. We have two children. And, do you know, I cannot recall a wedding ceremony or cradles or cribs, and I certainly cannot recall a honeymoon. I don't believe there ever was one."

"How did you let that slip past you?"

"I think the marriage just came upon me too fast. I was overwhelmed. A husband, a son, a daughter, it all happened at once. There never was time for a honeymoon."

"A woman like Conner Wyoming, I think she'd rectify that."

"Hold up!" called Stan from the driver's box. "We're clear!"

Zeph and Charlotte stopped walking and so did the team. Stars were shining like lanterns. The moon was shaped like a silver cradle. The wind had dropped to a cool breeze. The road ahead was open and dry.

"Looks like we came down some," remarked Zeph.

Stan nodded. "A drop in elevation did the trick." He climbed down from the coach and shook Zeph's hand. "I'm obliged to you, young man. Missus."

Looking like walking, talking snowmen, Stoner and another man got off the coach and came over.

"Thank you, mister," said Stoner.

"Name's Bert. You got a way with those beasts," said the second man, his beard glittering with icicles. "You ought to be head wrangler with some big outfit down in Pecos, Texas."

"I'd like that warmth right about now," Zeph replied.

Bert grinned through the ice. "So would I."

"You're quite the lady, missus," said Stoner. He took off his hat and whacked it against his leg. Snow flew in all directions.

Charlotte inclined her head. "Thank you."

"Both of you got a way about you," nodded Stan. "Nice to see a couple that got so much in common hitched and filling up the West with children."

"We have always thanked God for our marriage," said Charlotte.

"We got time for coffee?" called Slick as he opened the coach door for Cody and Cheyenne.

"Why, you got your fixin's?"

"I do."

Slick had a sack out of which he pulled wood, newspaper, matches, coffee, a coffeepot, brown sugar, and tin cups. "A habit I picked up during my gold rush days." He lit a fire at the side of the road, melted snow in the pot, boiled it, added the coffee grounds, let it steep, added sugar, and started pouring.

"The kids have some?" he asked Charlotte.

"A little bit would do them no harm."

"And I have some cocoa to sprinkle into it, for Slick and those under twenty only." He winked, producing a can and a thick block wrapped in paper.

"What's in the paper, Slick?" asked Stoner.

"Only for those under twenty, ladies and gentlemen."

He opened the paper, broke off chunks of dark chocolate, and dropped them first into Cheyenne's cup and then Cody's. "Give it a minute to melt some," he told them.

Stan laughed and tilted back his hat. "Slick, I got to say, you are some ball of fire."

Bert snorted. "Missed your calling. Should've opened up a stage station. People'd take the trip through Apache country just to sit down to one of your hot drinks."

"When I retire from keeping you alive, Bert."

Zeph sipped at his cup. The heat was giving him new life. Charlotte still had her arm through his. A scarf was wound around her head, just leaving a space for her eyes, nose, and mouth. Snow was melting on the scarf and the loose strands of hair that had slipped out from under.

Moonlight and starlight always found her eyes. She was more beautiful than God's heaven and earth. Now how was he supposed to tell her something like that with all these men standing around and the horses snorting and blowing and stamping and steaming? He gazed at the mountains to the east.

"Were you going to say something?" she asked.

"The moon makes the mountains look like mother-of-pearl."

"Is that what it was?"

"And you," he said so the others could not hear. "The moon makes me see a beauty in you I've never seen anywhere else on earth."

Her lips parted, but she didn't answer him. Instead she looked away.

Stan glanced over and poured the dregs of his coffee on the ground. "Let's get on board, ladies and gents. Mister and Missus Wyoming have a train to catch in Utah."

Chapter 11

The locomotive stood hissing and trembling, like a blackened and smoking arrowhead quivering on a bowstring, ready to let fly at the snowcapped Rockies and the hundreds of miles of open plain that stretched east of them.

Zeph and Cody stood together and stared at it. US GRANT was painted in white italic script on the side of the locomotive's cab.

"Is that the president?" asked Cody.

"That's right," replied Zeph. "Though maybe this locomotive was commissioned while he was still commanding the Union army."

"That is simon-pure."

A man in striped overalls with a striped hat, clean white shirt, and bright red scarf climbed down from the cab, pulled off one of his thick tan gloves, and put out a hand for Zeph to shake. He turned and shook Cody's hand, too, a big smile playing over his sun- and windburned face.

"Bobby E. Clements," he said with a grin, "kind of like Bobby E. Lee, what folk in Carolina called me during the war, though now most call me by the name the railroad hung around my neck, Cannonball Clements."

"Fremont Wyoming. And my son, Cody."

"Proud to meet you. You two on board?"

"All the way to Omaha," said Zeph.

"I take her more than halfway to Cheyenne. Cody, I will cut her slick as river water through the valley, you'll have a fine ride."

"Will we see buffalo?" asked Cody.

"Buffalo? Well, who knows. Now and then we might see a small herd south of the tracks. I see any coming up, I'll blow the whistle four times, how's about that?"

Cody smiled. "Thank you, sir."

"I heard you talking while I was up in the cab. You bet, Mister Wyoming, the Union Pacific had this engine named for the president before he ever was a president. Might seem funny to have an old Rebel like me driving a locomotive named after a Yankee general, but I got no quarrels with Grant. He treated Lee fair at Appomattox. Treated us all fair, for that matter, back in '65."

Zeph thought he was going to say something else about how Grant had treated the South since '69 when he'd become president, but Cannonball squinted up at the sun and shook his head. "It ain't all what presidents do or don't do that makes the South what it is, or the whole country for that matter. We do plenty of harm on our own." He looked Zeph in the eye. "I don't think much of these armed gangs decidin' who gets to vote and who doesn't in Carolina. I won't go back unless my own people make it right. Maybe I'll never go back. I guess I'm three parts a westerner by now anyhow."

He walked over and patted the side of the US Grant. "She's

a good one. Danforth Locomotive Works, four drivers five foot in diameter, twenty-four inch length of stroke. There's ones with more drivers, but Grant holds her own. She does well, very well."

"Cannonball!" called the fireman from the cab. He had his pocket watch open in his hand. "We're burnin' daylight."

"Easy, Dan," said Cannonball. "We'll make it up."

He shook hands with Cody and Zeph again. "You two enjoy the trip. Got sleepers?"

Zeph nodded.

"The rails'll rock you like babies. Good day, gentlemen."

Cannonball climbed back up into the cab. Zeph put his arm around Cody, and they started walking back to their car where Charlotte and Cheyenne were waiting. The air had frost in it, but the day was not uncomfortable.

"How long will it take for us to reach Omaha?" asked Cody.

"I'd say about three days."

"It took us a lot longer to come out by wagon from Pennsylvania."

"I guess it did. Train goes from California to New York in a week and a day."

Charlotte was at the window, smiling down. They could just make out her voice. "I thought we might have to haul everything out of the baggage car and wait for the next train east."

"We met the engineer!" said Cody excitedly. "A very nice man named Cannonball. He will blow the whistle four times when he sees buffalo!"

"Will he?" Charlotte laughed. "I hope he doesn't spot a herd at midnight."

Zeph and Cody swung up into the car and sat in their seats facing Charlotte and Cheyenne. The car was crowded with people heading east for Cheyenne, Omaha, Chicago, and New York. Charlotte handed them each an orange. Cody's eyes lit up.

"Something special," she said, offering the boy her black-handled John Petty & Sons penknife. "Real William Wolfskill oranges from Los Angeles, California."

Zeph glanced at the knife. "Where's that from?"

"It was Ricky's. He had it in the army."

"Sheffield, England?"

Charlotte looked over at him. "What a question. I never examined it with a magnifying glass. I just use it."

Zeph took out his own pocketknife, a J. M. Vance with a spear point and a small saw people called a cockspur. V&Co was stamped on the blade. He began to peel his orange. He noticed that Cody was more interested in the knives than he was in the oranges.

"Where did you find the fruit?" Zeph asked Charlotte.

She was helping Cheyenne use another knife that looked to be German made with mother-of-pearl handles. "There was a market downtown. I purchased more apples, too. In case we run into another blizzard."

Zeph grunted. "You think the locomotive will eat apples?"

"The engineer might."

Cody opened the knife Charlotte had given him and started poking at the skin on his orange, but he kept glancing up at Zeph.

"What is it, boy?" Zeph finally asked, popping a few orange segments into his mouth.

"What do you use the saw for?"

"Every now and then it cuts something better than the straight edge of the big blade."

"Where did you get it from, Mister—"

"What's that, son?" Zeph interrupted.

"Pa, where did you buy it from?" Cody's face reddened.

"Well, I picked it up in Pennsylvania, Cody." Zeph winked to ease the boy's discomfort at calling him Pa for the first time. "Here. Made in Philadelphia. Why don't you try it on that William Wolfskill?" He folded in the blade and saw and handed the pocketknife to the boy.

Cody's discomfort vanished as he held Zeph's knife with the warm honey bone handles.

"Thank you. . .Pa."

"You're welcome, son."

Charlotte glanced up from Cheyenne's orange. "I didn't know you'd been to Pennsylvania."

Zeph finished eating his orange and looked out the window at Ogden. "I've been."

"You've never mentioned it. Here I thought we had a great surprise in store for you."

Zeph could see she was miffed. He stared out the window at two men hitching a horse to a small wagon. "Sorry."

"When was that?"

Zeph watched the men load what looked to be sacks of lettuce into the wagon. "The war."

She sat stock-still for a moment and took this bit of information in. Cheyenne slipped the knife from Charlotte's hands and cut away at the orange.

"Gettysburg," Charlotte finally said.

"That's right."

Now it was her turn to look out the window at the men loading the wagon. "My father was killed at that battle."

Zeph didn't know what to say. "I didn't want to be there, Conner."

"Nor did he."

The edge was back in her voice. There was nothing he could do. It was over and done. Was she going to sit there and worry whether he was the man her father died beside? He thought it best to stand up.

"Wonder why we haven't started yet?' he said out loud.

A man in a white suit and gold paisley vest turned around and glanced up at him. "I just asked the conductor the same question. Apparently they're taking another stack of wood into the tender."

Zeph eased himself into the aisle. Charlotte reached out a hand.

"Where are you going?"

"The smoking car."

"But you don't smoke."

"Maybe Fremont Wyoming does."

She got up and slipped her arm through his.

"I'll walk with you," she said.

"Are you sure you want to?"

"Perfectly sure. Cody, help your sister finish peeling her orange."

"All right. . .Ma."

They walked arm in arm down the aisle of the car. There

was scarcely room to do this, but Charlotte was determined. Zeph kept banging into seats and people's knees and elbows. The smoking car had about half a dozen men in it who all stood up as Charlotte swept through.

"Good afternoon, gentlemen," she said.

In another car they sat down briefly in a set of vacant seats. She took his hand and squeezed it. Her eyes were dark violet.

"I am sorry. You were not responsible for the war or my father's death. You caught me off guard, that's all. I didn't know about Gettysburg."

"I don't talk about it."

"Is that battle the reason you won't wear a gun?"

"One reason."

"But a big reason."

"Yes."

"I admire you all the more for it."

Zeph looked down at the floor.

"Is there something else bothering you?" she asked.

Zeph lifted his eyes to hers. "When you and Cheyenne were having baths, Cody and I walked to the telegraph office."

Charlotte's gaze became more intense. "Was there something there?"

He nodded.

"Another Bible passage?"

"No. Nothing from Raber. This one was from Matt."

"What did he say?"

"The gang never came by Iron Springs. Matter of fact, they never came within a hundred miles of Iron Springs."

"Then where are they?"

"Nobody knows." He took her hands in his. "We have to stick together on this, Conner."

"I'm sorry. I didn't realize you had been in Pennsylvania during the war. I hate that conflict and everything about it. It was jarring to think about Gettysburg again. I was just out of sorts for a few minutes. I trust you, Fremont, and I know we will make it through this. I believe God meant us to see it through together."

"I haven't had a lot of time since I read the telegram to figure out what it means," he told her. "But I have prayed for wisdom about this."

"And what has God shown you?"

"I think that as soon as their accomplice telegraphed them we were headed for the railroad at Ogden they stopped thinking about Iron Springs. They knew they couldn't catch us. So they changed direction."

"To where?"

"If you wanted to make good time on horseback and try to get ahead of the train what route would you use?"

"I'm not sure." Zeph watched her brow wrinkle and the freckles gather tightly together around her small nose. "You can't ride through the Powder River Country. It's been closed to white travelers since the '68 treaty with Red Cloud."

"Are you sure?"

A flash of anger darkened Charlotte's eyes. "I'm the town librarian, remember? I read about these things all the time."

"What I meant was, do you think that treaty would keep Seraphim Raber and his crew off the Bozeman Trail?"

Her eyes widened. "But President Grant closed the forts along the Bozeman."

"All the better. No military patrols to slow them down."

"What about the tribes?"

"Raber and his men will move fast. Steal or buy fresh horses. Move by night as much as they can. I think Raber's more worried about the kids than he is the Indians."

The whistle blew. There was a jerk and a jolt, and Charlotte gripped Zeph's hands tightly. The train began to move forward.

"We should get back to the children," she said, getting to her feet.

She linked her arm through his again. They came back through the smoking car. It was empty. They reached their seats just as Cody sprinkled water from a canteen over Cheyenne's hands. She looked up at Zeph and Charlotte and smiled.

"My fingers are pretty sticky. Sorry."

"That's fine," said Charlotte as she took her seat.

Zeph noticed right away it was a Union army canteen covered in blue cloth. Charlotte caught his look.

"I used it on the stage," she said.

"I guess I didn't see it too clearly in the dark."

"It was Ricky's. He always carried it."

"I remember it now. How do you keep it looking so new?"

"I wash the cloth regularly."

The train gathered speed. Cheyenne and Cody had the window seats and eagerly gazed in all directions. Cheyenne said, "Buffalo, Indians, cavalry, US Grant, buffalo, Indians, cavalry, US Grant," and Charlotte arched her eyebrows.

"That's quite a chant, Miss Wyoming."

"I like the rhythm. Cody taught me."

Cody looked embarrassed. "I didn't teach her to chant.

I just told her that Cannonball would blow the whistle if he saw buffalo and that I hoped we'd see Plains Indians and cavalry, too."

She squeezed his hand. "That's all right. It might be nice to see all those things. Provided everyone comes in peace."

An hour passed. And another. Cody fell asleep with his head propped up on his hand and his elbow planted firmly on the windowsill. Cheyenne slumped into Charlotte's side. Charlotte placed her arm around the girl.

"Aren't they precious, Fremont?"

"They are. More precious than gold dust."

"That's a sweet way of putting it."

She stared out the window as the sun dropped lower and grew more golden. "Where do you think they'll show up?"

"They're going to keep riding the Bozeman and cutting a diagonal from west to east. They'll come out in Nebraska. We won't see a sign of them until well after Cheyenne."

"How long will that be?"

He shrugged. "Depends on where they want to make their move against us. They might wait until Omaha."

"You don't think that, do you?"

"No."

"How long, Fremont?"

"They'll want to put Fort Laramie well behind them. Catch us between Omaha and Cheyenne."

"You mean they'll try and stop the train?"

"There's six of them. Fewer men than that have held up trains."

Charlotte felt a shiver go through her like ice water. "Where are they going to block the tracks, Fremont?"

"The way I see it, they'll stick to the North Platte River after the Bozeman plays out and follow it right to the rail line. That'll put them far enough away from the law and the army to buy them some breathing room."

"Where and when, Fremont?"

"There's a little spot named Alkali that will suit them. Big Spring. O'Fallons. Maxwell. Any of them. Two days from here."

"Two days? Are you sure?"

"Less than two days."

She reached for his hand again. He held hers in both of his. The sun was beginning to set. The Rockies in the east were flames of crimson and bronze and made her cheeks shine.

"What will we do, Z?" she whispered.

He gave her a small smile and shook his head. "I don't know yet."

To himself he thought, *I can't say that I'll ever know, Charlotte.*

Chapter 12

Charlotte watched Zeph sleep.

They had enjoyed a fine supper the night before at the Green River Dining Hall in Green River, Wyoming. For the first time since she'd taken Cheyenne under her wing, the girl had taken a pencil to paper and tried to make a sketch of Castle Rock, a large hill in the vicinity. The sketch had been done so well it surprised Charlotte. Now they were through the high mountains and traveling across the plains.

The red light of dawn played over Zeph's eyelids and down over his mouth and the growth of beard that had begun in Virginia City, but he did not stir.

Somewhere in that head of his, she thought, *he is coming up with a plan to save us. Lord help him,* she prayed.

They had been so tired they hadn't bothered folding down their seats and making up their beds after Green River. All the others in their sleeper car had done so. Many of the temporary partitions that created a flimsy illusion of privacy were still in place. Charlotte yawned, with her arm over her mouth. They had all slept pretty well just the same. Perhaps tonight they might set things up so they could stretch out their legs and put their heads down onto soft white pillows.

Cody was up and whittling with the pocketknife Zeph had lent him. It looked to her as if a pretty good horse was emerging from the chunk of wood he'd picked off the ground in Green River. Cheyenne was still sleeping, nestled against Charlotte's side.

Charlotte gazed at the sky as it gradually turned blue like a fabric dipped in dye.

She opened a book in her lap and tried to read.

"I remember that."

She flicked her eyes off the book and up at Zeph. "Remember what?"

"*Great Expectations*. I took it out once."

She smiled. "But did you read it?"

He smiled back, sleep still in his brown eyes. "You think I didn't?"

"I'd just like to know. You borrowed a number of books from Iron Springs Public Library. I've often wondered how many of them you finished."

"Often?"

"Often. Your titles were intriguing. Let's see, *Oliver Twist* and *Barnaby Rudge* by Dickens. *The Three Musketeers, Twenty Years After,* and *The Count of Monte Cristo* by Dumas. I think you read everything by James Fenimore Cooper."

"I kept hoping you'd call me Natty Bumppo."

"I recall you took out *The Deerslayer* more than once."

"My favorite."

"So you read it?"

"Three times. I even read *Pride and Prejudice* like you wanted."

"Like I wanted?"

"'Mister Parker, you will find some interesting male protagonists in her novels, as well as others not to be emulated.'"

She laughed and put a hand over her mouth, as there were still so many people around them sleeping. "I don't know if I should believe you."

"'It is a truth universally acknowledged, that a single man in possession of a good fortune must be in want of a wife,'" he said, reciting the opening line of *Pride and Prejudice*.

Her hand was still over her mouth. "'I strive to do right, here,'" he continued, only this time quoting from *The Deerslayer* by Cooper, "'as the surest means of keeping all right, hereafter. Hetty was oncommon, as all that know'd her must allow, and her soul was as fit to consart with angels the hour it left its body, as that of any saint in the Bible!'"

Charlotte dropped her hand and gave a squeal of surprise and delight. The heavy man in the white suit and gold paisley vest snorted in his sleep. She clapped her hand over her mouth again.

"Mister Wyoming," she said through her fingers, "how can you play with such a good woman so? Have you really read all those books after all? Have you truly memorized all of Natty Bumppo's lines in *The Deerslayer*? Every day you become a different man than the one I imagined you were. I don't think I can bear it. You make my head spin as if I were waltzing."

"'Lord, Judith, what a tongue you're mistress of! Speech and looks go hand in hand, like, and what one can't do, the other is pretty sartain to perform! Such a gal, in a month, might spoil the stoutest warrior in the colony.'"

"Oh stop! I completely misjudged you. I thought you were a good-hearted cowboy and Christian."

"That's all I am."

"I did not think you carried Shakespeare in your saddlebag."

"'Shall I compare thee to a summer's day? Thou art more lovely and more temperate.'"

She dropped her hand from her mouth, her lips curved upward in a permanent smile, and shook her head. "You are incorrigible. And all this time it was my belief you took those books out of the library just to see me."

Zeph nodded. "That's exactly why I did it."

"And that you chose authors I mentioned I liked just to please me."

"That is the only reason I chose them."

"But you read them!"

Zeph shrugged and squinted at the ball of fire that was the sun lifting off the prairie. "Well, at first I read them because I had all these ideas of going on long evening rides with you and quoting the books to you."

"So you did want to impress me." She felt happy inside at this thought.

"Sure I did. Just didn't realize I'd like the stories so much. Mom was a great reader, and we had a fair-size bookshelf in the house. I read books about King Arthur and William Tell and Robin of Sherwood. We had books bound in leather that put the plays of Shakespeare into story form, so I read *Macbeth* and *Hamlet* and *King Lear*. My favorite was *Henry V*: 'once more unto the breach, dear friends, once more. . .' I may dress cowboy and talk cowboy and act cowboy, but I have a first-class education in me, Missus Wyoming. I just like to hide it the way a Cheyenne brave hides himself in the buffalo grass."

"Why?"

"Because no one would understand."

She gazed at him. Zeph had already shown himself to be more of a man than she had ever dreamed he was during their flight from Iron Springs—the way he'd listened as she told about her Amish past, how he'd ridden after her and brought her horse to a halt, when he'd climbed out of the stage in a roaring storm and led the team of horses forward and saved them all. Now he was sitting in front of her and quoting lines from books and poems he'd memorized just so he could speak them to her on evening rides in the mountains at sunset. It was too much for her to take in, an answer to prayer beyond what she could ask or imagine. Yet the promise she had made to her brother bound her, and the binding must keep them apart. She felt a wetness slip down her cheek, but she did nothing to brush it away.

"Here now," he said softly and leaned across to wipe her face with a clean blue bandanna. He had the scent of apples and woodsmoke on him, as well as the pleasant smell of fresh soap that he'd washed up with at Green River.

"Z," she whispered.

"It's gonna be all right now. See? I'm talking like a cowpoke again."

She laughed and shook her head. "It's all so beautiful, and it's more than I ever dreamed. It's too good to be true. I just know something bad is going to happen to take you away from me like Daddy was taken and Ricky and my mother."

"Shh. Shh. It doesn't have to happen that way again just because it's happened that way before. Chapters have different endings. Not all books leave you feeling sad, do they? *Pride and Prejudice* has a good marriage to bring the story to a close. Two good marriages, as a matter of fact."

"Those are just books, Z. This is real life."

"Books are written by people who've lived real life, Char. That's the kind of thing a librarian like you should be telling me. What can a busted-up old cowpuncher really know about it?"

She laughed. "Some busted-up old cowpuncher."

The whistle suddenly shrieked four times in a row. Zeph and Charlotte jumped. People stirred all around them and asked what was going on in confused and belligerent voices. Partitions came down. Cody's eyes went wide in disbelief, and he pressed his face to the window.

"Buffalo!" he shouted. "Buffalo!"

Cheyenne woke up and looked out. Their seats were on the south side of the car, and the four of them could see the herd clearly.

"How many, Pa?" asked Cody.

Zeph was leaning over him to gaze out the window. "I'd say seven or eight hundred. Maybe a thousand. Isn't that something?"

"Did you ever see more than this?"

"Son, I've seem 'em so thick there was no grass for a hundred miles, just buffalo moving like a wide and muddy brown river, like some kind of prairie Mississippi of hair and horns."

Cannonball had slowed the train down so passengers could get a better look. The man in the white suit stooped in the aisle to get a look out their window.

"Amazing!" he said. "I thought there were only a few left."

"Mister," Zeph said, "compared to what there was twenty years ago, this is a few."

Charlotte found herself fascinated by a grand bull at the edge of the rolling herd. It seemed to be staring at her and at the locomotive with a grandeur and defiance that impressed her, as if the sturdy old bull were declaring, "You will not defeat me. I will endure. You may have your hour. But I will not be vanquished." Then he and the herd were gone, a dark shape moving slowly over the plains and raising a small haze of dust, not much, for there was some frost on the ground. Finally, there was only a black speck that could have been anything.

"What does buffalo taste like?" asked Cheyenne.

"Good," said Zeph, sitting back down, "it's very good."

"I'd like to try it someday."

"Well, my girl, we'll see what we can do."

Charlotte looked at the health in Cody's face and in Cheyenne's and thanked God. She also saw the sparkle in Zeph's eyes and realized how much he loved the West and the things that were part of it that few easterners understood. How would he feel being cooped up in Pennsylvania—the quietness of the land, the softness of the snow and winds, the lack of mountains and sharp peaks, and the impossibility of a chance glimpse of bison thundering over country that stretched for hundreds of miles without a building or a road or a sign?

If we get to Pennsylvania.

The fear fastened its teeth into her heart and mind, and she swiftly lost the peace and joy she had just been delighting in. Zeph was watching her face. She felt his gaze and looked over at him, not bothering to hide the cold, dark sensations that were paralyzing her thoughts and her happiness.

He understood. One hand went into the pocket of the coat she had sewn for him and came out with his brother's Bible. He opened it but did not bother to look down as he said, "'The Lord is my shepherd; I shall not want. . . . Yea, though I walk through the valley of the shadow of death, I will fear no evil: for thou art with me. . . . Thou preparest a table before me in the presence of mine enemies: thou anointest my head with oil; my cup runneth over. Surely goodness and mercy shall follow me all the days of my life.'"

She sat and listened and waited. Suddenly she realized how much she liked his voice and how much it soothed her to have him read to her.

"Go on," she said.

"That's it in a nutshell, Conner." He smiled. "I'm getting used to that name. It's not half bad."

"Please go on."

"Only way to beat this fear is to face it. We can't keep running. We'll be running forever as long as Raber's alive: Wyoming, Nebraska, Illinois, Pennsylvania. He'd follow us all the way up into Canada or down into Comanche country. Probably cross the ocean to England to corner us in a back alley in London. Only one thing we can do."

Charlotte felt goose bumps on her arms under the sleeves of her dress, as if she knew what he was going to say before he said it, as if the same words were in her mind, too.

"What is it?" she asked.

Zeph rubbed the beard on his jaw and looked away from her out at the miles of sunlit prairie glittering with morning frost.

"We're going to have to make sure he knows where we are and where we're going and when we'll be there. We're going to have to draw him out and then face him down. We're going to have to put the kids and ourselves right out there in the open as bait. Bait for a mad wolf named Seraphim Raber."

Chapter 13

Zeph stood at the door to the telegraph office. He thought a moment and then pulled the badge from his pocket and pinned it on his coat. Then decided to remove his coat and broad-brimmed hat. Charlotte had plucked a spare from her luggage to replace the hat the winter storm had taken. He draped the hat and coat on a bench just outside the door, took the badge off the coat, and pinned it onto his shirt instead.

"Afternoon, deputy," said the elderly man at the counter.

Zeph nodded. "I'll need to send telegrams to the federal marshal in Iron Springs, Montana Territory, and another to the commander at Fort Laramie."

"Sure enough. Here's the pad."

Zeph hunched over the countertop with a stub of pencil and began to print.

Marshal Matthew Parker
*   We have had no trouble and are carrying on into*
Nebraska, kids are fine, will telegraph from Omaha.
*   Deputy Marshal Zephaniah Parker*

He and Charlotte had decided to make sure Raber knew

where they were headed and when. They counted on the accomplice, whoever it was, to get ahold of Raber and let him know what their plans were and that the children were with them.

Then he wrote another telegram out for Fort Laramie. Once again, he and Charlotte had talked it over. There was no guarantee the commander would do what Zeph asked. He only hoped the chance of nabbing Raber would make the fort commander cast all other plans to the wind. At the bottom he wrote, Zephaniah Truett Parker, Deputy US Marshal.

He put a few dollars on the counter, but the elderly man waved him off. "No charge, Deputy."

"Well, then, consider it a lawman's contribution to your retirement fund."

The man smiled. "Why, thank'ee kindly, Deputy."

Outside Zeph suddenly noticed the chill in the bright blue air and pulled his coat back on. With the large hat on his head and the badge in his pocket, he began to walk toward the shops on Main Street, no longer Deputy Marshal Zephaniah Parker, but Fremont Wyoming, farmer, father of two, and husband to one. He began to whistle a hymn without thinking, "Shall We Gather at the River?"

He found Charlotte and the children in a general store, one he remembered from '73, the year he buried his father, except the shop was much larger now. Cody was staring at the six-guns locked under the glass countertop and Charlotte was saying, "Never mind those things, Cody, they're nothing but death and destruction. Let me buy you something sweet instead. What do you think of these candies? Wouldn't you like a big bag of them?"

Cody stared at the small colored objects in the jar. "What are they?"

"They call them jelly beans."

"What do they taste like?"

"Oh, they taste very good, son," said Zeph putting an arm around him. "First had some when I was in the army. A fellow named Schrafft used to have them sent down from Boston for the troops. The boys'd fight over these more than they'd fight over coffee. Yellow is lemon, red is raspberry or strawberry or cherry, black is licorice flavor. A big bag'd keep you smiling all the way through Nebraska."

"Excellent," Cody said with a grin.

"I'm happy to do it for you, dear," Charlotte replied. "What about you, Cheyenne? A Silverhair and the three-bears size of bag? One that's just right, not too big, not too small?"

"I'm too old for that." Cheyenne's eyes blazed up and then settled. "I'll be eleven in a few months."

Charlotte and Zeph glanced at one another.

"Well, then," said Charlotte, "what would you like?"

"Chocolate would suit me."

Charlotte snorted briefly. "I'm sure it would. Pick out what you'd like."

She pointed at a large bar of dark chocolate, and the shopkeeper took it, wrapped it, and placed it in a paper bag.

"Thanks," said Cheyenne to Charlotte.

"You're welcome, dear."

Cannonball had left them shortly after the buffalo sighting. Another engineer was running the US Grant into Nebraska. As they climbed back into their car, Zeph noticed familiar faces that were carrying on, as they were, for points farther east: there was a family of five headed for Florida who always smiled at Zeph and Charlotte and the children; a man and wife who bickered about returning to Liverpool, England, or taking a train back to Sacramento, California; and the portly man in the white suit and gold vest who always tipped his hat to Charlotte.

"Where you headed?" he asked them as they resumed their seats.

"As far as the rails will run," said Zeph.

"I see." The man nodded. "Henry Chase, by the way."

"Fremont Wyoming. My wife, Charlotte, and my two children, Cody and Cheyenne."

"How do you do?" said the man, standing up.

"A pleasure, Mister Chase," responded Charlotte, inclining her head.

Zeph knew his sudden good cheer came from having written out those two telegrams. Instead of running and hiding, he had a chance to fight back and protect Charlotte and the children. It made him feel better than he'd felt in a long time. If only the plan would work. If only Raber would take the bait.

He settled himself in his seat. He could see the length of the car and everyone coming in and out from the front of the train. Opening a package of Adams New York No. 1 chewing gum, he handed each of them a piece, though Cheyenne preferred her chocolate. Then he glanced out the windows on the north side of the train across the aisle and watched two cowboys, covered in dust, ride past the depot.

Suddenly a pang of fear stabbed him like a sharp knife. Suppose those two had just come off the Bozeman Trail? How would he know who were just ordinary cowpokes and who were Raber's gunmen? Just then a man stepped into the car. He was dressed in black from head to foot except for a few silver conchas on his hat and one on his holster. Tall and lean, strength coiled under his clothing. He glanced around, black carpetbag in his grip, met Zeph's gaze with a look like a gunsight, then took an empty seat halfway down the car, his back to Zeph. He pulled off his dark sheepskin jacket and rolled it up on the seat beside him, tipped his hat to an attractive young woman sitting opposite, and gazed out the window to his left at the same two cowboys Zeph had been watching. The cowboys had stopped and were sitting on their horses, staring at the train.

For the first time in over ten years, Zeph wished he'd gone heeled, wished he'd bought a small pistol at the general store and slipped it into his coat pocket. What would he do if the man in black was one of Raber's crew? If he came at them in the night with the train clicking through the wide-open Nebraska miles? If the cowboys were there to back him up and they meant to make their move before the US Grant pulled out of the station?

There was nothing Zeph could do. Pinning on his badge would not stop them. If he made his way back to the baggage car to get the gun, he was pretty sure the car would be locked. And even if he got the conductor or one of his assistants to open it up and found his father's Remington, what good would that do when the cartridges that made it a threat to be reckoned with were rusting in the snow and mud on a road that ran north out of Iron Springs?

Charlotte read his face. "What's wrong?"

Zeph had stopped chewing his gum. "Too many strangers."

She glanced out the windows across the aisle. "Those two men on horseback?"

"They just sit and watch the train."

"No harm in that."

"They showed up the same time a man who looks like a gunslinger got into the car. He's sitting just ahead of us, and he's dressed to kill."

Charlotte looked over her shoulder and back at him. "They wouldn't do anything now."

"Why not?"

"The law in Cheyenne. They'd be caught."

"Char," he said in a low voice, "they'd gun down the law as quick as they'd gun down us."

They were silent a few moments. Cheyenne was taking bites of the bar of chocolate and sketching on a pad of paper. Zeph watched her scribbles turn into mountains and horses and buffalo. She was very good. He looked up at Charlotte.

"Even if we had a picture," he said softly, "and it was posted in every town and village and railroad crossing, it would make no difference. Raber would come for us anyway. Out of revenge."

The whistle blew. The car shuddered. The train began to move.

Zeph kept his eyes on the cowboys and on the man in black. The cowboys kept staring but made no attempt to follow the train. The man in black shifted his weight and pulled his hat down over his face and went to sleep. The train picked up speed.

Charlotte gave him a look that said, "You see? You're getting all worked up over nothing."

Zeph shook his head. "It can happen anytime," he whispered, "day or night, when we're asleep or awake. The man in black can make his play for us whenever he wants, and there's nothing I can do to protect you."

"Unless the plan works," she said quietly.

"If the plan works. If we even get to the only place in Nebraska where the plan has any chance of working at all."

"How long?"

"I'm not sure."

"How long, Z?"

Zeph shrugged. "We'll be out of Wyoming Territory in no time. There'll be some night travel. It won't be long. Well before noon tomorrow it'll be all over. One way or another."

"May I borrow your brother's Bible?"

Zeph handed it over.

"I'm going to mark a place with this leather bookmark I have. Ricky brought it home from Denver. I'm tucking it in right here. Now tomorrow, when this is all over, I want you to take this Bible out of your pocket, open it to where I've placed the bookmark, and read the passage out loud to us. But I don't want you looking at it before that, promise?"

"I swear."

She gave it back to him, and he slipped it into one of his outer pockets. Then he narrowed his eyes and looked her over from bonnet to boots.

"What on earth are you doing?" she asked.

"It's not the same dress."

"No, it's not."

"It's a lighter shade of gray."

"Yes."

"When did you do that?"

"I changed at the last meal stop before Cheyenne. Glad you've finally noticed."

"It's very pretty."

"Really? It's supposed to be very plain."

"I'd like to know whatever would look plain on you. You'd make rags look like silk."

Charlotte smiled. "Why, that's quite a compliment, Mister Wyoming. I'm glad the gentleman rancher has returned. I thought I'd lost him."

Zeph looked at the children. Cheyenne had put aside her drawings and nodded off, and Cody had his head on his hand and his arm propped on the window ledge, snoring quietly into the glass. Zeph leaned over toward Charlotte.

"If they stop the train tomorrow," he said, "go with the kids back to the baggage car. I'll make sure it's open. Hide there. They may not think to check it or have the time. All right?"

"I'm not leaving you, Z."

"You will. For the children's sake. All right?"

Charlotte looked sadly out the window at the fields of snow and grass. "All right."

Zeph slid down in his seat and closed his eyes.

Lord, went the words through his head, *I'm not the kind of praying man Jude is, but You've got to help us out, You've got to bring things together, or we're not going to make it. Have mercy on us. Have mercy on the kids. May Your holy angels defeat the angel of death. In the name of Jesus.*

He felt the slightest bit better and the slightest bit calmer. Sleep began shutting him down. He heard the rustle of Charlotte's dress and caught a whiff of her perfume. Part of him thought of the man in black, but the larger part thought of Nebraska and the morning and Seraphim Raber. Then his mind was filled only with the rhythm of the train and the *click-click-click* of the iron wheels as they ran over the rails, taking them closer to the east and closer to Nebraska and closer to the day which the Lord had made, a day on which they might live or they might die.

Chapter 14

When it happened, it happened so quickly Zeph barely had time to take it in.

That night they had turned their seats into beds and pulled another bed open above their heads. Cody had taken that one, Cheyenne was with Charlotte, Zeph slept on the outside close to the aisle. They had not set up the partition people often used for privacy because Zeph wanted to hear and see everything that was going on.

Something made him stir. He glanced out a window and saw a sign roll past that said ALKALI. Light was beginning to flood the east, and he wondered about a breakfast stop and why they hadn't pulled into the small town. Then he remembered the names Alkali, O'Fallons, and Maxwell. He sat up, fully awake, and looked for the man in black. Too many partitions were in the way. For all he knew, the man had changed seats to get even closer to them.

"Charlotte!" he whispered urgently.

"Mmm," she mumbled.

"Charlotte! Wake up! We're here!"

"Where?"

The car shook and squealed and slammed to a stop. People

were thrown out of their beds and into the aisle. Partitions collapsed. A woman screamed, and several men began to shout for the conductor.

Charlotte was awake now, her hair in disarray, looking, Zeph could not help but notice, warm and childlike and wonderful; but when someone yelled, "There's men on horseback in masks; the train's being robbed," he thrust her sheepskin jacket at her and said, "Get the kids to the baggage car."

Shots were fired outside the window. Cody came sprawling out of his bed above them. Zeph put Cody's jacket over the boy's thin shoulders. "Go with your mother and sister to the baggage car behind us. It's two cars farther on. You lead the way. Go now."

"No!" Cody pushed away from Zeph with all the strength a burst of anger can give a twelve-year-old boy. "They killed my mother. They killed my father. I'm going to fight."

"Cody, you have to get to the baggage car."

"I'm not hiding anymore, and I'm not running. I will face them."

Zeph saw the blaze in the boy's eyes. He meant it. But Zeph didn't have time to argue this through. There were two more gunshots. He gripped Cody's shoulders.

"Who is going to protect Miss Spence? Who is going to protect Cheyenne? If they are in the baggage car and we are both here, who will save them if the gang breaks into their car first?"

The boy hesitated.

"Take them to safety," Zeph urged. "Fight for them."

"All right," Cody said.

Charlotte was on her feet, holding a sleepy Cheyenne by the hand, her face and eyes a strange mixture of fear, anger, and defiance. "I am not happy about leaving you," she said to Zeph.

"I'll be okay."

She looked at him in the half-light as the sun began to slip over the rim of the prairie. People cried and shrieked all around them.

Cody seized her hand and led her and Cheyenne to the door. Then he turned.

"Is the baggage door open?" Cody asked.

"Yes," Zeph said. There was another gunshot. "I got a steward to open it for me last night after you'd all fallen asleep. Then I jimmied it, so he couldn't lock it back up again. I saw some saddle blankets in there. Maybe get under a bunch of them. Hurry now."

"Z!"

Charlotte's eyes were like twin fires in the dawn light coming through the windows. "There's no man like you, mister. No man ever."

And she was gone.

Zeph spun around and looked for the man in black. He was sitting in the same seat, cool as ice, while pandemonium reigned left and right of him. The pretty young woman, her face flushed, suddenly asked, "What do we do? Where do we go?"

"Just sit tight," Zeph heard the man say in a deep voice. "Give them your diamonds and pearls, and they won't take anything more."

Zeph clenched his fists. Sure, easy for him to say; it was his buddies that were going to board the train and shove their gun barrels into innocent people's faces. *Maybe I should try and take him from behind.* He took a few steps forward and then looked out the windows on both sides of the train. Men with flour sacks for masks were riding up and down the line. There were four or five of them, and every few moments another one of them would fire into the air with a pistol or rifle.

Some children had begun crying. He saw the family that was bound for Florida huddled in tears at the front of the car. Zeph looked in vain on both sides of the railway for any sign of troopers from Fort Laramie. It looked like they were going to have to bluff their way out of this one. *Lord, the baggage car has to work. Help us.*

He saw a tall man ride up to their car and swing down from the saddle. He wore a long white duster that was covered in dirt and grime. The door at the front of the car banged open. The woman who couldn't make up her mind between Liverpool and Sacramento shrieked. The outlaw had a flour sack with two ragged holes cut in it for his eyes and a third for his mouth. A short-barreled pistol was in his left hand. In a voice like stones dropping in a bucket he said, "I'm lookin' for a man goes by the name Zephaniah Parker. Any of you folks know if he's in this car?"

No one spoke, but the sobbing and crying carried on.

"How 'bout Charlotte Spence?"

Again, no one spoke up.

The man dug a small bag out of one of the pockets of his duster.

"Gold nuggets," he said. "It's yours if you point either of 'em out to me. And then I won't have to kill no one neither."

Zeph was sure a number of people would have jumped at the chance if only they knew who he was. One thing he couldn't figure out was why the man in black and the outlaw hadn't acknowledged each other, but he figured that when the time was right they'd hitch up and make their play. They were probably waiting to see if they could flush their prey first.

"There's two kids traveling with 'em. The man and woman abducted 'em. You'd be doing us all a favor if you pointed the kids out to me. I got to get 'em back to their rightful parents."

Who would buy that story? thought Zeph.

"The kids' names are Cody and Cheyenne Wyoming."

Fear ran through Zeph. How could the outlaw know that? The answer came quick as a peal of thunder—Raber's accomplice in Iron Springs.

To Zeph's dismay, the heavy man in the white suit and gold paisley vest, who'd introduced himself as Henry Chase, stood up, body shaking, and pointed a finger at him.

"There!" he squeaked in a high voice. "That's him! He goes by the name Fremont Wyoming! But he calls his children Cheyenne and Cody! He told them to hide in one of the other cars!"

"Is that a fact?"

The outlaw moved toward Zeph. "Well, Mister Parker, I got a bone to pick with you. Riding the Bozeman night and day ain't no Presbyterian picnic. Injuns killed my best horse. I've already taken a great dislike to you. So here's how it's gonna play out. I got questions; you got answers. The sooner you give me the kids the easier your pain's gonna be—"

A black leg shot out, and the outlaw tripped and fell on his face in the aisle. He was a tough one though. Zeph watched him twist like a snake and come up with his gun ready to fire. A black hand grabbed the outlaw's gun, so the hammer wouldn't go down, and clamped onto his wrist at the same time. The outlaw yelped. His gun fell to the floor. Another black hand swung at his head with a pistol butt. *Thunk.* It sounded to Zeph like a hammer hitting a stump. The outlaw lay still.

The man in black quickly put handcuffs on the unconscious gunman. Zeph heard him mutter, "One for the hangman," and then he stood up, tall, dark, and dangerous. He gave Henry Chase, quivering in his white suit, a piercing glance—"I want to have a word with you"—and came toward Zeph. Suddenly he smiled and touched the brim of his hat.

"Mister Parker, I am Marshal Michael James Austen. Your brother Matt thought I might find you on the train to Omaha, Nebraska."

Chapter 15

The marshal shook Zeph's hand. Zeph was still trying to take it all in.

"My brother told you I'd be on this train?" he finally got out.

"He did. I work out of Cheyenne, and I got a telegram from him. Took me three cars, but I finally found you. Family of four. Handsome woman. He gave me a pretty good description of your face and build, though I have to say he got your clothes all wrong. Where are the others?"

"In the baggage car."

"It'll be chilly in there. Best get them out before the kids catch their death."

"But what about the rest of the gang?"

The marshal looked out the windows. "They don't know what's going on in here. Besides, they'll have their hands full shortly."

"What do you mean?"

"Do you have a pocket watch handy, Mister Parker?"

"Lost mine in a roundup last fall. Never got around to replacing it."

"Occupational hazard, I guess. I punched cows once."

He pulled a gleaming silver watch from his black vest pocket and flipped open the top. Glancing at the dial he said, "They're five minutes late. Anytime now. Maybe wait on the kids a little bit."

There was a flurry of gunfire just as he finished his sentence. Somebody cheered. North of the tracks cavalry was pouring out of a gully and pounding down on the outlaws. Several were firing carbines as they rode. More gunfire from south of the train made him turn his head. Dozens of blue uniformed cavalrymen in brown buffalo coats were charging across the prairie at the outlaw gang from that side as well. Puffs of gun smoke erupted from their rifle and pistol barrels. A man cheered again, and soon the whole car was bursting with shouts and whistles. Zeph felt relief wash through him as if he'd just taken a large drink of cool water.

"Folks!" called the marshal. "You'd best get yourselves down on the floor! A stray bullet may come through one of the windows!"

When a bullet smashed one of the windows, Henry Chase almost pushed himself through the floorboards. Marshal Austen chuckled, and Zeph wondered if that hadn't been one of the reasons he wanted everyone on the floor to begin with. As for himself, the marshal remained standing and watching the action, so Zeph stood with him.

Horses raced back and forth, clods of frozen earth flew up into the air, smoke from the gunfire billowed and floated in the morning frost. One outlaw had been shot out of the saddle and stood with a hand clamped over his bleeding shoulder. The others had laid down a blistering fire, wounded several soldiers, and made a run for it on horseback. Gradually the shooting petered out. An officer shouted, "It's all over, folks, all over. You can rest easy now!"

Henry Chase slowly raised his head, *like a turtle,* Zeph thought. Marshal Austen had the satisfaction of glancing at Chase and seeing the grime and stains covering his white suit and gold vest. He nodded and smiled and went out the front door of the car. Turning his head, he called back to Zeph, "Now's the time to bring your family out." He stepped outside to speak with the officers from Fort Laramie.

Cody was right at the door when Zeph opened it and ready to brain him with an iron bar.

"Whoa, cowboy." Zeph held up his hands. "I'm one of the good guys."

Cody's eyes were like steel. "What happened?"

"They shot one. Caught another. The rest of the gang ran."

Cody brought Charlotte and Cheyenne out from under a stack of saddles, blankets, and harness. Charlotte gripped a pitchfork in her fists. Cheyenne held a steel currycomb and had the face of a cougar.

"I wouldn't want to tangle with you," he said.

"Where are they?" asked Cheyenne. "Are they right behind you?"

"They wounded one, the others ran, they caught two, the army has them."

Cody perked up. "The army?"

"That's right. Cavalry in blue uniforms and riding horses and blowing trumpets and everything. Go and take a look."

Cody flew out of the baggage car. Cheyenne ran after him,

still holding the currycomb. Zeph and Charlotte had a moment alone in the dim light.

She anxiously studied his face. "Are you all right?"

"I am."

"Did any passengers get hurt?"

"Well, maybe Henry Chase's pride, but he'll live."

"What do you mean?"

Zeph explained how Chase had pointed him out and that the gunslinger-turned-marshal had taken great delight in watching Chase soil his white suit squirming about on the floor to avoid gunshots. Charlotte's face brightened with anger.

"He told the murderer who you were and that Cody and Cheyenne were with you? What a despicable rattlesnake!"

"Go easy on him. He's just a frightened little man."

"Go easy on him!"

"You have that thunderstorm blue about you."

"What?"

"You know that dark blue of thunderclouds when they're coming at you full of wind and hail and fury? That's the color of your eyes right now."

"How can you tell what color my eyes are in here?"

"They glow."

Charlotte smiled. "Oh yes?" Then she had a look of concern. "You're sure you didn't get hurt?"

"Well, the outlaw meant to give me a going over. But the man in black took him down."

"What's the marshal's name?"

"Austen. Michael James Austen."

"Your brother telegraphed him?"

"Yes ma'am."

"'Yes ma'am.'" She made a face that brought her freckles tight around her nose. She kissed him on the mouth and then pulled away. He put one hand gently behind her head and brought her lips back to his. He expected the moment to be brief. But she slipped her arms about him and held him close. They kissed a second time.

"I was worried," she whispered.

"I know."

"Were you ever afraid?"

"Only that he might get past me."

"He'd never have gotten past you."

She gave him one more kiss and then stepped back and smoothed her gray dress. "The children will be wondering where we are."

Zeph felt light-headed. "After you."

When they got back to the car, three cavalrymen were talking with passengers, and Cody and Cheyenne were glued to one of them. They all wore buffalo coats over their uniforms. The unconscious outlaw had already been carried out. Marshal Austen touched his hat brim at Charlotte's entry and introduced himself and the officer standing with him. "This is First Lieutenant Robbie Hanson."

"Ma'am," said Hanson, giving a short tug on the brim of his cavalry Stetson. The number two stood out over the crossed sabers on his hat.

"Lieutenant. I see you're with the Second Cavalry. One of the best."

"Company K. The best I believe, Missus Wyoming. I hope

I find you well after your ordeal?"

"Quite well, thank you. The greater part of my ordeal consisted of hiding under a musty saddle blanket and trying hard not to sneeze."

The men laughed.

"Well, ma'am," said the lieutenant, "I think I can safely say that your saddle blanket days are behind you. We have two of the gang in custody. The others are probably halfway to Mexico. We have already thanked your husband for relaying the information to us at Fort Laramie that permitted us to be at this location today to capture them. There was a score to settle."

"You gentlemen have done an admirable job. I thank you with all my heart for protecting us from these savages. I especially thank you for delivering the children from their hands."

"It was an honor, ma'am," replied the lieutenant.

"Very much so," responded Marshal Austen.

"Were any of your men hurt or wounded, Lieutenant Hanson?"

"Five, thank you for asking, ma'am. They will be all right."

"I am glad to hear it. Well, Lieutenant, what happens now?"

"Now, ma'am," said Lieutenant Hanson, "we will take our prisoners ahead to the depot at Maxwell where a special train that set out from Omaha yesterday will meet us. The train will take the prisoners and their guards to Cheyenne where they will be put on trial. Then there will be a public hanging."

Charlotte's face whitened. "A hanging? Both of them?"

"Yes ma'am."

Charlotte recovered and patted him on the cheek. "I understand, Lieutenant Hanson. Thank you again for all you have done for us. I'll let you carry on with your duties."

"Thank you, ma'am. Will you be riding with us, Marshal Austen?"

Austen shook his head. "I'll take this train and go ahead to Maxwell. I'll meet you there when you arrive."

Lieutenant Hanson saluted and turned to leave the car, tapping his two men on the back as he did so. Cody and Cheyenne walked with their trooper to the door. He shook Cody's hand and gave Cheyenne a kiss on the cheek. Then, as he turned to go, he suddenly planted his Stetson on Cody's bare head and, whipping off his yellow scarf, tied it around Cheyenne's neck. Grinning, he climbed down from the car, swung up into the saddle, and galloped off with a wave of his hand and a shout.

Cody and Cheyenne came running back to Zeph and Charlotte.

"Look at this!" cried Cody. The Stetson had flopped down over his eyes.

"Very handsome," said Charlotte, "but you will have to let me put some paper under the sweatband, so it will fit."

"He gave me his scarf," said Cheyenne. "How does it look?"

"Wonderful. On windy days you could use it to keep your hair in place as well."

"No, it always needs to be around my neck." Cheyenne's face was set. "Just the way Trooper Johnny wore it."

"Trooper Johnny, is it? Suit yourself."

The whistle blew. People were tidying up their seats and putting away bedding. Charlotte began to do the same as the train lurched and started forward. Cavalrymen walked their horses on either side of the train. The two prisoners, unmasked, were escorted between them. Neither of the outlaws had boots. The breath of men and of horses hung like a white haze in the cold air.

Charlotte said to Zeph, "I can't see either of the outlaws' faces, only the backs of their heads. Did they catch Seraphim Raber?"

"I don't know."

"Did the others get away?"

"Yes."

The train left the cavalrymen and their prisoners behind. Marshal Austen watched the morning sun run over the prairie for a few moments, and then he said to Zeph in a low voice, "Your brother told me you don't go heeled."

"That's right."

"What would you have done with that outlaw if I hadn't been in the car?"

"I guess I would have tried to wrestle him to the ground if he got close enough."

"What if he kept his distance and just kept putting bullets into you?"

"He wouldn't have done that. He needed to know where the kids were at."

"He only had a couple more cars to search. He would've found the baggage car and gone through that, too. He didn't need you. If you'd told him where they were it would've made his job easier, that's all."

"I would never have told him."

"That's right. And once he'd put enough holes in you and realized that, he would've gone looking in the cars behind you and left you on the floor to bleed out."

"It's personal."

Austen nodded. "Most of us have our war stories, Mister Parker. I wouldn't touch a firearm going on five years after Appomattox. Worked cattle in Texas and then ran a dry goods store in Missouri. Had a friend elected town sheriff nearby who swore off killing after Lee surrendered. Never wore a sidearm or carried a rifle or shotgun, though his deputies did. This all works out fine long as you've got outlaws that respect the code. There's many won't draw on an unarmed man. But the day comes you've got a gang that will. Perk was healthy up until a Sunday the Murfreesboro Gang were out hunting men that had been Union officers. Shot him full of holes and left him lying in the street. He lived. Lost all but one arm. Perk's not a lawman anymore. Can't take care of himself or his own family, let alone the citizens of a town that would be counting on him."

Charlotte stuffed paper inside the cavalry Stetson's sweatband Cody wanted to wear. "And what became of the dry goods merchant Michael James Austen?"

Austen fixed his gaze on her. "Why, missus, the same gang rode back into the neighborhood a month later when someone told them I'd been a Yankee colonel. They laughed when my wife pleaded that I didn't have a gun. Strung me up by my feet and covered me in flour and molasses. Said I wasn't but half a man, and they wouldn't even waste half a bullet on me."

Charlotte felt a sadness go through her. "At least they let you live."

"Did they, Miss Spence? They snatched up my wife and two

children when they left. The kids are hollering, and I'm hanging upside down, choking on the molasses they poured into my mouth—I couldn't do a thing. Never saw them again. I hired Pinkerton's to track them down. Pinkerton's followed their trail as far as Arizona Territory. Then the gang vanished. I did some searching on my own. The story went that the gang had been wiped out by Mescalero Apache."

Chapter 16

Charlotte did not know what to say. She wondered what Zeph would have done under similar circumstances. Neither of the children was listening. Cody had his hat on and was drawing cavalrymen on the pad of paper with strong, dark strokes, the man back to being a boy. Cheyenne was daydreaming and fingering the yellow scarf tied around her throat.

Austen coughed. "There's something you don't see every day."

Out the windows that looked south, a line of Indians on horseback were trotting single file.

"A war party!" cried Cody.

Austen shook his head. "No war paint. A hunting party. They're heading west. I expect they're following a herd of buffalo."

All the Indians were men, all were wrapped in buffalo robes or red point blankets, all had repeating rifles. A few wore eagle feathers in their hair. They did not look at the train. It was as if the railroad did not exist. There were about fifty of them. They stared straight ahead and their heads were erect.

"Lakota Sioux," said Zeph.

Austen nodded. "Allies of the Cheyenne. Looks like Oglala, some of the Kiyuksa band. I recognize a few of them. They're a ways south of the Black Hills."

"What will happen when they run into the Second Cavalry?" asked Cody.

"They'll ignore one another," said Austen. "The Sioux haven't been raiding, and Hanson has to get his prisoners to Wyoming."

"At least the gold rush in the Black Hills is over," said Zeph.

"For now."

Austen tugged his pocket watch from his vest and consulted it. "We'll be into Maxwell shortly. It's only a half-hour run." From another vest pocket he brought out his badge. He smiled at Zeph. "I guess I've played a gunslinger on his way to points east long enough. I like black, but I like silver, too."

He stood up and pulled on his dark sheepskin coat. Then he clapped a hand to Zeph's shoulder. "No man can tell another man what to do. I admire your sand, Parker. And I wish you all the best. I pray to God it will be a clear run for you into Omaha and Chicago. If there's anything I can do, telegraph me at Cheyenne."

He began to walk up the aisle as the train slowed and the brakes squealed. Charlotte reached out and touched his arm.

"And are you a praying man, Marshal Austen?" she asked earnestly.

"On occasion."

"Then let's pray your family is alive. Isn't it possible the Mescalero have adopted your children and are raising them? And that your wife is with them in some Apache camp?"

He nodded. "It's possible."

He continued walking. When he reached his seat, he bent

down and picked up his black carpetbag. The pretty young woman who'd sat across from him rose to say something with a most engaging smile. But he touched his hat brim and said, "I am a family man, miss," and carried on to the door. He stood there as the train came to a stop. Then he looked down the length of the car to Henry Chase.

"Mister Chase."

The man looked up in surprise and a bit of fear. "Yes sir?"

"You'd best be coming with me."

"But, sir—"

"Aiding an outlaw gang, Mister Chase. You and I need to talk."

"I need to get to—"

"Come along, Mister Chase."

He pulled aside his sheepskin coat just enough for Chase and everyone else to see the silver badge he'd pinned to his vest. Chase looked around him for support, but there was none. Reluctantly he got to his feet and walked in his stained suit and vest to the front of the car. Austen stepped to one side. "After you."

Chase climbed down the steps and Austen followed him. Then they walked back toward the baggage car. No one boarded the train. After a minute or two, the whistle shrieked and the US Grant began to pull out of the small town.

Zeph watched Marshal Austen—lean, tall, in black—standing beside Henry Chase—portly, short, in white—on the station platform with three gold carpetbags at Chase's feet. Then the train left them behind, and there was only a row of large bare-branched cottonwoods rolling past the windows.

"I feel alone," Charlotte said.

Zeph nodded. "I know. I trusted that man."

"It's chillier in here than it was yesterday."

"Mercury's dropped, I expect. Maybe put your sheepskin coat on. Here." Zeph brought a white blanket with colored stripes out from under his feet. "One of these'll help, too."

"Why, it looks new."

"I believe Marshal Austen left it for us."

"Marshal Austen?"

"Who else would have done it?"

"But we were both here—"

"He did it while we were in the baggage car, I expect. He left this also." Zeph held the silver pocket watch in his hand. "And this." A package of Black Jack chewing gum.

Tears sprang to Charlotte's eyes, and she took a handkerchief out of a pocket in her coat. "Of course a gunslinger in black would chew that kind of gum."

"Could I have some?" Cody has his eye on the package.

Charlotte reached over, still sniffing, and plucked the Black Jack from Zeph's lap. "If the blanket was meant for me, and the watch was meant for your father, then I'm sure the chewing gum was meant for our two troopers from the Second Cavalry."

Zeph was examining the watch. "Don't know why he did that. It's a Waltham and it's engraved under the lid."

"To you?" Charlotte was surprised. "He didn't even know you before today."

He went silent as he read the entire inscription on the watch lid. Then he blinked several times and snapped the lid shut.

"Well, what does it say?" asked Charlotte impatiently.

He handed her the watch. She looked at him a moment and

then opened it up. The etching on the underside of the lid was very fine. She turned the pocket watch toward the sunlight.

FOR CAPTAIN ZEPHANIAH TRUETT PARKER. WHO FOUGHT SLAVERY. AND WHO STILL FIGHTS FOR OUR FREEDOM. THE OPPRESSOR SHALL FEAR THEE AS LONG AS THE SUN AND MOON ENDURE. COLONEL MICHAEL JAMES AUSTEN. PSALM 72:3–5.

Charlotte looked up. Zeph was rubbing his eyes in a peculiar way.

"What's wrong?" she asked.

"Nothing. I'm just tired. I kind of had a rude awakening." He smiled.

"But this inscription is beautiful. Don't you think it's beautiful?"

"Sure."

"And he hardly knows you. But he's right, isn't he?"

Zeph did not answer. He leaned his head back and watched the prairie slip past. "They've got more snow here," he finally commented.

"Where's your brother's Bible?"

Zeph tugged the small Bible out of the pocket of the baggy coat she'd made him wear since Ogden. She took it from him and flipped pages. Then she read the passage inscribed on the watch: " 'The mountains shall bring peace to the people, and the little hills, by righteousness. He shall judge the poor of the people, he shall save the children of the needy, and shall break in pieces the oppressor. They shall fear thee as long as the sun and moon endure, throughout all generations.' "

"My goodness," she said when she had finished, "He is paying you quite a compliment."

"For all his gunslinger looks, he is a kind man."

"And to say these things about someone he'd never met when he had the watch engraved."

"He was one of my commanding officers."

"Pardon me?"

"Look, I didn't want to bring it up. I had him pegged for a gunslinger at first. Then there was the holdup and all the excitement. I only figured out who he was a few minutes before he got up to leave. He had a beard back then—it was twelve years ago. I just wasn't sure."

"Obviously he was sure."

"Matt's doing, I expect. He sent the telegram asking Austen to help me. Likely mentioned I'd served in the war and wouldn't carry a gun now. The mention of the war would have jarred his memory, and then he would have made the connection with my name."

Charlotte's eyebrow arched. "Why? He must have known scads of soldiers."

Zeph was slow to answer. "Because of what happened. There was an incident he wouldn't have forgotten."

"What incident?"

"I don't want to talk about this, Charlotte."

She stared into his eyes. "Z. What incident? Tell me. Please."

"A night in Virginia. There'd been a clash. My boys had managed to free a dozen men, no, fourteen—it was fourteen men they freed from a Rebel company. They were freemen, African men, but they'd been captured when Lee invaded Pennsylvania, and the Rebs were taking them back to be slaves. There was a lot of that even though Lee forbade it and never kept slaves himself. We'd caught them out in the open, in a meadow; it was raining so hard the field was flooded. We could see the kind of men they had as prisoners, they weren't even soldiers. It was wrong.

"This was just after Gettysburg, and Lee was retreating. I guess he never stopped retreating from Gettysburg to Appomattox, and my boys were fed up with the whole Army of Northern Virginia and that attitude the Confederacy had about Africans and slavery. They went at the Rebs hand to hand—they wanted to make sure they didn't kill any of the freemen by mistake. It was after the fight I stood in front of Austen's tent in the rain with the Africans until he could see me. He had no idea yet of what had happened, but I brought two of the men with me into the tent once the orderly called my name. The orderly tried to stop me from bringing the Africans in. I just brushed him aside."

Zeph stopped, gazing out the window.

"Please continue," Charlotte urged.

"Well. Austen was a lot younger then of course, but just as slender, and he had a dark beard, like I said. One arm was in a sling from a wound. There was a lamp burning on his table and a Remington New Model Army revolver by his elbow. I noticed that because Dad had the same gun. Austen's uniform was buttoned right to the top."

Zeph stopped a second time, his thoughts far away. Charlotte put a hand on one of Zeph's.

"Do you remember what you talked about?" she asked gently.

"It's funny. You know how some things you've gone through come to mind again and again? You go over every word each time your memory calls those experiences up, and you can see every face? I haven't thought about that tent in twelve years—I haven't wanted to. I see the freemen; one was a lawyer, he's talking to Austen, Colonel Austen, and the other is waiting his turn. I don't remember anything Austen said. But he got the men into a couple of large tents, made sure they were served hot food and coffee, put them on horses at daybreak, gave them a mounted escort back to Pennsylvania."

"You can't recall even one sentence of what he said?"

"Have you got a piece of that black gum for me, Cody?"

"Yes sir."

Zeph chewed slowly. "It's very good."

Charlotte was staring at him. The edge came into her voice. "Z."

He shook his head. "It's like I buried it." He chewed a little longer. "All I can bring back is Austen saying, 'You did the right thing, Captain. Your men are to be commended.'" Then Zeph's face clouded over. "He asked if we had taken any Rebel prisoners. I said we had not. He thanked me and dismissed me." Zeph looked over at Charlotte. "Not one."

"I see. So that explains the inscription and him having the watch ready for you. Not an incident a man is likely to forget, even in a war full of them."

"No."

There was silence between them. Around the car others talked and laughed, and Zeph heard a woman say a meal stop would be coming up soon. Charlotte was opening Jude's Bible to the spot where she had placed the bookmark. She held it out to him.

"Are you a praying man, Captain Parker?"

"I try."

"Then read this. Out loud. Remember, I marked this passage before the outlaws assailed our train."

Zeph took the Bible from her. "Which psalm?"

"Number one hundred twenty-four, please."

"'If it had not been the Lord who was on our side, when men rose up against us: then they had swallowed us up quick, when their wrath was kindled against us: then the waters had overwhelmed us, the stream had gone over our soul. . . . Blessed be the Lord, who hath not given us as a prey to their teeth. Our soul is escaped as a bird out of the snare of the fowlers: the snare is broken, and we are escaped. Our help is in the name of the Lord, who made heaven and earth.'"

Charlotte leaned forward. "We prayed and the Lord rescued us, Z. Sending those telegrams, one to Fort Laramie and the other to Iron Springs, so Raber's accomplice would read it, that was the right thing to do. Now we're free." She took one of his big hands in both of hers. "I'm sorry about what happened in the war. About what happened to my father and what happened to you. For the killing that happened in that meadow in Virginia. But I'm not sorry you rescued those men from being taken down to Alabama or Mississippi and turned into slaves. You did the right thing. You fought to set them free, and that was the right thing to do. It's hard for me to admit, it's hard for me to accept, but if there was one good thing that came out of that terrible war, it was just that—some of you soldiers fought to end the enslavement of a whole race of men and women and children that God had created to be a blessing to the earth."

Zeph leaned back and closed his eyes, the Bible open in his hands. "Rich words, Miss Spence."

Zeph's jaw muscles tightened and then relaxed. He opened his eyes and tried to make light of the moment. "Pretty soon there won't be one secret of mine left hidden. I'll be an open book. Then I'll just be this dull person you know inside out and that you're bored to death with."

She smiled. "I doubt that."

"But what about all your secrets? Do I know any of them? Am I ever gonna know any of them?"

"Why, Mister Parker"—she fanned her face—"us girls have to keep our deepest secrets close to our hearts until the day we die."

Chapter 17

Snowflakes were swirling down and mingling with the gray billows from the smokestack. Charlotte found the rolling plains a welcome relief after so many days of flat prairie. The farm buildings were also a pleasant sight, with their rows of windbreaks and their red barns and livestock. She was not sure Zeph would agree with her. Once the US Grant had pulled out of Omaha and crossed the Missouri River, he had groaned and said, "That's it. We've left the West."

They were halfway through Iowa, and she felt her apprehension growing with every mile. They had left the US Grant and the Union Pacific behind in Omaha and were traveling with the Chicago and Northwestern Railroad now. The train would pass over into Illinois in no time, and then they'd be buying tickets for a different one to take them from Chicago to Pittsburgh and Harrisburg. Before she knew it, she would be facing her old neighbors at Bird in Hand in Lancaster County, and she had no idea what she ought to say or do once she met them face-to-face. It was something she had pressed to the back of her mind because of the imminent danger from the Raber Gang. Now that the danger from the gang was past, other worries came crowding in to engulf her thoughts.

It was not just Bird in Hand. It was undoubtedly God's will that she deal with her past and confront the Amish community of her childhood and, it was hoped, learn to forgive and perhaps even love those men and women once again. What worried her far more than that was whether she could graciously give up Cheyenne and Cody to the Amish world and its ways—and whether that world would keep her darkest secrets hidden or bring them out into the open for all the world to see, including Zephaniah Parker.

She began to argue with herself.

Why not tell him those darkest secrets instead of waiting for the Amish church to break the news? It would come across much better that way to Zephaniah. It would build trust.

No, I can't; these are terrible things to tell someone. It would be better if they were left unsaid.

It is your Christian duty to tell him.

I don't care.

The Amish will tell him who you are if you don't.

I can't risk it.

Just by being silent you are risking it. You are risking everything.

The snow was falling more thickly and more swiftly now. Cody and Zeph were leaning against one another, practically head-to-head, breathing in and out through open mouths, fast asleep. Despite her anxiety and inner turmoil, Charlotte could not prevent herself from smiling. Oh, they looked so much like father and son. During the robbery, Cody had acted just like a fiery young Zephaniah. How could she let Cody go? How, for that matter, could she let Zephaniah go?

Beside her, Cheyenne had been drawing all afternoon:

cavalrymen and men being captured. Charlotte supposed it gave her a considerable amount of peace and freedom from fear, even some healing in her heart, to know the men who had killed her mother and father had been taken prisoner by the army and were never going to be able to harm her again. Yet, for some reason Charlotte could not yet fathom, Cheyenne's drawings were adding to the emotional stress she herself was experiencing.

The ten-year-old suddenly held up a full-page drawing of a man's face. Like all her work, it was well done. Charlotte could see Cheyenne had meant to portray someone friendly and kind.

"That's very good. Who is it?"

"His hat has a number two on it and swords. And here is his scarf."

"Your Johnny?"

"Yah." She smiled. "It was easier to draw his horse than to draw him."

"What else do you have?"

"I drew some of the wicked. Two of them had long beards and long hair. They looked like bears."

Charlotte glanced at the drawings and felt a chill. "Don't you find it icy in here today, Cheyenne? There must be a new draft coming in from one of the doors or windows." She took the white point blanket Marshal Austen had left with them and bundled herself in it. A corner was lifted for Cheyenne. "Do you want to get warmed up?"

"I'm fine."

She lifted up another drawing. "This one had red hair. It was very short. This other was fat and always yelling." She shuddered. "I was really scared of him."

"I'm sorry, honey. Maybe we should put the drawings away for now."

"They are all in jail. Or they've run to another country." She pulled two more drawings from her pile. "These are the only other ones. This man was so skinny he made me think of a hoe. The others kept calling him Lunger."

"I see."

"And this was the leader. He told everyone what they should do. He shouted that he would kill us all." Her eyes narrowed. "Trooper Johnny said they had caught him and tied him up and put a gag in his mouth. He said they would hang him."

Ice went through Charlotte. "That's the leader?"

"Yes."

That's the Angel of Death, Charlotte thought. *That's the killer.*

She kissed the girl. "You are very brave to make this picture, very brave. But if they've caught him, you don't need to think about him anymore, not at all. It's over, honey. So I really think this is enough. No more drawing, all right? See, you're trembling."

"I hate him. I hate him. I don't ever want to see him again."

"Shh, shh, you won't, not ever, not ever again. Put the pictures down and get under the blanket."

Cheyenne shook her head. But she allowed Charlotte to put her arms around her. Then she laughed.

"What is it?" asked Charlotte in surprise.

"Pa and Cody look so funny with their mouths hanging open."

Charlotte smiled. "I guess they do. If this was the summertime, a big old fly could buzz right in there."

"Yah, a lot of flies!"

Cheyenne slept in Charlotte's arms. Charlotte watched the snowfall, but after a while her eyes fell on the picture of the gang leader. Cheyenne had given him long hair past his shoulders and tried to make it look light colored. The eyes bulged a bit, and the twist of his mouth gave the drawing a nasty feeling. Down one side of his face Cheyenne had drawn a long line that started in his eye and ended somewhere under his jaw. At the bottom of the page she had neatly printed ANGEL.

Charlotte stared at the line that ran from eyeball to chin. So he had a long scar. From what? A knife? A sword? That would have made him easy to identify anytime he did not wear a mask. Well, it didn't matter now. That story was over. For a moment she indulged an image in her mind of a man standing on a scaffold with a black hood over his head and a thick rope around his neck. A minister who looked like Jude was reading the Bible to him. Then she made a noise as if something was caught in her throat and shook her head to shake off the picture in her imagination. It was finished. She and Zeph and the children were safe and on their way to Pennsylvania.

Yet once she thought of Pennsylvania and Lancaster County, a knot began tightening itself in her stomach again. *Lord, help me get free of these fears,* she prayed. It was not a very satisfying prayer, because she knew there were things she herself could do to rid herself of some of her anxiety. She blew out a breath. Then she picked up Zeph's Bible.

Don't be afraid. Don't be afraid. Her hands turned over page after page. *What am I looking for?* A part of her wanted to sleep. Another part felt her dreams would be stressful and unpleasant.

A third part of her felt the right passage from holy scriptures would give her some measure of peace. But which one? There were so many.

Zeph had mentioned how Jude had used certain parts of his Bible so many times during the war it naturally fell open to several of these places. Now it happened to her. She was leafing through the New Testament when the book seemed to stop on its own and open where it wanted. The verse her eyes fell upon, 1 John 4:18, was underlined by sharp lines of black ink. *"There is no fear in love; but perfect love casteth out fear: because fear hath torment. He that feareth is not made perfect in love."*

Charlotte leaned her head back and closed her eyes. She listened to the *click-click-click* of the iron wheels over the rails. The sky darkened in the east, and the train moved into that darkness.

She knew what she had to do. But she did not think she had the courage to do it.

Chapter 18

Once he'd told her it would take another two days to reach Harrisburg—"Well, just under"—she'd insisted on having a bath, even if it meant missing a connection. Which it did. Since there was no help for it, he and the kids had baths, too. Zeph even treated himself to a shave. "But not the whole beard," Charlotte had protested, "just the upper lip. That sort of beard goes with the clothes I made for you."

"You mean it makes me plain?"

"Yes. You will go over very well with the Amish in Lancaster County."

"Why does it matter if I go over very well with the Amish in Lancaster County?"

She'd patted his cheek. "Because, my dear, we have enough to overcome in Pennsylvania without having to worry about what the in-laws think of you. I want them to see that my Fremont is humble as well as handsome."

They had reverted to their Wyoming names again. He touched the broad flat brim of his hat. "As you wish, Conner."

Clean as a whistle, upper lip shaved, the beard trimmed, he stood with Cody in their sheepskin coats and plain clothes and hats on one of Chicago's main thoroughfares and watched wagons, carriages, horse-drawn tramcars, and people stream past without ceasing. Steam and breath rose from the street like a fog. Zeph wanted to tilt his hat back on his head as he watched, but the hat Charlotte had given him did not work as well at this as a Stetson, so he was left with nothing to do except rub the beard on his jaw.

"It's like standing on the banks of a Mississippi chock-full of people and teams of horses," said Zeph. "Makes a fellow dizzy."

Cody had been to Chicago several times. "Pittsburgh is not so full. And Harrisburg has more trains than people."

"That so?"

"There was a great fire here four years ago. All of this has been rebuilt. And they're still building." Cody pointed down the street to where two steam cranes were hard at work and new buildings were rising into the cold winter sky.

"I guess you could say the mountains around here are man-made," mumbled Zeph. "I miss the real thing."

Cody nodded. "I do, too, but sometimes I like the excitement of the cities."

"Excitement! You call Chicago excitement?" Zeph lifted Cody's hat and rubbed his knuckles into the boy's hair. "Excitement is having a Sioux war party breathing down your neck and bullets and arrows making a colander of your clothes."

Cody laughed and fought back. "I wouldn't care. I hate these clothes."

"Me, too."

Two policemen in boots and belted overcoats with brass buttons and large stars over their hearts approached them. They wore revolvers in holsters at their sides. One policeman touched the brim of his cap. "Everything all right here, sir?"

Zeph was confused and released Cody from a headlock. "Sure."

"You all right, lad?"

Cody's face was red. He put his hat back on his head.

"Everything is fine, Officer."

"Where are you two from?"

Zeph straightened up. "Just off the train from Omaha. We'll be pulling out for Harrisburg in a few hours."

"That's a long trip."

Zeph nodded. "Three states. But not as long as coming all the way from the Montana Territory."

The other officer spoke up. "Did you?"

"Picked up the Union Pacific in Ogden, Utah."

The officer whistled. "We had a telegram about a wee bit of excitement down that way, was it yesterday or the day before that, Pete?"

The older man grunted. "They caught the Angel o' Death and that whole murderin', thievin' gang o' his."

"I'm glad to hear it," said Zeph.

"The noose is too good for 'em and all the savages like 'em," the older police officer went on. "Burn 'em at the stake would fix 'em. The Ind'ns understand that."

I know this accent, thought Zeph.

"You two sound like a man I was friends with back in the gold rush days of Iron Springs," he said. "Seamus O'Casey."

The older officer beamed. "A fine Irish name. Seems our people are everywhere, Pat."

The younger officer nodded. "Irish like to travel. And when

they don't, someone always plants a boot in their pants and gets them moving." He laughed. "Oh, I think about going west someday. I have a cousin in Dakota. He joined the army. He's with that Custer."

"Fort Abraham Lincoln," said Zeph.

"I believe that's it. What's it like out there?"

"It's wide open and free, Officer. Everything's big. The prairies, the mountains, the rivers. Room to ride a hundred miles and never see another human being."

"Lots of outlaws?"

"A fair amount."

"Indians?"

"Plenty."

"Is there desperate need for lawmen in the West?" asked the younger officer.

"My brother's a federal marshal in the Montana Territory. He could use a fine young officer like yourself."

"What's his name, if you don't mind my asking?"

"Matthew Parker. You can always telegraph him at Iron Springs. Acres of train robbers and bandits for you to chase down and slap behind bars."

The older man snorted. "Ha! We got our own bandits and robbers thick as summer flies on a mule. We don't need to be chasing 'em all the way to the ends o' the earth in Utah and Montana."

The younger officer smiled. "Sure, Pete, but I get restless just the same. The Irish in me gets awful cramped in Chicago when the spring comes. I wasn't from Dublin or Cork like your kind, y'know; I grew up under the stars of Connemara."

The older man put his hands behind his back. "Suit yourself. I'd miss my baseball games. And the wife would miss her church teas."

The young officer put out his hand. "Pleasure to meet you."

Zeph gripped his hand and shook it. "If you ever make it out west, look me up in Iron Springs. Zephaniah Parker."

"I may just do that. Pat Cavanaugh."

The other officer nodded. "Pete Cassidy. A safe trip to Pennsylvania to you both. And"—he winked at Cody—"no more horseplay on the streets o' Chicago, if you don't mind. It looked to me like you were layin' an awful lickin' on your poor father here."

They all laughed.

"Come along and let's walk, Pat," said Pete. "It's getting nippy, and I want the blood moving in my veins to warm myself up."

Zeph and Cody watched them march away down the crowded sidewalk. Then Zeph dug the silver watch Austen had given him out of a pocket of his sheepskin coat. He opened the lid, looked at the time, whistled, and snapped the lid shut. "We'd better find our womenfolk and escort them to the evening train, pronto."

Charlotte and Cheyenne were in one of the shops down a block that Charlotte had indicated to Zeph earlier, dressed in matching navy blue dresses and bonnets with white lace, their arms full of bags and parcels.

"We were just coming," said Charlotte. "Here." She handed several brightly wrapped packages to Zeph.

"What is all this?" he demanded.

"Gifts for the Amish families in Pennsylvania."

"You mean peace offerings."

"Call them what you will. Cody, help your sister with her bags. What were you two gentlemen up to?"

"Just watching the locals."

They were walking briskly up a street toward the train station. Charlotte glanced over at Zeph. "Did you get a chance to get to the telegraph station?"

"There were no telegrams for us. Wrote Matt and told him we'd be in Harrisburg in two days—"

"I know we go left here," she interrupted.

"You're right. There's the Pennsy Station. I'd better make sure they've put our luggage on the right train. That's our locomotive there, I believe, Missus Wyoming, am I right?"

"Well, the number is correct. Unless they have two engines using exactly the same numerals."

"Do you have the tickets?"

"You have the tickets in your pocket, and you know it perfectly well."

"Here." He gave Charlotte the boxes he'd been holding. "Find us some good seats in one of the sleepers."

After talking with an official for the Pennsylvania Railroad who looked over a sheet of paper and nodded his head— "Harrisburg, the Wyomings"—Zeph made his way back to platform four. A young boy was selling the Chicago Daily Tribune and hollering at the top of his lungs, "Double hanging in Wyoming! Raber Gang plunged into eternity!"

The feds sure didn't waste any time, thought Zeph.

He bought a paper and opened it up. Above the fold were

large black letters: HANGED! There was a photograph of two men hanging from ropes with black hoods over their heads. He kept walking toward the train as he read the story under the grim picture.

Charlotte was standing behind Cody and Cheyenne on the steps of one of the cars. Her arms were full of bags and parcels. She was rolling her eyes at a heavy woman who was taking her time making her way into the car. "Move ahead, Cody," she was saying, "move on ahead, son."

"I can't budge."

"Just push a bit, a little bit. Let them know we're behind them and that we need to get on board the train, too, before it leaves without us."

"Conner," said Zeph as he came up to the car.

"Oh, thank goodness. I thought you'd taken a horse back to the Montana Territory. Can you help me with these boxes again?"

"Conner, it's over."

Charlotte looked down at him from the steps. He held up the newspaper. She saw the headline and the picture. The blood ran out of her face. "Oh my Lord Jesus," she said. Her eyes rolled back white, and she collapsed, falling down the steps onto the wooden boards of the station platform, cracking her head and lying still. Her bags and parcels tumbled out of her arms and over the toes of Zeph's boots. Five or six dropped down onto the tracks and lay under the wheels of the 5:17 to Harrisburg, Pennsylvania.

Chapter 19

Zeph watched her sleep, listening anxiously for changes in breathing that might signal she was in some sort of distress. He had not bothered to transform their seating area into beds, so Cody had rolled his sheepskin into a pillow and leaned his head against it and the window. Cheyenne was awake. She slowly and continuously stroked Charlotte's hair.

Lights flickered in the dark square of the window. Zeph supposed they would be coming into Fort Wayne soon. The morning would find them well into Ohio and through the Great Black Swamp. Travel would be a bit slower through the swamp, but vast sections of it had been drained for the railroad, and Zeph didn't think there would be much trouble. He smiled briefly when he remembered a story of how the Michigan and Ohio militias had tried to fight a war with each other over a boundary dispute, but each had gotten lost in the swamp and had a hard time finding one another. What if the Union and Confederate armies had kept missing each other on their marches north and south? But there had been no Black Swamp between Virginia and Maryland to confuse them.

Gently he put one hand on Charlotte's wrist. Her pulse was not too weak, not too strong. On her forehead was a large bump with a plaster on it, a real goose egg. She would not be too pleased when she woke up and examined it in the mirror, but her anger would not chase it away. That would be difficult for her, not being able to rely on her strength and determination to deal with a problem. He smiled.

Take care of her Lord; she is one special lady.

A small crowd had gathered around Charlotte after she fell. An army surgeon had been among them, and he had Zeph hold her up while he administered smelling salts. She inhaled sharply, coughed and sneezed, and demanded to know who had struck her. When Zeph reminded her softly that she had fainted when he showed her the newspaper headline, her face had reddened. She told the people looking down at her, "I know those men were evil, but I have always found hangings brutal and upsetting. The mere mention of it causes me great distress."

She had rested there for about five minutes while the surgeon cleaned the cut on her forehead with alcohol and put a sticking plaster in place, then had leaned on Zeph and struggled to her feet. She almost fell a second time, and the people reacted with "oh no" and "keep a good grip on her," but with Zeph's help she regained her balance and thanked everyone for their concern.

"You have been most kind. But I fear I have delayed your travels long enough, and I am certain the engineer of this locomotive would like to have pulled into Pittsburgh Station ten minutes ago." The people had laughed. "Please have a safe journey, and may God bless you all."

Once Zeph had helped her into her seat in the car she had groaned, "Oh, I made a perfect spectacle of myself."

"Char—Conner, no one is going to remember this incident a week from now," he'd soothed her, "except maybe the army surgeon and four or five of the young men who fell in love with you and wished I was your brother."

"Oh, for heaven's sakes, Zeph—Fremont. The crazy things you come up with."

"Well, I'm a man, and what they were feeling when they looked at you, lying there unconscious in my arms, was written all over their faces, plain as day. Once the surgeon asked who I was and I told him I was your husband, their faces went flat as pancakes."

"They did not."

"You bet they did."

"How can you know what's in another man's heart?"

"I'm a man, and it was in my heart, too."

"What was in your heart?"

"Your face so white and the blond hair falling over your cheek and forehead, your hands so calm, your lips quiet and pale, freckles sprinkled on your skin, your soft breathing. There was a sweetness and a youngness. We could all see your beauty, and we could see the sleeping child in your closed eyes and small hands."

Charlotte's face had taken on color for the first time since she had fainted. "I doubt too many of the young men you say fell in love with me while I lay prostrate on platform four had those precise thoughts in their head. You sound like a blend of William Shakespeare and James Fenimore Cooper."

"Maybe they couldn't have put it into those exact words, but that's just about where their thinking was at."

Charlotte had ducked her head and tried not to smile. "The notions you get in that mind of yours, Fremont."

"Would you like some fresh Chicago water?"

"Yes, thank you."

He'd handed her the Union army canteen. She had sipped at it, made a face, then sipped at it again.

"Well, it's not Montana mountain water." She'd handed the canteen back to Zeph. "Thank you, my dear."

"Are you feeling better?"

"Yes, yes, I'm so sorry about all that, Fremont."

"I'm the one who's sorry, Conner. What was I thinking? Flapping that photograph in front of your face. I apologize."

"There have been enough public hangings in Iron Springs and Virginia City. I shouldn't have been that squeamish."

"I'm sure you've attended exactly none of them."

"There were always better things to do. Not that I'm saying some of those men didn't deserve it. Especially that hoodlum Skipjack William, who shot the woman teller."

Zeph had nodded. "Hard to find room in your prayers for that man."

"Yes, and hard to find room for Seraphim Raber or any of his gang of beasts."

A spark of her old vehemence had flared. Zeph stared at the dark fire in her eyes. She had glanced out the window at an engine building up steam on another track.

"Though it is my Christian duty to pray for their black souls."

She had no sooner said this than a tear slipped down her cheek followed moments later by another. In a burst of anger, she struck at them with her hand. "Oh stop it!" she snapped.

"Take it easy, Conner," Zeph said. "There's nothing to get upset at yourself about."

"How would you know? Or do you have total knowledge of my thoughts like you do of those young men?"

"I just meant it's not the time to get all worked up. Rest easy and get your strength back."

"I have plenty of strength, Fremont Wyoming."

"No one's denying that. Just like to see you with more."

"More?"

"You seem so fragile right now."

"Fragile?"

"Just joking, Conner. Anyone could see—"

"No one's ever used the word fragile to describe me in my entire life."

"You're building up a head of steam powerful enough you could roll over a buffalo herd. Don't want you to burst a boiler, that's all. Why don't you try and get some sleep?"

"What makes you think I'm tired?"

"Well, you got that knock on your head—"

"I'm perfectly fine. I don't feel a thing. I could waltz all night."

"I'm sure you could."

"Why hasn't this train left yet?"

"I don't know. Want me to walk up the track and give the engineer a dressing-down on your behalf?"

Cody had caught Zeph's eye. He raised his eyebrows. Zeph shrugged. Charlotte saw the interaction between them. Her eyes had narrowed.

"What are you men up to?"

Zeph had touched the brim of his hat. "Polite conversation, ma'am."

An hour after the train had left Chicago, Charlotte had fallen asleep. Over time the blow on her head had swollen while her breathing had relaxed and become deeper and more even.

Now he gazed at her pale face in the dark of the Indiana night and hoped when she woke up she'd be on the right side of heaven. His hand was still on her wrist. Thank goodness she was warming up. Cheyenne had stopped smoothing down Charlotte's hair and was asleep against her shoulder.

A lot of things didn't add up. He'd never known Charlotte Spence to faint over anything during all her years at Iron Springs. When he'd brought Ricky through the door that night, spitting blood, she'd scarcely blinked. She'd been thrown by broncs hard enough to knock the wind out of any ten men and swung right back into the saddle. Had cracked ribs once that she got Doc Brainerd to wrap tight, and Doc said she never dropped a tear or lost color in her face. So why had she fainted when he showed her the newspaper?

He blew out his breath suddenly and shook his head. He hoped she'd feel better after a couple of days' rest and a few decent meals. The train had a dining car and hot food on board.

"You're thinking about me, aren't you?"

He looked at her, surprised. "How long have you been awake?"

"Long enough."

He smiled crookedly. "I guess I'm hoping you feel a lot better by the morning, Conner."

"Conner."

He heard her sigh in the darkness. Her face was a pale smudge.

"I have so many names, don't I? Conner. Charlotte. Miss Spence. Missus Wyoming."

She was silent for a few moments. He could feel something building up in her, but she didn't speak. Finally he heard the rustle of her dress and blanket, and she leaned forward in the dark. He felt her soft, warm hands on his.

"Z," she whispered, "I think you care a little bit for me."

"Char," he responded, "I care a lot more than a little."

"I've cherished the way you've treated me ever since we left the Sweet Blue. Your words, the gentle way you look at me, your kisses, your courage. I'm sure God has a special woman for you somewhere. I just don't think it can be me."

Zeph felt his heart drop and black dismay roar through his head. He opened his mouth, but felt her hand touch his lips.

"Don't say anything. All the names you call me by, but you don't know who I am. The day you find out will be the day you turn your back on me forever."

Chapter 20

Another day and then a night and a morning and the train slowed as it came into Harrisburg, Pennsylvania. Cody and Cheyenne knew the city well and had their faces pressed eagerly to the windows.

"We are almost home," said Cody. "Soon I'll be able to introduce you to my aunt Rosa."

Zeph smiled. "I look forward to that."

"Her apple pies and cherry pies are excellent."

Zeph watched the buildings slip past as they slowly moved toward the train station. Charlotte looked at his face and eyes. Cheyenne was fastening a white bonnet.

"You have been to Harrisburg before," Charlotte said.

"My brothers and I were trained here," he responded. "Camp Curtin. It would have been back there. They closed it in '65. The city's changed a fair bit."

"When are we home?" asked Cheyenne.

"Well," replied Charlotte, "there is one more train to take after we leave this one. But that will not be a long trip, less than two hours. Lancaster is only forty miles south and east of here."

"Then we will see everyone? All our old friends? My playmates?"

"Yes, darling, you will."

"Who will pick us up at the station? How will we get to Bird in Hand?"

Charlotte leaned over and kissed her on the forehead. "Remember when we stepped out for a walk in Pittsburgh and bought some ice cream? We telegraphed Aunt Rosa at the same time and told her which day we would be in Lancaster. She will watch the trains this morning and this afternoon."

"I want to show her my yellow scarf."

"Oh no, dear, remember? Soldiers are not something Aunt Rosa and the others get very excited about."

"Why not? The soldiers saved us from the outlaws."

"I know they did. And we thank God they did. But soldiers and their guns and swords do not go down well with the church. You know that. I will keep the scarf and hat safe in my luggage, all right?"

Cheyenne sulked. "All right."

Charlotte smoothed down her own hair, placed a few more pins, then put on a white bonnet and asked Cheyenne if it was straight or crooked. The girl said glumly, "Straight."

"It will be fine, dear," soothed Charlotte, holding Cheyenne's hand. "I will keep your scarf safe, and one day we will show it to Aunt Rosa. You'll see."

"Why white all of a sudden?" asked Zeph, looking away from the window and seeing her bonnet.

She smiled. "That is the Amish way."

"How are you feeling today?"

"Here and there. Thank you for asking."

"It is not easy for you to come back to these people. They

excommunicated your family. I pray for you day and night."

She touched his cheek with hers and whispered, "I know you do."

It seemed strange to Zeph to step off the train and stand on the platform and remember being a soldier here in 1862. He stretched in the cold sunlight and buttoned his sheepskin coat. No warmer in Pennsylvania than it had been in Nebraska. He and Cody freshened up and got all the luggage on the train to Lancaster while Charlotte and Cheyenne were still using the restrooms. Then the four of them took a few minutes to stroll up and down the platforms and look at the different locomotives.

"How are we fixed for chewing gum?" Zeph asked.

"One stick of Black Jack left," said Charlotte.

"Well, I'd better take a quick hike into town and get some. What do you say, Code? Want to come with?"

"Sure."

"You ladies need anything?"

"No," said Charlotte, "we did our shopping in Chicago."

Zeph and Cody found a store that sold gum and candy. They not only bought gum for themselves, but also for Cody's old friends and Cheyenne's, too.

"Who else do you think would like chewing gum at Bird in Hand?" asked Zeph. "I mean, among the grown-ups?"

"Oh, Augustine Yoder for sure, that is Aunt Rosa's brother. And Martin Hooley, the farrier. And I think also Sarah Beachey, the schoolteacher."

They went back outside and shoved their hands in their pockets when an icy gust struck them.

"We should check the telegraph office before we go back," said Zeph.

"Sure," responded Cody.

They asked directions once or twice and made their way to the right building. Zeph fished his badge out of his pocket, unbuttoned the top of his jacket, pinned it on his shirt, winked at Cody, and then they both walked in the door.

"Deputy," greeted a man with no hair on top, but plenty on the sides and chin. "What can I do for you?"

He slid a pad over to them. Zeph considered sending Matt a note, but then decided against it. He didn't plan on being in Lancaster County more than a few days. There'd be time enough to telegraph his brother once he was on his way back west.

"Just checking to see if there are any telegrams," he said.

"Name?"

"Fremont Wyoming. Zephaniah Parker."

"Which one are you?"

Zeph shrugged—they weren't on the run anymore. "Both."

The man grunted. "Well, I got something for Parker, so I guess that's one of you. Here you go."

"Thank you. Where from?"

"Omaha."

"Omaha?"

Zeph was puzzled. He picked up and read the telegram the clerk had placed on the counter.

PARKER
REVELATION 9:11 & 12
ANGEL

His head felt as if he'd swallowed ice water too fast—it went cold and numb. Without thinking, one hand reached inside his sheepskin jacket and pulled the small Bible out and the other hand worked with the eyes to find the passage. *"And they had a king over them, which is the angel of the bottomless pit, whose name in the Hebrew tongue is Abaddon, but in the Greek tongue hath his name Apollyon. One woe is past; and, behold, there come two woes more hereafter."*

"When did this come in?" Zeph asked the clerk.

"Oh, six, seven hours ago."

They left the office. Zeph walked swiftly with long strides. Cody had to scramble to keep up.

"What's wrong?" he asked with a worried look on his face. "What was in the telegram?"

Zeph didn't answer. He continued to walk as quickly as he could to the train station. A part of him wanted to run.

There they were! *Thank You, Lord.* He hurried to Charlotte's side.

"We were beginning to wonder when you two were going to show up," said Charlotte. Then she saw his face. "You look like you've seen a ghost."

Zeph passed her the telegram.

She read the telegram. Her face went white. "I don't understand these words, Abaddon and Apollyon."

"Jude talked about them during a sermon once," Zeph replied, his face grim. "Abaddon means 'The Place of Destruction.'"

He could see fear creeping back into her eyes. "What about Apollyon?"

Zeph did not flinch from her painful stare. "It means 'The Destroyer.'"

Chapter 21

Three buggies with matching dark horses were waiting at the train station in Lancaster. When Cody and Cheyenne stepped onto the platform, a short woman with a big smile climbed from the first buggy and came toward them, opening her arms. She was all in black—dark bonnet, long dark cloak with a cape at the shoulders, dark woolen shawl that fell down almost to the hem of her dark dress, and dark boots. The children ran into her arms, and there was laughter and a great deal of fast speech. The language was not English.

It was the first time Charlotte had smiled since she'd read the telegram from Omaha. "Pennsylvania Dutch," she said to Zeph.

Another woman, much younger and very tall and slender, approached from the second buggy. She came up to Charlotte, inclined her head, and began to speak in Pennsylvania Dutch as well. Zeph noticed that the only difference between her clothing and that of the older woman was that she wore a lighter colored bonnet.

Charlotte turned to Zeph. "This is Sarah Beachey, the schoolteacher. I will be staying with their family. Her father is in the buggy."

"You mean we're splitting up?"

He said it as a joke, but Charlotte could see a flash of disappointment in his eyes. She gave a small smile and put her hand on his arm. "Yes, we are no longer Mister and Missus Fremont and Conner Wyoming. That journey is ended. Now I am Charlotte Spence again, and you are Zephaniah Parker. But I will never forget our short marriage. Don't worry, we will talk again in a few days."

Zeph was taken aback. "A few days?"

"I'm sorry. There are some things that have to be done. There will be meetings."

"And I can't be at the meetings?"

"You are not Amish."

Zeph felt a mixture of hurt and anger rising in him.

"So we go through all that trouble and hazard to get you and the kids here safe and sound, and the best these Amish can do is give me the boot?"

"They are not giving you the boot."

"I'll get your things. I take it the kids are going with Aunt Rosa, if that's her name?"

"Yes."

She sighed as Zeph stalked off to the baggage car.

A man climbed out of the third buggy in a black coat wearing a cape and a flat-crowned, broad-brimmed hat identical to the one on Zeph's head. He was tall and massively built, with a beard that did not cover his upper lip. He followed Zeph to the baggage car.

Zeph was taking bags from the steward who was hauling them out of the car. The man reached forward and took two heavy carpetbags.

"Thanks," said Zeph curtly.

"I am happy to help. My name is Augustine Yoder. Rosa's brother. You know Rosa?"

"I've heard about her."

"I am the blacksmith. Also one of the ministers. Welcome. Thank you for bringing the children home safely."

Zeph grunted and took two more bags from the steward. "Miss Spence thought we might be here as long as four months."

Augustine gave him a puzzled look. "Miss Spence?" Then he shook his head. "Four months? I think she will be at Bird in Hand longer than that."

This was something Zeph did not want to hear. "I'll take these bags to her and come back for the others. Perhaps you could take those others to the children?"

"Of course. Did you notice you and I are wearing almost the same clothing? You might be one of us."

"Well, I'm not one of you."

"Where did you come by your clothing, if I may ask?"

"Miss Spence made it. Except the sheepskin jacket."

"This woman you call Miss Spence. Her mother was a wonder with the needle and thread. I see God has passed it down to the daughter as well."

"You knew her mother?"

"Yah. The father and brothers, too. A good family, you know, hardworking. But we had our differences."

Zeph carried four of Charlotte's carpetbags to the buggy where she stood with Sarah Beachey and her father. Aunt Rosa had also walked over with the children to speak with Charlotte. The Pennsylvania Dutch ceased once Zeph showed up.

Charlotte took Zeph by the arm. "Aunt Rosa, this is Zephaniah Truett Parker. He is the brave young man who saw us safely from the Montana Territory to Lancaster."

Aunt Rosa smiled a smile full of brown and white teeth and took one of Zeph's hands in both of hers. "Thank you, Mister Parker. We are so grateful. So much we wished to see the children again, Samuel and Elizabeth. And, you know, the last time I saw our girl she was only fifteen years old. Now look at her. A woman. A beauty."

Zeph found he had a hard time keeping his anger stoked with Aunt Rosa smiling up into his face and clasping his hand. He touched the brim of his flat-crowned hat with his free hand. "I believe she is God's masterwork, Aunt Rosa."

Charlotte flushed and Sarah Beachey dropped her eyes, but both Mister Beachey and Aunt Rosa laughed heartily. Mister Beachey climbed out of his buggy and stretched out his hand. "If God has a good eye then so do you, young man. *Velkommen.*"

Zeph shook the man's hand. "A pleasure to meet you, Mister Beachey."

"Moses."

To his surprise, Zeph found himself saying, "Thank you all, *danke schoen,* for finding homes for Miss Spence and the children. It has been a long and exhausting journey for them."

"Ah," said Moses Beachey, raising his eyebrows, "you know some of the language?"

"When I was a boy, there was a rancher in Cheyenne by the name of Mueller. I listened to him talk the talk. His was not exactly the same as yours, but sometimes I remember a word or a phrase."

"Gute," said Aunt Rosa. "In no time you will be talking like one of us."

This rankled Zeph, but he covered it up with another touch to his hat brim. "I must get Charlotte's other bags. Excuse me."

Charlotte followed and stopped him a short distance from the others.

"Z, be patient with them. They are trying to be kind."

"I know it. I just don't like them always assuming you've come back to live here or that I'm anxious to become one of them."

"Who knows what will happen over the next few weeks?"

"Weeks?"

Zeph glanced over at the others. They were obviously listening. Without thinking, he began to speak to Charlotte in Spanish. "Senorita, what makes you think we have weeks? Have you forgotten the telegram?"

Charlotte's face clouded over. "No."

"It came from Omaha."

"The accomplice—"

"The accomplice is in Iron Springs. That's how Seraph Raber knew we would be in Harrisburg. How could the army or Colonel Austen have known if they had Seraph or not? The others wouldn't tell them he was one of the four who escaped. For all the army knew, he was one of the two they hung. Omaha, Charlotte. He's three days away. Four days, maybe, but that's stretching it. You think it will be hard for Seraph to locate a man and a woman who just came into Bird in Hand with two kids in tow from Montana?"

"What are you going to do?"

"At least I can tell them what Seraph looks like now. We have Cheyenne's drawing. The army will know if they hung him or not. If not, we'll know he's still at large. I'll telegraph Colonel Austen. I'll telegraph Matt, too. I'll try and throw some grit in that accomplice's eyes. I'm going to tell Matt we're pushing on to Philadelphia because the kids have relatives there."

"Aren't we going to tell the Amish that Seraph Raber is hunting us?"

"What can they do? Throw stones? Why, they wouldn't even do that. No need to get them and the kids all worked up. You know we can't stay here after three days, not if they haven't caught Raber. We'll have to run."

"No."

"To save others' lives. You know he won't care who he murders to get to us."

"No."

Zeph stared at her and the blazing lights in her blue winter eyes. "I guess I've run out of Spanish," he said in English.

"Where did you pick it up?" she asked, also in English.

"Same place as you. Ricky hired on that Vicente when you were still a girl, didn't he? You've been learning Mexican since you were a kid on the Sweet Blue. Well, Dad brought in a hired hand to help on our place in Wyoming when I was no bigger than a cricket. I learned from him, same as you. Pablo was his name. A great man. A true vaquero."

"I was fifteen when Ricky brought me to the Montana Territory. Hardly someone you'd call a kid, senor."

He smiled. "I'll get your other bags. Adios."

She gave his hand a squeeze. *"Vaya con Dios."*

In another ten minutes the three buggies were rattling east over the rutted road and slush to Bird in Hand. The long fields were sheeted with snow. Zeph sat next to Augustine Yoder in his buggy. There was only one carpetbag, a bedroll, and a pair of saddlebags for luggage.

"It is not far," said Augustine. "My house and smithy are on the edge of town and closer to Lancaster. You will want to lie down, I think, and get some rest. Long journeys can be tiring."

"Mister Yoder—"

"Augustine."

"The last thing I want to do, believe me, is lie down. Back home I ride the land every day. I felt like a fox locked in a coop on that train trip. I want to use my muscles. You're going to put in an afternoon at the anvil, aren't you?"

He nodded. "That I am. I must put some iron rims on several wagon wheels."

"Can I give you a hand?"

"Have you worked with a blacksmith before?"

"Not much. But it's always fascinated me."

"So. No food? Straight into the shop?"

"*Bitte.*"

Augustine smiled at Zeph's use of the German word.

"And Mister—Augustine—thank you for taking the time to come to Lancaster and fetch us. And for giving me a few minutes at the telegraph office. I'm very much obliged. Danke."

"*Bitteschon.*"

After Augustine had turned the buggy onto his property, Zeph jumped down and led the horse toward the large, gray barn. Augustine took Zeph's belongings.

"Shall I remove his harness and rub him down?" asked Zeph.

"Yah. There are stables at the back of the barn and hooks for the tack. Please give the gelding some oats. The buggy stays in the barn as well."

Augustine watched Zeph gently begin unhitching the horse, smiled, and nodded. Then he went to his house—white, plain, sturdy, two stories. At the door he leaned in and called to his wife in Pennsylvania Dutch. He put Zeph's carpetbag, bedroll, and saddlebags in the hall and shut the door. Then he jerked his head toward a small building which stood about a hundred feet behind the house. "You will meet Rebecca at supper."

Chapter 22

Augustine showed Zeph how to work the bellows to keep the furnace red-hot. "My boys used to do this. But now they are grown. One has a dairy herd; the other is a carpenter. And my daughter, my Katie, she is married to Amos Zook— he is the honey man, he has the beeyard, what do the English call it?"

"Apiary?"

"Yah. Big word. Why not just say hives?"

They set to work, Zeph pumping, Augustine hammering the strips of hot iron into hoops. In no time Zeph's sheepskin jacket was on a peg, soon followed by the black coat Charlotte had made for him. Augustine looked at his clothing and pointed with his smoking tongs. "Who you call Charlotte?"

"Yes."

"She has made for you a perfect mutze, a dress coat, do you know that? The vest, the broadfall pants, all from our people. Comfortable, eh?"

"Sure, but a little loose."

"Your shirt, no collar, just like mine. You see that?" Augustine had stripped down to his shirt before he'd struck his first blow with the hammer. "But you need suspenders. Your pants want to sit around your knees." He barked a laugh. "How did she miss that?"

"By not having to wear them herself."

"Yah, but you are plain, very plain, alle ist gute."

Sweat made their faces shine, the heat and wood coals made their skin glow crimson and bronze. Zeph helped Augustine fit one, two, three, four, five wheels. Then the big man sat and mopped his brow with a towel before tossing it to Zeph to do the same.

"Do you have a watch, Zephaniah?"

"Mm." Zeph walked over and pulled the watch from a pocket in his vest, which was hanging from a hook. The silver gleamed in the light from the furnace. "Five thirty."

"Not so plain."

"A gift."

Augustine grunted. "Enough for today. At six, Rebecca will be wondering if we mean to make a night of it. Come, I'll show you where to wash up."

When they stepped outside the shop, the cold made Zeph suck in his breath.

Augustine grinned. "I have a good trade for the wintertime, eh?"

"Your smithy is as warm as California."

"But in the summertime, I am always drinking water, gallons of it, and lemonade. It's a different matter then. I feel like a ham dangling in a smokehouse."

After he had cleaned up and changed into another shirt, equally as plain as the one he'd taken off, Zeph came to the table. Augustine and his wife were waiting patiently for him.

They rose, the wife coming around the table to greet him and take one of his hands in hers.

"Velkommen," she beamed. "Our home is your home as long as you remain under our roof. My name is Rebecca."

She was short and slender, and dark red hair gleamed under the dark mesh covering on her head.

Zeph lifted his hand to touch the brim of his hat, but it was hanging on a peg in the hall. He touched his forehead anyway and smiled. "Danke, Missus Yoder. I feel very much at home already."

"We will pray and then sit," said Augustine. "Everything is cooling off."

Rebecca laughed. "Just because the food does not smoke like your blacksmith shop, you think it will turn to ice in a few minutes."

"Still, we'll pray."

Zeph bowed his head as Augustine prayed in Pennsylvania Dutch. At his "amen," Zeph added his own and sat down with them to the meal: chicken, dumplings, a soup.

"This looks much better than train food, Missus Yoder."

"Rebecca. Well, I am glad to hear it, but it is only a small supper."

"She means there are only three of us," said Augustine. "She is happiest when she is cooking for our sons and our daughter and their families. Or for the whole church."

"Well, once you have put the pot on the stove it is as easy to cook for fifty as it is for five."

"Start with the sauerkraut soup," suggested Augustine. "Do you have sauerkraut out west? Very good. Cabbage that is pickled. Great flavor. And the chicken and dumplings, go ahead, fill your plate, taste one of the dumplings, very good—"

"Augustine, for heaven's sake," Rebecca said with a laugh, "leave the poor boy alone. It sounds like you are trying to sell him something you have made with your hammer and tongs. Let him eat what he eats. Would you like some coffee with your meal, Zephaniah?"

"Why, thank you, Rebecca, I would like that very much. You're right, Mister Yoder, the soup is full of flavor."

"Ah, you see, Rebecca. Now a dumpling—"

"Augustine, enough. Zephaniah, how was your trip?"

"Well, the children saw buffalo and a Sioux hunting party, and they met some cavalrymen from Fort Laramie, so I guess for them it was pretty eventful."

"It is a lonely land, they tell me."

Zeph ate and swallowed and then spoke.

"Well, there are vast stretches of open country with not a building or a person in sight, Missus Yoder, but some folk like it that way, and I have to admit I'm one of them. The wind and rain are fresh out of the Lord's kitchen, and you can see the rims of heaven and earth, sitting astride your saddle in the tall mountains."

"I am told your Charlotte has a property out there."

"That's true. Her brother Ricky made the purchase, but she has been running it since his death."

"Dairy cattle?"

"Beef."

"How long since her brother passed away?"

"Only a few years, ma'am."

"I remember Ricky well," said Augustine. "A fine boy. Very loyal to his father. That is why he left us."

"Zephaniah, will you have some *snitz* pie?" asked Rebecca, changing the subject. "It is a pie made with plenty of dried apples and brown sugar and butter."

"I'd like a slice very much."

"And perhaps some of our vanilla and mint ice cream with that? Augustine makes it."

"Thank you."

She placed the pie and ice cream before him and waited like a mother waits for a favorite child to eat hearty.

"Is it to your liking?"

"I haven't tasted a better pie in years, Missus Yoder."

"Now you are making a joke."

"Ma'am, I am a bachelor, and I am telling you the plain truth."

"But don't you meet with your Charlotte socially? Surely she would bake a good Amish pie for you now and then."

"At the church picnic I generally have a good feed. But no, ma'am, Charlotte and I do not see one another socially. Until this train trip east, I guess I haven't spoken more than two dozen words to her in the past year."

Rebecca frowned, her eyebrows coming together. "Why is that?"

"Well, I suppose we are both very busy. I have a ranch and she has a bigger one. It takes a lot of hard work, dawn to dusk."

"Is it common for a woman out west to run a ranch and a household?"

"No, Missus Yoder, not common, but Charlotte is very

good at it. And her spread is no small enterprise. She has ten men working for her."

A sudden chill descended on the table. Zeph felt it at once and looked up from what was left of his pie and ice cream. Rebecca and Augustine were looking at each other with the kind of expression on their faces that Zeph would have translated as, "You see what becomes of our women when they leave the church?"

Augustine pushed his chair back. "Will you walk with me to the barn, Zephaniah? I want to check on the horses. It will give my Rebecca time to clean up in here and also to prepare your bedroom."

Augustine tugged on his overcoat with the cape and Zeph his brown sheepskin jacket. The stars were glittering in the cold night sky like broken glass. Augustine carried a lantern to the barn and looked carefully at all three of his horses, each in its own stable. He rubbed their ears and spoke to them soothingly.

"Shall I pitch them some hay, Mister Yoder?"

"Yah. How many horses do you keep at your farm, Zephaniah?"

Zeph located the pitchfork and set to work. "Well, if I have a good spring, I hope to have eleven."

"Eleven? Yah? And what about your Charlotte? How many horses will she have this spring?"

"Well, if she has a decent spring, my guess is she will have around ninety-five or so."

"What? So many? Is it true?"

"Some of the spreads down around Texas have remudas that number in the hundreds."

"Remuda?"

"Spanish for a change of horses. It's the horse herd the hired hands get their remounts from. We do as much as we can with our horses out west, Mister Yoder. There's friends of mine who think if you can't do a job from the back of a horse it ain't worth doing."

Augustine barked his laugh. "So you care very much for your horses in Montana and Texas?"

"A man that doesn't care for his horse is a fool, Mister Yoder. They are the difference between life and death when you're out on the prairie."

They walked from the barn to the blacksmith shop. Augustine wanted to make sure the coals were well banked and there would be no danger of a spark starting a fire.

"You did not mind working with me today, Zephaniah?"

"I enjoyed it very much, sir."

"You would do it again?"

"I would."

"Well, I have meetings in the morning, but I hope to be back in the smithy after lunch. How does that suit you?"

"I'll meet you there."

"Or at lunch. Rebecca will certainly be expecting you at our table."

"All right."

Augustine glanced up at the February stars. "I never tire of God's handiwork. In my own poor way, I try to do what I can to emulate Him in my shop. I try to make everything come together just so."

"I know what you mean. But when I look at the Rockies

it puts me in my place, Mister Yoder. On moonlit nights, with the peaks glowing with snow, you kind of feel you've died and gone to heaven. I do the best I can with my hands, but it'll never be like the work of the Master."

Augustine looked at him. "You think about such things?"

"When you spend whole days in the saddle, you get to think about a lot of things."

Inside the house, Rebecca was waiting with an armful of towels. "Zephaniah, I have your room ready. Here are some towels when you wish to wash up."

"Thank you, ma'am."

"Now just follow me."

He walked after her down a short hall to an open door that looked to be about three inches thick. Inside was a bed; chair; desk; washstand with basin and jug; and a freestanding, full-length mirror. A candle burned beside the bed.

"Well, that looks mighty cozy, Missus Yoder."

"Rebecca. It was our Daniel's right up until the day he was married. This room has many good memories for Augustine and me."

"Thank you for fixing up such a special place for me, ma'am. I could've made do in the barn."

"The barn!" she snorted and then said something in Pennsylvania Dutch. "You are not a cow."

"I sure admire that quilt you put on the bed."

"It is the lone star. Those are log cabin blocks around it."

"My Rebecca made this only last winter," Augustine spoke up. "Many hours, many fine stitches sitting by the fire."

"Hush, Father, there is no need to say all that."

"It will keep me plenty warm, I can see that, just as if I'd made my bed in the stove."

Rebecca smiled. "Well, good night then. If you need anything, we are upstairs."

"I'll be fine, Missus Yoder. Good night."

"God bless."

When they had left, Zeph shut the heavy door and sat on the edge of the bed. The mattress felt pretty firm, and he was glad for that. He watched the candle burn and let what thoughts he had been holding back for a quiet moment come tumbling into his head. He was pleased that the first ones were images of Charlotte—her blue eyes, her golden hair down around her shoulders and uncombed, her lips, her smile.

What was she doing right now? What would she be doing tomorrow? When would he get a chance to see her again?

He lay back on the bed, his feet still planted on the floor.

No way around it. This was her childhood home. Shunned or not, she was an insider; he was an outsider. She fit in; he was like a donkey kicking up its heels among palominos.

It's Thursday night, another part of his mind cut in, *so that gives you the weekend, and then you'd better be gone.*

"I know it," he said out loud.

But gone where?

He thought about the passage from Revelation again. Raber calling himself the Destroyer made sense enough, but what was the Place of Destruction? The first woe was past—the holdup at the train? But what were the second two woes? Especially if Raber only meant to see them one more time and then kill them.

The Place of Destruction. The two woes. Zeph felt there was a message from Raber for him in those phrases, but he couldn't figure it out. There was a knock on the door, and he almost jumped.

"Mister Parker." It was Augustine's voice. "I am sorry to disturb you. Could you please come to the front door? There is someone here to see you, and it is urgent."

Zeph sprang to his feet. Had something happened to Charlotte or Cheyenne or Cody? He came out of his bedroom. Augustine was gone. The house seemed deserted. He made his way to the front door and stepped outside. A person was standing by the road.

"Who's there?" he asked.

The person did not answer. Zeph walked up to them in his shirtsleeves. A woman in a bonnet turned to face him.

"Charlotte." He wanted to hug her, but her face was like rock, and he hung back. "I thought I wouldn't see you for days. What's wrong?"

She reached out and took one of his hands in hers. Her fingers were like ice, and her eyes like dark pits.

"I thought I could keep my secrets forever. But I realize it cannot be done. God will not have it."

Fear tore down the track of his heart like a wild horse. "Charlotte. What is it?"

"You call me Charlotte. No one else here does, do they? Why is that, Zephaniah?"

"I thought it was because they know you by another name, a childhood name."

"Oh yes. They know me by another name." She reached a

hand to his cheek. "Thank you for all your gallantry and kindness. And now it is finished between us."

"What are you talking about? What have I done?"

"No, it is nothing you have done. It is I. My hair should be sheared in shame. You know me by the name Charlotte Spence. But that is not who I am. I have another name I thought I could leave buried in Pennsylvania, but I find I cannot. Now everything in my life has caught up with me, and you will see I am nothing more than one great lie."

"Charlotte—"

She put her fingers to his mouth. "Hush. No more of that. My real name is Lynndae Raber. The Angel of Death is my brother."

Chapter 23

Lynndae finished buttoning her sky-blue dress and then put the long light blue apron over it, fastening the apron at the back with pins. She looked in the mirror and placed the white prayer covering on her head—her blond hair had been pinned up as tightly as she could manage. *Perhaps too tightly,* she thought, *I am going to get a headache.*

The tabby with the coffee-colored fur on her tummy rubbed against Lynndae's legs, purring like some sort of small train engine. She smiled, bent down, picked the cat up, and cuddled her.

"*Guten morgan,* Snitz,*" she cooed. "It would be nice if they would let you into the meeting with me." The cat pushed her head against Lynndae's face.

There was a tap at the door. "Lynndae, the pastors are ready."

"Thank you. I will be right out."

Lord, please be with me at this hour. Help me to be honest with them and also with myself.

She opened the door with the cat still in her arms. Mary Beachey, Sarah's mother, smiled. She took the cat from Lynndae and handed it off to her daughter, who stood nearby. "Sarah, please take care of our little Princess Snitz."

"Yes, but she will be on the loose once I leave to teach school, Mama."

Mary came with Lynndae into the room where four men were waiting, closed the door, and sat beside Lynndae in the center of the room. Augustine Yoder nodded and stood up. He prayed for several minutes and then sat down again.

"Do you know all the pastors, Miss Raber?" he asked in Pennsylvania Dutch. "Here to my right is David Lapp. On my left, Malachi Kauffman. And Moses Beachey you know."

Lynndae inclined her head.

"We wanted first of all to offer thanks to you for bringing Samuel Troyer and Elizabeth Kauffman back to us. It is our understanding that your journey was not without its hazards. We are grateful God's hand of protection was upon you."

"Thank you, Pastor Yoder, but I must tell you that God worked through the person of Mister Zephaniah Parker in a very great way—"

Augustine held up a hand. "We will speak of your young man later, Miss Raber."

"Pastor Yoder, I would not call him 'my' young man, but I would be happy to speak about him later and at great length."

Mary Beachey squeezed Lynndae's hand as a warning, but did not look at her.

Augustine looked to Moses Beachey. The older man spread his hands. "Miss Raber, let us come right to the heart of the matter. Your family was asked to leave the church because your father and brothers insisted on going to war. Some of our people do not think it is right that the sins of the father were visited upon his womenfolk. Nevertheless, we must ask you, do you support your father's actions, or are you opposed to them?"

Lynndae looked calmly at Moses. "I respect my father, as God has taught all children to respect their parents. But I look at that war, and I see only pain and bloodshed and the loss of life. I hate war, Pastor Beachey. I hate what it does, and I hate what it takes away from God's earth. My father and brothers were wrong to take up arms."

"So you are opposed to your father's actions?"

"Yes."

"You are opposed to his defiance of the Ordnung and his dismissal of the teachings of our pastors and bishops?"

"Yes."

"We must also ask about your brother; I am sorry."

"I understand perfectly, Pastor Beachey. It is a necessary question."

"Bishop Schrock wished to be absolutely clear on this and on the matter of the children. He is on a business trip to Philadelphia and New York. Otherwise, he would have been here this morning."

"What about the children?"

"First we must discuss your brother Seraphim."

"No, first we must discuss the children."

Mary Beachey hissed under her breath, but Lynndae was in no mood to listen to her warnings.

Moses considered Lynndae for a few long moments. "Very well. It is only that with their parents dead, we feel it is best Samuel and Elizabeth remain here with their relatives and their church. Bishop Schrock was quite determined about that. As are all of us. We know they have grown attached to you. But if you choose to return to the Montana Territory, we want you to understand we believe they belong with us."

"Perhaps if you had not excommunicated their parents, we would not need to be discussing their fate this morning."

"They violated the Ordnung. They were warned on several occasions. The matter was handled properly. It is none of your concern."

"Excuse me, Pastor Beachey, but it is my duty, my Christian duty, to be concerned. You punished my mother and sister and me, as well as my youngest brother, for something our father did, not us. Then you punished Ricky and me for something our brother continued to do. Has it occurred to any of you that there might not have ever been an Angel of Death if you had shown love to my family instead of judgment?"

"We are a church who love one another."

"Yes, you love those who are like you. Everyone does that. You do not need Jesus Christ to help you do that."

"We do not need to be lectured by you, Miss Raber." Malachi Kauffman spoke up. "Take care."

Lynndae turned on him. "Those were your own relatives you sent to their deaths, Pastor Kauffman."

Malachi reddened. "It was their choice to travel west. I did not want them to do that."

"What did you expect them to do? You shunned them to such an extent they could not live here anymore. Where would they be able to find land where they could afford to start over again except by going into the Territories? The terrible irony is, they were excommunicated Amish who were murdered by another Amish man who had been excommunicated. All from the same community and the same church."

"That is enough, Miss Raber," said David Lapp softly.

"You sit and speak of judgment and shunning so calmly and easily, even though many have died due to your decisions. I wonder what you will do when God faces each of you on your own day of judgment and passes sentence on your lives? What will you do if He has as little pity on your souls as you have had on the souls of others?"

Mary had her head down and her eyes closed, but Lynndae could see that her lips were moving. Across from her the men were stone-faced and silent. Then Augustine cleared his throat.

"Miss Raber, still we must clear up the matter of your brother Seraphim."

"Pastor Yoder, with all due respect, what do you expect me to say? That Ricky and I believed in what Seraph has done for the past ten years? You must know we have never condoned any of the terrible killings he has participated in."

"Seraphim Raber was ushered into the presence of his Maker only last week. There he will receive a just judgment for the deeds he committed while in the flesh. But we must hear from your own lips how you felt about those deeds."

"I have told you how I feel."

"Did you ever encourage or assist him in his activities?"

"How can you ask this?"

"Do you know about John Wesley Hardin?" said David Lapp.

Lynndae felt confused. "The outlaw from Texas?"

"We read in the New York and Philadelphia papers about the men he has killed, more than forty, and this despite the fact his father is a Methodist preacher and that he was named after the founder of Methodism, John Wesley, a God-fearing minister."

Lynndae waited.

Malachi Kauffman spoke. "We read how his brother helped him, how even his father, a Christian man and a minister, assisted him in eluding the law. Time after time family and relatives kept him out of jail and hid him, and time after time he killed more men because of this. Today he is still on the loose and will destroy more lives. So we ask, did you or Ricky assist your brother Seraph in his crimes?"

Lynndae sensed a tightening in her throat and a burning in her eyes. "No, never."

"Did you ever help him to elude the law?"

"No."

"Did you ever go to the police or the sheriff and tell him what you knew of his whereabouts or his plans?"

Lynndae bent her head and felt the streaks of warm tears on her cheeks. Mary's hand rested gently on her arm. "We never knew of his whereabouts or his plans. He never wrote, and he never came to our house. I tried, Ricky tried, several times, to get messages to his camp, asking him to stop the raids and turn himself in, but we never knew where to send them. Sometimes the messengers found Seraph and sometimes they didn't. Two or three times, a reply made its way back to us, months later. They always said the same thing—as far as he was concerned, the war was not over, the war would continue until the day God told him to stop."

Augustine held up his hand. "I am sorry. It is our duty to

ask these questions. Why did you not make a sketch of him for the police?"

"For the same reason you didn't, Pastor Yoder," moaned Lynndae. "I did not know what he looked like. The last time I saw him was the last time you saw him—a tall boy, too tall for his age, skinny as a stalk of wheat; yes, just a boy with a pet dog and a pet raccoon, you remember, only twelve. What could I give to the police? A drawing of a young boy, when it was a man who was leading the raids, a man whose face was no longer that of a youth's, who may have gained weight, grown a beard, perhaps lost one of his eyes in battle and might now be wearing a patch? My memory of a child would have served the law no good purpose. That is why I did not go to them. And that is why no one in Bird in Hand went to them. None of us knew him anymore."

"Calm yourself," whispered Mary in her ear.

"I do not mean to be disrespectful. I am still tired from the journey and the danger, but that does not excuse my tongue. None of you passed judgment on my family in 1861, none of you were pastors at that time, and I know that not everyone agreed with the shunning, the streng meidung. I am told several families left the church because of the decision to excommunicate my family and because of the judgment passed on other families. I came back to talk these things over with the church, and so many words have just come tumbling out. I accept that the children must stay. I only ask that you consider the circumstances of my life when you come to make your decision about whether I may come back into the church or not. I do not know whether I will stay or go. I myself have not been able to make up my own mind, but I ask that you consider what my brother Ricky and I went through and how we had no other choice but to leave and start again in the West."

Lynndae cried with a down-turned face. Moses nodded and got to his feet.

"We will talk alone now, Miss Raber. My Mary will stay with you. When we are done we will ask for you."

Mary and Lynndae put on long dark mandlies, the woolen cape coats the Amish women wore in the winter season, and thick bonnets and walked out into the road. They held each other's arms.

"I am sorry, Mary," Lynndae said.

"Hush."

"I spoke too much. I cried too much."

"Hush. None of us have ever been through what you have experienced all these years. None of us have had such a train journey as you had this past week. Hush now. We will not talk. We will walk and pray in our hearts. They are good men; they have wisdom among them. And Moses and I want you to know, we did not agree to the shunning of your family, nor to the shunning of the Kauffmans, Troyers, and Millers. Moses only drew the short straw to be a pastor last month. God have mercy on us all."

It began to snow gently from a sky that was both blue and the color of woodsmoke. Lynndae hoped they might see Zeph or Samuel or Elizabeth, but the muddy track was deserted. Over their heads, now and then, a few crows flew back and forth. Gradually the snowflakes covered up the mud and ice like a clean blanket.

When they returned to the house in an hour, the ministers were still meeting behind a tightly closed door. Yet no sooner had Mary and Lynndae sat down to coffee, Snitz happy in Lynndae's lap, than Moses came out to the kitchen.

"Yes, we are ready for you now," he said.

Chapter 24

O nce the two women had sat in their chairs, Augustine stood up and prayed again before they began. Then he sat and nodded at David Lapp.

"Miss Raber," said David, "we understand the young man Zephaniah Parker was instrumental in seeing you safely to Bird in Hand."

"Yes, Pastor Lapp. God alone knows, but I do not think we would have arrived here in good health were it not for Mister Parker."

"Is it true the Raber Gang stopped a train you were on?"

"Yes. The Union Pacific between Cheyenne and Omaha. They wanted Samuel and Elizabeth because the children had seen their faces."

"How did you escape?"

"Zephaniah told us to hide in the baggage car. When outlaws boarded the train, he refused to tell them where we were."

"Did he shoot them?"

"Zephaniah does not carry a gun, Pastor Lapp."

"Yet he sometimes wears a badge, the children tell us."

"He was deputized by his brother before we left the Montana Territory. If he needed to ask for help from government officials, he put the badge on. Being deputized was not his idea. But his brother insisted on it."

"His brother is. . . ?"

"A federal marshal. His other brother is pastor for the church in Iron Springs."

David nodded slowly. "Why does he not carry a gun when so many other English do?"

"The war."

"So it is not a religious conviction?"

"I cannot say it is or isn't, Pastor Lapp. You must speak with him."

"Have you never discussed it?"

"Not at length, no."

"Yet you were on a train together for so many days."

"We read the Bible together a good deal, spoke with the children, looked at herds of buffalo. We slept. No, we did not spend any amount of time discussing firearms and killing people."

Another squeeze from Mary Beachey's hand.

"Tell us, what do you think, can you see yourselves as a married couple, raising children, starting a farm?"

"I have thought about it a little. But he has never declared such intentions to me in so many words."

"If you remained here and were welcomed back into the church, what do you think, would he wish to remain behind and marry you? Would he willingly take up our ways and ask for baptism?"

"Oh, I cannot answer that. He knows so little about our ways. He would need more time to think it over than a day or two."

"But would he stay behind for you?"

Lynndae felt her face growing warm. "I hope if he stayed behind it would be for God as much as it would be for me, Pastor Lapp. But I cannot say I matter to him anymore. He did not know my real name until last night. He did not know I was Seraph Raber's sister. Now I have told him, and I do not know if he can love me or forgive me."

"What did he say when you told him?"

"He looked at me in disbelief. 'Why did you hide the truth from me?' he asked. 'You were not the killer, were you? Why could you not trust me after all we have been through?' Then he turned and walked back into the house."

"He is a farmer in the Territories?"

"Beef cattle. A rancher. As I am."

"Yes. As you are. You have many men working under you, we are given to understand."

"I have ten hired men and a cook."

"And a cook?"

"I am often out and about on horseback, Pastor Lapp."

"Yet you found time to sew plain clothing for the children and for Mister Parker."

"I did."

"You own a good deal of land out there among the English?"

"Ricky bought it. It is in my name, yes."

"Can you give it up?"

"Pardon me?"

"If it were God's will for you to remain here and marry and raise a family, could you give up the land in the Territories? Could you give up being a boss—der chef—out in the West and be here a mother to your children and a helpmeet to your husband?"

"That is something I am praying about."

"Well, keep praying. I am sure the answer is not difficult to find, Miss Raber, not for an Amish woman baptized into the church as you are."

Lynndae sensed a fire rising up inside her, but she bowed her head, so the men would not spot it in her eyes.

Moses Beachey spoke. "You are not sure yet and neither are we. We hold nothing against you from your past, not from your father's decision to be a soldier or from your brother's decision to be an outlaw. What we are uncertain about is whether you can submit to a Christian life that sees you in the home instead of telling ten hired men what to do. It does not sound as if you are certain you can see yourself in that Amish home yet either. So we must proceed slowly. There is plenty of time. We hope you can remain here indefinitely—or at least until a decision is made on your part."

Augustine Yoder coughed. "It is something you must come to terms with in your own time and through your own prayers. Of course, we will be praying with you. But it must be your decision. If you can be that Amish wife in an Amish home, we will bring you back into the church. Meanwhile, the ban is lifted. There will be no more shunning directed toward you from anyone in the community. This Sunday the church gathers for worship and teaching at Amos Zook's house. You are welcome to join us; the door is open to you. It is also open to your young man. He is welcome to attend. We owe him a great deal. It would be good for him to see how we come to God and good to have him worship alongside us. Though it will be in our heavenly tongue and not the tongue of the English—or the Spanish."

The men laughed.

"Thank you all for being patient and gracious towards me," said Lynndae. "It means a great deal to feel I have been heard, forgiven, and embraced by my childhood friends and neighbors and Christians."

"There is so little to forgive," said Malachi Kauffman softly. "But there is much to give thanks for in heaven this day. Personally, I must thank you, from my heart, especially for young Bess's safe return. She lights up our home like a hundred lamps."

"I grew to love her very much. It was a privilege to bring her home to you, Pastor Kauffman. I hope I will see her again very soon?"

Malachi nodded. "We have told her she will see you on Sunday. We will make sure it is a long and wonderful day spent with God and with one another."

Moses stood up. "So we will conclude." He prayed and then the meeting was over.

After a quiet lunch with Moses and Mary and a short walk to the barn to look at the dairy cows, Lynndae took the cat with her into the bedroom that the Beacheys had set aside for her use. She lay back on a quilt with a brown and navy mariner's compass design, Snitz purring and licking herself. Lynndae had borrowed a Bible and was leafing through it, thinking about reading some of the Psalms and the Gospel of John.

She found she missed the days on the train when, for the

better part of a week, she had been wife and mother in a family of four. Every day she had spoken with Zeph. Every day she had laughed with Samuel and Bess. Now she felt lonely without them. She drew a circle over and over again on the quilt with her finger. At first the cat was interested in this movement, but after several minutes without any variation on the part of the circling finger, Snitz chose to tuck her tail around herself and doze off.

Lynndae found herself wondering if the kisses in the baggage car had been real. Had Z meant them, or was it just the relief they both felt once the gang had been captured? They had said so many wild and crazy things to one another on that trip, all the way back to Virginia City and the days on the stagecoach—did any of them matter now? Zeph felt so far away from her, it was as if he didn't exist.

Lynndae propped her head up on one hand and gazed out the window. It was snowing heavily now, like salt pouring out of a shaker. She had a view of the barn and the sloping land behind it. A lovely place. But then, so was the Sweet Blue a lovely place. Could she leave her cattle and horses behind, her mountains and rivers, the heart-stirring bugle of the elk, and the chilling night moan of the wolf?

What about Z? How was he feeling about her now that he knew who she really was? Did he hate her? Could he forgive her? The woman he had cared about was the sister of a monster. Did that make her a monster in his eyes as well? Was he willing to wake up every morning and look in her eyes and see Seraphim Raber? How could he forget she shared blood ties with a cold-blooded killer?

She stood up and began to pace, squeezing her hands together.

A killer who still hunted them. She felt no fear. Yet she had experienced moments of great fear on the journey from Iron Springs to Bird in Hand. Was it this place, with all its prayers and faith and open Bibles and absence of violence, that calmed her spirit? She glanced down at the Gospel of John and picked the Bible up. It was chapter 14 and verse 27 that caught her eye, underlined as it was with a neat black line of ink and marked with a date in equally neat and precise handwriting, August 17, 1863, probably by Mary Beachey: " 'Peace I leave with you, my peace I give unto you: not as the world giveth, give I unto you. Let not your heart be troubled, neither let it be afraid.' "

She laid her head back on the pillow and watched the snowflakes pelt against the window and the frozen earth. Her fingers stroked Snitz's fur.

Please protect Mary and Moses, Lord. Bless and protect Samuel and Bess as You have already done. Watch over these homes and these families. Watch over Zephaniah—and grant this peace You speak of to all.

Chapter 25

Even with the bellows making the forge roar and Augustine hammering a section of an iron plow on his largest anvil, Zeph could still hear the horse walking carefully up the icy track to the Yoder shop. Was there some sixth sense of his that had come back into operation since they'd ridden out of Iron Springs in the middle of the night? He'd had that feeling for things during the war, but had been determined to bury it once the fighting stopped. Yet there it was, back again. He could see that Augustine didn't realize a horse and rider were coming. He tapped him on the shoulder, and the big man looked up, face and beard dripping sweat. Zeph indicated the visitor with a jerk of his chin.

Augustine stared at the man on the tall chestnut horse and said something in Pennsylvania Dutch. Then he spoke in English for Zeph's benefit. "Big R. What brings him out?"

"Hello, the smithy!" called the man. "A good Saturday morning to one and all in the Yoder family."

"Velkommen, *wie geht es dir*?"

"Gute."

The man swung down from the saddle. He was taller than Zeph or Augustine by half a foot. He squinted up at the

February sun as it pulled free from a cloud bank and made the snow and ice dance. Then he took off his dark brown Stetson and ran a gloved hand over his iron-gray hair—it was cut close to his scalp, Zeph noticed. Under his earth-brown duster he wore a lighter brown, three-piece suit. A star glinted on its lapel.

"Always the Lewis Tweed," complained Augustine with a smile.

"Not plain enough for you?"

"The pattern—"

"Houndstooth? I have seen your women wear calico that makes my tweed look Amish enough for the bishop."

"Only the young, maybe you've seen."

"Depends what you call young, August. Well, the day you strap on a six-gun and clean up Lancaster County is the day I wear Amish black. How are you?"

He and Augustine shook hands.

"The Lord is good," said Augustine.

"I feel the same way."

"Is there something wrong that you are up and about on your best horse?"

"Shotgun and I are just doing our duty, August, working hard to keep you Amish out of trouble."

The man turned to Zeph. "Mister Parker? I asked for you at the house. Sheriff Friesen. Lancaster County is my jurisdiction."

Zeph took his hand. "Sheriff."

"Folks call me Rusty. Or Big R. Take your pick."

"Rusty?"

"No, it's not too red anymore, is it? Someone sticks a handle on you when you're young, and it's yours for life."

"He came to us with the news of what had happened in your territory," said Augustine, looking somber.

The sheriff nodded. "I had to find out who the kids' relatives were. August, we're going to walk a bit, is that all right with you?"

"Sure, sure, I'll go inside for a coffee; take your time."

"Danke."

Sheriff Friesen led his horse back toward the main road, and Zeph walked with him. Augustine suddenly clapped Zeph on the shoulder, and he turned around. The blacksmith put his cape overcoat in Zeph's hands.

"One of you must be plain," he said.

Zeph shrugged it on and immediately felt warmer in the cool winter air. He caught up to the sheriff. They went a ways in silence.

The sheriff didn't appear to be armed. Zeph wondered if that was because he harbored the same sentiments about guns and violence the Amish did.

As if sensing his thoughts, the sheriff spoke up. "I go heeled, Mister Parker. But it doesn't seem right to aggravate these good folk unnecessarily. I have a Smith and Wesson Schofield snug in a holster that's sewn into my suit jacket, just inside on the left, and unseen. It's the Wells Fargo model, barrel cut to five inches and the whole revolver refinished in nickel. I favor a cross draw; I believe it's faster. Only had to use it twice in Lancaster County. Which makes my parents happy. I am of Mennonite stock, and a good many of them hold to the same opinion of guns and shooting our fine Amish friends do. I appreciate my parents' point of view, but considering the evil I've seen men do, I beg to differ on what's best needed to quell some of that wickedness. The lawful authorities have the power of the sword, and sometimes we need to use it. How does the Bible put it?"

There was a long pause. Zeph decided to quote the verses he felt Sheriff Friesen had in mind. "'For rulers are not a terror to good works, but to the evil. . . . For he is the minister of God to thee for good. But if thou do that which is evil, be afraid; for he beareth not the sword in vain: for he is the minister of God, a revenger to execute wrath upon him that doeth evil.' Romans, chapter thirteen, part of verse three and all of verse four."

Sheriff Friesen chuckled and glanced over at him. "That's pretty good. You go to Sunday school?"

Zeph laughed. "Yeah, my brother Matt's Sunday school. He's drilled that passage into me ever since he became a lawman back in the '60s. My other brother's a clergyman, and Matt always tells him he's a minister of God, too, the Reverend B. A'Fraid."

Friesen laughed along with Zeph and nodded. "Well, it's God's truth, even my Mennonite relatives admit that. They question whether a Christian man ought to be caught up in it; that's the issue they have. I say to them, 'Would you rather have outlaws pinning on sheriff's badges and enforcing God's laws for you?' That's usually when they tell me to take a second helping of chicken and dumplings to shut me up."

They walked a little farther, and then the sheriff spoke again. "I had a telegram from a Marshal Austen in Cheyenne, Wyoming. It seems we are about to have some unwelcome visitors in Lancaster County."

"I contacted Marshal Michael James Austen from Lancaster. Seraph Raber wasn't hung, Sheriff. He slipped through K Company's fingers the day they caught two members of the gang."

"Mm."

"Raber knows we're in Lancaster County. I told my brother in Iron Springs, Montana, we'd be pushing on to Philadelphia. Raber has an accomplice in Iron Springs. He will pass on the news to the gang."

Sheriff Friesen shook his head. "Raber won't buy it. You tricked him at the railroad. He'll come here."

"What do you plan to do?"

"Well, if I thought it was just Raber, I'd sleep a lot easier. No, he's got the rest of his men with him, the ones that got away after they held up the train."

They reached the road and stopped.

"Raber telegraphed you from Omaha on Thursday, is that right?" asked the sheriff.

"Him. Or someone else. He could have already been far up the line in Chicago."

"Well, let's hope it was him and that he really was in Omaha. He could be here Monday if that's the case. What am I looking for?"

"He has a cut that runs from his eye to his chin."

"Which side?"

"I can't tell you that. I've never seen him. The girl did a drawing of his face and put it in. The left side maybe."

"Mm."

"He could have covered it with a beard by now."

"Or a woman's makeup."

"Sheriff, if he knows I'm not here, he won't stop in Lancaster. The information about his scar is going to be right across the country after a couple more days. Killing the kids won't change anything now. But he has a score to settle with me. Two of his gang were hung. I helped the army trap them. He wants me. I've got to be bait again."

"I told you. He's not likely to go for it a second time."

"If I pick a spot he can check out before he makes his play, a spot that will make him confident, I believe he may go for it. He has to prove to whoever's left in his gang that the people who cross Seraph Raber die hard deaths. He'll build another gang around that reputation."

"How do you expect us to protect you if you go someplace where he can see gophers and wood ticks for a thousand miles?"

"I don't."

"What are your intentions? To be a holy sacrifice?"

"He murdered Amish in Iron Springs. I don't intend to let him do more of the same here in Lancaster County. If he wants me, I'll make sure he knows where to find me."

"Have you got a place in mind?"

"Not yet."

"And you won't tell me when you do anyhow."

"No sir. I'd rather have you keeping an eye out for the good people of Bird in Hand. In case I get it wrong and he comes here to work mischief, regardless of where I'm holed up."

The sheriff swung up on his horse. "I'll have some deputies riding the roads hereabouts. And I'll have men watching that railroad station the way a hawk watches a pigeon. Raber doesn't get by with anything in Lancaster County, not without a fight. To quote that verse, I don't bear the sword in vain."

Friesen rested his hands on the pommel of his saddle and looked at the snow-covered landscape. "I always hoped the James-Younger gang would try to take the bank in Lancaster some fine day, but it's never happened yet. Things are so quiet here among the Germans it gets a lawman hungering for action, even the most hazardous kind. I may never get Jesse James, but the Lord has so arranged matters that I may just get the Angel of Death instead." He smiled down at Zeph. "I need to go tell my good wife, May, what's going on. She'll be fussing with our horses and dairy herd. Mister Parker, I wish you all the luck in the world." Then he spoke to Shotgun, and the big chestnut began to trot along the road back to Lancaster.

Zeph walked back to the smithy. Augustine called to him from the front door of the house, his hands in his pockets.

"How about some coffee?"

"Sure, I'd like that."

At the kitchen table Augustine worked a toothpick back and forth in his mouth. "So? Did you have a talk with Mister Friesen?"

Zeph smiled. "How does Romans thirteen, verses three and four suit you?"

Augustine paused and thought. Then he shook his head and growled, "Yah, yah, *flammenschwert*." Then he barked his laugh and slapped the table and shook his head again. "*Ach*, we need more coffee."

"Zephaniah," he said, when he had poured both of them another cup, "tomorrow we have worship at our Katie's home, at Amos Zook's. We would like you to join us. It will also give you an opportunity to see Samuel and Elizabeth. And Lynndae Raber, if you are interested."

"I'd be happy to join you."

Augustine stared at him. "How do you feel about the woman now?"

"I don't know."

"She did not do what her brother did."

"I didn't know who she was all those years. I don't know who she is now. She made a fool of all of us. She made a fool of me."

Augustine sipped at his coffee.

"This afternoon, the wife and I will take the buggy into town to buy some things she needs for baking. I also have a few items I must look at. Do you wish to join us?"

"What about the plow you have been working on this week?"

"The plow? Spring is months away. Smucker has time. I have time. Everyone will bring their plows for repairs and sharpening in March. There will be plows from here until spring planting."

Zeph hitched Matchbox up to the buggy, and the three of them went into Lancaster. After stopping in a few shops, Zeph excused himself and walked over several streets to the telegraph office. When he was given the pad of paper to write on, he leaned against the counter and thought as hard as he'd thought about anything in his life.

What will flush Raber? What will make him risk coming out into the open?

Getting his hands on Zephaniah Parker of course.

But where? Where will Raber feel safe enough to show himself?

Zeph went over the verse from Revelation in his head. Again and again he came back to Abaddon, the Place of Destruction. Did Raber have such a place in mind? Or was he going to create such a place, maybe turn Bird in Hand into a location fixed for slaughter and devastation? How could he get Raber and his killers away from Lancaster County and spare these people's lives?

Lord, I need Your help with this, one way or the other. I don't care if I make it through. But I care if Lynndae and the kids and all these decent folk do.

After several minutes, images began to form in his mind, images of death and suffering he had worked hard at suppressing for more than ten years. Soon his head was flooded with them. He could hear the *crack-crack-crack* of thousands of muskets and the roar of cannon, and he could smell the stink of smoke and sulphur and blood. He almost gasped, the memories were so raw and overpowering. The telegraph clerk glanced his way once or twice. Finally Zeph leaned over and wrote a message on the pad.

Raber
    I will come alone to the Place of Destruction. It is only forty miles south of Lancaster. You know the location I am talking about.
    If you have the courage, meet me there.

                                          Parker

"Send this to the office of the federal marshal in Iron

Springs, Montana Territory," Zeph said to the clerk. "Matthew Parker."

"Very well, sir."

Zeph paid him and left. Then he walked quickly to the station and purchased a ticket for the Sunday evening train to Gettysburg, Pennsylvania.

Chapter 26

Several dozen buggies were already lined up outside the Zook house when Augustine and Rebecca Yoder and Zephaniah came down the road, Matchbox trotting cheerfully through the sparkling frost and blue sky of a Lancaster winter morning. Rebecca carried in several snitz pies, and Augustine walked carefully, with a large container of bean soup. Zephaniah came through the doorway balancing several loaves of heavy brown bread and a massive pot of beef and cabbage, still warm, against his chest.

Zeph had risen early, bathed in a large wooden tub with water heated on the stove, trimmed his beard, and shaved his upper lip clean. Put on a fresh shirt. Used the suspenders Augustine had lent him to hold his pants up. Brushed his dress coat and pulled it on over a plain Amish vest Augustine had also lent him. Wiped muck off his black boots and polished them to a gloss. Exchanged the hat Lynndae had purchased for him in Ogden for a hat the Yoders' son Daniel had left behind. Rebecca Yoder called it a piker. It had a crease in its crown that gave it, Zeph thought, a bit of dash. He placed his silver watch in a vest pocket.

"How do I look?" he asked Rebecca.

She had smiled and nodded. "Very plain. A good Amish."

When Zeph entered the Zook house with the food, there were people everywhere, talking in Pennsylvania Dutch, at least a hundred of them, he figured, probably more. He noticed when he glanced out a window that a number of boys had gathered near the barn. Some of the older horses were being stabled there. Women were rushing about in the kitchen organizing the food. Several men were carrying benches into the house. Elizabeth found him and wrapped her arms around him. He kissed her on the top of her head.

"Hello, Mister Parker."

"Hello, Miss Kauffman. Are you well?"

"Very well. But I miss our train rides."

"I do, too. Where is Master Troyer?"

"With the other boys at the barn."

"And Miss Raber?"

"Oh, I saw her outside walking with Sarah Beachey and Rachel Otto. But then Aunt Rosa called them into the kitchen to help."

"I didn't notice her there."

"Well, she is dressed very plain and is in and out of the pantry with things."

Zeph looked toward the door of the large kitchen and thought about invading the Amish women's domain on some sort of pretext. But he didn't know if he was even halfway ready to make peace with Lynndae Raber. Maybe he never would be. A hand fell heavily on his shoulder. He turned around and it was Augustine.

"Mister Yoder," he said by way of greeting.

"Come. I have some men I would like you to meet."

He was introduced to the pastors, David Lapp and Malachi Kauffman. Moses Beachey he had already met at the train station. Then in swift succession, he met a number of Zooks, Hooleys, Umbles, Petershwims, and Planks, until he could no longer match faces with names.

"I am James Lambright," said one thin man, taking Zeph's hand in a tight grip.

"A pleasure."

"They tell me you are from the West."

"Montana Territory."

"Do you farm there?"

"I raise horses and graze beef cattle."

"Who do you sell them to?"

"Some of my horses I sell to officers in the army. The beef goes east to feed people in New York and Boston."

"What about Indians?"

"All is quiet, sir. I am hoping we may have found a way to live at peace with one another, something that will last."

"I pray so, I pray so."

Another man with glasses and red hair and pale skin came up.

"I am Jonathan Glick. All praise to God."

"Yes."

"I hear you have become quite a blacksmith, yah?"

"Oh, I wouldn't say that. So far, all I have done is pump the bellows."

"Do you like to work?"

"I do."

"A smithy is a wonderful place on a cold day."

"It is."

"I have been cutting and storing ice for the summer. Chills you to the bone."

"It would."

"Do you do that out west?"

"We cut the ice from lakes and rivers, yes."

"Store them in sawdust and straw?"

"Please, everyone, it is time to meet with God." This was said in Pennsylvania Dutch, but as people began to move toward the benches, Zeph followed them. His pocket watch read eight o'clock. He caught a glimpse of Lynndae and felt an unpleasant darkness inside himself. She saw his glance, but he looked away and bowed his head. She looked so Amish in her dress and head covering, Zeph would not have been able to tell her apart from any of the other young Amish women.

He felt a sting in his heart. Lynndae was one of them. She had returned to her home, and this was where she belonged and where she was going to stay. All her years in Iron Springs she had been one of them, but he had never known it. He shook his head. There couldn't be any future for them as man and wife. All the things he would have done for Charlotte Spence, he could not do for Lynndae Raber, the sister of a heartless killer, a woman who had lived so many different lies he no longer knew who she really was. The only thing he was sure of anymore was that he had a date with her brother in Gettysburg.

People continued to find places to sit all around him, but he scarcely noticed. His thoughts had made their way to Gettysburg. Monday night could find him buried with Union soldiers in southern Pennsylvania. Strangely, the thought of that had not yet frightened him. Still, now that it had surfaced, he was glad to be in a place of worship where he could hand everything over to God among a people of faith and goodwill.

"The men sit together," said Augustine, who was suddenly at his side. "Here, sit with my son-in-law, Amos. I must join the pastors in another room during the singing. We need to decide which of us will preach today."

Zeph sat next to a tall, straw-blond young man who smiled and shook his hand.

"Amos Zook."

"Zephaniah Parker."

"The cowboy?"

"Yes. And you are the honey man?"

"For sure."

A young man came and stood by them, uncertain of his welcome. It was Samuel. "Good morning, Mister Parker."

Zeph shook his offered hand. "Why, good morning, Master Troyer. You're looking very well. Where have you been hiding these past couple of days?"

"I have been with my friend Nathaniel Mast and his family, Mister Parker. I hope I may introduce you to him at lunch if that is all right with you?"

"I'd be glad to meet your pal, Samuel—"

"Shh," came a woman's voice behind them.

Zeph shrugged off his cape overcoat. Hymnals were passed down the rows. They were thick and heavy. When Zeph opened his, he saw that it was in German, but he left it open in his lap anyway. A man began to sing. All around him men and women and children joined in. There were no fancy notes,

Zeph noticed, no harmonizing or polished transitions, just a simple strong melody that was carried by earnest voices far beyond their hearts or the roof of the house. No piano played, neither was there an organ in the room. He closed his eyes, listened, worshipped, and prayed.

After about half an hour, Moses Beachey came into the room with the other pastors and began to preach. He had a lilting way of talking, almost like chanting, and Zeph watched, fascinated, as he wandered about the room and then disappeared into other parts of the house where people were seated, still preaching. It was as if his voice were floating far away in a cave or catacomb. Then he returned. It seemed as if he was pleading with them. A man groaned out loud and sunk his head into his large hands. A woman nearby began to cry openly. Next to him Amos Zook was nodding his head, mesmerized, and biting his lower lip.

Lord, I am not used to this, prayed Zeph.

Moses sat down. There was the sound of sniffling and amens for a few moments, and then Amos stood up and began to read from his black Bible. Once he had finished, another man's voice came from a room Zeph could not see. He presumed the man was reading scripture as well, his tone rich and deep. Then everyone went to their knees and Zeph did likewise. A man prayed out loud, then another. When Amos rose, so did Zeph.

Augustine Yoder was preaching now. He, too, moved from room to room, his voice now booming, now scarcely more than a whisper. He began to cry, tears rolling down his broad cheeks and into his dark beard. Again and again, Zeph caught the words, Jesu Christi am kreuz, and he realized Augustine was talking about Jesus Christ on the cross. Women and men began to weep. This went on for more than an hour. It was as if the hearts and souls of the congregation were suspended in the air of the house and God was personally touching each one as He walked among them. Zeph understood nothing— yet, it seemed to him, he understood everything, far more than he might have understood in a calmer worship service in an English church.

When Augustine sat down, David Lapp got to his feet and seemed to Zeph to be addressing himself to various points Augustine had raised. Malachi Kauffman got up and did the same. Then everyone went to their knees to pray again, and after that the hymnals were opened and there was more singing. Once they began to clear the rooms to set up tables for lunch, Zeph felt he needed to be alone with God and not sitting and talking with the men again, as good-natured as they were. So in the moving of the benches and the setting out of breads and jams and soups and meat dishes, he slipped out the back door of the kitchen and walked off across the fields of snow without the long overcoat Augustine had lent him.

He did not mind the chill. The presence of so many people had made the house very warm. It had been quite an experience. Zeph sensed God was trying to say something important to him through it all.

Jesu Christi am kreuz.

Jesus on the cross—for Zeph, for Augustine, for Sheriff Friesen, for Colonel Austen. For Lynndae Raber. Yes, even for Seraphim Raber. The Angel of Death had heard sermons like this. In some corner of his heart, they were still lodged there. He had chosen to ignore them.

Jesu Christi am kreuz.

Was it possible? Could God be expecting him to say something about this to Raber when they met? Would Raber be in any kind of mood to hear it? What if Raber just shot him or hanged him before he had a chance to open his mouth?

There was a cluster of barren winter trees, heavy branches outstretched, and Zeph found a patch of dry earth and sat in their midst. He looked back at the house. It was perhaps two hundred yards away. He could see some people moving about in the snow, crossing between the barn and the outhouses.

Lord, he prayed, *if there is something You want me to say to Seraphim Raber, then please give me the words. Yes, bring us together and give me the words. May Your hand of mercy be upon him, may it be upon me, may it be upon all the people of Lancaster and Bird in Hand, may it be upon the woman I care for more than anyone else in the world even though I myself must release her.*

He changed position so he could look out over the fields and sky rather than watch the smoke rising from the house chimney. His thoughts wandered back to Montana, back to the long train trip, back to the moment he put his lips to Lynndae's in the baggage car of the train. Maybe he was just meant to get Lynndae and the children safely to Pennsylvania, and that's all there was to it. It felt like there should be more when he turned everything over in his mind and remembered the feelings that had poured through him, but maybe that was the whole story. It hurt a bit, but a man got used to hurts or he died young. After all, she had never trusted or loved him enough to tell him the truth about herself—that she was Amish, that she was the Angel of Death's sister. A darkness settled deeper inside him as he turned this bitter pill over in his mouth. No, there was nothing between them now. It was over.

Zeph checked his watch. Two o'clock. His mutze dress coat was no longer proof against the cold. Nor did he want to appear as if he had disliked the worship service. He started back through the snow to the white, two-story house.

He had only been walking for a minute when he noticed a figure coming over the fields toward him. It moved lightly and smoothly. His heart quickened—Lynndae Raber.

She stopped and looked at him in her white prayer covering and black dress with its gray apron. The sun brushed against her cheek and lit up her blue eyes.

"I have come to ask on this Lord's Day," she said, "if you can forgive me and we can start again."

And she stretched a hand toward him.

Chapter 27

The feeling in him was to take the hand. He fought it. Dark feelings and sensations of light whirled around in his head and heart. She watched the struggle but did not drop her hand. It remained suspended in the cold afternoon air, fair, ungloved, lovely. Finally Zeph realized he wanted her and wanted to forgive her more than anything else in the world. He stopped resisting and reached for her hand. In taking it, he drew her closer to himself.

She squinted up at him and at the sun that rode his shoulder. "Are you forgiving me?"

He nodded. "You had your reasons. It's not like I was your husband or lover. I'm sorry I've been so harsh."

"Thank you, Zephaniah." She touched his cheek with her free hand. "Everyone was asking about you."

"I found the worship service to be a powerful experience. I just had no appetite for talk or food afterwards. I needed to be alone with the Lord. So I came out here to pray and think myself clear. Listen, we haven't got a whole lot of time."

"Z, we have all the time we need. The Amish like things to happen at a slow pace."

"I'm leaving on a train in a few hours, Lynndae. I've got to go alone. You can't come with me. Though I do pray to God you'll let me take you with me in my heart."

Her stomach went cold. "Are you heading back west?"

"No."

"Then where are you going? And why are you going?"

"I can't tell you everything. But I need your prayers. If all goes well, there's no reason I won't see you in a day or two."

"A day or two?" She studied his eyes and every line in his face. "It's something to do with my brother, isn't it?"

"Yes it is. Lynndae, I can't have him coming in here like he meant to do at Iron Springs and shoot everyone on sight and burn every house to the ground."

"He won't do that—"

"He will do that. He wants revenge for the men that were hung, and he wants revenge against the people who shunned him and his family for taking up arms for the Union. He will come here and set houses and haystacks ablaze. Unless I draw him off."

"You?"

"He doesn't want the kids anymore. I telegraphed his description to Colonel Austen and my brother. He knows the information will be right across the country and through all the Territories over the next couple of days. No, he wants the man who set him up at Alkali and had troopers ready to gun down his men or take them west to Cheyenne for a hanging. He wants me more than anyone else I guess he can think of right now. If I get him away from here, the people will be safe."

"Z, I don't want you to do this."

"If I don't, the Mary Beacheys and Aunt Rosas and

Augustine Yoders are going to die."

"They have Sheriff Friesen."

"A good man, but he's not enough, nowhere near enough to take on a killer like Seraph Raber."

"And you are? Unarmed? Alone?"

"He wants me—Z. He'll come after me. And he knows where I'm going."

"But I don't."

"You can't. You might be crazy enough to follow me."

"I have things to say to my brother that have been left unsaid for too long."

"Yeah, well, that's exactly the way I feel about you and me."

"Pardon me?"

"It was no game for me on that train, Lynndae. I never had to act one moment since we became Mister and Missus Fremont and Conner Wyoming. For me, it was all for real."

One hand touched her chin and lifted her face toward his.

"I love you, Charlotte. I love you, Conner. I love you, Lynndae. I forgive you. Just as Christ on the cross has forgiven me. I want you to be my wife. I want to marry you and take sunset rides in the Rocky Mountains. I want to fill you with God's happiness. I want to raise a family with you and have a house full of good words and good laughter and good loving. That's all I want."

He paused.

She looked straight into his eyes. "Z, do you really mean all that you're saying?"

"I mean it. But you can't give me your answer yet. I know you've got your Amish ties to think about. Your home on the

Sweet Blue. I guess, in a way, I've got no right to be saying these things to you when I might not be alive a day from now. But if I never said them today I might not ever get another chance. If things don't work out the way I've planned, well, I want you to know that this cowboy really did love you, Lynndae. I love you more than heaven and earth."

She touched his lips. "You're a crazy fool, Zephaniah T. Parker. Do you think I'm going to wait another day to tell you how I feel when I've been waiting so long to hear you say the words you said to me just now? Amish are slow, but we're not that slow. I'm not waiting another moment."

She threw her arms around him with a strength that made him gasp. "I love you, I love you, yes, yes, yes, a thousand times yes. Marry me, take me back to our Rocky Mountain sunsets, and let's ride until we find a stream where we can toss down our bedrolls and sleep under the stars and thank God for everything."

Her face was close to his, and he could see the light dancing in her blue eyes like sunlight sparkling on water. "I guess I'm kind of confused right now, Lynndae Raber."

"Why's that?"

"I'm not sure how to kiss in Amish."

She laughed. "Slow, and you take a long time at it."

Zeph did as he was told. He had stopped feeling the cold of the afternoon air ever since she'd walked out to meet him. Now he felt heat roar through his lips and head and heart. Once he'd started, he had no idea of stopping and neither did she. He tasted her sweetness and her love, and there was nothing like it on the face of God's good earth, nothing.

"Who needs breath?" he finally asked her.

"That's why God gave us noses."

A long time later they walked back to the house. Many of the buggies had left. By common consent, they did not touch or hold hands, nor did they have any intention of telling anyone anything yet. A hundred feet from the house he stopped, and she turned to look at him.

"I've got to go to the station now," he told her.

She held his gaze and her eyes were violet. "You've given me the happiest hour in my life, Z. The hours to come will be the longest and the hardest."

"But you understand, don't you?"

"I do understand, my love. And I'm proud of you."

"You'll pray for me?"

"How can you ask that? I'll be praying without ceasing." Then she placed a hand on his heart. "Listen. Long ago, in Montana, I made a promise to my brother on his deathbed. The promise was that I'd never marry outside the family, never split up our ranch or join it to another's, never let a marriage contract threaten the land. Never."

A chill swept through him. "I'm no cousin of yours."

"I've fought with Ricky's words for years. Should I keep the promise, should I break the promise. Why do you think I never let you get close to me? Why do you think I never responded to your warmth and friendliness in a way a woman who adored you would? I made a promise to my dying brother."

He was confused. "Didn't you just say you'd marry me?"

"Yes, I did. And I meant it. But I need some time to make peace with Ricky. I need time for his spirit to understand. I want to go ahead and have a life with you. But please don't ask for the wedding ceremony to be tonight or before you get on that train. I need time to work this through with him and God."

Moses Beachey came around the corner of the house. He smiled. "There you are, Lynndae. We are just about to head home."

She dropped her hand from Zephaniah's heart but held his gaze. Neither she nor Zephaniah were smiling. "Yes. All right. I'm coming."

"Mister Parker," said Moses. "I have not seen you since the morning worship."

"I found it a very moving and very meaningful time, Mister Beachey. Please convey that to the others. I don't want my absence to be misunderstood. Those hours of worship and preaching meant more to me than many a church service has in a long time. I needed to be alone to pray and think over what I had heard taught and sung and prayed."

Moses looked surprised. "But you do not have the language."

"Today I understood the language of God's Spirit, Mister Beachey, and that was all that was needed."

Moses nodded and looked at Zeph for several moments, thinking. Then he said, "I sense God will bless you in the days to come."

"Why, thank you for that, Mister Beachey."

Zeph walked out to the buggy with the two of them and touched the brim of his piker hat. "Miss Raber, I wish you every goodness Christ has to offer those He loves."

She inclined her head. "The Lord be with you, Mister Parker, night and day, day and night."

Their eyes locked for a brief instant, and then Moses shook the reins. The buggy moved off down the rutted track of snow and mud. Zeph stood watching.

A hand came to rest on his shoulder. It was Augustine. "So. It was a good day for you?"

"It was a holy day, Mister Yoder. Thank you for your sermon."

"What? You understood some of it?"

"Jesu Christi am kreuz."

Augustine had been working a toothpick around in his mouth. He stopped. "I saw you under the trees. I thought the morning had disappointed you."

"No. I was greatly blessed. I needed a place to pray."

Augustine grunted. "So, what did prayer help you to figure out?"

"I would be much obliged if you took me to the station after we've dropped off Missus Yoder and I've picked up my luggage."

Augustine looked hurt. "You are going back west so soon?"

"I'm not going west."

Augustine narrowed his eyes. His toothpick began to move around again. "All right. We should go."

At the Yoder house, Zeph said good-bye to Rebecca and picked up his carpetbag, bedroll, sheepskin jacket, and the saddlebags, which he had stacked just inside the front door. She remained at the roadside while the buggy rolled over the mud and water to Lancaster.

"I hope to be back Monday or Tuesday," said Zeph as Augustine hunched over the reins and stared straight ahead.

Augustine flicked the reins and sat back, appearing to relax a bit. "Gute. For Rebecca it is like having one of the boys back in the house again."

"Mister Yoder, I am grateful for your hospitality and the kindness of the Amish community. Thank you for allowing me to worship with you this morning. My few days here have been very pleasant and invigorating. Now I must tell you something you will not want to hear. Seraph Raber is still alive."

Augustine glanced at him in astonishment. "No, he was hanged with the other outlaw—"

"They didn't catch him. He's still at large. I am going to meet him."

"What are you saying?"

"He is angry with me for trapping his men at the train last week. I am going to meet him and talk. But that does not mean he will not send some of his gang here after the children or to seek revenge against the Amish for shunning his family. You must get everyone to a safe place."

Augustine considered this and worked at his toothpick. "He has no gang left."

"Sheriff Friesen thinks he has a few that weren't captured at the train. I believe he's right. They did not vanish across the Mexican border. They may come here."

"You want us to gather in one place?"

"Maybe not one place. It would be better if you used three or four houses. All at the same location. That way Sheriff Friesen will be able to keep an eye on all of you. You will need to tell him where you are."

"When should we do this?"

"Now. Tonight. As soon as I've left on the train."

"There are animals to take care of."

"Let the men do that and then join their families in the houses."

"In the morning also there are chores—"

"The gang may come at daybreak."

"We have our farms and livelihood, Zephaniah."

Zeph reached over and gripped Augustine's broad shoulder as tightly as he could. Augustine looked at him in surprise.

"Mister Yoder. Seraph Raber has killed people past counting. He murdered the Kauffmans, Troyers, and Millers at Iron Springs. All that for no more reason than wanting to hurt and destroy. Now his men have been shot and hung. So he has a bigger reason. How much worse do you think he can be when real fury is in his heart?"

Lancaster was in sight. Matchbox quickened his pace. Augustine worked at his toothpick and flicked the reins to keep the horse moving smartly.

"You think Raber will meet you?"

"I'm counting on it."

"Where?"

"South. A place I swore I'd never go back to."

"He will want to kill you, Zephaniah."

"That's why I'm sure he'll be there."

"This is something for the rulers God has appointed over us. You do not carry a weapon."

"Not since the war. Another thing I swore I'd never go back to."

"What can you do against his hate but remain among us and pray?"

"If I remain among you and pray, he will come right to where I am and cut through all of Bird in Hand to get to me—every man, woman, and child."

"No, Zephaniah, this is not something you can do; this is for the law."

"Mister Yoder, I am the law." He brought the badge out of a pocket in his mutze and pinned it on his vest. "I swore an oath on the Bible I would protect people like you from people like him."

"We do not swear oaths."

"But I did."

They were at the station. Zeph stepped down and pulled his luggage out of the buggy.

"Thank you, Mister Yoder. God bless you."

Augustine sat in the buggy and looked down at him. His toothpick had stopped once again. "I will tell the pastors what you have said. We will move everyone before sunset."

"That sounds right."

"We will see you Monday or Tuesday."

"I look forward to it."

"Don't forget your coat." Augustine tossed him the overcoat he had left on the bench at the Zook house. "It is best to dress plain among the English."

Zeph smiled and touched the brim of his piker hat.

The sun was an orange and purple blaze only a little ways above the horizon. Zeph walked into the station holding his gear. A clerk nodded at him and said the train south for York and Gettysburg would be along in forty-five minutes. Zeph thanked him and went into a restroom, where he uncinched one of his saddlebags and drew out his father's Remington revolver. He turned it over in his hand. It was empty, and no stores were open on a Sunday where he could purchase ammunition. But maybe it would slow down Seraphim Raber just enough if he saw its butt sticking out of the waistband of Zeph's pants. Which is where he put it, the long barrel grazing the inside of his thigh. Then he walked back to his seat in the station, checked his watch, and waited.

If he had glanced east out of one of the windows, he would have seen that Augustine Yoder had not yet left. What he had done was climb out of his buggy and kneel by its side in the snow and ice and pray for God to spare the life of the young man from the Montana Territory. He stayed on his knees in the cold for at least ten minutes. Then he rose and got back into the buggy. Matchbox stamped his front left hoof, but Augustine did nothing. He waited until the train arrived and Zephaniah boarded. Not until the black smoke of the locomotive was a distant pillar in a sky rapidly losing its light did he flick the reins, turn the buggy around, and set Matchbox on a fast trot for the village of Bird in Hand.

Chapter 28

He came to the cemetery at night after he stepped off the train. Stars were white and sharp and pointed in the chill air of the February night. He walked through the tall brick arch of the cemetery's gatehouse. Sometime ago back in the Montana Territory, he had read in a paper about the project, how the Union dead had been moved from other locations on the vast battlefield and reburied here, state by state, over three thousand of them. The moon rose like a bonfire and lit the white headstones, row upon row, and they suddenly gleamed like candles. Zeph put down his gear and moved among them like a spirit.

He read the names. *I know none of them,* he thought, *yet I fought beside them all.* Up and down the rows he went. *We fell here and there like sacks of corn, all jumbled up with one another and with dead Rebs, yet now we lie in straight lines without a hint of confusion or messiness.* Zeph touched a headstone. He let the cold work its way up his fingers to his arm and shoulder and heart, so he could remember this place was about death, not order and decency.

No Confederate soldiers were buried here. They had been unearthed and removed to cities like Charleston and Savannah. He kept walking through the snow. At one point he stopped and began to look past the naked branches of trees to the fields and hills that were white as open bone. It looked different from those hot July days, yet it seemed right to him that he should be here in the season that allowed no growth or green or lushness. He strained his eyes.

Where was the wheat field and Emmitsburg Road? The McPherson Woods? Devil's Den and Little Round Top? The peach orchard? The clamor of battle and the cries of dying men assailed him. Zeph groaned and put his hands to his face. Wednesday, Thursday, and Friday. The only respite at night when lamps floated over the carnage as men looked for missing friends and wounded comrades.

Why couldn't Raber let the war go? Hadn't once been enough? What could possess a man, any man, that he would want to relive the battles and the horrors, the death of companions, and the slaughter of boys no older than fourteen, fifteen, or sixteen, their young faces motionless against the tall hay and moist summer earth?

They had almost lost Jude in the orchard. And Matt at Cemetery Ridge—he had taken a ball in his leg and come close to bleeding out. Three, four, five times over the three-day battle Zeph was certain he himself was in a fix he could not get out of and that he was finished. It was a miracle he had survived. Yet here he was at the battlefield again, and it was not clear at all whether he would walk away unscathed a second time.

He had no idea what he would say to Raber or if Raber would even give him a chance to speak. Well, as long as the hope of getting his hands on Zeph drew Raber out of hiding and away from Bird in Hand, that's what mattered. He was not interested in dying only hours after the most beautiful woman in the world had said she would marry him, but he was even less interested in seeing her and twenty or thirty men, women, and children die along with him. Gettysburg was where he had to be. If only Raber felt the same way.

Zeph cleared away a patch of snow and laid his sheepskin coat down over the frozen soil. Then he untied his bedroll and spread it out, placing the Amish overcoat on top of it for extra warmth. Raber or no Raber, he was cold and tired. He removed his boots and climbed into his bedroll, tugging his father's pistol free and holding it in his hand under the blankets. Then he put his head on his bent arm and lay down to sleep among the Union dead.

When he woke, he could not remember having dreamed. The morning chill had woken him. The piker hat had fallen off, and the cold had gnawed at his skull. He sat up, found the hat, and crammed it back on his head. Then he put the revolver inside the top of his pants just near one of the suspenders. Tiny snowflakes melted against his forehead and cheeks. The first proper thought that came into his mind was a verse from Psalm 23: *"Yea, though I walk through the valley of the shadow of death, I will fear no evil: for thou art with me."*

He heard a footstep in the snow. A heavy coil of rope landed on his legs with a thump. At one end of it was a hangman's noose.

"Good morning, Captain Parker."

Zeph looked up. A tall man stood over him in a long sheepskin coat and Union slouch hat that reminded Zeph of Samuel's cavalry Stetson. Sideburns curled down both sides of his face.

The man smiled. "Looks like you could use more sleep. Well, I believe I can help you with that. Give me a few minutes, and I'll see what I can do to help you find that long, deep rest you seem to need."

The man looked out over the fields and slopes covered in white. "I was here the whole three days. You?"

"Wednesday, Thursday, Friday."

"Lee always felt he would have won if he'd had Stonewall the Presbyterian. What do you think?"

"I think if we'd had Grant the war would have been over on July fourth."

The man snorted. "Is that what you believe? The war ain't over for me yet." He looked around. "Thank you for being a man of your word. This will be an honorable exit, even if it is at the end of a rope. We spent an hour scoping this place before we came down. Been here for a day, truth be told, keeping an eye on things. No cavalry, no lawmen, just you and your piker hat. Get up and let me take a look at you."

Zeph climbed out of the bedroll in his bare feet. He and the man were about the same height. Just under the sideburn on the left side of the man's face Zeph could see the trace of a scar it covered up.

"Raber," he said.

"I am. Sideburns grow faster than a beard. You'll recall it was a Union general who started the fashion."

A man stood a few feet behind Raber. He held a pistol in his hand and wore a long woolen coat and slouch hat like Raber's, though it was quite a bit more battered and stained. Raber indicated him with a flick of his head. "Major Spunk Early of

Illinois. I have two more of my boys watching the approach to the cemetery with sniper rifles. Billy and Wyatt are death at half a mile."

"There won't be anyone coming."

"After the railroad I take precautions." Raber glanced about. "Is there a tree you favor, Captain? I don't want to prolong this. I'd like to take the train back to Lancaster. It was slow coming down by horse. I have work to finish in a timely fashion."

"What work?"

"Oh, rape, pillage, and plunder, I reckon, the same as we did on our immortal march through Georgia. You killed a couple of my men, Parker. There's a debt to pay."

"Those Amish are more your people than they are mine."

Raber exploded with rage. "They are not my people! They haven't been my people since the day they threw us out of their church and killed my mother and my sister Mary! I hope they will take a picture of their bodies swaying in the breeze just as pretty as the one that graced the front page of the Chicago Daily Tribune!"

He glared at Zeph. "Get the rope, Major Early."

"Yes sir."

"I know you came here on your own to draw me away from Bird in Hand, Captain, and you must understand I admire that. You're a man of substantial courage. I salute you. It did the Amish no good, they will die anyway, but no one can say you did not make the most valiant effort. So I offer you a final opportunity—is there a view you'd like to see one last time while you're swinging from your neck? Little Round Top? The peach orchard? McPherson Ridge?"

"Someone coming!" yelled a man by the cemetery gatehouse.

Raber looked at Zeph. "Just one?"

Zeph shook his head. "I swear, I have no idea—"

"You swear, do you? On a stack of Bibles?"

"It's a woman! No one else! Just a woman in them funny clothes!"

Raber drew a revolver from a holster under his sheepskin coat. "Let's go take a look. After you, Captain. Put on your overcoat first. I wouldn't want you to catch your death and cheat the hangman."

Zeph threw on the cape overcoat and slogged through the snow to the gatehouse. Two men in blue were using it for cover. The woman was about a hundred yards away, head bent, doggedly marching through the snowdrifts. A white bonnet, a long cape coat, very plain.

"Amish," said Zeph.

"She your cavalry this time around?" Raber reholstered his pistol. "Didn't think you'd get a woman to do your fighting for you."

"I don't know who it is, Raber."

"Major General Raber."

"I didn't tell anyone where I was going."

"Well, then I guess a little sparrow told her."

As Zeph watched her come toward them, his heart began to sink. He had seen that very walk only the day before as he sat under a cluster of trees on the Zook farm and waited while a person made her way across the snow toward him. He hoped he was wrong. But the closer she got the more certain he became.

Oh Lord.

As she approached the gatehouse, Raber swept off his slouch hat. "Good morning, ma'am. Where have you come from?"

"Good day to you, sir. I have just stepped off the early train from Philadelphia, Lancaster, and York."

"Perhaps you have come by to place some flowers on a brave soldier's grave, even at this chill winter hour?"

Her head was still down. She kept her eyes on the steps she took through the snow and ice. "Not entirely. Although I have come to find and speak with a brave soldier if one may be found."

Raber smiled broadly. "Look no further then, ma'am, you have found what you seek."

"Why, a brave man, sir?"

"None braver."

"And a soldier?"

"All my adult life and most, I may confess, of my youth."

"I am glad to hear it. Because then we may actually be able to hold a Christian conversation and you can explain to me where that brave soldier has been hiding these ten years. You have certainly not been him, and he has most certainly not been you."

A frown covered Raber's face. The woman lifted her face defiantly and let him stare at her in astonishment.

"Good morning, brother. It has been a long time since our good-bye in the summer of 1861, when you snuck out of the house to enlist in the Federal Army."

Raber looked as if he had been bayoneted. "Little L," he finally whispered.

"Seraphim." Her blue eyes crackled with fire.

"What are you doing here?"

"Well, since you have made up your mind to hang my husband, I thought I should at least come along to pay him my last respects. Isn't that what a good Northern woman would do, Major General Raber?"

"Him?"

"He declared his love for me only yesterday, brother, and I accepted. It was he who protected me and the children all the way from Iron Springs. Don't you know my name? Charlotte Spence, the woman you threatened to kill in the Montana Territory."

Raber stood rooted, taking it all in like a boxer standing stunned and still absorbing fresh blow after fresh blow.

Lynndae stepped closer to him so that they were only inches apart. "My brother. The boy I played with. The boy I read to. The boy with a dog named Sparkles and a raccoon named Jingles. The boy who became a man amidst the horror of war and led his men, Ricky said, like King Arthur leading the knights of the Round Table—brave, gallant, chivalrous, merciful to the defeated, courteous to the prisoner, noble, unconquerable, the very flower of manhood. What happened to that officer and gentleman, brother? Who stole his soul out of your body and replaced it with the spirit of a demon?"

She drew back and slapped him across the face with all the force she could muster, which, Zeph knew, was not inconsiderable. Blood sprayed from Raber's lips. Still he did not move or speak. His men looked alarmed, and Spunk Early took a step toward Lynndae.

"Child killer!" she spat. "Woman killer! Thief! Murderer! Is this how you honor our father? Would he be proud to stand up among the saints in heaven and have them look toward earth with him? 'There is my youngest boy, Angel. There is my pride and joy. There is my heart and soul, my righteous and holy Christian son?' Do you remember nothing of the prayers he prayed over you or the Bible stories he read to us by the fire at night? Have you forgotten your own baptism or the day you kneeled before us all and said Jesus was your Savior and Lord?"

Raber continued to stare at her, his face white, blood trickling from the cut on his mouth.

"What about our mother? They say there are no tears in heaven—oh Seraph, how could she have no tears when she looks down on the babies you have murdered and the mothers you have slaughtered and the fathers you have put in early graves—unarmed, unwilling to fight, innocent—yet you butchered them like cattle and hogs, no remorse, no conscience, not a drop of pity in your heart. Oh, stop it, stop it, put away your guns and ask God's forgiveness and give yourself up. End this bloodshed, and even if you find death in this world for your sins, you will find eternal life in the next in the presence of God. Angel, I beg you, don't go into eternity an unrepentant killer—"

"Shut up, you devil!" shouted Early.

Raber turned to him. "No, Spunk, don't—"

But Early's gun swung up on Lynndae, and his face was a mask of hate. "I'll close that mouth forever and thank the good Lord in heaven I did it!"

Chapter 29

Early was going to shoot. Lynndae didn't even notice him; she was still looking up at her brother's face, tears springing into her eyes, her gloved hands on his chest.

The snow was pouring down. Raber drew his revolver as he turned toward Early. But Early caught the movement of Raber's hand and flicked the barrel away from Lynndae. He fired and Raber went down. Lynndae cried out and knelt over her brother. Early shifted his pistol back to her.

Zeph pulled his father's gun free from under his vest and overcoat. He knew there were no bullets in it, but there was nothing else he could think of to do that might save the life of the woman he loved. He hoped Early would see him draw the revolver and swing his weapon away from Lynndae a second time. But Early ignored him, yelling as he aimed his pistol to fire. Zeph squeezed the trigger of the six-gun. A roar filled his ears, and the bullet caught Early high up on the shoulder of his gun hand. He flew backward into the snow, and his pistol went spinning into the air.

Dad loaded six chambers, Zeph thought in astonishment as the gun smoke burned his nostrils.

But now the two men at the gatehouse had decided to shoot.

"I got him!" shouted one, aiming his rifle at Zeph.

"I got the woman!" shouted the other.

Zeph ran at Lynndae and drove her backward with the weight of his body. Something like a hot knife went through his clothing and into his arm. The force of the blow spun him around and hurled him onto his back. Snow stabbed at his neck and made him wince.

Lying in the snow, he thought he could hear cannon fire, the shouts of men charging, the crack of muskets, and the whiz of minié balls as they scorched the air over his head. He glanced to his right and saw Raber push himself up on an elbow, his revolver flashing. All of earth and heaven seemed to be roaring, seemed to be on fire.

Where was Lynndae?

He struggled to sit up. One of the men at the gatehouse was lying in the snow. He was not moving. The other was wounded in his leg and leaning against the brick of the arch and fumbling to reload his rifle. Finally he tossed it to one side in frustration and dug a small pistol out of a coat pocket. Zeph watched him aim it at Raber and fire twice. Then he pointed it at Lynndae, whom Zeph saw was only a few feet to his left. She was struggling to get to her feet, bracing both hands against the snow and frozen earth. All he could think to do was roll. In a sudden swift movement, he came at her. Again, he felt heat cut through his clothing and sting his flesh. This time it was the back of his leg. She fell as he smacked into her.

"Stay down!" he hissed.

There was still firing. Snow and dirt spat into his face from a near miss. A ricochet whined nearby. He lifted his head and saw that Spunk Early had climbed back to his feet and was trying to cock a revolver with his one good hand. Early ignored Raber and Zeph. He was clearly interested only in getting a shot off at Lynndae. Zeph squirmed through the snow and placed his body between Lynndae and the gunman. A bullet smacked into his boot, but he felt only a short stab of pain. Early fired again, and Zeph heard it go past his ear like a wasp.

Zeph glanced at Raber, who had pulled another pistol from a holster under his arm and was aiming it at Early. Zeph saw him shoot three times. Then an invisible hand seemed to lift Raber off the ground, shake him, and drop him into the snow. He fired a final shot in the direction of the gatehouse and then lay still, snowflakes covering his face and hands so rapidly that soon all his flesh had vanished.

The roaring stopped.

Zeph was on his stomach. One arm would not work, so he used the other to push himself up. The man at the gatehouse had slid to the ground with his pistol in his hand, and his eyes were closed. He could see Early sprawled on his face and the snowfall burying him as it came down thicker and thicker. Zeph tried to reach out to Lynndae with a hand that would not respond to his commands.

"Are you all right?" he asked.

She looked at him. "There's blood on your coat."

"No matter."

He turned and began to crawl toward Raber, propelling himself with his good arm and leg. When he reached Raber's side, he collapsed.

"That you, Captain?" asked Raber in a raspy voice.

"Sure is, General."

"How're we doing?"

"Lynndae's fine. You saved her life."

"I saved her life? I recall as you were the one who pulled a pistol out from under all those Amish clothes and stopped Early from shooting her."

"The same way you stopped those two sharpshooters at the gate from killing all of us."

"It's strange the things a man will do for family, Captain."

"I know it. Are you hurt bad, General?"

"No, no. Early always was a poor shot, and Billy and Wyatt were only reliable if the target was a thousand yards away."

"Never thought I'd have to come all the way back here to Pennsylvania just to get a proper wound."

Raber laughed and coughed up blood. "Ain't it the truth? The ways of God are past finding out."

Lynndae was at their sides. "Oh no, oh no no no, my Angel, my Z," and she began tearing at the hem of her dress to make bandages even though both Zeph and her brother protested. She moved swiftly to staunch the flow of blood from her brother's two leg wounds, and then she bandaged Zeph's shoulder, leg, and foot. Turning back to her brother, she whipped the bonnet off her head and pressed it down over a large wound in his chest. But he firmly placed a hand on her arm to stop her from doing anything more.

"What I really need, Little L," he whispered, "is someone to pray with me."

"There are three or four other wounds—"

"Let it be. I've only got time enough for one good confession and one good prayer, so pay attention to my words and not my wounds. The holes in my spirit are bigger, and you need to tend to them first."

He reached up a hand to her face. "I haven't felt shame in more years than I can count, but I felt shame today when you spoke to me like you did. It's as if your talk snapped me out of some kind of spell. Seems I haven't been able to see straight or think straight for a long time. I fooled myself into believing God approved of what I did because He never meant for the war to end until all slavery was vanquished. Now here I'm about to meet Him, and my hands are smothered in blood. I can't undo the wickedness I've done. I can't stop what my men are doing right now at Bird in Hand. All I got to offer up in place of all my murders is saving your life today. That's a big thing to my way of thinking, but big as it is, I know it's not near enough. Little L, can God forgive me?"

She kissed the hand against her face. "Oh Angel, if you are sorry for all the killing you've done—"

"I believe I am."

"—and you know you've committed terrible sins—"

"That I am certain of."

"—and you repent of all the crimes and bloodshed—"

"I do, I do repent. When you spoke to me, I wished again and again I had laid down my sword at Appomatox."

"—then the Lord has promised to forgive you and cleanse you. Jesus has died for your sins on the cross. You know that, Angel, you know that."

His whisper grew harder and harder to hear. "Sure, I know that. I just needed to hear it again coming from Little L."

He turned his head. His eyes were almost colorless.

"Captain?"

"Yes sir," responded Zeph.

"Pleasure to soldier with you, Captain."

"Pleasure to soldier with you, General."

"They say we're all of us Americans now, Captain. What do you say?"

"I believe that's so, General."

"Then you take good care of my sister and you raise a good American family, y'all hear?"

"I will do that."

"Got any names picked out? For the first one?"

"How's Angel suit?"

Raber smiled and closed his eyes. "Works for a boy or a girl." He drew a deep breath. "Lord Jesus, have mercy on my soul, have mercy on me a sinner." His breath came back out in one long sigh, and he was gone.

As Lynndae cradled her brother's body in her arms and wept, Zeph looked on and felt a great sadness well up inside him. Here was the man they had been fleeing, who had sworn to kill the children, who had left a trail of innocent blood behind him all of his adult life, and now Zeph wished, like Jesus with Lazarus, he could bring the man back to life. He groped for one of Raber's hands with his good hand and held it tightly. A verse passed through his mind: *"And the publican, standing afar off, would not lift up so much as his eyes unto heaven, but smote upon his breast, saying, God be merciful to me a sinner. I tell you, this man went down to his house justified."*

Zeph felt a pounding in the frozen earth he was lying upon.

Horses. There was nothing he could do if this meant more of Raber's men. He could scarcely move. Turning his eyes to the left, he saw three men ride up through the snowstorm and dismount, each of them bristling with guns. They stood over Lynndae and him, and he could tell one of them was surveying all the bodies and trying to figure out what had just happened.

"What in the world? Did you folks have a need to refight the battle or something? Can either of you explain to me just what went on here?"

Zeph looked up into a face with a chin beard and a mustache that drooped around the corners of the mouth. "Who are you?"

The man pulled aside the flap of his winter jacket so Zeph could see the star. "Sheriff Buck Levy. Gettysburg township. Adams County. Elected, genuine and official. These are my full-time deputies, Mister Flint Mitton and Mister Josh Nikkels. Our citizens heard the gunfire and became concerned that Lee and Meade were going at it again."

"These men are the last remnants of the gang that Seraph Raber led."

"Is that a fact?"

"I am Zephaniah Parker, Deputy US Marshal. This woman has just lost her brother. He died defending us."

The man stooped over Zeph and flipped both the front of the overcoat and the mutze open and found the badge on his vest. He grunted. "Kind of a funny occupation for an Amish man like yourself, isn't it, Mister Parker?"

"I'm not Amish, though this woman is. It was simply a way for me to travel unnoticed in these parts."

"That so? Maybe you can explain to me how your travels

brought you to my battlefield cemetery and involved the deaths of four men."

"That's a long story, Sheriff, and I'm not sure I'm up to telling it right about now."

"Maybe not. But I need some kind of explanation to take back to the town fathers."

For the first time, Lynndae pulled herself away from her brother, laying him gently back on the ground, and turned her grief-stricken face toward the sheriff and his deputies. Her features were so distraught and broken that all three men took off their hats and bared their heads to the snowstorm.

"Sorry for your loss, ma'am," mumbled Mitton. Snow had already made his red beard white.

Lynndae stood to her feet, snowflakes catching in her pinned-up hair and eyelashes. "Deputy Parker came from Lancaster to Gettysburg to apprehend these members of the Raber Gang, Sheriff. They were supposed to talk, but the gang members chose to ambush him. I traveled down on my own to see if I could be of assistance. I can assure you, the first shots were fired by the gang members and my brother, and Mister Parker returned fire only in self-defense."

"I'm sure that's the case, ma'am, but we do have to check the facts. Flint, Josh, make sure all those bodies are armed and that their weapons have been discharged."

The deputies placed their hats back on their heads and made their way through the blowing snow to the bodies by the gatehouse and to Early. Sheriff Levy returned his hat to its rightful place as well.

"Sorry, ma'am, I realize this is a bad time to question

someone who has lost a loved one under such circumstances—"

"Do your duty, Sheriff," replied Lynndae coolly.

"But what brought your brother into this fracas? You make no mention of him being a lawman or being deputized by Mister Parker here. Was he your escort?"

"No, I escorted myself from Lancaster."

"Very well."

"My brother was in the company of the gang itself, Sheriff, but it was his express desire that he disentangle himself from his involvement with notorious criminals and take that opportunity to live an honest Christian life."

"That so?"

"His dying wish, Sheriff."

"And the point of your traveling from Lancaster County to Adams County unescorted was perhaps to coax your brother to initiate this disengagement from the remnants of the Raber Gang?"

"Quite so."

Levy scratched the scrap of beard on his chin. "Maybe this will all come together for me if I start with your name."

"I am Lynndae Raber."

Sheriff Levy stared at her through the shower of snowflakes. "And your brother?"

"Seraphim Raber."

"The Angel of Death himself."

"So the newspapers called him. At the end, if anything, he was an Angel of Life."

Levy shook his head. "This has to be some story you're spinning me, Miss Raber, and I'm not exactly sure why, unless it's meant to cover up the murder of these four men—"

"This is no cover-up, Sheriff, I assure you."

"Seraphim Raber and his whole crew were hung by the neck until dead in Cheyenne, Wyoming a week ago. You must've missed that little bit of news before you concocted this yarn of yours."

Even through the snowfall Zeph could see Lynndae's eyes turning to blue ice. "I haven't missed a thing, Sheriff, and you'll look the fool when you speak with Sheriff Friesen of Lancaster County or Colonel Austen, a federal marshal out of Cheyenne, or the commander of K Company, Second Cavalry, at Fort Laramie. I think you'd be better off taking my story to heart just as I've told it to you."

Levy nodded. "I'm sure you think so. But the way I look at it, I'd be better off getting you and Mister Parker down to my humble accommodations in town while I send out a few telegrams to the sort of people who can offer me a yea or nay on all this stuff you've been selling. If you're on the money, I'll know about it in a few hours and, by way of apology and redress, I'll buy you steak and eggs for dinner. If you're not on the money, well, you'll have to settle for whatever's on the jailhouse menu for Monday night."

"All of them had guns," said Flint Mitton, walking back through the snow, "and all of them have been fired recently."

"Well, that's something," grunted Levy.

"Something else. Josh noticed the two guys who had rifles, well, they're for sniping, Federal Army issue, the sort of guns Raber's men'd be toting."

The sheriff wasn't impressed. "Maybe."

"They're Sharps rifles and they fire a big cartridge. We pull a bullet like that out of one of these two, it'll go a long way to making their case for self-defense."

"Hm."

Zeph saw the sheriff look down at him, but it seemed like Levy was at the end of a long hallway with white walls, a hallway that was getting longer all the time. It came off as comical to him when the sheriff's face took on a sudden look of concern.

"How many times was he hit?" he heard the sheriff ask Lynndae.

"I bandaged three bullet wounds."

"Three! Flint, you get this man over your saddle and in to Doc Murphy as fast as you possibly can. We're standing here yapping and the man's losing blood. Look at him—you can see how much blood he's lost. Josh!"

"Yes sir."

"Help Flint get him over the saddle. Then you go in and get a wagon for these others. You understand? Pick up the horses they staked out yonder. And that bedroll and those saddlebags."

"Yes Sheriff."

"Come on now, get him up, get him up. This ain't no Presbyterian picnic, get moving."

Far away Zeph heard Lynndae asking, "Is he going to be all right?"

The last thing he could make out was the sheriff's response: "I hope so, ma'am, I hope so, but I had no idea he was losing so much blood."

Chapter 30

The feeling came over her that she liked least of almost any feeling she had to deal with, including grief—the feeling of being utterly and unbearably alone.

She was sitting in a straight-backed wooden chair outside one of the rooms in the doctor's three-story brick home, which also served as his surgery. Across from her was Flint Mitton, an apologetic look on his face, left by Sheriff Buck Levy as her guard. The fingers of her hands kept knotting and unknotting. Behind the closed door, Doctor Clyde Murphy was working feverishly, along with his wife and an assistant, to save Zephaniah Parker's life.

Lynndae could not stop condemning herself for putting Zephaniah in this situation. She had been so stricken by her brother's death she had sat crying and rocking him when she knew with every fiber of her being his body was only an empty shell and that his spirit had left to be with God. Yet while she wept over Angel's body, the man who was to be her husband was bleeding to death in the snow. How could be she be so thoughtless?

To make matters worse, she had then proceeded to argue with Sheriff Levy, too proud to back down, too headstrong to wait for the truth to come out later, stubborn to the point of stupidity. Ten minutes or more lost for no good purpose other than to satisfy her own vanity, wanting the final word, while Z continued to lie cold and bloodless, snow covering his body like a winding sheet.

Oh Lord, forgive me. Spare his life, oh, please, spare his life. Do not pile sorrow upon sorrow.

She wiped away tears quickly, not wanting the deputy's sympathy.

The door opened and the doctor came out of the room, his shirt red with blood. His young face was lined with sweat and worry. He was holding a pan in which several small objects rolled back and forth.

"The bullets are out," he said.

She was not interested in the bullets, instead looking at him with fear and hope for news about Zephaniah, so he handed the pan to the deputy. Flint Mitton fished out the larger of the three bullets and looked at it closely.

"That's no .44," he said. "It's like Josh was talking. One of the men at the gatehouse got him with a Sharps."

"That came out of his shoulder," the doctor told him.

Flint eyed the other two bullets. "That woman's brother was using a .45 and these are both .44 caliber. Had to come from their pistols and not his. The evidence is backing her story more and more."

"Where is Sheriff Levy?"

"Getting Lance to take care of the bodies. Sending and receiving telegrams." He flicked open the lid on his watch. "It's half past five. He'll be by shortly, I expect."

The doctor turned to Lynndae. "Miss Raber. We are doing the best we can. His blood loss is acute." She felt a sting in her heart as Zephaniah's bleeding was brought up before her yet again. "We may be able to save his arm and leg; it's too early to tell."

"Oh, please try, doctor."

"There's massive tissue damage to his left shoulder and the back of his right leg. I may have to remove the limbs to avoid gangrene. I'm going to get some coffee, and then I'll take another look. My wife and Tommy are cleaning his wounds as thoroughly as they can right now. Deputy, we need more ice to keep the fever down."

Flint Mitton looked confused. "I have to watch Miss Raber here."

"I need the ice. Either you go or she goes or you both go together."

"For heaven's sake," cried Lynndae, "where do you think I am going to run to when the man I hope to marry is fighting for his life in the next room?"

She saw Mitton glance at her empty ring finger and said, "He only asked for my hand yesterday afternoon. There hasn't been time for any of the formalities yet. In fact," she added, her eyes meeting those of Mitton and the doctor, "you are the first people to know. We never told a single soul, everything happened too fast."

The doctor nodded. "Congratulations. Flint, I'll be responsible for Miss Raber. Go get that ice. We have a wedding to look forward to."

The deputy got to his feet and placed his hat on his head.

"Sorry, ma'am, I'll go get the ice."

Suddenly there was a knocking on the front door. The doctor shook his head. "I need to coffee up and get back into the surgery. Miss Raber, could you see who that is?" He vanished into another room.

Lynndae stood up, and she and Flint Mitton walked down a hall to the front of the house. Before they could get there, the door burst open and Aunt Rosa rushed in, followed by Augustine Yoder. Behind them were Sheriff Rusty Friesen from Lancaster County and Sheriff Buck Levy, who looked like he'd been kicked in the stomach by a horse.

Lynndae and Aunt Rosa flew into each other's arms.

"Oh Rosa," cried Lynndae, a little girl again, allowing the tears to streak down her face, "he's in the surgery. He covered my body with his. Oh Rosa, he took the bullets meant for me." She sobbed in the older woman's arms.

"Hush, hush," Aunt Rosa soothed, patting Lynndae on the back, "everything will be all right. That is why the train brought us. We are in this place to pray with you; God will hear."

"He took the bullets meant for me."

"Hush, hush." But tears sprang into Aunt Rosa's eyes as well.

Augustine Yoder was pale, watching the two women hold one another with large liquid eyes. Snow melted on his hat and overcoat.

Flint Mitton looked at Sheriff Levy. "I was just going out to get some ice. The man has a bad fever."

Levy nodded. "Go quick and get it." As Flint stepped around him, Levy took him by the arm. "I got telegrams back from everyone and their horse. Seems I heard from every person in the country but President Grant. Her story checks out. This is Sheriff Friesen from Lancaster. He confirms those were the last of Raber's gang."

Lynndae broke away from Aunt Rosa. "What happened? Was anyone hurt?"

Mitton hung back to hear the news, but Levy fixed him with a glare. "We caused enough heartache for these folk, Mister Mitton, what with doubting their story and leaving a good man to bleed out in the snow." He looked down at the floor, disgusted with himself, and muttered, "While we argued for points like some Harvard debating society playing to the gallery." He glanced up at Mitton and growled, "Get."

Flint rushed out the door into the swirl of snow.

Sheriff Levy removed his hat. "Miss Raber, I apologize for the way I acted early this morning. I confess I was bewildered by the scene we came upon, but it would have been better to have helped you out first and asked for your story later. I hope I will be able to make amends to you and Mister Parker over the course of the next few days. It's my prayer he will pull through as fine as sunshine."

"Thank you, Sheriff," Lynndae responded. "I admit I had my back up pretty quickly, and I don't think that helped you any. I appreciate your concern, and I believe both Mister Parker and I will be able to take you up on your offer of assistance before the week is out."

The doctor came down the hall with a fresh shirt on. "Miss Raber, I am going back in now. Are you folk in some need of medical assistance?"

"We are here for Miss Raber," explained Augustine Yoder.

"If you need extra chairs, there are plenty in the front room."

Aunt Rosa spoke up. "We will pray for you, doctor."

He smiled. "Why thank you, ma'am, I am grateful. My father is a Presbyterian minister. He would be glad to hear you offering me that sort of divine aid."

As he strode off, Lynndae turned back to Sheriff Friesen. "What happened at Bird in Hand this morning?"

Friesen removed his hat and knocked snow off with the flat of his hand. "Miss Raber, is there some place we can sit? The doctor mentioned the front room."

"Right through here," said Sheriff Levy, making a gesture with his hat.

They went down a short hall into a room that looked out over the street. A fire was in danger of going out in the fireplace. Levy began to stir the ashes with a poker and place on more logs. Aunt Rosa found a coatrack and began to peel a wet, black shawl from her shoulders.

"Come, brother," she said to Augustine, "don't drip over the doctor's nice wood floor."

The men removed their coats and hung them on the rack while the fire burst into life. When everyone was seated, Lynndae leaned forward anxiously.

"Please tell me what happened," she asked again.

"Lynndae," said Aunt Rosa, "you must first tell us how Zephaniah is doing. I am sorry, but we cannot go on and talk about anything else until we know that."

Sheriff Friesen nodded. "I agree."

Lynndae passed a hand over her eyes as the tears welled up

again. "The doctor doesn't know. It's too soon to tell. There was so much blood loss. So much damage from the bullets to his arm and leg. They may have to amputate."

She broke down. Aunt Rosa left her seat to put her arms around Lynndae. "Yes, yes, that is why God told us to come here. We are going to pray. We do not leave until everything is all right, even if it takes days or weeks. You will not be alone."

"That is so," agreed Augustine.

"My brother defended us," blurted Lynndae.

Surprise crossed Friesen's face. "What?"

"At first he was going to—going to hang Z. But when I walked down from the station, one of his men took exception to the things I said to Angel—things about his life of crime, his murders, his sins—and this man pulled his gun out to shoot—to shoot me, but Angel tried to stop him. And he shot Angel. Then the man aimed at me again, and Z had his father's old revolver. He fired and the bullet knocked the man down. Then the other men from the gang, there were two of them, tried to shoot Z and me, but Angel began to fire at them from where he had fallen to the ground when he had been shot. Oh, there was so much gunfire back and forth—it was like a small war. That was when Z covered me with his body to keep the bullets from hitting me. Angel stopped the men of his gang from killing us, but he died from his wounds—not before he confessed his sins and repented and asked God's forgiveness in the name of, the name of Jesus—"

Lynndae could not continue. Aunt Rosa held her and shook her head at the others. "Hush now, that is enough, your Angel is with God. That is enough, do not speak anymore.

We have heard you." Then she prayed, "Lord, spare young Zephaniah's life. You know him. He was Your chosen instrument to bring Lynndae and her brother together again and to help save Lynndae from death and her brother from damnation. Restore him to us, dear Lord; give him many more years among those he loves. Guide the doctor's hands; bless his healing work done in Your holy name. Oh, You who healed in Galilee, will You not heal this night in Pennsylvania as well?"

No one spoke for several minutes, then Lynndae lifted her head from Rosa's shoulder, her eyes crimson and swollen. "I must know. Did Z's sacrifice change anything? Did it matter that he brought my brother here, my brother and his three gunmen? Did it make any difference at all, or was it just wasted effort? Sheriff? Augustine?"

Augustine and Sheriff Friesen glanced at one another. Augustine nodded at the sheriff to go ahead. Friesen leaned forward in his houndstooth suit, brown Stetson in his hands.

"Miss Raber," he said earnestly, "I'll give it to you straight. If Raber, your brother, if he had come up to Bird in Hand leading the men that were left of his crew, and he was the Raber who shot, murdered, and maimed, not the one who repented, there wouldn't be a stick of Bird in Hand left standing tonight. They'd have burned every house in the village to the ground. They'd have killed us all."

Chapter 31

Lynndae sat holding Aunt Rosa's hands.

"I had found out from Mister Simpson at the station that Zephaniah's ticket was for Gettysburg," she told her. "I left well before six. There was a train from Philadelphia that was heading to York with connections to Gettysburg and Baltimore."

Friesen nodded and looked at Aunt Rosa. "It was still dark, and one of my deputies escorted the buggy Mister Beachey used to take Lynndae to Lancaster."

Lynndae protested. "I did not want Mister Beachey to take me. I was afraid of putting him in harm's way."

"But he insisted," said the sheriff.

Lynndae smiled weakly. "Many of the good people of Bird in Hand insist on things."

"My deputy saw him back safely."

"You had men all around the depot." Lynndae leaned forward. "Surely you stopped some of the gang members when they came off the train?"

"I'm afraid not, Miss Raber."

"Why on earth not?"

"For the simple reason that none of the gang members came by rail. They came by horseback."

"Oh—"

"Now that doesn't mean they didn't take a train part of the way. For all I know, they might have been lying in wait a day or two in advance. Two came up the road from the east, from White Horse and Intercourse, and two came up from the south, by way of Paradise and Gordonville. Not a shot was fired. So we didn't know there was trouble until a house went up. I saw the flames and hurried some of my deputies in that direction.

"This would be about a half hour after your train left for York, Miss Raber. I had five men at the station, and they might just as well have not existed for all the good they were to us. I couldn't spare a rider to get a message to them. So I hoped they'd see that a house was burning and make for Bird in Hand to help us. But they never did. They were afraid to leave the station unguarded in case more outlaws came in by rail. I honestly can't fault them for that line of thinking. That's why I had them there, armed to the teeth. In retrospect, I should have given them more leeway in making decisions to stay or go. The mistake rests on my shoulders. I was convinced Raber's men would come in by means of the Lancaster train."

Lynndae felt her anxiety grow as the story unfolded. "What houses were burned?"

"The Ottos' went first. That was done by the two that rode up from Paradise. We were no sooner trying to deal with the Otto place when another house went up in flames from the direction of Intercourse. I had seven men in all—there would have been twelve of us if the boys from the station had ridden in—but I'd already sent a couple south to the Otto house. So I ordered three toward the new fire, and that left just me and Joseph Sheridan to keep an eye on the two homes that had fifty people crammed into them. You can imagine how difficult it would have been for us if all the families had remained on their own properties. Your Zephaniah's idea to get the people into one spot saved lives."

Lynndae felt a surge of pride, but the feeling was quickly lost as she remembered the danger Zeph was in. Aunt Rosa squeezed her hands. A part of Lynndae did not want to hear the rest of what Sheriff Friesen had to say for fear the story of the raid on Bird in Hand might get worse. But she steeled herself and said, "Please continue, Sheriff."

"The Bender house was burning east of us, the Otto's to the south. Joe and I stayed put. If there'd been another bunch of Raber's men coming at us from the west or north, say those three at Gettysburg and Raber himself, we'd have been done for. There was nothing more we could do. My men ran off the two that had set the houses on fire to the east, but my two boys that had gone south were ambushed."

Fear hit Lynndae again like an icy gust of wind. "Are they all right?"

"One died in the saddle. That's how we found him. The other was wounded. But he fought back from behind a clump of trees. He dropped one before the other rode off and left him."

Friesen stopped and his eyes took on a haunted look. "I thank God your brother wasn't there to lead them, Miss Raber, and I thank God that was as far as they got."

Lynndae waited.

"I don't know what idea they had in their heads. That no one would be armed? That they'd only be fighting Amish and the Amish wouldn't fight back? Maybe they didn't have a plan, I don't know. But they sure didn't take us as seriously as they should have, that's for sure.

"They had expected there to be people in the houses of course, and some of them out doing their morning chores. But by the second house, they could see they were torching empty homes, and with the sun up now, they could see there wasn't a soul for miles, not on the roadways, not in the lanes, not in the fields. There weren't even any animals out; we had them all locked up tight in the barns.

"So they didn't know what to do. It seemed as if they didn't even have a leader of any kind. They hit on racing from property to property, hootin' and hollerin', shooting their guns in the air, hoping, I guess, to stir something up, bring the people out of hiding, frighten some animals out into the open. I don't know exactly what they had a notion of doing. But they paid my deputies and me no mind. Maybe it was just that they only saw me and Joe sitting there on our horses and thought that was it. Maybe they could see we were too far away to do them any damage. I don't know. They kept on riding back and forth like madmen, doing their yell as if Sheridan and I didn't exist. As if doing the devil's business was all the protection they needed.

"Well, in the clear light of day, galloping or not, they made fine targets, and although they might have felt they were out of range, Joe and I jerked our Sharps carbines clear of their scabbards and proceeded to target the three of them, one after another. The Sharps can send a bullet a long way, Miss Raber, even the shorter barreled carbine's a shooter, and Joe's been handy with one since the war. Long story short, two of them went down, and the last one lit out towards Intercourse and ran into my three deputies, who saw him coming. They all cheated the hangman, Miss Raber, but none of them will hurt innocent people anymore."

"No one else was hurt except for your deputy?"

"I had another man wounded, but he's doing fine."

"The man who died, was he a family man?"

"No ma'am, Frank wasn't the marrying kind."

"What about the houses?"

"We get spring and a spell of dry weather, I believe the Amish will be having a couple of house raisings."

Augustine nodded. "Everyone has a place to go. Each family is moving in with another family. It will be all right. They did not touch the barns. The children are safe. We thank God. The killing we do not like, but we are grateful for the lives spared."

Lynndae's head was in turmoil. "I wish there never were such men."

"So do I, Miss Raber," said Sheriff Friesen quietly.

"I wish we did not have to fight. I wish there were no fighting at all."

"I understand. But you know as well as any of us here that this is a sinful world where people are permitted to follow the devil's ways if they choose. In matters like this, Miss Raber, lawful authorities must bear the sword and protect the righteous and the innocent. That is what we have done. My deputies and I were, as the Bible puts it, ministers of God, revengers 'to execute wrath upon him that doeth evil.'"

"I know, Sheriff, I know," sighed Lynndae, "and I'm thankful you saved the lives of so many good people. I suppose I am just wishing it was a different sort of world altogether, one where the swords are beaten into plowshares and the spears into pruning hooks."

"Ma'am, the Lord hasten that day when it is true for the entire earth."

"Amen," said Rosa and Augustine together.

Sheriff Levy had left the room to look for his deputy, Flint Mitton. He walked back into the room with Mitton in tow. It looked like the deputy had something to say.

"Go ahead," urged Levy.

Flint held his hat in his hands, turning it over and over in his nervousness. Again, Lynndae endured the cold blast of fright. She got to her feet.

"What is it, Deputy?" she asked, a bit more harshly than she intended.

"Ma'am," Flint finally got out, "I came back with the ice about ten minutes after I left. Had to get some from the hotel a few blocks over. Doc Murphy asked me to help in his surgery. He gave me an apron to wear over my duds. He was—he was going to use his saw."

Lynndae felt her legs grow weak, but she was determined to remain standing and take the news Flint had come to give her. "Thank you, Deputy. May I ask why the doctor isn't out here giving me this news himself?"

"Why, I guess he would be, except that he's still busy in there, what with your husband, that is, your fiancé—"

Lynndae had a momentary image of Zeph with an empty sleeve pinned to his shoulder and a wooden leg replacing the one of flesh the doctor had cut free of the bone. Blood roared through her head. She felt Aunt Rosa's firm arm steady her. "I understand, Deputy. There's no need to speak any further—"

"—sitting up all of a sudden and talking, well, pretty much of a whisper, I would say, but I could understand him. He was asking about you and asking for water in about the same breath, said the ice felt good against his skin. Well, Doc wanted you to come right quick while he's awake so's you might say hello—"

Lynndae ran from the room and down the halls to the surgery door. Behind her she heard Aunt Rosa say, "Oh, thank You, Lord." When she entered the surgery, the assistant, Tommy, was holding up Zeph's head with one hand and a glass of water for him with the other.

"Z!" she called to him, unable to contain her excitement.

The doctor and his wife were washing their hands at a corner sink. She looked up and smiled at Lynndae. "I am so happy for you, dear. We are so pleased he pulled through."

The doctor nodded. "He is a strong man, Miss Raber. He wanted to come back. If you work in medicine long enough, they tell me, you see everything. Well, his recovery is nothing less than a miracle, and I haven't seen anything like it. This man was definitely meant to live."

"And his arm and—"

Murphy shook his head. "The way he's coming around, I wouldn't touch them."

She rushed to Zeph's side and said to Tommy, "Thank you so much; I'll do that," and put her arm under Zeph's head and shoulders.

He smiled up at her weakly. "Hey, I know that face," he whispered.

"You gave us quite a fright," she said softly.

"I wanted to stay awake and help you handle that ornery sheriff with the rug on his chin—"

"Shh. He turned out all right. Got his deputy to fetch you extra ice."

"Well, good for him. Good to know a leopard can change its spots." He held her gaze. "I am sorry about Seraphim, honey. He saved us."

It was all too much—Zeph dying and now sitting there alive, her brother fighting to protect her and now silent in a pine box. Tears filled Lynndae's eyes. "He is coming home with us to Lancaster County. The mortician has taken good care of him, and Seraphim will be ready anytime you are able to board a train."

"That won't be for a few days, I'm afraid," the doctor spoke up, "but as soon as he is able to handle a short train journey, he'll be all yours."

"I need to lie back," said Zeph, so Lynndae gently put his head down. "Now stay with me, Conner, and hold my hand awhile."

"You like that name, don't you?"

"I like all your names."

She kissed him on the forehead. "Choose whichever you like."

"Can I make one up? Like a nickname?"

"That would be sweet. My brothers always had nicknames for me."

"What about your oath to Ricky?"

"My big brother is looking down from heaven and saying

to me, 'Lynndae Sharlayne, what the heck is the matter with you? That promise was never meant to keep you from the arms of a good man like Zephaniah Truett Parker. Have you abandoned all the common sense I raised you with in the Montana Territory?'"

Zeph tried to laugh and choked out, "Is that a fact?"

"It is."

"In that case, if there's a cloth handy, and your brother has cottoned to me, I'd be grateful if you would bathe my forehead with cool water."

"Of course."

Lynndae reached across a small table next to the bed. She noticed that a tall, broad figure had filled the doorway.

It was Augustine. His large eyes seemed to sparkle in the lamplight from the surgery. A toothpick was going back and forth in his mouth.

"So, so, so," he said, "I have come here in the hopes that someone will introduce me to the bride and groom. The doctor made a point of telling me that Gettysburg has a pair and that they are both dressed very plain."

Chapter 32

Four days later Zeph hobbled on board a train bound for York, Lancaster, and Philadelphia, one arm in a sling, a leg in a leather brace, and a wooden crutch to lean on. Augustine helped him to his seat while Aunt Rosa stayed by Lynndae, who was making sure the pine coffin that contained her brother's body was securely stored in a freight car. Sheriff Friesen had returned to Lancaster the morning after his visit to Gettysburg, but Sheriff Levy promised to provide an escort in his stead. He saw Aunt Rosa and Lynndae safely to their seats with the men before settling back with his 1873 Winchester and a dime western with the title *The Blazing Guns of Texas, A Kid Comanche Adventure.*

At the Yoder house, Levy enjoyed three bowls of sauerkraut soup and several thick slices of smoked ham before heading back on an evening train with connections to Gettysburg and Baltimore. As he left the house to ride to the station in the Yoder's buggy, he touched the brim of his hat to Lynndae.

"I hope you will fare well," he said, "and that your marriage will be everything a young woman like you dreams of."

"Thank you, Sheriff. I'm grateful for all your help."

Zeph was placed back in his old room at the Yoders', and

Lynndae was set up in the room Katie had grown up in. For the first few days, Zeph slept off and on around the clock as his body worked to heal itself. Rebecca and Lynndae cooked pots of chicken and beef broth and fussed at him to eat bowl after bowl from morning to night. Lynndae often sat at his bedside and read James Fenimore Cooper out loud.

"Where'd you get those books?" he asked. "Were they in your three months' of luggage along with everything else?"

She smiled. "If I'd known when I packed that I was traveling with the Yale professor of early American literature, yes, I would have found room for some of the Leatherstocking Tales. As it is, now that I know you better than I did in Iron Springs, way back when I thought you were just a cowboy with sweet eyes—"

"I am a cowboy."

"—I took the liberty of borrowing these from the Lancaster Library. Do you know who started the library in Lancaster? William Penn's daughter-in-law, Juliana. She gave books and money. They showed me her Bible while I was there. Two volumes. I opened the first one, and where do you suppose I found myself?"

"The wedding feast in Cana?" Lynndae gently hit him with the book in her hand, *The Last of the Mohicans*. "You think you're funny? I was in the Old Testament. The book of Ruth."

"So?"

"Oh, for heaven's sake, I thought you were a literary scholar."

"I am. Jude's the Bible scholar."

"Don't you remember Ruth's words? 'Intreat me not to leave thee, or to return from following after thee: for whither thou goest, I will go; and where thou lodgest, I will lodge: thy people shall be my people, and thy God my God.'"

"I have heard that."

"I want to use those words in my wedding vows."

"I've no objection, as long as the words are spoken to me."

Lynndae found the Cooper book useful for another swat at Zeph's healthy arm.

The Tuesday after their return to Bird in Hand, while Zeph slept, Lynndae sat in a rocker in a corner of his bedroom writing a letter with a steel nib pen and using a lap desk to support the sheets of paper, ink bottle, and blotter. That morning she had joined the other Amish families who had gone into town for the funeral of the deputy who had been slain defending their families and homes. After lunch back at the Yoder house, Augustine had lingered, and now he tapped gently on the open bedroom door. She glanced up and smiled. He gestured with his hand for her to come with him.

He sat at the kitchen table with a cup of coffee and asked quietly if she wanted one. She shook her head and took a seat. Rebecca had cleared up the lunch dishes with Lynndae and then disappeared upstairs. Augustine ran his fingers through his beard.

"He is getting stronger."

"Oh yes. We are going to start taking walks this evening. It is warming up now that we are into March."

"It may rain. Keep his hat on."

"Of course."

Augustine played with his coffee cup. Looking into it as if he might find the words he needed there, he cleared his throat and said, "So, we have met, the pastors, and we talked about your brother and his burial."

Lynndae sat up. "Please don't trouble yourselves. I accept the restrictions for Amish burial that my brother's life have placed upon you. Mother was buried in the Lancaster cemetery. I intend to place him beside her as soon as Z is strong enough to join me at a graveside ceremony."

Augustine held up a hand. "We wish him to be buried here at Bird in Hand at our cemetery in the fields. It is also our wish to have your mother's remains returned so that she may rest beside him. Your brother Ricky's as well, if you would permit it."

Lynndae was astounded. She sat and stared at Augustine, who looked up at her and nodded. "Yes, it is not just the wish of the pastors and the bishop, but of all the people. We believe Seraphim truly repented, just as you described it, and that he is with the Lord. The excommunication has already been lifted from your family. Let mother and son be at peace, together again with their friends and neighbors."

Lynndae looked down at the tabletop. "I do not know what to say. I had not expected such an offer of—of—"

"My son David works well with wood, it flows in his hands. He will complete the coffin for Seraphim tonight, your mother's tomorrow. We will lay them by your grandparents. I would pray at the graveside, if that is agreeable to you."

"Oh yes, oh yes, Mister Yoder." Her eyes glistened. "I had not expected this."

"It is not simply our will, Miss Raber. It is the Lord's will." He stood. "Trouble yourself with nothing. I will go into town now and make the necessary arrangements for your mother's remains. Seraphim we will lay out in our doed-kammer, our dead room. The men will dig the necessary graves."

"When shall we do the funeral, Mister Yoder?"

"Is Friday too soon?"

"No, no, that is just fine."

"You will tell me, who you would like for pallbearers? We will need four carrying each of the coffins."

"Yes. I will make a list for you."

"Gute."

On Thursday evening men and women, dressed completely in black, walked or drove their buggies to the Yoder home. They sat on chairs and benches that had been brought to the house for that purpose. People spoke in hushed voices. Lynndae went from family to family, thanking them, asking if they wished to see the body of her brother.

Zeph sat in a chair in the dead room by Seraphim's body. Seraphim was in a coffin with a lid that had been left open to show the upper part of his body. When people arrived in the room in the company of Lynndae, Zeph nodded gently and pulled a sheet back from Seraphim's face and chest. His blond hair had been neatly combed and his body was dressed in a white shirt, vest, and pants. No cosmetics had been applied by the mortician, that was the Amish way, but Lynndae had requested the long sideburns be shaved off. The long scar was visible on her brother's pale cheeks, but Zeph considered that it did not look so long or so vicious as he had imagined. It seemed to him to be as thin as a faint line from a graphite pencil.

None of the neighbors had seen Seraphim since he was thirteen. Many wept silently. One older man gripped Seraphim's hand and said something in Pennsylvania Dutch, his tears dropping onto the corpse's cheeks, so that Seraphim, too, appeared to be crying.

The next morning began with a silver rain that washed over the fields and the remnants of snow. A number of women arrived early to help Rebecca cook food. They tried to chase Lynndae away, but she insisted on working alongside them. It was better for her to do something with her hands than to just sit and wait, she told them.

The carved coffins containing Lynndae's mother and her brother were placed side by side in the dead room. Augustine stood in the room and began to preach while the others sat without. He did not speak about Seraphim or his mother. He spoke about Christ, about His resurrection from the dead, about the resurrection of those who believe. "'Verily, verily, I say unto you,'" he quoted from the Gospel of John, without looking at his Bible, "'He that heareth my word, and believeth on him that sent me, hath everlasting life, and shall not come into condemnation; but is passed from death unto life.'"

It was all in the Amish tongue, but Zeph found himself experiencing a touch from God much the same way he had experienced it during the worship service almost two weeks before. So many things had happened since then. Yet God remained the same God. Zeph closed his eyes while Augustine preached.

Jesu Christi am kreuz.

A long line of buggies followed the two horses pulling the hearse from the Yoder house to the cemetery out in an open field. At first the rain rushed against them. But once they had reached the graveyard and were hitching their horses and buggies in the large fenced area set aside for that purpose, the clouds became silent, simply sitting over them, brooding and watching.

The four pastors carried Seraphim's coffin from the hearse—Augustine, Moses Beachey, David Lapp, and Malachi Kauffman. Lynndae's mother was lifted out by Bishop Schrock, Augustine's sons Daniel and David, and Aunt Rosa's husband, Aaron Christner. The graves were open. The men lowered the coffins with ropes. Augustine prayed. Then he opened the thick book, the *Ausbund*, and read a hymn while the people listened, heads bowed, and the pastors and bishop took shovels and covered the coffins with earth.

The headstones were the same as all the others in the cemetery, curved stone two feet high, set to face the gate, beautifully hewn. The name Angel Raber was on one and his mother's name, Sarah Raber, on the other. Once the graves were filled, Augustine invited everyone to recite the Lord's Prayer silently in their hearts.

Zeph waited, leaning on his crutch. People began walking back to their carriages, and a scattered line of buggies formed on the road, most of them heading back to the Yoder home for the meal. It was clear Lynndae wanted to be alone for a few minutes, so Augustine and Rebecca and Zeph held back. Zeph moved awkwardly among the rows, seeing the same names over and over again—Smucker, Zook, Glick, Riehl, Esh.

He gazed out over the broad fields of brown grass. They worked the land, and then they rested in the land. From the earth they were created, and to the earth they returned. There was a goodness to the pattern. So many men's bones were never gathered into one place and never remembered, left scattered among stones at a mining site or washed by cold waters to oblivion in some lonely mountain place.

"Hello," said Lynndae, taking hold of his good arm.

"How are you?" he asked, looking at her face.

"It is a sad day and a glorious day at the same time. My emotions are up and down and all over the place."

"But you are glad your mother and brother are resting here together?"

"Oh, very glad. I never imagined it. I never prayed for it. It seemed to me to be an impossibility beyond even the grace of God."

Zeph looked around him. "All the farms seem to fit into the folds of the land as if a master joiner and carpenter had put everything together. Even the graveyard seems right, though I've never been one for such places."

"There is a peace here."

"In this one. I've seen plenty of bone orchards that made a man restless, as if none of the spirits were content."

"I suppose some of the boot hills are like that."

"All of the boot hills are like that. The graves of the murdered and the hanged."

"I thank God that Angel can lie here and not in some hole in a prison yard or out under a desert sun that has no pity."

"Yes. This is a good land. It hasn't got mountains and

panthers, but a man could settle in and do some solid living here all the same."

"Is that something you're thinking about, Z?"

"I like it here. But I miss the Sweet Blue and the Two Back Valley."

"Well, me, too. I see the good in both Lancaster and Iron Springs. But sometimes missing the Sweet Blue can be almost painful."

"I know it."

Zeph continued to lurch on his crutch among the head-stones. "Yoder, Mullet, Beachey. Anyone that's anyone is buried here."

"You, too, someday, if you live right."

"Well, you'll pardon me if I don't seem eager to rush on in, Miss Raber."

"I'd like to have you above ground a few more years myself, mister."

Zeph stopped. "I didn't know King was an Amish name."

"One of the finest and oldest."

"So William King, the attorney in Iron Springs, is Amish?"

"Well, I don't think he follows the Ordnung. But he has Amish roots. There's Kings he's related to in Lancaster County."

"Would they have known your family? Would they have known your father and brothers and Seraph?"

"The Kings? Of course. Some of them were very close to us before the excommunication."

Zeph had a flash of memory. Billy King had the two pack-horses that had been unloaded of their baggage. He raised his hat. "God bless you, folks, God bless you, Cody, Cheyenne.

I pray time flows like a fast river for us all while we're apart."

"Seen enough, Z?" asked Lynndae. "The Yoders have the carriage ready."

"Yes, I'm done."

Zeph began to move toward the Yoders with Lynndae beside him.

"How's your leg holding up?" she asked.

"Give me a month, Miss Raber. I'll be right as rain, and you'll have a brand new name."

She laughed. "I've had so many, Zeph. I don't mind another."

Chapter 33

I swore I would never come back here. Now I find it almost impossible to leave.

Lynndae sat by the train window, looking down at the families she had just finished saying good-bye to. Zeph was doing a final round of handshakes, including Samuel, tall and thin, and giving Bess a kiss on the cheek. Sheriff Friesen stood among the Amish in his three-piece houndstooth suit. His wife, May, was by his side, and she was no elf either, easily past his shoulder in height. Long brown hair framed her weather-tanned face. Her strong hand took Zeph's. Lynndae could just make out their voices through the open window.

May said, "My husband will be bored now. Nothing but horses, milk cows, and me."

Zeph laughed. "Time for that second honeymoon. Make sure you join us in the Rockies this summer for our wedding. That'll liven things up."

Then he was being embraced by Augustine and his toothpick. Lynndae could hear Augustine perfectly.

"We are sorry to see you go, Zephaniah. You two belong with our people."

"Pray for us," Zeph responded. "You never know what will happen."

The whistle blew twice. Zeph climbed on board and sat opposite Lynndae. The train began to move. Aunt Rosa, Bess, and Samuel waved. Lynndae and Zeph waved back. They rolled west for Harrisburg.

The fields were dark with plowing. Horses and cattle walked back and forth on the green pastureland. Swallows swooped and darted in the blue sky. Amish children in a wagon bouncing along a country lane looked at the string of passenger cars solemnly. A man stood waiting for the train to pass with a long fishing pole in his hand and a wicker creel slung over his shoulder.

"Heaven," murmured Lynndae. She felt empty inside.

Zeph nodded. "It's fine country."

She turned on him. "Is that all you can say? It's a fine country?"

"And it's full of good people."

"If you think it's fine country and full of good people then why are we leaving?"

"Well, where we're heading is fine country and full of good people, too."

"Things could have changed in our absence."

"Not that much."

"Yes, that much."

"I need a nap. That farewell supper kept us up late, and before we knew it the sun was shining in the windows and the train was heading in from Philadelphia." He settled back in his seat, pulled his hat down over his eyes, and folded his arms over his chest.

Another sentence was on the tip of Lynndae's tongue, but she held it back.

Fine, she thought, *sleep then. It must be awfully nice to just trim your wick like that and shut everything down.*

The train carried them through western Pennsylvania, Ohio, and Indiana before they made a change in Chicago. Then they rattled and swayed on tracks that ran through Illinois and Iowa to Nebraska. In Omaha they booked passage on the Union Pacific to Ogden and had a three-hour stopover. Zeph touched the brim of his piker hat and vanished up a nearby street. "Meet you back here in an hour."

Lynndae protested. "Don't you want me to go with you?"

"No."

What was the matter with Z? In an unsettled mood, Lynndae wandered among the shops close to the station, but very little caught her fancy. She was in between two worlds and felt adrift. If only the train for Utah could have departed sooner. Restless, she paced back and forth on the station platform until she saw a man approaching with Zeph's carpetbag in his hand.

"Hello," the man greeted her.

Lynndae stared. "Zephaniah Truett Parker. What have you done with yourself?"

"Shave and a haircut, two bits. My Levi Strauss pants, my boots, my hat. We've crossed the Missouri, my lady. We're back in the West."

"I hardly recognized you."

"Weather's warm, so I don't need a coat."

"You haven't looked like this since—"

Zeph interrupted. "Now, this is a chit for a dress shop just two blocks thataway—"

But she wasn't listening. "—Eagle Rock or Ogden, I can't remember which—"

Zeph carried on. "—you can't miss it on account of how fancy the sign is. A Missus Willoughby will be happy to fit you into—"

So did Lynndae. "—but I would have to say it's a very pleasant change to have you less plain."

Zeph finished up. "—a brand new dress right off the rack, no waiting around for two or three weeks."

Lynndae finally listened to him, startled. "A new dress? Two or three weeks? Oh Z, the train will be leaving in less than two hours."

"No, I said it won't take two or three weeks. They have ready-to-wear dresses hanging up in the store. They just need to open some parts out and pin some others in, at least that's what they told me."

Lynndae repeated Zeph's words. "You went into a dress shop—"

"I did."

"—to buy a dress for me—"

"Well, I wasn't planning on trying any on for myself."

"—when you don't even know my size or what colors I like or—"

"That's why I'm giving you this chit. The dress is paid for. You just have to pick it out."

Lynndae looked at him in astonishment. Zeph touched the brim of his brown Stetson and placed the slip of paper in her hand.

"Two blocks north, right up that street, and then a left.

You can't miss it. Missus Willoughby. Can't miss her either. The kind of woman who fills a chair. Very sweet."

"Why, Z—"

He grinned. "It's your engagement present. I haven't seen you in anything but blacks and grays for more than three months. Time to let you be the wildflower you are again."

"What if they don't have anything suitable?"

"Get going, palomino. You're burning daylight."

Suddenly realizing what Zeph had done, and that she might not have time to pick a dress out and have it fitted in time, Lynndae began walking rapidly up the street.

Zeph watched her slender dark figure until she paused and turned left, and then he went to buy himself an Omaha paper and relax with it.

After he bought the paper and had read a few stories, Zeph remembered that he had gone past the telegraph station earlier. He was debating whether or not to send word to Matt that they were on their way back. If the accomplice was still around, he would be sure to read it. Zeph wasn't interested in being ambushed on the stage between Virginia City and Iron Springs.

Mulling it over, Zeph wandered into the office. After waiting behind two other men dressed in fancy suits and then asking for a pad, out of the blue the idea popped into his head to ask for telegrams for Parker. The clerk looked and said there hadn't been any.

"But I do remember the name Parker," he said. "I sent a

real odd telegram out to a Parker in Pennsylvania a couple of months back."

Zeph was hunched over the pad with a yellow pencil. His ears pricked up at the clerk's words. "Pennsylvania?" The older man chuckled. "Sure, hard to forget. It was a passage from the Bible, from Revelation. I never get anything like that."

Zeph stared at the clerk. "Do you happen to recall who sent the telegram?"

"That's just it, how could you forget someone that went by the handle Angel?" The clerk busied himself with some papers. "Not that it was his real name, anyhow."

Zeph put down the pencil. "What was his real name?"

"Oh, he never told me. Just laughed about it. But then he went and left his business card in that basket there. All sorts of travelers leave one behind. People go through them now and then. You never know. Someone might get in touch about a business deal. Let me see."

The man came out from behind the counter and went to the large wicker basket that sat on a table by the door. There were hundreds of cards, but he was not deterred. Zeph came and stood beside him. After several minutes of riffling through the pile, the clerk exclaimed, "Here we go!" and held a card up to the sunlight from the window.

"William S. King, Attorney at Law," he read out loud, "Iron Springs, the Montana Territory, Wills, Estates, Property. That's the one. You see, he puts a crown on the top of the card, his business logo, I guess, and that makes the card easy to pick out. Good head on his shoulders. Nice man. Gave me a tip, too."

"And you're sure this is the man who sent the Bible passage

to Pennsylvania? And signed the telegram 'Angel'?"

"T'weren't no other."

"And he sent it to Parker?"

"He did. That Parker kin to you?"

"Yes. He is."

Zeph walked in a daze back to the counter and the telegram pad. He kept thinking of how many times Lynndae and the kids had almost been killed because the Raber Gang always knew where they were going and what they were doing. He saw King grinning and laughing through his thick beard, and the heat rose in him and the blood pounded through his head. Raber's gunmen had been deadly, but they had been strangers to him. King was a friend, someone he'd dined with and sat next to in church. The sense of betrayal was strong. Zeph felt he could knock down an Omaha brick wall with his bare hands.

He wrote out two telegrams. The one to Matt had Zeph and Lynndae coming into Iron Springs at least a week later than he knew the train and stage would get them there. The other he sent to Colonel Austen at Cheyenne.

He was seated with his paper at the depot when he spied a tall, slender beauty in a dress of white, yellow, and blue silks almost floating down the street toward him. Men were stopping to turn and look at her, even men who were escorting other women. Zeph folded the newspaper and got to his feet. Not for the first time he marveled that this lady should be excited about marrying him.

Thanks for the train ride, Lord, he prayed. *It wasn't an easy trip, but I'm grateful for how things turned out, and I wouldn't change a thing.*

The sunlight danced all over Lynndae's hair and dress as if it were delighted to have a woman of her caliber back in Nebraska again. Zeph could not take his eyes off her. As she drew up to him, her face reddened.

"Must you stare so?"

He whipped off his Stetson. "I'm afraid I must, ma'am."

"Oh, don't act so foolish. You'd think it was the first time we've met."

"I've never seen you wear a dress like this in Iron Springs."

"Well, I never had the time to make one. And, I was never engaged before."

"I was looking forward to seeing the Rocky Mountains shining in the distance, and now I don't care. I got more of God's beauty in my eyes right now than any man has a right to see"—he put his arms around her—"and more of God's beauty in my arms than I'll ever know what to do with. I'll need time, a lot of time. Why, I expect I'll need a lifetime, and even then I won't get around to doing all the things a man would enjoy doing with a woman of such fine features and well-bred disposition."

She rested her head on his shoulder. "I'm sure it's the dress."

"No ma'am."

"Or the heat."

"I put you in sackcloth, your beauty'd still shine. For the past three months it sparkled, even in your Amish wardrobe. It's just that this dress and these silks bring out all the different colors in your soul, and they show who you truly are: a woman of vast splendor, of awe-inspiring magnificence, and of exquisite loveliness. I really don't know what to do with you."

"Why don't you just kiss me then and stop talking? It's embarrassing."

So he did, while trains shunted in and out of the station and whistles blew and people streamed past and locomotives hissed steam and covered them in white mist. Finally she pulled back.

"Was that a Western kiss?" She smiled.

"You only get those on this side of the Missouri."

"Well then, I think I'd like to stay on this side of the Missouri for a little while."

"I am glad to hear it."

The train pulled them through Nebraska all that day and into the night. At sunset on the following evening, it began to slow as it came into Cheyenne. Lynndae was patting her cheeks with a napkin dipped in cool water and passing it over her throat when she noticed a man in black standing alone on the platform. People rushed back and forth all about him, but he was like a rock in the middle of turbulent waters, fixed and immovable. It so happened their car came to a stop right in front of him. Lynndae leaned forward out of her seat.

"Why, Z," she exclaimed in astonishment, "that's Colonel Austen."

"So it is."

"Well, come, come, we must get off the train and greet him before we miss this opportunity. There's so many things he will want to know."

"You'll have plenty of time for that."

"What are you talking about? We don't have plenty of time at all. The train may only be here twenty or thirty minutes." She rose out of her seat and gathered her skirts about her, but Zeph placed a hand gently on her arm.

"Lynndae."

"What are you doing? Aren't you coming out with me?"

"There's no reason to do so."

"What do you mean?"

"He'll be coming on board presently, and he will be with us, by rail and stage, all the way to Virginia City and Iron Springs."

"What?"

Lynndae stared at Zeph and then out the window at Colonel Austen. He had noticed her once she stood up, and he met her gaze with a smile. Then he gently touched the brim of his black Stetson. Coming aboard, he greeted her with a kiss on the cheek and shook Zeph's hand.

"Thank you for the watch, Colonel," Zeph said.

"Thank you for the memory," Austen replied. "A strong one and an important one."

He settled in his seat and turned to Lynndae. "I have exciting news I think you would like to hear. My family is alive."

"What? Oh Colonel Austen, is it true?" She threw her arms around him and gave him a hug. "Where are they?"

"The Territory of Arizona and the Territory of New Mexico. I received the report from the US Army, which received the information from a trader by the name of Wilkes. They are indeed attached to an Apache tribe. I intend to go down there and get them back."

"Colonel, I thank God. You must feel like setting out this very day to bring them back."

"I do. But there is unfinished business in Iron Springs. And I intend to help Zephaniah and Matt set that to rights before

I make my way into the American southwest."

"Oh." Lynndae glanced at Zeph. "Will that take long?"

Austen shook his head. "I believe, Miss Raber, that it will be short and sweet."

Chapter 34

William King used a key to open the door of his law office. A passerby on horseback called his name, and he waved and went inside. It was early, only seven, and his secretary would not arrive for another hour. He checked her desk to make sure everything was in order. Then he went back to his own room and opened that door with another key.

Everything seemed to be as it should. His filing cabinet was in place and all the drawers intact. He moved around, going through his usual Monday morning ritual. His desk was neat and tidy, just the way he had left it on Saturday. He opened a drawer and brought out a short-barreled Colt .45 revolver that was deep blue in color. Turning it over in his hand, he admired the workmanship of the pistol then glanced at the cylinder to make sure it was loaded with six cartridges. He almost looked away before his eyes told him the gun was empty.

King frowned. The Colt was always loaded. All sorts of riff-raff went in and out of his office on a daily basis. He had to be sure he could protect himself as well as defend his female secretary from assault. He reached back in the drawer for the box of .45 cartridges he stored with the pistol. It was gone.

King's heart began to thump rapidly in his chest. His office might look undisturbed, but someone had obviously been in here. The Colt was always loaded and the box of extra cartridges was always in the same drawer with it. He remembered looking at the gun and the box Saturday afternoon. Something was wrong.

"Looking for these, Billy?"

King whirled around and met the flat stare of Matt Parker. He was holding six bullets in one palm and a box of cartridges in another. King began to sputter.

"Matt—what—why did you take the bullets? Who let you in here? Give them back—"

"Well, Billy, I normally don't give a loaded gun to a wanted felon."

"What are you talking about? Have you gone loco? I'm an attorney."

"So I'll just keep ahold of these a little bit longer, until Judge Skinner decides what to do with them. And with you."

"You're out of your mind. I don't know what's going on, but I'm not about to subject myself to some sort of frontier justice you've cooked up with that old fool Skinner. What is this all about?"

Zeph stepped into the room. "It's all about two Amish kids named Troyer and Kauffman, Mister King, and a man named Seraphim Raber who was hunting them down because they'd seen his face."

"Zephaniah! I didn't know you were. . . Welcome back. I was expecting you next week."

"Expecting me? Why, I didn't tell anyone but Matt when I was coming in."

626

"And I didn't tell anyone else," said Matt.

King looked from one of them to the other. Suddenly he yelled and charged at them like a bull. King was a big man and he bowled them over. Then he raced down the short hall for the back door of his office, threw the latch, and jumped outside, prepared to jump on the horse he'd hitched there and ride it bareback out of town. Colonel Austen stood between him and his mount.

"Mister King?" he said. "I am Marshal Michael James Austen out of Cheyenne, Wyoming. I am afraid I must detain you, sir. The charge is, I believe, accessory to murder and accessory to attempted murder."

King stared at the man in black. He glanced to his right.

Matt's deputy, Luke, came out from behind a nearby building, and he was holding a coach gun, a shotgun with two short barrels that was often used by Wells Fargo guards. He pointed the weapon at King. "I'm guessing you know what this can do at close range, sir."

Matt and Zeph rushed out the back door and then stopped. Austen strolled up to King and put his face right up to the lawyer's. "Mister King, you endangered friends of mine. You endangered women. You endangered children. I have little use or patience for men such as yourself, masquerading as a champion of justice by day and doing the deeds of darkness by night."

He pulled out handcuffs and locked them on King's wrists. "I arrest you as an accessory to the crimes of the Angel Raber Gang. You will be accompanying me to the jailhouse in Cheyenne."

"You can't do that!" protested King. "You're way out of your jurisdiction. I'm staying right here."

"For this transfer, I have a court order meant to prevent two possibilities from occurring. One, that your two brothers attempt to release you from jail in Iron Springs unlawfully."

"Leave them out of this. They don't know anything about Raber. They were never part of any of it."

"And two, that a lynch mob might storm the jail and hang you by the neck for assisting one of the most notorious and blackhearted gangs that has ever crossed the Missouri River."

King went silent as he turned this bit of information over in his mind. Zeph walked up to him.

"Was it the money, Billy?" he asked. "Tell me there was a better reason than the money."

King could not meet Zeph's gaze. He dropped his eyes and studied the dirt under his feet. "How'd you know? Did Raber tell you before he died?"

"The clerk in Omaha recalled you sending the Revelation telegram to me in Pennsylvania."

King snorted. "You'll never be able to prove I did anything else. You don't have any of the telegrams I sent Raber."

"The clerk here talked."

"No."

"Yes. He did. He'll say whatever he needs to say to save his own neck."

King looked up and pleaded with Zeph. "You have to understand, the Rabers and Kings go back a long way."

"I know that. The Kings in Lancaster County told me all about it. What I don't understand is how some old friendship turned you into a criminal."

"The Kings owed the Rabers. It's as simple as that. When my great-grandfather left the church seventy or eighty years ago, it was some of the Rabers who made sure my family had land and livestock and a roof over their heads. They saved us. When a telegram came for me demanding I return the favor, I couldn't refuse. I am a man of honor."

"Of honor!" Zeph was seething. "Helping Raber's cutthroats is your idea of honor? Helping them track us down so they could murder those children? Shoot Miss Spence? Shoot me?"

"It–it's complicated."

"No, it's simple. It wasn't just returning the favor. It was filling your pockets with gold, too, wasn't it? Your practice was a lot more lucrative in the gold rush days. This was a good opportunity to make up for the shortfall."

"I didn't take much."

"The clerk says you paid him ten thousand in gold. I'm thinking if you paid him ten thousand, well, you must have kept a whole lot more to yourself to live on."

King looked down again. "Just remember, my brothers didn't do anything."

"I guess we'll ask them for ourselves. Meanwhile, you've got a stage to catch."

They took him down the lane behind the buildings where the stage was waiting. It was empty. The driver saw King and spat down into the dust.

"We told the passengers there'd be another stage along in a few hours," he said.

"Thank you kindly," responded Austen, pushing King into

the stage ahead of him.

Zeph stood at the window. "Charlotte Spence has another name, Mister King, and it's Raber."

King looked at him in astonishment.

"She talked with Raber before he died. A brother and sister heart-to-heart. I thought you might like to know he apologized for all the wrong he'd done. I guess the better word is repented. You recall that word from church, don't you, Mister King?"

"I don't believe it," King growled. "A killer like Raber wouldn't turn unless there was money in it."

"Well, there was God in it, I know that for sure, and love for his sister, too. He had to fight off what was left of his gang in order to save her life. They took exception to her preaching. It shamed him, but didn't sit well with the others."

"Raber would never turn, I tell you."

"But I was there that day, Mister King, and I tell you he did. I guess you've got the same choice to make as he did, heaven or hell. I hope you make it before the trapdoor springs."

"They'll never hang me."

"Well now, don't you bet your life on it."

Zeph stepped back and looked up at the driver. The man nodded and flicked his reins.

"Hey yup, hey yup," he cried.

Austen leaned forward in his seat and touched the brim of his black hat. "My regards to Miss Raber. I will see her again at your wedding. It will be an honor to stand for you, Captain Parker."

"And an honor for me as well, Colonel Austen."

The stage rolled down the street, kicking up dust. Then it was gone. Matt was at Zeph's side.

"You still a deputy marshal?" he asked.

"I don't know."

"Well, let me know when you do know."

They walked back down Main Street with Luke. Their horses were tied off in front of the law office. All three of them swung up into their saddles.

"Luke and I need to pay a visit to the Kings," Matt said.

"You think there'll be trouble?" asked Zeph.

"I think they'll be as surprised and upset as we were. Don't know how they'll feel about it down the road."

"Will they hang Billy in Cheyenne, brother?"

"With his connections to the Raber Gang? I believe Wyoming might."

"None of this feels good to me. We were all best friends."

"I know it. Jude said something about it the other night, quoting the Bible of course. Zechariah, I think it was: 'These are the wounds I received at the house of my friends.'"

Luke and Matt rode off, and Zeph turned his horse toward the trail north that led to the Sweet Blue. The town was waking up and wagons went rattling past. People crossed the street in front of him and behind him. He didn't pay any of the hustle and bustle any mind. He was thinking about how much a life can change not only from one year to the next, or one month, but one moment to another. And how you hardly ever saw it coming.

Chapter 35

It was the middle of June and warm as a wood fire, Lynndae thought. She coaxed Daybreak along the ridge and looked at the mountains that seemed purple in the distance. A few still had snow, but most had sent it down by way of creeks and streams and rivers to water the valleys and pastures below.

"Heartland," she murmured.

"Why, hello," came a cheerful voice.

Lynndae smiled as Zeph cantered toward her on Cricket from across a small stretch of meadow. He touched his hat brim.

"Hey there, palomino."

"I'm never sure if you're talking to my horse or you're talking to me," she teased.

"Maybe both."

"Which is it?"

"I think you know."

"Hm." She glanced around her at the vista that surrounded them on all sides. "I had my head down most of the way up watching her steps. My goodness, this land gets more beautiful as each day goes by."

"This land. And some of its inhabitants."

Lynndae smiled over at him. "Always gallant."

"And always truthful."

Lynndae looked at her man, at the tan the western sun had already fashioned over the skin of his face and hands, at his brown eyes and hair, at his smile and rugged good looks, at the kindness as well as the strength that was there, and felt an enormous surge of gratitude toward God for the entire journey from the Montana Territory to Pennsylvania and back again. It had been fraught with danger, but the outcome had been blessing upon blessing. She needed to know if he felt the same way.

"Z?"

"Hm?" He was looking at the sun as it moved closer to the tops of the peaks.

"Was it worth it?"

"Was what worth it?"

"The trip, the journey, the whole thing we've been part of since February."

"What sort of crazy question is that?"

"My crazy question. If you had to, would you do it all over again?"

Zeph moved his eyes from the sun to her. "Let me see. You're in new denim pants, Levi Strauss, like mine, and a long-sleeved cotton shirt in pale white. You've got a black-and-white pattern bandana around your neck and your silver earrings are catching the sunlight. Your golden hair is pulled back and braided and dropping like a glittering rope down your back. Your Stetson is as new as your pants and black as midnight, and it ties together all your handsome whites and darks and golds at one beautiful summit."

Lynndae felt the heat in her face. "Z, please stop. A woman can only take so much of your chivalry in one go."

"Then there are your eyes. A man could live forever just gazing into that blue."

"Are you finished playing Romeo?" she asked. "When are you going to answer my question?"

Zeph smiled. "Was it worth it? Bess and Samuel are alive, so is the village of Bird in Hand, so are you. Your brother's in heaven, which he had small chance of getting into before, and the Raber Gang isn't around to terrorize innocent folk anymore. Colonel Austen and I met up again. I made a hundred new friends in Lancaster County, Pennsylvania. We discovered Black Jack gum."

She waited for him to continue. "So, is that it?"

"Our ranch'll be the biggest spread in southeastern Montana once we buy that little strip that separates Two Back from Sweet Blue. Your brother Ricky'd like that."

Lynndae felt an impatience stirring inside her. But she was also pretty sure he was toying with her. He laughed.

"What's so funny?" she demanded.

"You are. Because you think I'm done."

"Aren't you?"

"Not by a long shot."

He brought Cricket closer so that they were only inches from each other. "We finally got our sunset ride," he said.

"We did."

"Took a long time to get here."

"It seems that way, doesn't it?"

"Trains and stages and walking on foot. Might have saved

ourselves the trouble by just staying put."

He reached out a hand and ran it gently down one side of her face. "Except if I hadn't made the journey, I wouldn't have gotten to know you half so well. Wouldn't have seen all your courage and tenderness and charm. Truth is, before we left Iron Springs, I thought I knew you pretty well. But I didn't know you at all. There's a difference between looking at a stretch of heartland from a distance, thinking it's fine, and riding through that same country for a week and seeing every well and spring and blackberry bush, and knowing for a fact it's fine."

He leaned over and surprised her with a soft kiss on her lips. Then he kept his face near. "Well, I guess you could say God took me on a ride through a heartland till I got to see every stone, every flower, every ribbon of fresh water, every green place, and once I made that ride, I understood what He meant when He said He made that land and called it good, very good."

Lynndae felt a flush rising to her cheeks. How was he always able to do that to her? He kissed her again, and she wished he would never pull away, never stop. Then he was cradling her head against his chest, and she could hear the beating of his heart.

"Was it worth it? I fell in love with the most beautiful woman God has ever placed upon this earth, a lady who outshines Esther or Cleopatra or Helen of Troy. But what's even more astonishing is that this woman fell in love with me and said she'd be my wife. Do you know how long we'd been gone when she said yes? Maybe two weeks. Do you think she would have promised to marry me after just two more weeks of living in Iron Springs and neither of us setting a foot outside the Sweet Blue or Two Back Valley? If I'd come to your door with roses and daisies and chocolates and kisses and said, 'Miss Spence, will you marry me, it's been two weeks,' would you have thrown your arms around me and cried, 'Oh yes, oh yes, marry me, Z, it's been two whole weeks of courtship, and we've scarcely seen each other in all that time?'"

Lynndae laughed into his shirt. "I would have got the boys to throw you out on your ear."

Zeph carefully lifted the new Stetson and kissed the top of her head. "So there you have it. The journey was hard and not without its moments of great darkness, but in the end it was a miracle. With the kind of ending to the story I'm holding in my arms right now, I'd do it again. And again. There is no doubt of that in my mind, and there shouldn't be any in yours."

"There isn't."

"Then we are in agreement."

All the land was sheeted in copper and gold now, and Zeph tilted her face back into the sunlight.

"Look at you," he whispered, "my lovely palomino, ready to throw back her head and toss her golden mane and fly across God's earth like a shooting star. I love you."

Lynndae was about to respond with the same three words when she felt him slip something cool and round and thin on her finger. She pulled back in surprise and sat upright in her saddle, looking at her left hand. A ring and its jewels sparkled in the setting sun.

"Z!" she exclaimed.

"The sapphire is for your eyes of course, those eternal

windows to your soul. But the amethyst is there for the same reason. I was able to procure two of a deeper shade of violet, the shade that comes over your eyes in certain moods and changes in the weather. Did you know the British crown jewels have amethyst? I had them put these four stones in a circle around the diamond. You understand that the diamond is you, all of you, in one perfect gem? It catches the light, makes rainbows, shines like the moon and stars and all the heavens. That about says it all, don't you think?"

Lynndae didn't want to cry, but the tears came anyway. "Oh Z, what girl was ever given such a beautiful ring in such a beautiful place by such a beautiful man?"

"I just wanted to make it official. And I was waiting for the right moment." Zeph put his hand under her chin again and gently lifted her face toward his. "Lynndae Sharlayne Raber, will you make me the happiest man on earth? Will you be my bride?"

Lynndae cried out and threw her arms around his neck. She kissed him so hard and so long he didn't know if she would ever let him go. When she finally did, he caught his breath and asked, "Is that what you call a yes in Amish?"

She laughed a silver laugh and took him in her arms again. Just as she did so a shooting star streaked across the Montana night. A good shiver went up her spine.

"Don't ever leave me," she whispered.

He kissed her forehead so lightly she thought it was moonlight.

"Don't worry," he said, "in this story we ride as one from here on in."